Suzanne Rafalko

BITE

BITE

C. J. Tosh

NEW YORK LONDON TORONTO SYDNEY SINGAPORE

DOWNTOWN PRESS
1230 Avenue of the Americas
New York, NY 10020

ISBN: 0-7434-7764-2

First Downtown Press hardcover edition August 2003

10 9 8 7 6 5 4 3 2 1

Manufactured in the United States of America

For information regarding special discounts for bulk purchases, please contact Simon & Schuster Special Sales at 1-800-456-6798 or business@simonandschuster.com.

BITE

Chapter 1

Most days, Samantha Leighton knew she had the best job in the universe. Too bad this wasn't one of them. Because of post–Labor Day traffic, she barely made it to Kennedy in time for her flight to LAX, heightening her travel anxiety. She'd splurged on an upgrade—rationalizing that it put her more in the mindset of the absurdly rich people she was going to interview—only to find herself next to a monster whose nonstop snoring made her want to scream, despite her attempts to practice her newly learned, calming yogic breathing.

Samantha was a celebrity journalist. This meant that often, she got to travel to amazing places, talk to executives and directors, and cover studios' wheelings and dealings. But it could also mean what it felt like today: Being underpaid to talk to the actors the world most wanted to meet that month—no doubt, because they never would. Still, she got to wear jeans to work, keep hours that no other industry would stand for (no point in arriving at the New York office before noon, when it was only 9 A.M. in L.A.), and indulge in an expense account rivaled only by Bill Gates's.

The next morning, Sam was supposed to interview a bug-eyed young actor who had, at their last meeting, refused to answer her questions unless she literally held his giant, sweaty hand. It was good for the story, but the actor had apparently found it less amusing than her readers. (Tomorrow, he'd probably punish her by droning on about his method and keep his madness to himself.) And now, she was being led to her room at the Four Seasons by the bellhop who, two months ago, had accidentally walked into her room while she was standing and talking on the phone, buck naked. They had both been mortified, a feeling that apparently remained alive and well for at least one of them. *Mercury must be in retrograde,* she thought, as she followed him down the hall. On the bright side, while only 5 P.M. in L.A., it was three hours later in New York, which meant that having a glass of wine would be perfectly appropriate.

After tipping the bellhop, managing to smile without looking him in the eye, she started running the bathtub. Thank God for Elizabeth, her best friend on the West Coast, whom Sam was to meet downstairs at the bar in an hour. Elizabeth was spiritual, wise, and up on all the things anyone would like to know about daily living, like waxing, shopping, and men. It was a pretty impossible combination to beat.

"And thank God for Bulgari bath oil," she said out loud, pouring a healthy amount into the tub. Wait. First she had to check her messages. She lit a cigarette, stepping onto the balcony. Her mother, flaky but lovely, rambled on about some friend Sam should look for at the Four Seasons. What Sam was supposed to do with this friend if she saw him she wasn't sure, but then, her mother probably wasn't either. Then Tom, leaving her a detailed message about some guy he'd met at a party, which made her giggle and roll her eyes—as he probably knew she would. And, just as Sam stopped pacing the terrace and started to relax, one of her editors. "Sam. Tomorrow afternoon. We need you to do Mel Gibson." (God, how sexual it sounded. If only.) "On his latest movie. Can't remember what it's called, he's probably playing an admiral or a cop, some hero. I had the research center overnight you a packet. Later."

She peeled off her clothes and climbed into the bath. At least it was Gibson. The guy couldn't be nicer; he knew that talking to the press was part of his job, and he did it with a courtly, professional manner—there were no hip-checks or fake-outs that could suddenly get him crying about his first love, but he also knew it was his responsibility to serve up sound bites, and he did so without complaints.

Reaching for the phone without getting out of the tub—one could do far worse than having a stab of self-pity in the Four Seasons—she called Tom.

"Yeah?" He sounded cranky.

"Nice you," she said, laughing. "I'm suffering here."

"Let me guess," Tom said, his voice warming. "The paparazzi chased you at LAX, your stalkers discovered the alias you were staying under, and now you've taken to your bath, from which you'll refuse to rise until I get on the next plane and rescue you."

Sam thought about offering him miles for an upgrade, then thought better of it. "Hard day too?"

Tom groaned. An editor at a business magazine, Tom was in charge of the lifestyle section—a great job, if anyone who read the magazine had either a life or style. "Honey, you don't even want to know. I've been sitting here all day trying not to notice that Justin isn't in love with me."

"Justin? I don't know Justin. But then, I have been on a plane for six hours . . ."

"Trust me, he's worth it." Tom had a predilection for the most awful men out there—something that never failed to astound her, given that he was a man, and therefore, according to Sam's twisted logic, should know better. Not to mention, as far as she was concerned, he was a catch. At six-foot-three, he had a lanky elegance that meant on the seldom occasion he put on a suit, he looked like an old-fashioned movie star. Most days, it was jeans and a bowling shirt, but every time Sam saw him, tall and Nordic to the core, she felt lucky just to stand next to him.

"Look, Tom, just tell me what to wear. You know I can't get out of the tub without your guidance."

"Pants. Shirt. Shoes. And for God's sake, try to remember the underwear this time."

"Thanks, honey. When the paparazzi ask me who dressed me, I'll make sure to give them your name and number. Before I go, I have a great item for you." When Sam came across good gossip, she told Tom—but refused to say who it was she was talking about. It was a rip-off of the blind items in the *New York Post*'s legendary Page Six column. "Or should I say Page Sex. Which married business titan is finally settling down? During his last trip to St. Bart's, he spent all his time with just *one* Russian hooker."

"That one's easy!" he said.

"Right," she said. "But it's not who you're thinking of. Get back to me when you figure it out."

She hung up and crawled out of the tub. She had always dreamed of traveling for work—the glamour!—but she'd found that recently, she felt like she was missing her center. It was too many hotel rooms, and while she had to admit that it was all quite luxe in appearance, there was something about being in an anonymous space, no matter how decadent it was, that made her feel an aloneness she was able to keep at bay at home. Here, even amid the marble tiles and Frette sheets and view of the Hollywood sign, that ache seemed to resonate in a way that made her feel like a child on a bad play-date who called her mom and said, "Come get me!" If only it was that easy anymore. And having a bellhop seeing you naked, well, it wasn't quite the same thing as . . . Sam stopped herself. "Blah, blah, blah," she said. "This you can deal with later. Right now, it's time to get dressed."

She walked into the bedroom and surveyed the walk-in closet—larger than all of her small apartment's closets combined. She looked at her jeans—was it better to wear the Moschino ones that made her ass look good, or the Earl ones that were chic? (And when, she wondered, had something so inane merited an actual conversation with herself?) She threw on the Earls in disgust, only to be further disgusted that they were tighter than she remembered (she really did have to get to the gym), grabbed a white Petite Bateau T-shirt, and stepped into the black Manolo Blahnik pumps she had bought with her first bonus. Expensive but casual—that was the goal this season, right? Hell if she knew, but it made her feel better. She towel-dried her hair, ran her fingers through it to get out the knots, indulged in her addiction—Kiehl's lip balm—and headed out the door. If people noticed she didn't wear makeup, well, maybe they'd think it was a kind of retro glam. Only her close friends knew it was, more than anything else, total laziness and a tendency to run late. And if it didn't work, she thought, gathering all her bravado, tough shit. She could always blame it on jet lag.

Out on the patio, Sam saw at least eight people she knew, five of whom she knew well enough to actually have to say hello to. She paused to kiss a studio executive busy schmoozing up an agent, a wannabe actress who'd had a bit part in a movie Sam had been on the set of, and two publicists, both of whose calls Sam had forgotten to return. After offering apologies, she spotted Elizabeth across the room, and made a run for it.

"Girl, you are the light at the end of the tunnel," Sam said, giving Elizabeth a long hug. "Why are we so lazy we can't find somewhere small and romantic where we can just hold hands and stare silently into each other's eyes?"

Elizabeth laughed loudly, and everyone turned. "You're the sorry ass who doesn't want to have to do anything but stumble into an elevator. I merely sit and watch you hold court."

Sam grinned and sat down, intentionally putting her back to the room so she wouldn't be distracted. She had known Elizabeth since they were both assistants, Elizabeth to a rapacious publicist, Sam to an equally ambitious editor, and they had shared every humiliation and accomplishment since then.

"What are we drinking?" Sam asked.

"Wait! Did you cut your hair? It looks fabulous!" You were always allowed to interrupt someone if you were complimenting her hair.

"I did," Sam said, tossing her brown, longish hair over her shoulder with a bit of mock drama, "thank you very much. I got sick and tired of spending so much money on a trim, and finally went to a barber in the subway station at Grand Central. Fourteen dollars."

Elizabeth rolled her eyes at what was clearly an L.A. crime—trusting your dead ends to anyone who would charge less than a shrink. "Anyway," Sam said, remembering she was on the West Coast now, "what I want to know is, what are we drinking, what are we eating, and how much are we doing of both?"

Elizabeth lowered her voice to a conspiratorial whisper. "Sammy girl, let me tell you about my latest wax. Once I get to the part where Max went down on me and came up with a hot pink sequin firmly lodged between his teeth, my guess is you'll be doing a lot of drinking. Eating, I don't know . . ."

Feeling truly happy and at home for the first time that day, Sam relaxed into her chair. "Alright, baby. I flew across the country for this story, so give it to me good."

Chapter 2

Shit. After hanging up the phone, Tom realized he'd forgotten to tell Sam the story of the day. He emailed her:

> you'll die. i went to the dentist this morning. he looks in my mouth and says hmmm. then he says, "you have a cavity that needs to be filled." tell me something i don't know! come back soon

"That ought to cheer her up," he said to himself.

Lately Tom had been feeling like he had a second job—namely, to make other people laugh. He liked to make people laugh, granted, but all he really wanted was to find someone who would make him laugh. Actually, lots of people made him laugh. What he wanted was someone who would make him laugh then kiss him goodnight.

The bitch of it was that he had met that guy. Justin. Sam thought he always threw himself at unworthy men—the same way she thought she looked better without makeup, when a little mascara wouldn't kill her—but he really didn't. He was all talk, making fun of various obsessions just, well, to make his friends laugh.

He'd met Justin last weekend at a party. Francisco, the host, had told Tom that he had the perfect guy for him. There was a time when he heard that a lot; it had been a while. He was waiting in line for the bathroom when Francisco came barreling through with perhaps the foxiest man Tom had ever seen. Tall and meaty with a big nose—just the way Tom liked them (in theory; he'd never actually dated anyone who fit the profile). Like David Schwimmer, but less dorky.

"Tom!" shrieked Francisco. Never give a Puerto Rican rum; it's like giving a gremlin water after midnight. "This is the guy I was telling you about! Justin Miller, this is Tom Sanders. Tom, Justin."

Francisco wasn't done. "Isn't he perfect? You owe me a thousand dollars!" And he salsaed off.

"A thousand dollars?" said Justin.

"Is that rhetorical?"

"No."

"I have no idea." Tom was woozy. Smile. Say something. "Francisco is *loco.* I guess he has the idea that if he finds me a good man I'll give him money."

"What makes a man good?"

"It depends. What do you do for a living?"

And so it went. Or didn't go. Or whatever. They had talked a bit, laughed a lot, and then drifted apart. Tom didn't want to glom on (in truth, that was all he wanted).

The next day Tom and his best friend, Andrew, attended the gay man's Mass—brunch—with Francisco. He had told himself it was the right thing to do; people who throw good parties deserve to bask in their glory and rehash the night's events. All he could talk about, though, was Justin. Until Francisco said Justin had called Tom "dismissive."

"Don't worry!" said Andrew. "He just doesn't know you. Francisco will give you his number. You'll call him. And you'll go out." Sweet sentiment, Tom thought—dismissively!—but Andrew knew as well as anyone that Tom could be dismissive. The thing was, he had never in his life less wanted to dismiss someone.

A knock at the door. "Tom?" Veronica, his photo editor, poked her head in. "Am I interrupting anything?"

"Just thinking about the California condor." It was a game

they played—each would try to come up with the most ludicrous answer possible, even if it ultimately made them feel kind of shallow. "And love at first sight."

"Does it exist?"

"Only the unrequited kind."

She smiled. "The pictures of the new BMW are in. Want to come look?"

"You bet."

They walked down the hall. Tom thought once again how his office really should be down by the art department. He liked them more, and he fit in better there. The editors at *Profit* were kindly souls, mostly, but he could never shake the feeling that he wasn't one of them. "Are the pictures any good?"

She stopped, put her hand up by her throat as if to clutch her imaginary pearls, and shot him a look.

"Sorry," he said. "I didn't mean to give the impression that your work could ever be anything but perfect."

Veronica was a beauty—curly red hair that went to the middle of her back, pale skin, and big green eyes. At twenty-five, she was six years younger than Tom, though he rarely remembered it. She had the reputation around the office for being a bit of an ice queen, but in reality she was more unflappable than unfeeling. Tom always thought he could tell her the world was ending and she wouldn't blink. Come to think of it, she never seemed to blink. She wasn't particularly tall, but she came off tall anyway. She had a certain dignity.

"Sarcasm," she said, "is unbecoming in anyone over thirty."

There were times Tom believed that his generation—and hers—was indelibly screwed up by watching bitchy sitcoms. All those people showing their affection by verbally sparring had made it impossible for anyone to say anything nice. He considered telling her about Justin, then decided against it.

He talked every potential relationship to death before it even had a chance to live. If you sat and dissected someone before you had a chance to know him, he reasoned, you could always find enough evidence to warrant never seeing him again. *Liar. You tried to tell Sam today but she was in a me-mood. One martini with her and you'll be spilling your guts like an incestuous stepsister on the* Ricki Lake Show.

They looked at the BMW. "Nice," he said, wondering once again why they spent thousands of dollars to photograph a car when it always ended up looking like every other photograph of a car. Living in New York, of course, he didn't own a car, so that whole fetish had escaped him completely. Plus, he was gay. He'd met fags who cared about cars but he didn't trust them. His readers would love the BMW. In fact, they'd probably read the article with one hand and a Kleenex box at their side. *Goddamn it! Stop being dismissive!*

Veronica sighed. She couldn't give a hoot about cars either. She was still in the East Village phase of New York living—anyone who went to NYU first lives in the Central Village, then goes East, where all the cool young people were, even if it means living in a fourth-floor walkup that has the same stale hallway smell that all East Village apartments have. If they're lucky they make it to the West Village. "I know," she sighed again. "It's just a car. I tried. Smoke?" It was a ritual: when one of them was obviously obsessing over a guy—and Tom's blathering about unrequited love was clear evidence of that—they'd go outside and talk it out.

So much for not dissecting Justin. "The thing is," he said after getting through the party details, "on Monday I called him. Left a message. Then I literally sat down and read *Time Out.* That special Singles issue? Did you see it?"

She shook her head.

"Throughout the issue, they ran personal ads for various types of singles. A veritable Rainbow Coalition: black, white, straight, gay. Even our closet case ex-mayor was in there. And then I turned the page and Justin was one of them! His roommate works for *Time Out,* so I guess she asked him to do it."

"What's the problem? Besides the questionable idea of posing for *Time Out . . .*"

"He's gorgeous. I had a chance with him—don't give me that look, you know what I mean—when no one else in the city knew him. I told you he just moved here, right? From Boston? Anyway, now everyone's going to see it and want him, because he's the only hot gay guy in the whole damn magazine."

"Did your friends meet him? What did they think?"

As if. Tom had been like a dog keeping guard over its food. When he wasn't with Justin, he had gone around telling everyone to stay the fuck away from his new boyfriend. Only Andrew had dared to ignore Tom, probably figuring that if he was going to have to hear about this for weeks he might as well get some firsthand experience. Afterward, all he had said was, "I'm sure he's a nice guy."

Veronica tried to reason with him. "Look, Tom," she said. "I know you think he's above your level, whatever that means—"

"I know, I know, levels don't exist. But now he's sort of famous—in a localized way—and I just can't compete. He's newly single—did I tell you that?—and he's going to be running all over town with guys wanting the hot guy from *Time Out.*"

"You're crazy."

"And right."

"That," she said, stubbing out her second cigarette—she'd never seen him like this, and they almost never smoked two in a row—"I am not prepared to give you. Wait, did he call you back?"

Yes, he did. But Tom wasn't ready to talk about the "date" yet.

Chapter 3

Sam opened her eyes, stared at the ceiling, and groaned. She turned her head toward the bedside clock, and felt her brain rip into sinewy shreds of pain. "Oh, good God," she muttered, scanning back through the evening for where she had gone wrong. Somewhere between the third drink and . . . She couldn't remember. Not that her interview subject hadn't driven her to it, of course. He was so impossibly boring she had spent the second half of their two hours together weighing what, exactly, she would be drinking to celebrate the end of it. Luckily, it had been decided for her—by the time she turned off her tape recorder, Elizabeth and their mutual friend James had already been waiting for her at dinner for more than an hour, and had gotten their revenge by ordering her a very dry, very dirty, and very big martini.

"Help," she muttered weakly to herself, as she sat up in bed and tried to imagine how she was going to get herself packed up, checked out, and to the airport.

She called room service for coffee, and then reached Tom at home, waking him up. "Hello?" he said groggily.

Sam groaned again, this time for Tom's benefit.

"Didn't we just do this?" he asked.

Sam collapsed back into bed, happy for the excuse to pull the sheets up around her wrecked body again. "I can't help it," she said. "I was driven to drink."

"Uh huh," Tom responded, sounding like he was on his way back to sleep.

"I'm serious," Sam said. "Last night I went to Lucques with Elizabeth and James, and do you know what they told me? It's possible to come just by being kissed. I mean, James hasn't personally experienced this, but he said his girlfriends had. And just when I was thinking, 'Liar, liar, pants on fire,' Elizabeth grinned and asked me where I'd been for so long. I'd finally reached a point in my life of being superpleased with myself that I wasn't one of those girls who required a sex shop of toys stuffed under her bed, and now this."

A long silence. "That's nice, dear." Clearly, he'd fallen back asleep.

"Fine, be that way. I find out that after twenty-eight years I'm sexually deficient, and you take a nap on me."

"Sex is the least of your deficiencies, sweetie."

Sam laughed, feeling the sound painfully echo through her head. "You know, you tell me to report back the wonders of the world, and then you act all blasé. I have to move my very sorry ass into the shower now."

"Bon voyage," Tom said, and hung up the phone.

Sam gathered herself together, picked up the phone to call the bellhop, and then changed her mind. On this particular morning, she would rather carry her bags than face the bellhop again. She called her editor and left a message. "Bug Eyes was a freak. He wanted to talk about the metaphorical meaning of playing golf. And no, it will *not* make more sense when I elaborate. Gibson was his typical lovely self. I think he and his wife have had three more children in the last year, but other than that, no big news. Let's make the pictures really, really big so I don't have to . . ." She let out a long yawn. "Sorry. Write that much. Please. Oh and no, I don't think he's gotten hair plugs. He's getting older and he's still handsome beyond—impossible to imagine, I know."

Somehow, Sam made it to the airport, where she resisted the temptation to upgrade—the electric company might not be as understanding as it had been in the past—and headed for the executive lounge, where she propped herself up on a couch and weighed the pros and cons of puking. She put her head in her hands. Blood flow might help.

"Samantha!" bellowed a voice from across the room.

"Help, help, help," she whispered quietly, obviously her mantra of the day, and raised her eyes to look at perhaps the last human being she wanted to see at that moment. And the only human being she wanted to see at any moment. "Shit." *Shit*—she was trying to stop swearing.

Chris Foster always did this to her.

"Hi," she muttered weakly, quickly trying to remember exactly how horrible she'd looked in the mirror before she left the hotel. She hadn't looked in the mirror. *Shit*.

Here he was, walking toward her, like some stupid Hallmark commercial, all slowly and seductively . . . *Am I still drunk?* But there was no denying . . . God, he was beautiful. An Adonis if she'd ever seen one, with blond hair, blue eyes, six foot two . . . pretty much perfection, she thought, looking to see if everybody else turned around to see this miracle of human nature crossing the room. Interestingly enough, the answer was no. Sam stood and let herself be hugged by him, delighted that her hangover made her feel so toxic she didn't get the usual knee-clanging weakness from him touching her. Then again, maybe the nausea was responsible for that.

Chris and Sam had been in and out of each other's lives for years; he was the older brother of Sam's college roommate, and when she moved to New York, they found themselves hanging out in overlapping circles. Chris was an archaeologist for the Museum of Natural History, a modern Indiana Jones. For the last several years, he had commuted between New York and Egypt, where he was in charge of an expedition, and, Sam had heard through the grapevine, had some gorgeous Egyptian girlfriend.

Sam had always been infatuated with Chris—no, she had to be honest, she'd always been in love with him, since if you knew someone so well and still felt weak in the knees, that was probably more than infatuation. And to be brutally honest, she reminded herself through her clanking brain, despite what she felt like doing now, she had *actually* excused herself from her desk and puked when she heard about that Cleopatra bitch. Not to mention that the moment after she'd washed her face and returned to her office she'd gone online to check out airfare to Cairo, determined to win him back . . . Win him back from what? Sam stopped herself. When she was twenty-five, they had had an incredibly intense week-long affair. Sam had been at Chris's house for one of New York's snowstorms and been homebound with him for twenty-four hours (homebound in the sense that they pretended they couldn't leave). But then, damn him, Chris had come to his "senses" and gently dumped her. "You're only twenty-five, and it's time for you to be having fun adventures," he had said. "While I'm honored to have been one of them, I don't want to be the thirty-five-year-old boyfriend who's always out of the country and whom you grow to resent." Sam had assured Chris she was fine, then promptly took to her bed for two weeks. At times, she could still feel his legs around her—he had the strongest, most beautiful thighs, from riding his bike everywhere he went.

Chris was grinning. "You look terrible!" he said. "Not to mention," he added, starting to laugh, "you smell like you've drunk all the booze in L.A. Thank God we're getting out."

Please excuse me while I go kill myself, she thought. She mustered what energy she could to hold her ground. "What's going on?" she asked meekly, hearing her words echo in her ears. "This is sort of the last place I thought I'd see you." *Where had the scent of the Bulgari bath oil gone?*

"I'm heading out to Fiji today for a couple of months—a 'top-secret' project," he said. "Never thought you'd hear those words out of a ditchdigger's mouth, did you? The museum's found an old site, but we're having trouble with the government, so I've been asked not to say anything. But believe me, it's only exciting to me and the mayor, who's hoping he no longer has to work for a living. What's going on with you?"

Sam concentrated. She concentrated on standing there without swaying, she concentrated on not looking into his blue eyes, but also on not *not* making eye contact; she concentrated on not doing something, please God, that would make him go away and never talk to her again, but could he just stand here and keep talking forever? It was a lot to concentrate on. And then, suddenly—she couldn't help it—she wondered what he had meant that she was too young and he wanted to protect her? Obviously, if he'd wanted her, he wouldn't have said that. So he didn't want her. He'd never wanted her. Because she wasn't worth wanting . . . Did a hangover cause psychotic episodes? Sam felt like she'd read that somewhere. That must be it. A ministroke caused by too many martinis.

"I'm working for the magazine," she heard herself say, with a giant breath of relief. This was good. Deep breath. Oxygen to the head. "And . . ." she continued. What else? What else did she do? Sam had gone completely blank. All she could hear was, "Why don't you love me? Why don't you love me?"

Chris began to laugh. "Too raunchy to say in an airport lounge, huh? That's my Sam."

Sam blushed with agony. *Brain, please report immediately.* "I'm doing well. I miss you." *That's it,* she thought. *That is it, that is it, that is it. I have now officially bottomed out, and there's not one person in my life who wouldn't understand that there's simply no option. I will now go into the bathroom, swallow my entire pack of birth control pills, and hope for a quick, barren death. Please say nice things about me at my funeral . . . Oh, God, did I ever tell anyone that I wanted a party, and not a funeral?*

Reality interrupted. "I miss you too, Sammy girl," Chris said, putting his arm around her and giving her a way-too-brotherly squeeze. "Let's try to stay in better touch, okay?"

She nodded. *How could he be so out to lunch?* He couldn't be—he was brilliant—so clearly this had to be alcohol-induced psychosis. She'd open her eyes and be in LAX busy blathering to an imaginary ex-lover, and people would look at her like she was as crazy as she was, and everything would be groovy.

But no. Chris was still there, and he was still talking. And she was still the giant loser who had never been able to get the one guy of her dreams. Even worse, she thought, feeling herself turn crimson, she'd slept with him. So clearly, on top of everything, she sucked in bed. Great. She hadn't worried about that for a while, but there was no other explanation. Which would also explain why there hadn't been anyone else she'd ever felt so passionately about. Because she couldn't possibly feel passionately about someone who didn't feel passionately about her, and if she was horrible in bed, how could anyone be passionate about her in the first place . . . *Tom promised her she'd be a pro as long as she kept one hand on the balls and one hand helping, and she always swallowed, so it must be something after that . . .*

"I'll email you," Chris said, leaning over to give her a kiss on the cheek—why did he have to smell so good?—and turned away. *Hello? I'm in hell here!* Apparently, she didn't say that. Apparently, she kissed him on the cheek and nodded, and said something about emailing him back. She flopped onto the couch. It was too bad that she had a dinner party to go to tonight and a job to go to tomorrow, because she was pretty sure she would never be able to move again. And it would probably, for everyone involved, be for the best.

Chapter 4

Long after the answering machine should have picked up, R.J. answered the phone.

"In the middle of something?" Tom asked.

"Just reminiscing," R.J. replied. "Last night was . . ."

"Tell me over coffee."

"What's up? Is something going on?"

Nope. It was a Sunday afternoon, and nothing was going on. Tom was pretty much always busy except for Sunday afternoons. Every week he'd not plan anything for the dreaded Sunday afternoon, thinking that this weekend he'd want to relax, and every Sunday afternoon he'd get into a minor funk. This was usually exacerbated by the fact that every restaurant was full of couples who'd been happily fornicating all morning. (On Sunday afternoons, he actually used words like "fornicating.")

"I'm putting off writing," Tom said.

"I was hoping you might be wanting to tell me about your own decadent adventures."

"Sorry. I had dinner last night with Tracy and Evan, my married friends, then came home. I figured I needed to be good and ready to write today." This was a lie. He had dinner with Tracy and Evan, and then he trolled around a few bars in the East Village. No point in telling R.J., though—the futility of last night's mission would only make R.J. think once again that Tom was some sort of sociosexual nincompoop. On Sunday afternoons, words like "nincompoop" were also prone to come up.

"Why don't you just get it over with. Marry Andrew and move to Westchester. Raise babies."

"Fuck off. Andrew's a friend. Unlike you, I don't screw my friends."

"I know, I know. I screw everyone. I'm a slut. We can discuss it over coffee. Give me a half hour."

R.J. was Tom's oldest gay friend in the city. Not oldest in age, R.J. would hasten to point out. Successful in insurance or pensions or something—Tom always told R.J. to tell people that he was an entrepreneur—he spent most of his time, spare and otherwise, having sex. He had so much sex, of such wildly varying kinds, that at times it made Tom feel like a pariah for being relatively normal.

Even after having sex at least four times a week—usually with someone new—for the past ten years, R.J. still came off as innocent. There was something childlike about him: men forever got caught up in his gawky, wide-eyed looks, never realizing for a minute he was the gay Wilt Chamberlain, and not in height. In the past month alone, there was the Arab-Israeli three-way (Tom called it the "piece-of-ass summit"); the airline pilot, a man so insatiable that R.J. said he had to keep him away from parking meters, lest the pilot mount them; and Sean, the UConn freshman (R.J. gave him the bus fare). There were doubtless others, but R.J. would forget to tell Tom, even though Tom always pointed out that if he didn't tell Tom then he'd forget and no one would ever know.

Clearly there were emotional risks in seeing R.J. on a lonely Sunday afternoon, but Tom didn't want to think or talk about Justin, and he knew that R.J. would have some fresh exploit he'd much rather discuss. Sure enough, R.J. walked into Magnolia Bakery with the look of a man who'd been up all night having debaucheries. *This Sunday afternoon vocabulary has to stop . . .*

"Can you believe the smell in here?" Tom said. "It's like they aerate butter."

"Mmm," R.J. replied. "I love it. It reminds me of Sean's sweet, smooth—"

"R.J.! There are kids here!"

"Sorry."

They ordered coffee and muffins and went outside to the bench. "So," Tom said, almost dreading what he was about to hear, "what was last night about?"

"I fucked the New Houdini."

Tom held up a hand. "Before we go any further, I have to know—was that his phrase or yours?"

"His." It turned out the New Houdini was an up-and-coming magician who loved nothing more than self-promotion. Well, maybe not nothing. "He was a monster bottom!" R.J. said. "He wanted more and more and more!"

Tom knew that the best way to get the story out of R.J. was to ask straightforward, even naïve, questions. "Where did you meet?"

"At Splash."

"The New Houdini goes to Splash?" Splash was one of the cheesiest—and most popular—gay bars in the city. It had a new name but no one used it. The New Houdini was always in the *Post,* photographed with some starlet. "Wouldn't that pretty much out him?"

"I don't know." R.J. had lost interest momentarily, and was focusing on his muffin.

"So then what happened? Did he pull a rabbit out of your ass?"

"No, but he does have quite the magic wand." Tom set his coffee down. Clearly he couldn't risk taking a sip. "So how did you leave it?"

"He had to fly to L.A. to be fitted for a tank of barracudas he's going to swim in." This was unbelievable—except that while R.J. may have been embellishing a bit, he probably wasn't lying. He wasn't creative enough to make this stuff up. *Dismissive!*

"So that's what they mean by 'magic trick.'" Tom stuffed what was left of his muffin in his coffee cup and tossed it in the trash can. He was glad someone was having sex, but he wondered, as he had a thousand times that year, what was wrong with him. St. Tom, the Normal. He told himself once again that he was smart not to separate love from sex, that in the end it only made it hard to marry—bad choice of words—the two.

He walked down Bank Street toward his apartment. He had lived in the same apartment for nine years. Until last year, he'd had a series of roommates—two bad, one good. What did it mean that the one good roommate was a woman? Was he even capable of being close with a man? Was he a cliché straight out of *Will & Grace?* R.J. fit the part of Jack. . . .

Clearly, coffee with R.J. wasn't the best idea. He should've called Andrew instead.

When his last roommate moved out, Tom thought he'd be immediately happy, finally having the place to himself. Wrong. He took one look around and realized how much he hated everything he owned. He'd never put much money or effort into his apartment, because what's the point if your roommate is just going to ruin it all? So he'd spent the past year buying furniture to fill a two-bedroom apartment that no one but he ever saw much. And then he was forced to write freelance all the time, in order to pay for the furniture to fill the apartment that no one ever saw.

Shit. The freelance story. He'd gone to Niagara Falls for *Holiday,* the travel magazine, and the story was due tomorrow. "Great," he muttered to himself as he walked up the stairs to the apartment that no one ever saw. "Now I get to write about what's it like to go to the Honeymoon Capital of the World and spend a weekend alone in a room with a waterbed and a heart-shaped tub."

Chapter 5

Sam got off the elevator and stepped into the magazine's office, feeling, as always, a sense of relief to be back on safe ground after traveling. She walked down the hallway, lined with *Star Face* magazine covers (the staff referred to the magazine—out of the editor-in-chief's earshot, of course—as Star Fucker) and let herself into her airy office, which properly reflected a job that was all about glamour and veneer. Or it would have, if she could learn to be a little bit less of a slob. Piles of mail blocked the floor-to-ceiling windows that looked out on the Hudson River, papers with notes scrawled on them flooded the two desks, and her attempts to be responsible in the form of nurturing plant life were less than successful. She put her overloaded bag down and headed to the kitchen to get water for her brown-tinged orchids, bumping into Brian on the way back.

"Hey lady, we missed you around here. Tales of your adventures reached us before you did. Heard you met up with the Crowemaster again."

"Don't make me smack you," Sam threatened, trying to balance the water containers without spilling them on the pants of her Dolce and Gabbana beige cashmere suit, which was absolute perfection as long as she didn't eat, drink, or drool.

Several weeks earlier at the Deauville Film Festival, a nasty colleague of Sam's had spread the rumor that she had given Russell Crowe a blow job at a party; Sam thought it was a riot—she had met the man for thirty seconds, surrounded by his bodyguards—but her editor had been none too pleased when the news had somehow reached him. Explaining that she wouldn't have spent quality time with the star on her knees did little to lighten the situation—only a man would be egocentric enough to believe a woman would get a thrill out of giving a stranger a blow job and not insist on a little reciprocation. Still, with all the rumors that swirled around, one could do worse than being hooked up with the man who had dated Hollywood's most beautiful women. Sam's life, she thought, was always far, far more fascinating in people's fantasies than in reality, and at a certain point she'd stopped trying to correct the image. It was just a waste of energy. Well, that's what she knew she *should* feel, anyway, instead of wallowing in hurt feelings. Someday.

"Sorry I can't tell you more about the trip, but my mouth is still full." Five years younger than she, Brian, also a writer, was one of the only straight male friends Sam had ever had with whom there was no sexual tension. They were as close as siblings—or so she imagined, not having any of her own—and Brian had gotten her through many an all-nighter, thanks to his sense of humor and the bottle of single malt he kept in a desk drawer.

"Don't worry, I'll do the talking," Brian said, walking Sam back to her office. "Edgars"—the editor-in-chief—"is threatening that we're overstaffed, and that there are going to be layoffs."

"Are you serious?" Sam said, collapsing in her chair. Her plants could wait another sixty seconds.

"Extremely. And our hero Charles has decided he's sick and tired of running the magazine while Edgars hides out with his mistress in Boca, and he's threatening to quit." She couldn't blame Charles; the executive editor, he was the brains behind the magazine, and the reason everyone stayed at *Star Face* for so long. But as years went by and it became more and more apparent that Edgars wasn't going anywhere—except

Boca—Charles was getting fed up with not being recognized for his efforts.

"Oh, and Julie?" Brian continued, referring to the one woman in power on the staff, which was dominated by the kind of straight white men in their forties who believed a martini at lunch enhanced the creative process. "She's more of a nightmare than ever. Walking the hallways with that booming, bossy voice of hers, trying to figure out how she can make this work out to her advantage, and seeing who will be on her side when she does. Needless to say, yelling at the assistants a thousand times louder isn't getting a warm response."

"Well, thanks, I guess," Sam said gloomily.

"Anytime, babe," Brian responded, leaving Sam to face her email, voice mail, and regular mail—and dying plants—in peace.

She had come to *Star Face* right out of grad school, when the magazine was still in its infancy, and it had become, in that way work did for far too many ambitious young New Yorkers, a second home, a family as dysfunctional, but close, as any other, she supposed. Sam had thought about leaving over the years—several times, she had gotten job offers that had been tempting enough to lose sleep over—but had always decided to stay put. The devil you know, etc. Sam hated that phrase, perhaps because she seemed to be following it to a tee. It scared her that unlike so many of her friends, she didn't feel like anything significant was missing in her life—when she knew, at some level, that there were pretty big holes. There was a fine line between being grateful for what she had and exercising an ironclad case of denial, and sometimes in the morning, when her heart started racing before she had even opened her eyes, Sam knew there were some major life questions she needed to answer—and soon.

She absentmindedly scrolled through her emails, biding time until the morning meeting, and thinking about a conversation she'd had one afternoon not long ago with Jennifer Aniston. After the interview was over, Sam had turned off the tape recorder, and Aniston and she had had one of those discussions that always made Sam grateful to be a woman. Intimacy could be established so quickly, if fleetingly. The two women had sat outside at the L'Ermitage Hotel and talked about the difficulty of being content. How do you stop working once you'd achieved some of the things you wanted, and learn to enjoy the rewards? It didn't escape Sam that Aniston's overflowing plate included a husband who happened to be Brad Pitt, an obscene bank account, and a thriving career, but she was still comforted by the idea that even those things didn't necessarily bring automatic serenity. Was Sam just busy neurotically fighting contentment at Star Fucker, she wondered, or was she legitimately restless? And how ridiculous that when she considered this, she thought with a silent laugh, she referenced a conversation with someone who literally *played* a friend on TV? *What a demented job,* she thought with a laugh. Fabulous, but definitely demented.

Grabbing a cup of coffee from the kitchen, she made her way into the meeting. *Star Face*'s morning gatherings were a twenty-minute run-through of what was going on in the entertainment world, where the suited powers of the magazine sat at a conference table, surrounded by the serfs like Sam, who perched in chairs behind them and tried to pay attention, but more often than not passed notes like recalcitrant schoolchildren, or just daydreamed.

Sam was busy doing the latter when she suddenly felt all eyes on her. "Samantha?" Edgars was addressing her, and, judging from his tone, it wasn't his first attempt to get her attention. "Yes. Yes," Sam said, blushing. She'd read somewhere that there was a new treatment to stop blushing—kind of like putting Botox under your armpits to stop sweating. She made a mental note to do some research. "Lovely to have you back with us," Edgars said, with his usual snideness. "We were just wondering if you had any news from the West Coast."

Quickly gathering her wits, she related the gossip she'd heard from friends at studios and agents—who was in, who was out, and who was plotting. "Also, George Clooney might start talking to the magazine again, according to his publicist, if we'll issue an apology for saying his decision to leave *ER* was moronic, à la David Caruso, and that he'd never have a career in features. And in more good news, Will Smith is starting to see that *Wild Wild West* didn't tank simply because our reviewer hated it." Phew. Sam loathed speaking in these meetings, and was always relieved to have managed not to start babbling in tongues.

"Thank you for your great ambassadorship," Edgars said, moving his glare onto another hapless editor. Sam felt a surge of relief and started paging through the gossip pages that her assistant had copied for her, only half hearing Edgars' grilling of her colleague. There was Cindy Adams blathering on about something—*when* would the woman retire?—Liz Smith recounting a glowing tea meeting with Harrison Ford (that earring he'd just gotten was so wrong, Sam thought)—and Page Six posting its deliciously catty items.

Sam's favorites were the blind items, reported without names for fear of lawsuits, but usually accurate as far as she could tell. Sam scanned today's offerings—"What supermodel was caught with her pants down, literally, in the back of Bungalow 8? Which women's magazine editor—and new mother—horrified her staff by insisting her assistant clean her breast pumps?"—but didn't see any she could easily identify. Suddenly, Sam froze. "What personal publicist, who handles the most fabulous of fashionistas, fell off the wagon and into a keg of coke this weekend?" Goddamn it. It had to be Jen. One of Sam's closest friends since she was five years old—

they met in kindergarten at Miss Sheffield's, a private girl's school on the Upper East Side where both would stay until heading to college—Jen had been struggling with sobriety for two years. She had just gotten out of Betty Ford for the second time a month ago, and was having a really hard time of it, no thanks to a job that made it impossible to stay away from temptation. Sam had hoped this time she might be able to do it—what savings she hadn't wiped out on coke had been blown at $16,000-a-pop stints in rehab—but evidently not.

It took every ounce of willpower to sit through the rest of the meeting, and as soon as Edgars nodded his regal excusal, Sam race-walked back to her office. She called Jen at work, only to be told that she had taken a leave of absence. At least, Sam thought, putting the phone down, Jen had gotten herself on a plane and out of New York after only a weekend of backsliding. Sam closed her door, and, in direct violation of her building's fire code, lit a cigarette. Alright. She had a full day's worth of work—she had to write the Gibson profile at 3,000 words, despite her pleading—and then she was supposed to go have drinks with a VP from Sony at the Chambers hotel. But clearly, something had to give here. Sam was quickly losing her sense of humor about the world's funkiness this week. There was always Jack. . . .

Sam gave herself a mental slap. Jack was one of her closer friends—or would have been, anyway, if they hadn't complicated things by falling into bed together several years ago. They had continued to sleep together—always spontaneously and a bit regrettably, even if it was pretty damn fulfilling—about every six months. But a year earlier, Sam had realized that she and Jack were having a completely ass-backward relationship, as far as she was concerned: While Sam was delighted to be friends and have the occasional (and memorable) romp with someone she cared about deeply, she was getting the impression that Jack wanted a commitment. For whatever reason, she knew she couldn't, and would just ruin whatever hope they had for a friendship down the line. So she'd sworn off him—or tried. But when something like what had happened to Jennifer upset her, all she wanted to do was pick up the phone and hear his reassuring voice. *You promised you wouldn't,* she reminded herself sternly.

And just in case that didn't do the trick, she grabbed a Post-it pad from her drawer and peeled one off. "NO MEANS NO," she wrote, using a fat felt-tip pen for good measure. She stuck it on her phone.

Hey, whatever it took.

Chapter 6

A typical Thursday morning. Tom woke up, went to the gym—get it over with early—then came home and ate breakfast. He started this routine years ago. It was when he lived with the roommate he liked. She got up and went to work even earlier than he did, and he enjoyed the time in the apartment to himself.

He and Alicia had gotten along like an entire city on fire. It became a problem: both would rather spend time at home with each other than out trolling for love. They rarely went out, because she'd end up having an embarrassing giggle fit; instead, they boiled pasta and made separate sauces, moving through the tiny kitchen as if they'd been choreographed. They sat and compared lives, they rented movies, they argued about nothing. They were all but married. Eventually she had enough, and up and moved to San Francisco. She never said it was to get away from him, but they both knew. Within three months she had a boyfriend; within six months she was engaged; after a year she was married.

Tom finally finished reading the *Times*—the headlines, anyway—and weighed whether to scan the *Wall Street Journal* now or save it for later. "Save it?" he said. "Ha!" He hated the *Journal,* hated that he had to read it. But at a business magazine, even the lifestyle editor better know who on earth everyone is talking about. When he started at *Profit* he couldn't tell G.E. from G.M. (actually he still occasionally mixed them up). He decided to save it.

Even after being at *Profit* for two and a half years, he still had a tendency to giggle when he handed anyone his business card. "Tom Sanders, Senior Editor, *Profit."* It was ludicrous. He didn't know a thing about money. He'd only recently unearthed himself from a pile of debt. He had no investments beyond what was in his 401(k). And he generally made R.J. choose the mutual funds for him. But *Profit* didn't care. As far as they were concerned, he was irreplaceable. In the boom times of the late nineties, they had searched all over for someone to start a lifestyle section; every business magazine had one—if you wanted the lifestyle advertisers (cars, fashion, liquor) it helped to have lifestyle edit. He had worked at *Holiday* and knew someone who knew someone at *Profit.* He got the job, he figured, because he never really wanted it. The honchos at *Profit* were a swinging-dick bunch; if you acted needy they'd want nothing to do with you. "How much bullshit are you going to throw at me?" he asked in his second interview. "If we like what you do," the editor-in-chief had drawled, "we're not going to fuck with you at all."

Sure enough, they didn't. He created a lifestyle section that was like nothing else out there. It wasn't always useful—Tom hated the idea of service journalism (where to eat, what to buy), even if it was what he was supposed to be good at. Instead, he figured, these readers want to laugh, and they deserve it. *Profit* was a relentlessly smart magazine, but it wasn't always an easy read. So he named the section, which ran at the end of each issue, "Dessert." And he ran only stories that interested him, which meant no stories about cigars, or single-malt scotch, or golf clubs, or the latest in suits—in short, none of the things business lifestyle was supposed to be. Someday, he figured, he'd get to work at a magazine that actually related to his life.

"I can't even dress the part," he muttered as he opened his closet. "Now let's see, what do I have going on today . . . better make sure I can get away with wearing a rugby shirt." Talking to himself had become a problem, and he wondered—in conversations he had with himself, out loud—whether it would ruin his chances of ever having a boyfriend.

"Sam!" He'd totally forgotten that he was having dinner with Sam that night. "Hot damn!" Tom had only known Sam for a year, but she had already gained complete control over him. They met in one of those fluky New York ways. Tom was at a bachelorette party for a college friend. He hated being the only man at the bachelorette party, because you always had to explain that you're gay, and even then some of the women really didn't want you around. But you had to go, because the bride probably thought of you as one of her "fun" friends. White limousines, penis straws, silly dares—he could handle just about all of it, but he tried to draw the line at Hogs & Heifers, a rowdy bar in the Meatpacking District where bachelorettes tended to end up. He just didn't have the nerve that night. He sat in the back, tugging on a Budweiser, trying to pass for straight—but not so straight that one of the women would take off her bra and throw it at him. (It was that kind of place.) Despite his best intentions, he turned to gape at a particularly hot man walking outside, and his left hand, somehow, ended up resting ever so perfectly on the breast of the woman at the next table.

It was Sam. She raised her eyebrows. "Pleased to meet you," she said, and playfully slapped him. "If you're going to feel me up, I'd appreciate it if you didn't also cruise the passersby."

Sam breezed over his explanation. "Whatever," she said. "What in the hell are you doing here?" She was there on a tip that Cameron Diaz would be out carousing, and was about to give up. They got to talking, and he got to complaining about his job—in particular, having to always find merchandise to put in the magazine.

"Sweet Jesus!" she said. "If you'll pay me to go shopping I'll let you fondle me all night long."

They met for lunch soon after, and Tom walked away from the restaurant shell-shocked. He could see how she got good stuff from celebrities—when she turned her sights on you, you felt incredibly important, and she seemed genuinely interested. And everything she was feeling was right there, on her face. He preferred to keep his emotions close to his chest until he was good and sure exactly what he was feeling. Even though he didn't like mixing friendships with work—it always left him wondering if the friends were using him for freelance money—he assigned her a story anyway, she wrote it beautifully, and pretty much immediately they were the best of friends. Once, when introducing Tom to another editor friend of hers, she had said, "He's one of us." Tom hadn't known until that point how much he'd wanted to be part of an us.

In a word, they were both picky. Clothes, restaurants, liquor, hotels—they cared deeply, probably too much, about making sure everything they did was worth it. Why bother otherwise? For Tom it was a job requirement: if you're going to feature something in a magazine with a million readers, you better believe in it. They didn't always agree, but that only made it more fun. It was his turn to pick the restaurant, so that afternoon, he gave her a call. Since *Star Face* was owned by the same company as *Profit,* his name appeared on her phone.

"Baby!" she squealed.

"Are we still on?"

"God, yes. I need a drink! A really dirty martini. To go with all the stories you're going to tell me."

"Nothing dirty this time, I'm afraid," Tom said. "Sorry to disappoint. Still want that drink?"

"Even more. What's going on?"

"Justin."

She sighed in reply.

"I know," Tom said. "But we had a second date. And I'm miserable."

"Okay, no dirty martinis. Macallan fifteen-year-old. We'll sit at the bar and make like Sinatra. Tell me now about the date so I can come prepared."

Where to start? He and Justin had gone out once, and Tom had talked nonstop. He wished he could have blamed it on the liquor, but Justin hadn't ordered a drink, so neither did Tom. (Sam was appalled: "Major violation of first-date rules!") Francisco had mentioned that Justin liked writers, so Tom had gone on and on about all the fabulous writers he had worked with when he was at *Holiday,* rarely pausing to ask a question. It was a personality fault of his: generally, he preferred people who, if they had something to say, just said it. Combined with Justin's background as a lawyer—and proclivity to ask lots of questions—it made for a fairly one-sided date. Afterward, Tom said that he'd had a good time, that he'd like to do it again. "Guess what he said to that," Tom said.

"Tell me tell me tell me!"

" 'Really.' "

"Yes, really! Tell me!"

"No, Sam. That's what he said: 'Really.' "

"Ouch. He's a loser. Drop him."

"Sam, it's not that easy. I adore him. He's whip-smart. He's gorgeous. He has a huge nose. And he banters."

"Ooh." As a banterer herself, Sam could appreciate this last detail. It was rare to find someone who could keep up. "What else do you know about him?"

"Just moved to New York to work off his law school debt. Left freshly ex-boyfriend of four years back in Boston."

"But you went out again?"

"Yeah. We had dinner, which went better—I asked questions this time—and then to a movie. But first we killed time at a newsstand, which was bad, bad news for me, as it brings out all my bitterness."

"Magazines suck."

"I know! I pointed out every magazine's faults to him, then he insisted we look at *Profit,* and the current issue has a big story about cheese." Sam and Tom were in complete agreement that good cheese is hugely important, and both were vigilantly opposed to the government's outrageous attempts to stop the importing of unpasteurized cheeses. "But it made me look sort of silly. He's into politics and wants to make the world a better place. I want to save the brie."

"And the movie?"

"*The Pianist.* A serious movie, to be sure, and a good one, but there was no air-conditioning, and he's tall, too, so it was awkward, and the whole time I got the impression that he didn't think we were on a date. I went home—"

"Kiss?"

"God no. He patted me on the shoulder." She groaned. "I went home and felt worse than I had after the last one. This either must not be love—because it makes me feel so shitty—or it must be love."

"Because it makes you feel so shitty?"

"You got it."

"Macallan it is. Where are we going?"

"I was thinking Ilo. In fact I made a reso for 9 P.M. Had to mention *Profit* to get a table, and they'll probably kvell all over us, but it's supposed to be fantastic."

"Excellent. Don't worry. Two Macallans and everything will make sense."

"That," said Tom, "is exactly what I'm afraid of. Before I go, here's something for you to think about: which major magazine executive screwed around with an intern—"

Sam snorted. "Which one didn't!"

"—but was at least kind enough to pay for the abortion?"

At dinner, they talked about Justin until Sam couldn't take it anymore, and decided to get to the root of his relationship problems. "Tell me," she said, putting her elbows on the table and her chin in her hands. "Why do you go for unattainable men? What was your family like?"

Tom rolled his eyes. "Jesus Christ, Sam, if I wanted a therapist—"

She shushed him. "Seriously." Close as they were, the truth was that they didn't know that much more about each other's lives before they met. They could tell each other their deepest romantic secrets, but it was a rule of New York life that you never really talked much about the world that you came from. Starting with a sigh, Tom explained that he was never particularly close to his parents. He loved them, but they had him when they were fairly old, and he didn't connect with them the way he did with his friends. He figured it was because he knew he was gay by the time he was twelve, at which point he clammed up. "What I learned early was that I couldn't really trust anyone," he said. "There's nothing like keeping a deep secret for nine years to make you get by on your own." Independent to a fault, he called it.

"Would they have had a problem with it? With your being gay?"

Well, he said, his father had died when he was fifteen, so he didn't know for sure. "But is any parent thrilled to find out his son is gay?" With his mom, he could chatter away about school, the tennis team, whatever, but he never said much of anything about what was really going on in his mind.

"What did she say when you told her?" Once Sam was in interview mode, there was no stopping her.

"I guess I was shocked that she was shocked. I guess she

thought I was just really shy. Eventually she became cool with it, but we don't really talk about it."

"But you've had boyfriends . . ."

"And?"

"You've never talked to her about them?"

God, no. He never got the impression that she was completely comfortable with the details of his gay life—and if he was to tell her about a boyfriend (none of whom had lasted long anyhow), he'd worry she would visualize him getting penetrated.

"Well," Sam said, "I don't think you're giving her enough credit. You need to open up, sweetie. You're her son."

"It's not that easy," he said. "What should I do? Say, 'By the way, I'd like to open up to you. Let's take a walk on the beach and really get to know each other. I can tell you all about Justin, and you can tell me if you're seeing anyone.' "

Sam reached out and grabbed his arm. "I know it's hard, but really. You should."

"All I really wanted to talk about was Justin, you know. Can't we change the subject?"

Even though they were stuffed, the waiter, knowing that Tom was from *Profit,* refused to let them go before sending out one of each of the five desserts. Tom took a bite of lavender crème brûlée, and pushed the plate away. "What an absurd occupational hazard," he said. "Death by dessert."

"There are worse ways to go," said Sam, pulling the crème brûlée her way.

Tom's cell phone rang. He pulled it out of his pocket, and checked the number. He looked confused. "It's my brother," he said.

Sam yelped. "You have a *brother?*"

Sam led Tom to a taxi, helping him in like she would a sick child. She climbed in beside him and gave the driver his address.

"We're going to take you home," she said, "and you can pack while I make your reservations." Tom nodded mutely. She looked at him carefully to see if he was going to cry, but he was clearly too deeply shocked to do anything but stare ahead. Yes, Tom indeed had a brother. And that brother had just called Tom to tell him that their mother, who lived in California, had died.

When they got to the apartment, Tom disappeared into the bedroom while Sam worked the phone. She got him a reservation on a flight the next morning, and called the car service. Then she got his brother's number from Tom's cell phone and dialed it. Unlike Tom, Trevor had clearly been weeping.

"Hi," Sam said, introducing herself and offering her condolences. "I've gotten Tom on a flight tomorrow morning, American number 39, arriving at 1:15 P.M."

"I'll pick him up," Trevor said.

"Good. What else can I do for you in terms of helping with arrangements? Can I do anything to plan the service?"

There was a pause on the other line. "No, I'm taking care of that now," Trevor said. "I need something to do to take my mind off of it anyway."

Sam went to find Tom, who was staring at his closet. "Let me do this," she said, and pulled out a suit. She went into his drawers and got out underwear and socks. Tom just sat on the edge of the bed, still not speaking. "Do you want me to come with you?" she asked.

He shook his head. "No, I'll be fine. I need to just be by myself right now."

She nodded and put her arms around him. "I'll call Andrew. I got his number out of your phone. Anyone else?"

Sam felt Tom's body begin to shake. "I think I need to be alone right now," he repeated.

"Okay," she said, giving him a final squeeze as finally, he began to cry. "I'll be staying in touch. And you do the same." She gave him a kiss and left.

Chapter 7

Tom checked in at the airport, annoyed that the world didn't know that his mom had died. It was stupid, he knew, and overly dramatic, but he wished that he would find a way to tell everyone he came into contact with, if only because it would make it more real. He went and bought a bag of peanut M&M's, like he always did before a flight, and a bottle of water. The M&M's reminded him of his mom, who used to serve them when her bridge group came to their house, then hide the leftovers from his dad. *Was it always going to be like this?* he asked himself. *Every little thing reminding me of her?* Followed quickly by: *Don't be maudlin.*

His cell phone rang.

"Am I interrupting anything?" It was Veronica.

He cleared his throat.

"Are you okay, Tom? I was wondering why you aren't at work."

"I guess I won't be in the office all week. I'm at the airport right now. My mom, um, died. Don't you think it's better to just say 'died'? 'Passed away' sounds—"

"Oh, Tom," she cut him off. "I'm so sorry."

Tom explained he was fine, that she had been sick for a long time, though of course that didn't make it any easier.

"I wouldn't worry about *Profit,* Tom. I wish I could give you a hug right now. I'm so sorry. If there's anything I can do—"

"Thanks," he said quietly. "I'll call you from California. And promise me that when I get back you'll take me out for a big old drink."

"You bet. Hang in there, hon."

He tapped his foot. He needed something to do. *No point in waiting for the flight.* He opened the M&M's, and called Sam.

"How are you?" she asked in her most serious voice.

"Shitty, thanks. Can we talk about something else? I can't think about this anymore." He laughed at himself for bemoaning the fact that he had no one to talk to about it, then insisting Sam avoid it. "What's going on?"

She obliged in spades. "Take your pick. Topic A: the entire Hollywood community thinks I gave Russell Crowe a blow job."

"Another one?"

"Very funny. Topic B: I finally talked to Jen, and sure enough, it was her in Page Six."

"Jesus. I'm sorry."

"Me too. I can understand why boring people do coke, but why do people who are already interesting feel the need? Topic C: I can't stop thinking about Chris."

"I'm not sure I have anything left to say about that one."

"I know, I know. I wish you could meet him. He makes Indiana Jones look like a eunuch. I want to eat him. Somebody get me a spoon!"

"Watch it, Sam. That's how rumors get started . . ."

"I'm glad I can amuse you. Wait, I didn't mean that to sound sarcastic. I really am glad I can amuse you."

"Me too. Is there a Topic D?"

"Well, totally unrelated to yours truly, I hear that a certain major actor has a fetish of a most unseemly sort. He makes his actress girlfriend bleach her ass, so as to improve the view when she defecates on him."

Tom cackled, scaring the bejesus out of the woman next to him. She moved over a seat. "Unbelievable!" he said. "Except I totally believe it. Of course if you tell anyone they'll think you came about this knowledge firsthand. Which leads us back to Topic A."

"I feel like Tom Cruise. But taller, of course. I don't want to dignify the rumor by denying it, but I'm beginning to feel like I'm covering something up by being silent. It's bad enough having to suck up to Hollywood flacks without having everyone think I'm sucking off their clients."

They called his row. "I have to go. My veal crate awaits. You'll be fine, I have no doubt of it. Thanks for cheering me up."

"Anytime. Call me from California, okay?"

On the plane, he wished for so many things. He wished he'd spent more time with his mom, that he'd told her he was gay when he was much younger. He wished he was closer with Trevor, his brother, whom he was now going to spend a week with for the first time since he was thirteen. He wished he'd taken Andrew up on his offer to come out to the funeral with him. He wished he had more of a family in New York. Friends were great, but not enough. It was the big lie, really, about single, young city life. Your friends are your family, people constantly said. And they were, in a fashion, but ultimately you went home alone.

One of his wishes was coming true: He was getting to spend a lot of time with his brother. Trevor was five years older than Tom, and their relationship had always been strained. The thing about Trevor was this: everyone loved him. L-U-V. He was a snack, even Tom could see that (though he preferred not to dwell on it), and it was simply galling how even though they were both starting to lose their hair, just a little receding in the hairline, on Trevor it looked good. Like he was Sting or something. And he was smart—Tom hated how he'd say he went to school "in Boston," when it would be so much less pretentious to just say Harvard. He was one of those people to whom everything just came effortlessly. Tom hadn't suffered much, but at least he'd been gay, so he had that. Trevor was as straight as could be, and had glided through life. A rising star in the San Francisco advertising world. And the fact that it was such a cliché to be envious of your big, beautiful older brother only made it worse. He hated clichés.

Tom was sitting at the kitchen table, where he'd done his homework as a kid. It was weird not having his mom around, popping in to see how he was doing, offering to do some typing if it would get him to bed sooner. He marveled for a second about how they'd actually used typewriters back then, before realizing that he was off point. He tried to think about his mom some more, but found that you couldn't will it to happen. *Is this what grief is like?* he wondered. *Random bursts of unhappiness?* Plus, he was so sick of hearing people say they were sorry. The funeral was one big procession of sympathizers. He knew they meant well, that he would say it if he were in their position, but that didn't make it any easier to hear.

"Yo, Mr. T." Only Trevor called him that. Tom felt like Trevor had been following him around all week, taking his emotional temperature like an overzealous nurse. For some reason, this made him think of Sam. Trevor, who had pulled out a chair and sat down, knocked on the table to get his attention. "What are you pondering?"

"Typewriters, actually. And Mom."

Trevor laughed. "She hated doing your typing for you, you know that?"

"What the fuck, Trevor? If you're trying to make me feel good, it's not working."

"Relax, Mr. T. I'm just reminiscing. She hated it but she did it anyway." Tom could feel a rebuke coming, and sure enough, it did. "What's your problem, anyway? I'm cutting you a lot of slack because of Mom, but I am your brother.

Why are you being such an ass?" The way he said it, Tom could tell Trevor thought about adding the word "hole" to the end. That he had been so perfect as to not do it just pissed Tom off more.

"Look, everything's been . . . perfect. The funeral was . . . perfect. Really, Mom would have been very happy. You've taken care of everything." Tom hated the way he sounded, how this whole exchange was straight out of an afterschool special, but he couldn't stop himself. This was why he rarely came home—he always felt like a child again. "And I shouldn't be surprised, because you're always perfect, and I'm just the immature little brother who can't even avoid having a stupid adolescent confrontation with you. But I wish you'd stop it. Just leave me alone, okay?"

Trevor didn't move. He raised his thumb to his mouth and chewed on a nail. Tom smiled bitterly, happy at least to remember that Trevor had always had that one flaw.

"Tom, this is hard. For you, for me, for everyone—except I guess there isn't anyone else. We're all that's left of the Sanders—"

"And we sure as hell know I'm not going to have kids."

"Give the chip on your shoulder a rest, would you? I've never given a shit that you're gay."

Tom stood up. "You're a saint, Trevor." He went to his room and slammed the door.

Chapter 8

Post-its sucked. They were too small, they never stayed put, and whoever thought that yellow was a good color for notepaper anyway? Actually, Sam knew, it was she who sucked. *Superhero of Shame!* Sam thought to herself as she walked up Madison Avenue. *Queen of Mean!* The phrase had totally been wasted on Leona Helmsley, but that's only because the media hadn't known, when they had nicknamed the infamous hotel boss a decade later, that someone as truly awful as Samantha Leighton would come along.

There was no other way for Sam to explain to herself that here she was, headed to the Carlyle to meet Jack, and—this was the proof she was evil—both relieved and excited at the thought of seeing him. The thing that scared Sam the most about the fact that she had ultimately called him, despite her promises to herself, was that she couldn't even blame it entirely on living an unexamined life. Or maybe her life was unexamined, she thought as she walked past the hotel doorman and turned into Bemelman's Bar, but her actions certainly weren't. She had known she shouldn't be calling Jack, even as she picked up the phone and dialed his number, but she couldn't help it. The death of Tom's mother had shaken her more than she would have thought—had she taken her own parents for granted?—and her need for comfort had outweighed any kindness she might have exercised instead. Sam couldn't pretend that she was hoping it was just going to be a friendly chat—not when she found herself, lying spread-eagled, in Joyce's cubicle at the J Sisters, getting a Brazilian bikini wax. True, she hadn't had sex for a year, and that was a long time for someone entering her sexual prime. On the other hand, wasn't an adult supposed to have some semblance of self-control? The next day, Sam promised herself, she would search the Web for a support group, whether it was for sex addicts, screw-ups, or just plain bad people. Then she spotted Jack sitting there at a table, smiling.

How could she not love that face? It was, she had to admit, one of the kindest faces she knew. Boyishly handsome, with brown hair and brown eyes and dimples in exactly the right places, Jack had that combination of good looks and goofiness that reminded her of Matt Dillon. Sam's friends couldn't understand what her problem was—come to think of it, she couldn't either—unless it was that she was incapable of true intimacy. She'd check into support groups for that, too.

"Hi," she said, feeling herself relax immediately as she slid into the banquette next to him. "I'm so happy to see you." She kissed him on the cheek.

"And you, Sam. It's been a long time." Jack motioned the waiter over for a drink and ordered her a dirty martini, three olives. "So what's going on in your crazy life?"

Sam sighed. "Well, not much you haven't heard before. Still at the magazine, still traveling like a lunatic. In fact, I just got back last week from L.A. and found out that Jennifer is back in rehab."

"I'm so sorry." Jack said, touching her hand gently. "I know she's one of your closest friends. What happened?"

"It's always the same story." She reached into her bag to grab her cigarettes, and felt herself blush red with shame.

"What?" Jack asked. Sam shook her head. How could she possibly explain that attached to her Kiehl's lip balm was a Post-it that read, "Free Jack!"

Another martini helped her get over the embarrassment. For the next two hours, Sam and Jack talked about their lives, their work, and nothing at all. Sam let herself go completely, kicking off her shoes under the table.

And then, she found herself half-listening to Jack talk about what was going on at NBC News, where he worked as a producer chasing down the latest tabloid stories for an anchor whose talent at making her interview subjects weep was matched only by her ability to make her colleagues do the same. Sam was only half-listening because the other half of her was wondering if Jack might . . .

And there it was. She cursed silently as she felt the warmth flood her body. Jack had placed his hand on her leg—casually, tentatively, as if maybe he was just emphasizing his story about his boss's latest scare tactic and then it would go right back where it belonged. Lord, that hand. Sam often felt that Jack was searching for himself, needy for assurance, but his hands told a whole different story. Long, tapered fingers, delicate but strong, his hands were nothing less than magic. How often had Sam blessed those hands, at the same time she wished—and there it was again, sliding up the inside of her thigh. She felt her legs part, while she tried to keep up her end of the conversation, managing to say something especially insightful, like "Uh huh," as Jack's hand slipped farther, farther up her leg, until his voice only echoed in her head, until he had pushed her underwear aside—the lavender La Perlas she, the evildoer, had bought for the occasion. And there were his fingers inside of her, gently pushing further up, until she heard a groan escape her lips. Jack smiled at her.

"Shall we go?" he asked, placing a $100 bill on the table. "This place can be so stifling." They had made it as far as the bathroom, one of the few civilized places where a bathroom's door locked the entire world out. One stall, one sink, one marble space meant for two. Jack kissed Sam until she thought she'd lose her breath, then lifted her—again, so gently, how did he know how to be gentle, but confident, when he seduced her?—until she was rested on the sink. He lifted her skirt, and parted her legs, groaning with pleasure as he lowered himself to kiss her. Sam grasped the faucets, and bit her lips, and tried to think about how rude they were being hogging the bathroom—anything to distract her from the extraordinary feeling that Jack was giving her, a feeling Jack seemed to be sharing. She felt her breath catch, beginning to come, when he suddenly lifted her off the sink, turned her around, and entered her from behind, all so fast that she had no chance to object. So there they were, Sam's hands on the mirror, Jack behind her, his hands on her hips, guiding her towards him, guiding her until her knees gave out, and he had to hold her up, and then, finally, with a shiver and a low growl, he let go, holding her hips and resting his head on her back. And now was supposed to be the awkward time, and Sam felt a surge of frustration that it wasn't. Why couldn't she feel uncomfortable, untwisting her underwear from her shoe, cursing as it caught on her heel, reassembling herself as Jack did the same? This, as far as Sam was convinced, was the most intimate act in the world—the aftermath of sex, where both partners stood there, flushed, empty, done with each other. But Sam didn't feel that with Jack, she didn't feel it as he smiled at her in the mirror, as he kissed the side of her neck. As he gallantly, but with a devilish smile, held the door open for her to leave the bathroom, as if he were a kind stranger holding open the door at Bloomingdale's. He reached for her hand as they walked down the hallway, and for one brief minute, Sam felt a kind of total happiness.

Even if it was just the grownup equivalent of playing house—playing boyfriend and girlfriend—she experienced flashes of this with Jack. Such a good friend, such a good man. But something was just missing. Something kept her from being able to imagine making it more . . . complicated, for lack of a better word.

But this, their sex life, was one of the few areas that Sam felt—at least in the moment of it, and the moments following—couldn't be less complicated. Their sex was affectionate and just too damn good. And she was, she told herself, a grownup who, after years of teenage Episcopalian guilt, finally figured she could indulge as liberally as her male friends—or so she rationalized. Yeah, right. And that's why she hadn't had sex in a year. Still, theoretically, Sam believed two things: There was sex with love, and there was sex for sex. Two fine things not to be underappreciated, but as different as a shopping trip to Milan and a shopping trip to Filene's Basement. Excellent shopping, both, but—but Jack was different somehow. He fell between the cracks, and Sam didn't know how to move him in her heart in either one direction or the other. She hadn't known how since they had first met several years ago through friends. They'd never talked about what, exactly, their relationship was or wasn't—had never even broached the topic, Sam realized. It was as if they were married to other people and having an affair—no discussions of future or intentions, just a series of passionate, intense, momentary meetings.

Still holding hands as they headed quietly out of the Carlyle, Jack began walking Sam the two blocks home. Still flushed, she didn't protest. After a few minutes in silence, she began, "Jack, I don't want—"

He placed a finger to her lips. "After that," he said with a smile, "what could you still want?"

Sam smiled back. What had she been about to say? She had no idea. "Save me?" "Rescue me from myself?" Sam laughed out loud at the idea. "Would you like to come up for a sleepover?" she asked instead, standing in front of her building. "I promise I'd let you sleep in peace—for an hour, at least."

Jack leaned down and kissed her on the lips, only brushing

them before he took a step back. "Good night, Sam. Thank you." She looked at him, wanting to grab him and flee at the same time.

"Good night, Jack."

Sam walked upstairs, shedding her suit as she strolled to the bathroom, turning on her stereo, and ran the bath. She needed quiet to figure out what had happened—what had happened so many times—with Jack. She stepped out of her ruined underwear. Funny how she spent so much money on La Perla, when men, she felt pretty sure, didn't care what women were wearing as long as they got out of it pronto, and slipped into the hot bubbles. She heard the phone ring in the other room, and the machine pick up. "Sam, don't even try to pretend . . ."

Ugh. How did the man know? She raised herself from the tub, trailing bubbles across the living room until she found the phone.

"What do you want from me, boy?"

"Every detail, and no less, thank you very much."

Sam got back into the tub with a sigh. "Nothing, nothing, nothing."

"I think my lady doth protest too much."

"Aren't you supposed to be with your family now? Is this really what you want to talk about?"

"Without a doubt," Tom said. "I can't feel sad for one more second today."

"Tom," Sam began, "you need to talk about this. Or I need you to talk to me about this. It's too strange and sad to think of you going through this alone. I want to help, however I can."

"So dish for me, please," he responded. His tone was still light, but there was a sternness to it that Sam recognized. Tom's wall of defense had gone up, and the U.S. Army couldn't have battered it down.

"Okay, fine," Sam said. "If that's what you want." She was met by silence. "I'm becoming a parody of myself, I really am," Sam said. "I'm like those women on *Sex and the City.* You watch them and say, "Phew, thank God they're just caricatures, but I'm starting to feel like that. Perfectly accessorized, but—"

"No soul," Tom interrupted. "My only question is, what took you so long? The rest of us have known that about you for years. Without your labels, darling, you are an absolute zero, and I do not mean in size. Actually, I've been meaning to talk to you about your ever-growing girth."

"Tom!" Sam laughed. "Okay. I give up. I went to the Carlyle with Jack, we schtupped our brains out, and that's it."

"More so-called 'meaningless sex,'" Tom said. "You don't believe in it any more than I do."

Sam thought for a second, grateful that Tom was one of those friends with whom silence could be comfortable. What did she think? Tom was a hopeless romantic—she wished he'd just go off and get laid, for God's sake—but she wasn't proving to be much better at it than he was.

"Listen, buddy, this is women's lib at its best. My mother marched many a mile in protest to allow me this evening—sex for sex, and that's it. And yes, it was worth it."

"Right. Which is why you're in the bathtub yet again, soaking your sorrows. Never a good sign, Sam, never a good sign. Sorrow floats. And don't think I can't hear that good-to-kill-yourself-by music in the background. Are you listening to the fucking Indigo Girls again?"

"You got me there. I figure if I listen to enough lesbian music I might be able to cross over to the other side and rid myself of all my troubles."

"You know you love 'em. Too bad that love goes unreturned."

Tom had taken Sam to a lesbian bar once—Sam had been

game to be a tourist, if not ready to apply for a green card—but not one single woman had looked at her. Not for the entire two hours, not when she made Tom tell her some stupid joke so she could laugh loudly to get attention, not when she had catwalked to the bathroom.

"Here's the thing," Sam said, sitting up straighter in the tub. "If I could just figure out how to love a man who loves me, or how to make a man I love love me back."

"You'd win the Nobel Prize. Love you, Sam," Tom said. "Sleep well."

Sam slipped under the water and let out a scream. This love thing was very, very tricky.

Chapter 9

Four o'clock. Tom was killing time. He had spent the day finishing up the closing of a section, tweaking the headlines, making sure the photo credits were in, getting changes from the factchecker, taking his top editor's fixes. Like most office jobs, editing was mostly about making sure everyone was doing his part well, and on time.

But now, there was nothing to do. *Profit* came out every two weeks, which meant seven days of pure hell followed by three of boredom. He thought about ditching work early today, but he didn't have anything to do at home either, and at the office there was less likelihood of thinking about his mom. He considered going through his files and throwing stuff away—that always made him feel better—then decided against it for no good reason. He sat at his computer and clicked constantly on his email inbox, hoping for a message from Justin. Occasionally he moved the mouse around and watched the arrow glide across the screen. *Magazines are so fucking glamorous,* he thought.

His email beeped. It was Trevor.

> Mr. T! You can't be mad at me forever. Don't make me come out there and get you. Seriously, give me a call. I need to talk to you about some of Mom's stuff.

A knock. "Hey." It was Ethan Foxman, the other gay editor at *Profit.* They'd become fast friends, at first because they were both gay. Ethan, who had been at the magazine for five years, had long ago made sure everyone knew he was gay;

Tom would have preferred to wait until it seemed relevant to come out at the office, but as the lifestyle editor, he was simply presumed to be gay. Their friendship grew deeper when they shared a room at the magazine's retreat in Puerto Rico. The whole event was like a wedding in that you partied with the same people at one meal after another. After the first day they more or less ignored the agenda and watched morning television, then went to the beach. (Consequently, everyone thought they were getting it on.)

He lay down on Tom's sofa. "What are you up to?" Ethan asked.

"Admiring your tan, Foxman. You look more Latino than ever."

"I know. Two days in South Beach and I got called 'Papi' more than you can imagine." Ethan was Jewish but to his everlasting mortification passed as Latino. He was happy to pretend for a while but eventually the truth had to come out, so why bother. Plus he didn't speak Spanish.

"I'm telling you, just say that your mother was a Nicaraguan whore." Ethan frowned: he was practically a lesbian in his opposition to the straight white patriarchy. "Sorry."

"That's okay." Ethan got serious. "How are you feeling?"

God, not again. He understood why people wanted to talk about his mom, or that they thought he would want to, but he didn't. "Better, thanks."

Ethan got the hint. "What are you up to tonight?"

"Dinner with Andrew. And you?"

"I'm having a mevening." The word made them both smile. They loved to invent words. 'Mevening' was one of Tom's. A combination of 'me' and 'evening,' it meant you were going to stay home and probably watch TV, most likely rent a video (and if so, almost definitely it'd be a romantic teen comedy, with a fifty-fifty chance of it climaxing at a prom), and for sure you'd eat ice cream. In theory, if you were doing it with someone, it became a wevening—but in modification the word lost some of its allure. In any event, staying home for Tom and his friends was a rare treat.

"Delicious. Renting?"

"I think so. I'm leaning toward *Picture Perfect.*"

"Again!" Tom loved Jennifer Aniston, but hated watching movies more than once. Although come to think of it he did own *Picture Perfect* . . . He'd bought a prewatched copy at World of Video, and was saving it for a night of pure desperation. "I should give you my copy."

"What can I say," Ethan said. "I'm feeling clooney." Another invented word, of undetermined provenance. Tom had wondered why there was no word that meant "horny for love," and for a while he'd ask everyone he ran into what word they would use: A word that expressed the yearning all single people had—for Tom, it was usually on Sunday afternoons—to be in love, to be loved, to love. "Moony" had come to mind, but it sounded too much like you were lost in the stars. Then one morning, waiting for the 10 A.M. meeting to start, Tom was telling Ethan about the dream he'd had the night before. In his dream, Tom and George Clooney were a couple. There was no sex in the dream, but George Clooney was very much Tom's boyfriend. George Clooney was home. Tom was whispering this to Ethan, saying how he'd always found Clooney attractive—who didn't?—but that he'd never thought much more about him than that.

"Clooney!" Ethan said.

"Right, Foxman. George Clooney. Have you been listening?"

"No, that's the word. Clooney. It means horny for love. 'How are you handling your breakup? Well, I'm feeling a bit clooney.' "

At least that's what Ethan claims had happened. Tom

remembers the dream but not exactly who thought clooney should be an adjective. It didn't matter except until one day Tom said he thought he'd try writing an article for the *New Yorker* about words he'd invented, and added clooney to the list. Ethan got petulant, and they never mentioned it again.

"Speaking of which," Ethan said, "any word from Justin?"

Tom moaned and swiveled in his chair; an obvious no.

"Why don't you email him?" Ethan liked to torture Tom. They had had this conversation several times that week, but Ethan was a bit of a romantic, convinced that good things happen to good people, as long as good people are upfront about their feelings. The great part about it was that Ethan never tired of talking about Justin. Tom briefly wondered if Ethan didn't somehow enjoy his misery.

"I told you! He doesn't want to go out with me. I could tell." Tom daydreamed for the umpteenth time what it would be like to be in Justin's arms. He didn't think lustful thoughts, which was strange. He wanted to sleep with Justin, sure, but that wasn't the part he was obsessing about. He just wanted to be with him.

"The 'really' thing."

"Yes the 'really' thing. You have to admit that's a pretty good sign."

"But he smiled as he said it?"

"Well, yeah, but it might have been more of a smirk."

"What do you have to lose?"

"My pride! And yes it matters! It's what keeps me warm at night." They looked at each other. They were both aware that eventually Tom would email Justin, if only for something to do. No one knew the horror of the three down days better than Ethan. "If I were to email him, what would I say? It would be so great if I just had a reason to email, if there was something I knew he'd want to know."

"Tell him he makes you feel like Courtney Love right after

Kurt Cobain's suicide, like you want to rip off your scabs just so you can feel something other than this sickening numbness."

"Wait," Tom said as he mimicked typing. "I lost you after 'suicide.' "

"Just say 'hey, what's up, want to catch a movie?' You know he likes movies."

"But they make such shitty dates. Still, I guess it's the best option."

howdy justin, what's up? want to catch a movie this week? t.

Tom read it to Ethan. "Perfect," said Ethan. "Keep it simple."

"I think it's too late to build a mystery."

"Send it."

"Wait. What if—"

Ethan got up, reached over Tom, and clicked on send. "There," he said. "It's in God's hands now."

"But I don't believe in God."

"You will if he says yes."

Chapter 10

Sam stopped to pick up coffee from the kiosk outside her office, praising herself for getting dressed and to work on time. She was halfway through the revolving door when she heard a cry. "Hey, lady! You forgot your coffee!" Great beginning, she thought, doubling back to the cup. She only had one more obstacle: slinking into her office unnoticed, drinking another shot of caffeine, and keeping the door shut until 6 P.M. How hard could that be?

"Never, ever ask a question like that," Sam muttered, as she saw a note taped to her door. She put the coffee cup between her teeth, hoping for the best, and grabbed the note with her free hand. It was from the editor-in-chief's secretary: "Roger would like to see you at 10:30 in his office." Naturally, this was the day when she had chosen to exercise her rights as a hung-over, sleep-deprived, just-been-screwed-at-the-Carlyle-by-a-man-she-could-maybe-but-didn't . . . something, and slipped into faded jeans and a T-shirt.

A meeting with Edgars was a guarantee of one of two things: a bonus (which happened to someone, once), or a firing (better statistics there). Well, at least Sam knew her job was safe. The studios had good working relationships with Sam, which had been her safety net for years. And she'd been at the magazine too long to have something bad happen to her without hearing it from the gossip chain first.

Everyone knew to avoid the editor-in-chief early in the morning—and 10:30 A.M. was definitely early for him. A notorious drinker, he was usually miserable and hung over from the evening before, until he went out for his martini lunches at 1 P.M. So right after lunch wasn't so good, either, because he'd promise the world and not remember any of it, and 4 P.M. wasn't good, either, because the hangover was setting in again, until 6 P.M., when he opened the evening's first bottle of vodka. By 6:20, the line of people waiting to see him stretched down the hallway. The smart ones brought a glass.

"Samantha, come in. Close the door," Edgars said, smiling from behind his massive desk. Damn, that closed door thing was never good. "Sit," he said, motioning to the chair across from his desk. Another bad sign. All pleasant conversations were held in the corner of his office with the couches. But Sam had done nothing but work her ass off and—

"I'm concerned, Samantha." Sam looked up, surprised. Had he been in the Carlyle? Good God, of course not.

"I'm sorry, sir?" Sam kicked herself. At the age of twenty-eight, why did she still fall back on her childhood manners, which only made her bosses feel like they were 175 years old? *Which,* she thought, *they were . . .*

"It's come to my attention that you, um, you . . . You may have crossed boundaries." Now what the hell was he talking about? Sam definitely hadn't had enough coffee, but even in her sleepy state, she knew she hadn't crossed any lines as far as her work was concerned. She had earned a reputation over the years as being an ethical and fair reporter.

"Sir?" Shit. She had to get herself together, and now. "I'm sorry, but I'm a bit confused."

"Well, it's come to my attention that you, um, that you, you violated a code that we all know exists, that you cannot, oh, well, Samantha, I don't know how to say this . . ." Edgars winced, looking pained.

Sam stared, confused and panicked. All her life, she'd been terrified of being caught breaking some code of behavior, thanks to her mother's strict upbringing of exactly how young ladies behaved. To this day, Sam couldn't eat on the street—not even so much as chew a piece of gum. Not that she would dare to chew gum.

"I would help you, I really would, but I have no idea what you're talking about," Sam said. She felt a surge of impatience.

"That business with, um, er . . . you know?"

"No, sir," Sam said, giving up and falling back into the formality that made her most comfortable when she was ill at ease. "I have no idea what you're talking about. I'm sorry."

"Russell Crowe."

She stifled a laugh. This was not actually happening. Man, this was going to be embarrassing. "Excuse me?"

"You know we can't be having this. I know this happened several months ago, but it just came to my attention, and it's my job to act when something like this crosses my path. I honestly wish it hadn't. You're one of the finest reporters I have, but I can't have you compromising the magazine like this."

"I didn't do anything!" Sam said, realizing she sounded like she was back in third grade, accused of stealing from the cookie jar. She let out a nervous giggle. "That was a rumor started by someone else. Everyone knows it isn't true! For God's sake, *you* know it's not true!"

"Well, unfortunately, I don't," Edgars said, "and I can't risk anyone else not knowing, either, and having you associated with the magazine. I'm sorry."

"You're sorry?" Sam said, feeling tears of rage build up in her eyes. "I didn't *do* anything. I interviewed the man for all of ten minutes at a party. I left. Nothing happened. He didn't even hit on me, for God's sake. This is lunacy."

But Edgars' jaw was set. "Samantha, I really am sorry, I'm going to have to ask you to leave. I've notified human resources, and we've arranged for two months of severance."

"What?" Sam stared at him, slack-jawed. Tears were streaming down her face, and she didn't care. "I've worked here for six years. You yourself just told me I'm one of your most valued employees. How can I prove to you this never happened?"

But Edgars just shook his head. "Even if it isn't—and I really hope it isn't, Sam—the harm has been done." Sam took a deep breath, wiped the tears away with the back of her hand, and tried again.

"Edgars. I understand that this isn't the kind of thing you like to hear, but my God—far worse rumors circulate about all of us all the time. And even if I *had* fooled around with Crowe, I wasn't writing a story about him! I was just getting a quote from him on the festival!" Sam could hear her voice start to rise, but she didn't care. "I have spent *years* busting my butt for this magazine. Surely you owe me more than this? You can't fire me just because you heard a rumor that has absolutely *nothing* to do with reality!"

Edgars sighed, and looked almost sorry. "Unfortunately, I not only can, I have to." And with that, he rose and stood beside her chair, resting his hand lightly on her shoulder. The conversation was over.

"How could you do this to me?" Sam sobbed. But Edgars merely gestured for her to get up, and escorted her to the door. Somehow, and she would never know how, she managed to stand and walk through it.

Chapter 11

Am I interrupting anything?" Tom was poking his head in Veronica's office, and the relief in her eyes was visible—he figured she had been afraid that their little joke was gone forever.

"Just thinking about how to clean up Wall Street," she said.

"Buena suerte," he said. "That means 'good luck' south of the border."

"Sí," she said. *"Quieres fumar?"*

Did he ever. This Justin thing was making him crazy, and most of his friends wouldn't talk about it. Andrew was sick of the topic, and Sam, in her funk, wasn't returning his calls. Neither was R.J., who was probably on a sex bender.

Justin had said yes to a date, then blown Tom off. Said he'd tried to call but Tom was unlisted (then had the nerve to express disbelief that Tom had in fact at one point warranted a stalker—a co-worker gone psycho, Tom didn't like to discuss it). They made plans for the next night, and Justin said he'd probably have to cancel, because he'd probably have to work. Then when he called to say he could in fact go out, he didn't say "Might as well," but he might as well have.

Tom could replay the whole date in his mind. He called it the Night of 1,000 Demerits. Justin, frankly, had behaved like an asshole. Examples?

1. When they met in the street, Justin was on his cell phone—and stayed on it for a good five minutes while they walked to the restaurant.

2. He said that if he had cable he'd be at home watching the Republican candidates for something-or-other debate.
3. He flirted with the waiter.
4. After pressing Tom for details on his last boyfriend, he asked if the boyfriend was cute. When Tom said "Damn straight," Justin said that maybe he should meet him—seeing as how he was single and all.
5. He looked at his watch. Twice.

"Twice?" Veronica was disgusted.

"I'm telling you, there were 995 more demerits. I think I have a list back up in my office."

"Maybe that's part of the problem."

He knew what she was saying: Maybe Tom was enjoying the misery a little too much. Maybe it was just the novelty. He dismissed it.

"Look, Tom, this guy's no good. He just doesn't want a boyfriend right now, and if he does, and I'm sorry to have to say this, he doesn't want you." She sighed. "But obviously he likes you, or he wouldn't string you along. I think you need to entertain the possibility that all he wants is a friendship, and he's trying to tell you that by being an asshole."

Great, Tom thought. *Another friend.* He loved his friends, he did, but he didn't need more. And he didn't need a friend he was in love with. It was bad enough that his relationship with his brother was one big cliché. The last thing he wanted was to be in another relationship that made him look like the smaller person.

"I don't get it, Tom," Veronica said. "What is it about this guy?"

Tom took one last drag off his cigarette. "He gets my jokes. I've never dated anyone who gets my jokes. And he makes jokes back—good jokes. He's big, and I've never dated anyone my height." He dropped the butt on the ground and stepped on it.

"Sam is convinced that I like unattainable men, but I don't. I hate it. I hate that he treats me like shit. But I swear to God, I've never felt anything so right. I tingle when I see him. I *tingle*. And the worst part is, even though half the time he's being a schmuck, the other half he's flirting."

"And you're never bored when you're around him."

"Exactly. In my mind, that's love. But have you ever been in love with someone who didn't love you back? I haven't. In fact, I've never been in love with someone at all. But I've read about it, I've seen the movies, and it's so much worse than I had ever imagined. And in the books, in the movies, the guy usually ends up with the—well, not the guy, but you get my drift. It works out. Part of me says go, but part of me says stay."

Back upstairs, he went through his emails. One from R.J.:

> I'm back! Ooh-whee! Do I have a great story for you! I didn't even know the circus was in town!

One from his boss:

> Excellent section this issue! By the way, did you see the piece in the Times about trapeze school, down by the river? Could be a good item . . .

Jesus, Tom thought. *Life is weird.*

And one from Trevor:

> American has a last-minute fare this weekend. $325 round-trip. Call me by 3 P.M. or I'm booking it.

Tom picked up the phone. He didn't want to talk to Trevor right now, but he really didn't want to see him this weekend.

Trevor's assistant answered. It didn't help his mood to be reminded that Trevor was successful enough to warrant an assistant.

"Hi, this is Tom Sanders, Trevor's brother. Is he in?"

"Just a moment." Tom took a pen and drew a line on his hand. *Be nice . . .*

"Well, well, well. The prodigal brother. I had a feeling that would get you to call."

"Howdy, Trevor."

"Listen, Tom, I hate that you're mad at me. I just want—"

"Stop. Let me. I've been an ass." Tom let the possibility of the second syllable hang there. He hadn't planned on being apologetic, but what the heck. Maybe he could use one more friend these days. Plus, they still had to go through the probate process, and there was no point in being at war with your brother. "And I'm sorry. This has been harder than I thought."

Trevor exhaled. "Thanks, Mr. T. It's good to hear you say that. Good to hear you speak at all. I know you're not one for all this family shit, but I don't think it would kill us to get a little closer." Tom had a creepy déjà vu sensation, and he remembered how awkward he had made the same sort of sentiment sound when he mocked it to Sam. "Just give it a chance, okay? I promise, I'm not all that perfect."

"I know," Tom said, a little too fast. Then, to sweeten it: "But who is?"

Chapter 12

Whoever said that your twenties was a great decade had clearly, and magically, skipped from being nineteen to thirty-two. Or had a serious case of Alzheimer's that made him forget the reality of those horrid years.

Sam was lying on her couch. *Damn it,* she thought, *I deserve a good wallow*. The last two weeks had been the most humiliating, depressing period in her life. After being escorted out of her office, Sam had spent most of the afternoon raging. Then she took herself for an exhausting, six-mile run through Central Park, racing up the hills until her need to throw up finally won out over the need to commit murder. Seizing the moment, Sam jogged back to her apartment and didn't even bother showering before she started logging calls.

To her friend who was an editor at *Newsweek.* To another friend who was the number two at *Marie Claire.* To a high school friend who worked at the *Daily News.* And so on and so on—heck, she even called someone who worked at *Redbook*—until, four hours later, she was calling friends of friends she had met at screenings and cocktail parties. It was absolutely amazing. She slunk down in her chair and called Tom. "You're not going to believe this," she said. "Some people won't even take my calls. And the people who are nice enough to speak to me do so in low, conspiratorial whispers, as if they're afraid getting caught talking to me will get *them* fired."

"What are they saying?" Tom asked.

"They're saying that they'd love to talk to me in a few months, but that right now, they can't touch me."

"What?"

"I know." Sam started to cry again, as much from disbelief as frustration and exhaustion. "Apparently, this rumor has been circulating like mad, long before I even heard about it, let alone Edgars. And while a couple of people were nice enough to say they didn't think it was that big a deal, apparently enough people *do* care that they're too nervous to go near me until the buzz dies down."

"That makes a little more sense then," Tom said thoughtfully.

"What?" Sam snapped at him in fury. "How could you say that?"

"Hey, hey, hang on," Tom said. "This *isn't* going to end up being a big deal, I promise."

"Yeah, easy for you to say," Sam muttered weepily.

"All I meant," Tom continued calmly, "is that this makes more sense in terms of your conversation with Edgars. From what you told me, he was uncomfortable and didn't want to fire you—it was almost like his hand was being forced. Now I'm pretty sure it *was*. If this came down from his bosses, that could explain things."

"No," Sam said, feeling herself get mad again. She had the sense he knew her parents had money, and worried that he was going to tell her to ask them for it—which she had always refused to do. "No, it does *not* make sense. If a male reporter had a rumor like this going around about him, he would be fielding calls from every headhunter in New York. Edgars would call him in and *promote* him. You know it's true. I fucking *hate* this." So much for not swearing.

Tom managed to calm her down a bit, making a deal with her that if she'd get into the shower, he'd take her for a BLT at her favorite diner.

That was twelve days ago, and nice as it was, it didn't help. In fact, it was the last time she had left her apartment.

She sighed and looked around her living room. It was disgusting. A couple pizza boxes littered the floor. The garbage pail next to her—she had given up days ago on actually going across the room to throw things away—was littered with Kleenex from her crying jags. On the coffee table was a bottle of Visine, a bottle of water, and a quart of vodka, which was being emptied at an alarming rate. Sam started to cry again, and then saw that she was out of Kleenex. Screw it. She wiped her nose on the sleeve of her sweatshirt. She'd been wearing it for three days anyway, so what was the difference?

Sam heard the phone ring but didn't bother to move. Other than calling her mother and pretending everything was fine—the last thing she could deal with was her mother coming in and attempting to save the day—she had let the answering machine pick up every time. "Sam, it's Tom, and I swear to you, if you do not pick up this very second I'm going to come over there." He paused. She didn't move. "I've given you ten days of not returning phone calls. Now you have to." He paused again. She rolled over, placing her back to the phone. "That's it, I'm on my way." Sam raced—rather shakily—for the phone.

"Don't you dare," she said, picking up. Her voice was hoarse from crying and lack of use. "I love you, but I'm of absolutely no use right now. But Tom?"

"Yes?" he said slowly.

"How are *you?* I've been thinking about you so often. Have you gotten my messages?"

"Um, the ones you leave me every morning between 3 A.M. and 5 A.M., when you know you can't possibly get me?"

"Yeah, those," Sam said. "I want you to know how much you're on my mind—how are you doing with your mom's death?"

Tom sighed. "I don't know. It's a little better most days, a lot worse some days. But you know I don't really want to talk about it. Otherwise you'd actually call me during daylight hours."

"I know," Sam continued. "But even if you don't want to talk about it that often, I still want you to know I love you. And I think it would be good for you to talk about it a little, no?"

"No," Tom said, "I'm not sure it would be. But if *you* do, you're going to have to actually be willing to be seen. I'll talk about it, but only in person."

"Can't right now, sorry," Sam said. "I'm busy." There was a slight teasing tone in her voice, which they were both relieved to hear.

"What are you so busy doing?"

"Oh, packing my bag," Sam said. "I just got a call from Sean Connery, who has realized the error of his ways. A limo is coming to pick me up in thirty minutes and take me to the airport, where I'll board a jet to Paris and our suite at the Bristol. There, Sean will be waiting for me with a bottle of Krug, ready to plan the rest of our happy lives together."

"He's a little old for you," Tom said slowly. "And now, if we may have a bit of a reality check?"

"Reality sucks," Sam said. "I've been in the same clothes for three days."

"That's not so bad."

"I'm so depressed I'm getting cigarettes delivered, so I don't have to go outside."

"Okay, still not completely awful . . ."

"I had ramen noodles, chicken flavor, for breakfast. And for lunch and dinner the day before. This morning, I didn't even bother with the flavor packet—I just ate the noodles."

"This is an emergency."

"I *hate* ramen!" Sam wailed.

"And you would be eating it why?" Tom asked unhelpfully.

"Perhaps you will notice, Mr. Fancy Pants Editor, that I no longer have a job. Perhaps you can bend your imagination around the fact that I do not, therefore, have an income. Nor do I, unlike *some* people"—Sam was practically spitting here—"have an expense account to go out and wine and dine the charming literati who might possibly change my pathetic existence. And even if I *did,"* she continued, "none of them would be"—Sam let out a howl and started to cry again—"willing to be seen with me."

"Oh, Jesus," Tom said slowly, letting out a little whistle.

"What?"

"You have truly gone off the deep end."

"Maybe it's the MSG in the ramen." Sam let out a little giggle. "Oh my God! Did you hear that?"

"Um, what?" Tom asked carefully.

"I giggled! I did, I did, I did! Okay, maybe it was a tiny one, it wasn't even funny, but it was definitely there." Sam sank to the floor. After days of silence on the couch, this standing-and-talking thing was killing her.

"I have a thought," Tom said. "While you are being wholly ridiculous and unpleasant, I understand that's because you've been taken over by aliens. Perhaps if you'll agree to see me, we can perform an exorcism? You know, detox the devil with a little martini, paid for by Mr. Fancy Pants Editor's expense account?"

Sam sighed again and lay down on the floor. "I can't. That will mean changing my clothes."

"Yes, it will," Tom said.

"Too tired."

"Tough shit."

"Can't."

"Trattoria Dell'Arte, 8 P.M."

"I told you . . ." Sam started to say, but realized she was

talking to dead air. Tom had hung up. Damn him. She rose to put the phone back on the cradle. Well, since she was already up, she thought, she might as well investigate what, exactly, that shower in her bathroom was for. After all, Tom needed her—even if he didn't know it. And she sure as hell needed him.

Chapter 13

Anyone who worked in magazines heard the same question as soon as he complained about his job: Where *would* you want to work? When Tom first joined the industry, Tom found that sort of thing fun—it was like trying on different clothes. He could imagine working at *Jane,* spending the day talking about boys, trading beauty secrets, and gossiping about Pamela Anderson. Or *Food + Wine,* where he'd learn how to cook and eat at only the best restaurants in town. Or *New York,* where he could have the freedom of a general-interest magazine—to assign stories about anything!—without having to really keep up on the rest of the country. Or *The New Yorker,* but fat chance of that.

Problem was, he didn't really like those magazines. Well, he liked a lot of things about all of them, and many more, but he was at the point in his career where he thought he knew better than the people above him, but was in no way near anyone actually giving him control.

He was at the gym, having abandoned hoping to achieve any sort of rhythm on the elliptical machine, which as far as he could tell was totally impossible, but at least he was lucky enough to get one without the flailing armpieces. As he usually did during moments of intense aerobic boredom, he thought about the magazine he would like to start.

Years ago, Tom had been called in for an interview at *FHM,* a crass British men's magazine that was staffing up for an American edition. The editor and he had hit it off, but both agreed that it wasn't an ideal match. Tom simply never would be a "lad" (a sports-loving, babe-chasing manchild). Still, they had had a long conversation about why American magazines refused to believe that it was acceptable to simply be fun. They either had to tell you how to live or insist on teaching you something. Even women's fashion magazines were so serious—if *Harper's Bazaar* ran one more piece about AIDS in Africa (a worthy topic, but in *Bazaar?)* Tom was going to puke. The conversation with the editor of *FHM* stuck with him, and had affected the way he looked at *Profit* when he moved over to start his Dessert section. It was a basic philosophy that most editors forgot: people liked to be entertained.

And, essentially, that was the idea behind the magazine he wanted to start. Not that it was a humor magazine; if the sharp kids at *Spy* couldn't make that work, Tom didn't stand a chance. No, it was a lifestyle magazine leavened with joy. "It'll fetishize experience," was how Tom described it to himself. "The same way *Wallpaper* fetishizes design."

He called it *Bite.* It came out of an idea he had for the first cover. A beautiful woman taking a huge bite out of a foxy red apple. Life is so tempting: why not dive in, muck around, take a big delicious bite of it? The Eve allusion was entirely intentional.

Other magazines either pandered to readers and/or advertisers, or they relentlessly tried to prove they were smarter than anyone who read them. Where was the joy? Was it impossible to be smart and sexy? He wanted to give Joyce Carol Oates ecstasy and have her write about it. Get sex tips from Bangkok hookers. Send a writer to massage school. Skip the traditional restaurant reviews (food/service/décor/yawn) for a setup in which the critic takes someone famous for good taste to the restaurant; simply print their conversation—about the restaurant, about food in general, about anything. Tom had spent so much time editing the same old lifestyle stuff that the very idea of breaking the rules was like unleashing a dam.

"Ten more minutes," he muttered.

He wasn't sure he could stand ten more minutes of thinking about *Bite.* It occasionally kept him up nights, drove him to distraction every time he read another lifestyle magazine, one that took its mission too seriously (he liked *Outside,* but just because people like to rock-climb doesn't mean they want to read 10,000 words on the conflict in the mountains of Kashmir). But how long would he have to be a drone, a cog in the machine, before he'd get a chance? And would someone else do it by then?

He had never mentioned it to Sam, mostly because he was afraid that she'd think it was stupid, or point out some way it would never work. But she'd be great to work on it with—she had celebrity contacts, which was something Tom knew nothing about (and didn't want to), and she loved life even more than he did.

Starting a magazine was something every editor dreamed of; the fact that it cost yachtloads of money kept it firmly in the dream category. Then again, maybe he could at least talk to Sam about doing up a prototype. They would never be able to start the magazine on their own, unless maybe they won Lotto, but they could maybe get an executive at Worldwide, which owned both *Profit* and *Star Face,* to look at it. It would be a good exercise, and as selfish as it may be, his bosses would learn that he wanted bigger things than Dessert. It would give Sam something productive to do until she regained her reputation (well, her good reputation, anyway). And it would be fun—and that was the whole point, right?

Chapter 14

Tom wasn't that comfortable with her overt affection, but at this moment, she didn't care. She threw her arms around him and gave him a giant, long hug.

"I don't think I've ever been so happy to see anyone in my life," she said, as they sat. "Now, how are you doing?"

"Soldiering on," he said. "You can't imagine how easy it is if you just don't ever think about it."

Sam raised her eyebrow. "I've never gotten this about you Tom, I really haven't."

"Trust me," he said. "Where there's a will there's a way. And lest you doubt that my way of coping with things isn't as good as yours, let's just hold up as proof the way each of us looks, shall we?"

"You do have a point," Sam said with a smile. Tom looked amazing, in a Calvin Klein suit. She, on the other hand, had thrown on a pair of cargo pants and an old sweater. And while she was finally clean, she knew the bags under her puffy eyes were a dead giveaway.

"You've got the pallor of someone who's malnourished," Tom joked. "Let's get you some real food."

They were seated at a quiet corner table in the back of the restaurant where Sam wouldn't embarrass Tom, who was always a little taken aback at Sam's utter lack of self-consciousness when it came to weeping vociferously in public. "I know why you seated us here," Sam said. Tom threw his hands up, busted. "But you know, Tom, a good cry every now and then isn't the worst thing in the world. How's your family holding up?"

He sighed. "You mean Trevor and me? We're fine, or at least better. I mean the thing is, all teasing aside about my man-of-steel approach, it still feels so unreal I don't think I fully accept it. I haven't lived with my mom in so long, it's not like anything has changed in my daily life, so it's more like I'll be sitting there, in a meeting or on the phone, and suddenly I feel like all the air has been knocked out of me, and I can't figure out why. And then I do, and I feel pretty shitty. But in terms of wanting to talk about it, there really isn't that much to be said, truly. I mean, it happened. It's over. And now I have to just get used to it."

Sam nodded. "What can I do to help?"

Tom laughed. "Oddly, your 3 A.M. phone calls are a blessing, because you totally understood—I just want to know that people are thinking of me and checking in, but I don't necessarily want to dwell on it." He paused. "Okay?"

"Absolutely," Sam said. "And when and if this changes, let me know."

"Deal," Tom said. "Now, can we please talk about your own hell?"

Sam smiled. "Because it's so interesting, right?" she said. "Girl lies on couch for twelve days, knowing she'll never be employed again. Now that makes for a fascinating conversation!"

"Seriously, what do your options look like?" Tom asked.

"I don't really seem to have any, although I will admit I haven't tried very hard since that first day I called everyone in town. I guess it's time to start hunting again. Maybe the *Des Moines Register* is looking for freelancers? I doubt they'll have heard of my escapades out there."

"Don't be so sure."

"It's too bad my eyes are so swollen I can't see you," she responded, "or I'd reach across the table and smack you."

"You know, you do have a case against the magazine. Sure,

you hate the idea, but everyone knows they have a terrible time with women, and this is some kind of reverse slander, since they've fired you with absolutely no proof and hurt your chances of being hired."

Sam grimaced. "Ugh. I hate the idea of spending any more energy going down to their level. And I'm sure there's a better way of getting what I want. If I could just figure out what I want . . ."

"You'll probably kill me, but I have to ask. Would you consider asking your parents for money? You think it's your dirty little secret, but the fact that you grew up on Fifth Avenue does kind of give it away . . ."

"No chance," Sam said firmly. He meant well, but no. "Never. No way. I've paid my own way since college, and that's not about to change now. I'll just have to make do. I'm never going to ask them to help me finance a life of sloth."

"Alright. But in the meantime, you'll just freelance for me to pay your bills," Tom said.

Sam reached across the table and held Tom's hand—damn his embarrassment at displays of affection. "You're an unbelievable friend. Thank you."

"And in the meantime," Tom continued, shrugging off both her hand and her gratitude, "I'm working on a plan. A project."

"Do tell!"

"Not yet," Tom said slowly. "But I promise it'll be worth waiting for. Promise."

Sam had to wait only as long as her cab ride home. As she walked in the door, the phone was ringing, and in a true sign of how Tom had lifted her spirits, she answered it without waiting for the machine to screen.

"Hello?"

"It's me. I couldn't stand it."

Sam laughed. "Thank you for such a lovely dinner. I can't tell you how much it meant to me."

"You're welcome," Tom said hurriedly. "Now, can I get to my point? My plan to save the world? Well, not necessarily the world, but the two of us?"

"Absolutely," Sam said. "I was hoping you'd think of something." Sam lit a cigarette and headed for the couch. At the last minute, she changed her mind and sat in the club chair. Better to avoid the couch for a while. It was a trap.

"Promise to hear me out without a word."

"Done."

"I'm frustrated by my job. You've been fired from your job."

"I know that—"

"Ssh. Hear me out. Now, this has always been in the back of my mind, but I just have never figured out how to actually make it happen. I mean, I still haven't figured out *exactly* how to make it happen, but I realize now I can't do it without you. Or don't want to do it without you."

"Tom, you're killing me."

"I know, I know. But just keep listening."

Sam nodded silently.

"First, I'll tell you the plan. Let's call it, for argument's sake, Plan Bite. Then, I'll tell you what I think we should do about it."

For the next week, Sam thought about what Tom had proposed. It was ludicrous. Why bother working on a nonexistent magazine that wouldn't pay her bills? Her skills were honed just fine, thank you very much. But the more she thought about it, it also sounded like fun. And it felt nice to dream. And more important, it's not like she was getting any nibbles on the job front. She had started to log calls again, with no better results than before, but at least she was being dogged about it. She even went to a benefit that her high school friend Martha—the *Daily News* editor—held to raise money for a neighborhood shelter. Sam realized it wasn't Martha's fault that she couldn't hire her, and she certainly didn't want to damage their friendship over it. And Sam spent hours at her computer doing battle with Quicken and her bank account, figuring out how long she could be unemployed without having to dip into her savings. And then, six days after Tom and she had first spoken of the idea, she joined her parents for dinner.

She sat at the dining room table, where she had always, even as a child, felt like a guest. Her parents were warm and friendly, but attached to that old-world way of wealth that seemed dated to Sam. As the housekeeper ducked in and out of the dining room, making sure the family's glasses and plates were filled, her parents gently began grilling her.

"You know you don't have to worry about money, Sam," her dad said. "I don't understand why you've put up with these people as long as you have, given that you could do anything that you want to."

Sam took a deep breath. This was not exactly a new conversation. Her father was still recovering from the fact that Sam hadn't shown the least interest in joining the family company, and nothing Sam said about not being the least interested in wall coverings—regardless of how profitable they could be—had made him understand. Recently, though, they had reached a truce. As long as they didn't raise the issue, they could have a nice relationship.

"Well, the thing is, this was the 'anything' that I wanted to do," Sam began. "And as for the money, it's incredibly generous, Daddy"—she hadn't been able to shake calling him that, even when she knew it made her sound, and feel, like a five-year-old—"but I'd rather see if I can figure out something on my own."

"Honey," her mom interrupted, "I don't know why you

don't start your own magazine. I know I say that to you all the time, but I honestly don't understand."

"Mom, you have no idea . . ." Sam stopped herself. She hated when she spoke to her mother as if she was a child. Which she was, but no need to encourage it. And then she realized that she was so busy reacting to the way her mother had just spoken to her, that she hadn't really heard what she had actually said.

"I'm sorry, what?"

"I asked why you don't start your own magazine."

Sam felt herself flush. This was really, really weird. And wonderful. It was weirdly wonderful. "Well," Sam said slowly, "it takes a lot of money, for one thing."

And as her parents looked at her silently, waiting for her to continue, Sam realized that the decision was totally hers. Her parents' generosity was hers to gracefully accept, an acceptance that could literally change her life—and Tom's too. In other words, Plan Bite wasn't just a dream, it was a total possibility.

Sam excused herself and ducked into the bathroom. She ran water over her face. She paced. She paced some more. And then she picked up her cell phone. "Tom?" she whispered, her voice echoing across the marble tiles. "Let's do it."

Chapter 15

Veronica was in her office, bored. Not with the job, though she supposed she was bored with that too. The magazine was so small these days—and fewer pages meant fewer photos.

She thought about checking out the website for Bar 89 again, just to get a look at the bartender she liked. What was the point? He flirted with her a bit every time she went there, but he never followed through. Even after she'd gone to the play he was in. Tom always told her that one day she'd snap out of her bad-boy phase and find a man with a real job, and she supposed he might be right. (Then again, his love life had taken a disturbing turn.) For now, though, bad boys were what she liked. Tattoos, long hair, that skanky look—she ate it up. It was like that Cowboy Junkies song "Misguided Angel." She loved the thought of being swept off her feet by a man who no one thought was right for her.

She pulled herself back to reality, and decided to go see Tom. He had seemed agitated when they had passed in the hall earlier; it was probably Justin. She was about to poke her head in his office when she realized he was on the phone.

"Sam, I'm telling you, this is going to change our lives! It's all I can think about. Can it really work? How much money will it take? We need someone to run the numbers. I mean, how do you just go and start a magazine?"

Someone came down the hall, and she tried to act like she had a reason for loitering outside of Tom's office.

"Okay, fine. We'll think about it later. Tonight?" A pause.

"Okay, but soon. I'm losing my mind." He hung up. Veronica made her move.

"Am I interrupting anything?"

Tom looked like a deer caught in the headlights. "Um, the world is running out of fresh water?"

"You look terrible. Don't tell me—Mr. Time Out."

"Gosh, thanks! No, not Justin. Well, yes—always, I think. But no. It's something else, too. Smoke?"

In the elevator, he hemmed and hawed. She thought about putting him out of his misery, but didn't really want him to know she was eavesdropping. Finally, he got it out. "V., if you had a chance to go off and start a magazine, would you do it? If it meant working closely with someone you really liked, but had never worked with, would you do it?"

"Tom, give me the specifics."

"I can't. Not yet. It's too embarrassing, like I'm Mickey Rooney suggesting the neighborhood kids join me and Judy in putting on a show."

When they got outside, she decided to push. "This must be serious, since you normally can't not tell anything. Let me guess: Sam wants you to start a magazine with her."

"How did you—?"

"Look. I'm a listener. I listen. And I remember—it's all part of what makes me so unforgettably fabulous." Veronica allowed herself a flick of the hair. "And I may have overheard you talking about it with her on the phone." She smiled guiltily. "But it's good to hear you excited about something. It reminds me of that book the two of you were going to write."

"*The Stud Ring?*"

"Right. This sounds like that. You get a look in your eyes. Anyway, I don't know what the story is with this magazine—what it's about, whether it's viable. I assume the money is coming from Sam . . ."

"How did you—?"

"Honey, you mentioned once that she grew up on Fifth Ave. Anyway, that's neither here nor there. What I'm saying is this: if you leave, I'm coming with you. One: I love working with you. Two: I'm good. And three: Because I'm young, I'm cheap."

Tom was stunned. He gave her a hug, then pulled back and looked into her big, beautiful eyes. And then he dove into his anxiety. "I didn't sleep at all last night. Would I have to quit my job? Should I? I have a good gig. And I love Sam, but what would working with her be like? Look what happened to *The Stud Ring!* And how much money does her family have, anyway? Does she have any idea how much money it would take to launch *Bite?* Do I? Neither of us knows a thing about business. Or, for that matter, managing people—let alone hiring them. If it didn't work out, would our friendship survive? Could ours? Am I really good enough to pull this off, even with Sam? And this is unrelated, but why doesn't Justin like me, anyway?"

Veronica smiled. "You forgot one," she said.

"What?" Tom asked, spitting out the word.

"What are you going to do about the fresh-water problem?"

Tom laughed. She was right. He was worrying about things he couldn't control—yet. "Now you have to meet Sam. I'll set something up."

"Hey," she said. "Aren't you going to tell me what the magazine is about?"

Tom thought about it for a second. "Nope," he said. "You'll just have to wait to bite into it later."

Back upstairs, Tom sent Sam an email. He was too scared to tell her over the phone that he had just gone and hired someone.

hey, sweetie. i'm so excited i can't stand it! in fact, i'm so excited i just told my friend veronica here all about it, and she wants to come on board as the photo editor. you'll love her, trust me.

He got a reply immediately.

delicious. but then you'll just have to trust me too.

Chapter 16

Liza was cruising through the fourth floor of Barneys, absentmindedly checking out the sale rack. Which would have been a wonderful hour alone, if it hadn't been the fourth time in the past month she'd done exactly the same thing.

Was she out of her mind? Liza was almost as bored of asking herself that question as she was bored of Barneys. But somewhere, she knew, she had gone wrong about three years ago, when she quit her job to begin living her true destiny: being a very rich wife.

Yes, she thought, as she stroked a Prada black jacket, size 12 (no wonder it was on sale—who dared step over the Barneys threshold if they were more than a size 2?), she had indeed screwed herself beyond measure. Everyone had assumed that her job as an art director was just a way of marking time until she found the right guy. Everyone but her, of course, but then, no one had ever asked her. And then she had found the right guy—Chandler was magnificent, she had to admit, as she thought back to last night at Petrossian, where he had surprised her with Tiffany diamond studs after his three-day business trip to L.A. defending some druggie lead singer from his latest DWI charges. But his work as a highly paid and in-demand lawyer meant that he was home about two weeks a month, if she was lucky. Friends joked that it sounded like the perfect marriage, but Liza wasn't so sure anymore. Frankly, she was lonely. It was getting harder and harder to connect with Chandler when he *was* around. It was an odd way to live, almost like having the worst part of being single and the worst part of being married, all wrapped up in one not-so-wonderful package. On one hand, she wasn't free to date, and Chandler didn't like her going out late with her single friends—it didn't "look good" for him—and on the other, she still had plenty of the downsides of marriage, like trying to keep a relationship together, without the comforts of someone to share her daily life. And as for that daily life, well, this Park Avenue wife thing, to be totally frank, was boring the shit out of her.

While Chandler made no secret out of the fact that it was important to him that Liza maintain her California-girl, healthy good looks, she had little interest in them herself. So there was the once-a-month appointment to return her hair to the color it used to be when she was fifteen, but that was about it. Chandler had once jokingly—at least she hoped it was jokingly—told her he'd be happy to pay for a "little" something to give her more cleavage, but she'd made it clear that if he valued his life, he'd never say anything like that again.

She did the mandatory volunteer work—helming boards along with women who had never met, nor ever wished to meet, the people for whose benefit they threw these galas. She had even taken on two other volunteer activities, coaching immigrant adults in English as a second language, and mentoring an inner-city teenager. But as much as Liza enjoyed the couple of hours here and there, who was she kidding? She was losing her marbles—and, she had to admit, only about two more lunches at La Goulue, the watering hole for equally rich, equally bored Upper East Side wives, from losing her hard-earned sobriety as well.

Liza had been a drinker until she was twenty-six, when Chandler came along and convinced her that there was a life worth living without always having a martini glass in hand. He was a new convert to AA, and his enthusiasm was contagious. Liza still attended AA meetings when she was feeling vulnerable. But now she was definitely losing her center, and no amount of counting days seemed to be changing that.

Even growing up "with everything," as her parents always reminded her, she struggled to find her way. Miss Haladay's, an equally exclusive boarding school, didn't expect much from their students than to sweat it out until they were of an age to marry. After graduation, Liza flew solo for several years, designing graphics at a hip downtown weekly. When she met Chandler at a cocktail party in Southampton, she finally fell in love and gave up—much to her parents' joy. She stopped working to set up a house for her husband. That they had only known each other for six months before they married seemed beside the point: Destiny was destiny. And if they never forged the intimacy she had dreamed of, they lived relatively companionably. Whenever she had longings for more, Liza simply looked at the marriages around her, and remembered that there wasn't one she envied.

Her cell phone rang. She pulled it out of her Louis Vuitton bag, the one Chandler had given her with its very own cell phone pocket, so she wasn't always scrambling around her mess of a purse and missing her call. "Hello?" she whispered. She hated it when people spoke in public on cell phones.

"Liza? It's Sam Leighton! How are you?"

"Sam!" Liza smiled. They had met through Jennifer. Liza liked Sam, but they never had a chance to really spend time on their own. And somehow, Liza thought ruefully, she was even busier now that she had nothing to do—how else to explain she hadn't called Sam and asked her to lunch? "Hang on one second," Liza said, wending her way to the dressing room, into which she ducked with the phone, plopping down on a stool.

"I'm so happy to hear your voice! What's happening?"

"Actually, I'm calling to ask you the same question."

"Honey, if I told you the truth, your eyes would roll back

into your head so fast you wouldn't believe it," Liza said. "But it amounts to nothing. Nada. Zero. With each dollar I spend, I lose a brain cell. You're lucky I still speak in complete sentences."

"I was hoping you'd say that!"

"Thanks, Sam," Liza said smiling. "Delighted you can revel in my misery."

"No, no. I'm delighted to hear that, because I think we should get together. Assuming, of course, you can meet me, what with all your Junior League activities."

"How about in fifteen minutes?"

Sam laughed. "I'm busy working on something right now," she said. "But speaking of working, what's your feeling about doing something like that these days? Is work a dirty word to you?"

"Um, did I mention I'd be free in fifteen minutes?"

"Make it next Tuesday, Liza. My apartment, 7:30. And start thinking about this: Bite."

Chapter 17

Sam did the thing that they never did: She mentioned *The Stud Ring.* "It won't be like that, Tom. I know it. That was a joke, nothing more. This is our lives."

The Stud Ring was Sam and Tom's first effort at working together (besides the stuff she wrote for him for *Profit).* They had decided that what the world needed was a gorgeous new beach book: Jacqueline Susann updated for the twenty-first century. They each wrote a few chapters before it dissolved. Tom had a hard time writing badly—on purpose, anyway—and they had more fun just having dinner and yammering. It was something they rarely mentioned, if only because the stench of failure hung over the entire endeavor.

"So let's talk about *Bite."* God, she was relentless. "I spoke with Liza, and she sounds bored out of her head. It's perfect, and she's so good. You're going to love her. Tuesday, 7:30, my place. Plus, she's filthy rich, so we won't have to pay her much. Her husband will probably want to pay us—it'll cost him less than her Barneys habit."

Tom trusted Sam's taste but was concerned that a teetotaler would be a less than ideal match for the team they were assembling. Veronica and Sam could drink Tom under the table, and he was no slouch. But how to mention it without sounding like a drunk? "Sam," he said hesitatingly, "about Liza. Do you think the fact that she doesn't drink—"

"It's so not a problem! Her mother's a lush and she deals with it. She'll be fine." Sam had a way of clearing things up.

"Here's my other thought. We need a money man. Your family—and our other many investors, whoever they may be—isn't going to just start writing blank checks. I want you to meet my friend Andrew. He's the most trustworthy, sensible person I know."

"Hey! What about me?"

"Sam, I love you. But no. Anyway, Andrew works at a tech company that probably doesn't have much life left—no fault of his—and he'd be fantastic for us. Not as publisher, but just as someone who can quickly look at the numbers and come up with a basic plan." Two years at *Profit* and Tom still didn't know what you'd call the money guy. "Don't you think we should run some numbers by your parents?"

Sam shrugged. Money wasn't an issue, but she had to ask about Andrew. "Is he one of us?"

"I think you'll really like him. He's a maniac for good cheese."

New York was funny that way. You could easily amass a dozen close friends, the intimate details of whose lives you could know everything about, and they would never meet each other. Tom had never met Jennifer, Sam hadn't met Andrew or R.J.—and yet Tom and Sam were practically each other's analysts. They had often joked about billing each other for hours spent dissecting their lives. It made Tom a bit uneasy to have Sam and Andrew get together, since on the surface they had nothing in common beyond cheese. He figured he should warm Andrew up on the idea.

Nursing a Maker's Mark, neat, Andrew was sitting at the bar at the Red Cat, a restaurant in Chelsea where he and Tom often met. *Thank God the medical establishment has come around,* he thought, *and realized that a drink after work is good for you.* Wearing a suit and sipping his drink, he was the very model of a yuppie—or guppie, as the gay yuppies were known, although Andrew didn't love the idea of being gay at the expense of being young. He had always been a straight arrow, sexuality notwithstanding. Raised on a commune, he was the child of hippies; his way of rebelling was to be fairly establishment. Tom teased him for the wild oats he had sown in high school—every now and then Andrew pulled out a story about how back then he'd snap out the car's eyeshade vanity mirror and snort coke off of it, just to remind his friends he had been crazy once—but since it was the eighties, it was actually very establishment to snort coke in high school. *Frankly, Tom could afford to have one friend who wasn't crazy.*

Speak of the devil. "Howdy!" Couldn't Tom dress up a little? He complained that he was never going to get promoted, but he dressed like he didn't want anything more out of life. They amused Andrew, these contradictions, but he wondered sometimes if Tom would ever grow up.

"Hey there."

The fierce lesbian bartender approached. "Ketel One gimlet on the rocks," Tom said. He looked at Andrew. "And menus?"

"Sure." You get much better service at the bar.

"How was your day, honey?" Andrew and Tom joked that they were married, except that they didn't have sex. (Then again, that might have made it feel even more like a marriage.) They ate dinner together at least twice a week, and it was rare that one did something without the other knowing about it.

"Don't ask."

"Too late."

"The usual. Whitford is a schmuck. I mean I like him, and I agree with his vision, but as CEO his job is to sell people on the idea that everything is fine. Everything isn't fine. You might have heard that we're in a recession."

Tom acted shocked. "I am an editor at *Profit,* you know!"

"Telling people how to spend their money doesn't require any business expertise, as *you* well know. The day was a drag.

I don't want to talk about it. Whitford makes my life hell, and I should just quit, but I keep hoping I'll get laid off and at least get some severance."

"I'm sorry." There wasn't much to say. "Nice suit, by the way."

If it was possible for a thirty-five-year-old man to harrumph, Andrew harrumphed. "I assume that's sarcasm. But my hair's a mess. I need to get it cut, or I'll have an Afro by next week." He smushed it down.

"You should let it grow! Be free! It's fun."

Another harrumph. "Maybe in the summer, when it gets blonder." It was Tom's turn to harrumph—he had heard Andrew postpone many things until the summer. "And how are things at *Profit?* Or do you even know?"

"Of course I know. They make me go to a meeting every morning. Things suck. Ad pages are way down—advertising, Andrew, is like the canary in a coal mine. The first thing companies cut back on in tough times is ad spending. So my section is now three pages an issue, sometimes two, whereas last year it was eight or ten."

"So you're bored."

"I'm so bored I'm bored with being bored. I'm bored, cubed. But, but, but: Remember my friend Sam? She writes for me? She's got this crazy idea that we should start a magazine."

Andrew rolled his eyes. This was classic Tom. Make a plan without thinking about the fundamentals. He figured it couldn't have gotten very far, since this was the first he'd heard about it. But did Tom have any idea how stupid it would be to start a magazine in a recession, how much money it costs, how it's virtually impossible to get off the ground when you don't have the resources—in circulation, in ad sales, in printing—of a major company? There were very good reasons that most every American magazine you'd want to read was published by four companies. And even though Andrew worked in finance, he followed the media world. As he liked to point out to Tom, he was one of those people whose reliance on magazines for whatever—glamour, advice, news—kept Tom and Sam afloat. He liked them so much his coffee table was a sheet of glass propped up on stacks of magazines. Most of which featured pretty young actors on the cover; Andrew was what the gay world calls a chicken hawk—an older, wiser bird who preys on innocent, young meat. (As long as the chickens were of legal age, of course.) Andrew particularly liked them when they were just discovering their attractiveness, getting a little puffed out with that silly young-stud bravado.

Tom smiled. "Don't answer me right now. We'll talk about something else. But listen to this: Sam got fired from Star Fucker, I mean *Star Face,* her family is stinking rich, and they've agreed to bankroll at least six issues." That last part was a lie. "You're going to be free of a job soon, you're the smartest person I know—at least when I'm not in the room—and if you agree to give us a little financial guidance, you can also be the food columnist." Andrew stared at the bar. Tom had him. Andrew loved good food more than anything else—even chickens—and the chance to go up against Jeffrey Steingarten, the food columnist at *Vogue* and his idol, was all but irresistible.

"But I'm not a writer!"

Tom leaned in. "Honey, no one is. That's why God made editors."

Chapter 18

Sam looked around her apartment. It was going to be hard to keep up this kind of enthusiasm with a wet towel and laundry on the floor. Now that she didn't have an office to escape to, she was keenly aware of how her living space had become a reflection of who she was. And judging from the way things looked, who she was wasn't pretty.

On the other hand, she was, much to her amazement, feeling fairly free of the depression that had haunted her. She still had moments where the horribleness of the Star Fucker situation could bring her to her knees—okay, so she had about forty of those moments a day—but she *was* feeling better. And the night before, she'd even gone out and not just muddled through, but had a wonderful, wonderful time. It was like suddenly, she was reminded there was a world out there where Star Fucker was a tiny entity, one that most people couldn't care less about.

The evening before, Jennifer, who had just gotten back from rehab again, had talked Sam out of the house, although at first Sam had insisted she couldn't leave. She'd been totally engaged with thinking of story ideas, calling Tom so often with questions and ideas that finally he had unplugged his phone. But Jennifer had pointed out that they hadn't actually gone out and had *fun* since she had been out of rehab and Sam had been out of a job. After all, Jen had said, if she could go to her first party with alcohol, Sam could be there to help her out. Just in case.

Sam relented, and the next thing she knew, she was cabbing down to Tribeca, dressed in a—she must admit—fabulous outfit (black Helmut Lang skirt, fishnets, and a fitted Donna Karan top), and entering a loft made to look like a Venetian palazzo. Votive candles were lit throughout the 2,000-square-foot space, and everywhere, guests wandered by like shadows, men and women all dressed in masks. Sam stepped back out to the foyer and pulled out her cell phone. "Jen," she whispered, "I'm sorry to ruin the romance, but I'm standing outside, and I have no idea how to recognize you. Can you come get me?" Just as Sam finished the sentence, Jen was at her side, dressed in a bright red bustier and black slacks, a red Venetian mask with feathers and sequins adorning her face. It was a little over-the-top, but then, so was Jen. Huge hazel eyes, with killer platinum hair she'd adopted at USC and grown attached to. "What was I thinking?" Sam said. "Of course you'd stand out in a crowd."

"I'm so glad you came," Jennifer said, linking arms with Sam and beginning to lead her back into the apartment. "I knew if I told you it was a costume party, you'd get shy and come up with some excuse."

Sam shot her an and-this-gets-better-how? look. "And," Jennifer said in response, "I knew you'd be too shy without a mask once you got here, so I have one for you."

Jennifer and Sam dodged into the massive kitchen, where caterers were preparing trays of caviar and crème fraiche, and Jennifer reached into a cabinet. "Voilà!" Out of a bag she pulled an extraordinary mask, appliquéd with black feathers. "Not hard to guess you'd be wearing black."

"Oh, Jen, thank you," Sam said, fingering the mask. "Now tell me, do I look like a fool?"

Jennifer surveyed her masked friend. "As if," she responded, leading Sam into the party.

The scene was awash with bodies, caped and masked, laughing as though they were having the conversations they'd meant to have all their lives. Sam felt that shyness overcome her again as Jennifer got pulled over by a group of friends, and she began walking across the room. She stood in front of the fireplace, holding her glass of champagne tightly, and wondered how and when she could make it back across the room and out the door.

"Madame, you're looking quite spectacular this evening." Sam heard the voice behind her, and it sounded so familiar she almost turned around, but given that her back was to the room, and she didn't know anyone but Jennifer here, what were the chances?

"I see. So it's a playing-hard-to-get evening, is it?" Sam was paralyzed. She did indeed know the voice, but she didn't want to be a fool and spin around, to find that she was a third wheel to a romantic hookup, and the guy wasn't talking to her, after all.

"Sam?"

She turned. What she saw was this: Six feet of spectacularness. A black cape. A black mask. Big thighs. And blue eyes. The kind of blue eyes she'd only seen on one man. The kind of blue eyes that made her stupid, and speechless, and brought her to her knees. The kind of blue eyes that were supposed to be in Egypt right about now.

"Chris?" Sam couldn't believe this. Was it not possible to have a little notice before running into the man? If only to rehearse her ridiculous patter in front of the mirror, and practice highlighting her different eye shadow shades? Or at least check out how her ass looked in this new skirt, for God's sake? Here she went—she could feel it—here she went getting stupid. "Chris. Aren't you supposed to be digging up dirt somewhere else?"

Chris smiled and reached for her hand. "I'd rather do some digging right here, if you don't mind," he said. "What have you been up to?" His eyes burned up and down her body. "You certainly look better than the last time I saw you!"

Sam felt herself go crimson. She suddenly felt very, very short, despite her heels. And very, very small. "Well . . ." She began, "I got fired . . ."

"What?" Chris put his arm around her and gave her a squeeze. "I'm sure you mean laid off, right? Either way it's awful, of course—"

"No, I was fired." Could she not stop herself?

"I'm so sorry. What happened?"

Oh God. Now she'd done it. What was she supposed to say? *Quick. Come up with some reason that sounds incredibly sexy and fabulous. Something that will make him want you. Then again, maybe he'd think it was sexy if she'd actually given Russell Crowe a blow job . . .*

"Oh," she stammered, trying not to look too deeply into his perfect eyes, "you know. I mean, you don't know, but . . ." she looked down at her feet. "It's a long story." She looked back up at him.

"Why don't we go somewhere quiet where you can tell me everything?" Chris said. Except, Sam realized, he didn't say that at all. What he was saying, in fact, was, "I wish I had the time to hear it all, I really do, but I have to run to a meeting. Oh"—he added, as his cell phone rang—"that must be it. Sorry, Sam. I'd love to hear about it next time. I'll be back in New York in a month or so—do you want to have dinner then?"

Sam nodded, torn between total misery and total joy. Okay, so he had to run to a meeting, but she would see him in a month! Over dinner! A date!

"A *meeting?* At 10:30 at night?" Jennifer asked incredulously an hour later, as they shared cheese fries at Moondance diner in Soho. "Who the hell would he be meeting with?"

"Trust me," Sam said knowingly, taking a sip of her Diet Coke. "He wouldn't lie to me. Plus, he's only in New York for a little bit of time, so he has to squeeze in a lot of appointments. Remember, this is the city that never sleeps."

"Because everyone is so busy sleeping together," Jennifer remarked.

Sam raised her eyebrows. "Look, I understand that you don't know him, and I can see that given the kind of men we've met it sounds fishy. But he really is different."

For once, Jennifer snorted Coke *out* of her nose. "You did not just give me the line that he's different. No, no you most certainly didn't. Because that would be too ridiculous for words."

"Well," Sam continued, realizing this was a losing battle, "we'll see who's right a month from now, when I call you after a grandly romantic dinner with him. I'm telling you, I have loved this man for years, and he's well worth loving. You'll see."

"I look forward to it," Jen responded. "But speaking of lovely men, what's up with Jack? I never did understand why you guys didn't click."

"Tell me about it," Sam said, rolling her eyes. "But we just don't. I mean, we totally do when we're together, but afterwards, I don't know . . . It's like I think of him often as a friend, but it almost seems too easy."

"Can I have him?"

"What?" Sam started to giggle.

"I'm just teasing—believe me, I wouldn't go there," Jen said. "It's just that he's the nicest guy in the whole world. He deserves better than you."

"That," Sam said, dipping her finger in the last of the cheese sauce, "I am fully aware of. Which is why I've been a very good kid the last month and not called him. I sent him an email telling him I'd left *Star Face,* and I'd be in touch when I got settled somewhere else."

"Ouch."

"Ouch? That's nice! That's respectful! That's acknowledging I can't just call him when I need a shoulder to cry on!"

"Yeah, but Sam, it's possible he'd *like* for you to call occasionally. Did you ever think of that?"

"Please, Jen," Sam said, motioning for the check. "I've thought of everything. But I think I'm right. Now, if you'll excuse me, I have to go home and dream of Chris. Do you think I'll be happy living in Egypt?"

Chapter 19

Tom and R.J. stood outside Mexicana Mama, waiting for a table for brunch. They always ate there, simply because it was where they always ate. You could take R.J. out of Minnesota, but not the Minnesota out of R.J.: his taste in food was forever suspect. Mexicana Mama was the one place they agreed on, even if Tom argued that it wasn't real Mexican food. People from California can be so tiresome on that topic.

"What you need," said R.J., "is a booty bump."

Tom should have known better than to ask.

"It's when you take an empty caplet, fill it with ground-up ecstasy or K or whatever—I recommend ecstasy—and stick it up your ass. It gets into the bloodstream quicker."

"What's the hurry?" Tom asked. "That was rhetorical." He had done his share of drugs—well, less than his share according to R.J., but more compared to lots of other people he knew—but unless he was fairly drunk and in a nightclub or at a party, he didn't really see the point. And talking about them made him feel pathetic. "Suppositories aren't supposed to be fun, R.J."

"Right." R.J. was cruising a delivery boy. "I could give him a tip," he muttered.

R.J. was always convinced that Tom needed to have more sex. He may have been right, there were certainly times when Tom thought he could be. Like now. *Maybe it would help me get over Justin . . .*

"What you need," said R.J., "is to get laid. Well, that and a booty bump. I could go online and get you someone! I have a shirtless photo of you from when we were in South Beach. I could just pretend to be you and have him show up at your door."

A year or two after every other gay man in New York had discovered AOL as a means of getting some tail, Tom finally bought a laptop. And R.J. showed him how it worked. For three straight days all he did was send and receive IMs to and from men on the prowl; it was all he could do, all he could talk about—even to his straight friends. Who, it must be said, were both grossed out and incredibly jealous that such a system didn't exist for them. But the whole thing made Tom very nervous, and while at first that was part of the thrill, it evaporated as soon as he had swapped photos with his first boss. It's one thing to be desperate, and another altogether for everyone to know it.

They were seated, finally. R.J. was blathering on about Cheryl, a big black woman he worked with who had promised long ago to take them to Harlem for a night on the town. She had said they'd be her skinny white bitches. Tom didn't have the energy to point out once again that the promise remained unfulfilled.

"Tell me sex stories," said Tom, because even if it made him feel sorry for himself at least he'd be entertained.

"Well, Sunday morning I went out to get milk at the deli. And I walked by the cash machine—"

"The one on 12th Street?"

"Yeah. And there was this guy, and he was hot. He was walking his dog. And we fucked for hours."

"Wait a minute," said Tom. "How did you get from there to here? What exactly happened?" Tom was the kind of guy who, when he watched porn—which was not often, he'd point out, even to himself—found the parts leading up to the sex much more interesting than the sex itself. He figured there were clues there on how to pick up guys.

"Well, I said, 'Hi.' And he said, 'Hi.' And I said, 'What are you going to do with the dog?' "

That was R.J. in a nutshell, thought Tom. He could simply walk down the street and end up having sex all afternoon. Tom wasn't sure to believe that the guy or the sex was hot—R.J.'s filter was famously askew—but he envied his friend just the same. He might not have wanted the sex, but he wouldn't have minded the opportunity, even if it was only to turn it down.

"Tom." Uncharacteristically, R.J. was whispering. "That woman outside is staring at me."

Tom looked over. "Sam!" She ran over and unleashed a monologue.

"I knew it was you! What are the odds? I was trying a new yoga place. It was insane. If I wanted to sit in a hundred-degree room, well, I would. But I don't." She paused, then turned to R.J.: "Hi, I'm Sam. I'm not usually this sweaty—it's like I've retained the heat, like I need a trivet to sit down."

"Please," said Tom, scooching over. "Sit!"

She did, then noticed the silver circle R.J. had laid on the table. "Wow. What a cool key ring," she said, reaching to touch it.

"So nice to meet you, Sam," R.J. said with what Sam thought was the grin of a lunatic. "But that's not my key ring. That's my cock ring."

Tom was pretty sure this was a good moment to die. Unfortunately, the fates didn't seem to agree, because a second later, he was still sitting there, watching Sam's face. Bless her, she started to laugh.

"God, Tom didn't make you up," she said, shaking R.J.'s hand. (A brave move, Tom thought.) "Tom, maybe it's the Bikram yoga, but I have to ask you—is this not the sex columnist we've been dreaming of?"

Just as Tom was about to protest, he stopped. It wasn't

because Sam and R.J. were looking at him expectantly. It was also because, in addition to being the most hackneyed idea he'd heard all day, also, just maybe, one of the best.

"R.J.?"

"I have no idea what you're talking about," R.J. said, "but any woman who doesn't know the difference between a key ring and a cock ring needs some educating, and if I have to be the one to do it, so be it."

Tom winked at Sam. "All right, I'm off," she said.

"Stay," Tom said. "Eat with us."

"Are you kidding? I had cheese fries at 3 A.M. I'm on food probation. And I need to be thin because"—she paused to pinch Tom's cheek—"I have a date with Chris."

"Get back here!" Tom yelled.

"Ta ta!" she trilled. "See you Tuesday." And she was out the door.

Chapter 20

Tuesday, 7:20. Good, Sam thought. Exactly a minute later than it was when she checked her watch . . . a minute ago. She couldn't believe how nervous she was about everyone meeting each other tonight. "They're your friends, Samantha," she reminded herself. "Get yourself together." Of course they were also her employees . . . Sam wondered when she would finally feel like a grown-up. Was it something just conferred upon you on your thirtieth birthday? She hoped so, as she changed the CD for the fourth time in the last fifteen minutes. Jeff Buckley was too mopey. No Doubt might be a little too . . . something. She finally settled on Dave Matthews. Screw what anyone else thought—that boy made her dream of nice things. Like Chris. *No Chris thoughts tonight.* Although he was coming back to town soon . . . *Dave Matthews, Dave Matthews. Think about Dave Matthews.* He could crash into her anytime.

Sam made sure the candles were still lit, and that the chairs in her living room were pulled up into a circle where everyone would be comfortable but not claustrophobic—a hard thing to achieve in a 600-square-foot apartment. Then she settled down to review her notes. 7:24. Five minutes later, the doorman buzzed. "Guests downstairs." Sam took a deep breath and opened the door.

"Sam!" Liza was standing there with Veronica, Liza looking hipper than thou in an East Side way, Veronica hipper than thou in an East Village way. Immediately, Sam got a burst of self-confidence. This could work.

"Lisa! And you must be Veronica!" Sam hugged them both.

"I assume you met in the elevator?" They nodded and each handed over a bottle of wine, while Sam led them into the kitchen in search of glasses.

"Alright, Sam, spill the beans," Liza pleaded. "What's up?"

"No, no," Sam teased. "You're just going to have to wait for everyone."

As if on cue, Tom walked in, Andrew in tow, R.J. trailing behind. As soon as Sam hugged Tom, all anxiety was gone. With Tom behind her, they could do this. "Alright kids, settle in," Sam said, pointing people to chairs. Andrew settled stiffly in the wing chair—perfect, Sam thought, for their future businessman. The stiffer the better, at least when it came to dealing with numbers.

Tom nodded at Sam to begin. "So," she said haltingly, "Tom and I have an idea. Some of you know a lot, some of you nothing. Regardless of what you know, Tom and I know we want all of you involved, if you're willing. Here goes. Tom and I are starting a magazine. We have our first backers, who really believe in the idea—"

"Yeah, parents are like that," Tom cracked, and Sam giggled.

"Alright, my parents love the idea. But we want you to, as well. We want to do a lifestyle magazine, but before you roll your eyes, this one is going to be different. The concept is this: '*Bite.* It's your life, live a little.' It will be fun, it will be irreverent, but it will be accessible. This isn't a *Vogue* or *Details* making you feel like a loser, but it also isn't going to treat you like an average joe. You want to travel? We tell you where you want to go—or rather, *we* don't, but people who are in a position to. We ask the concierge at the Bristol in Paris where he stays when he goes on vacation. Food reviews? We have a restaurateur talk about how he knows a reviewer the minute he walks in the door, and what tricks he pulls out. Then we have that restaurateur go review another restaurant. It's experts talking about their fields of expertise. It's a private club that you're invited to, but unlike any club I've ever belonged to, you're actually going to love everyone else who belongs. You're going to trust them, you're going to feel like they're your friends, and you're going to go back month after month to hear about the adventures they've had since you last heard from them." Sam stopped and looked up. "So there you go."

She looked around the room. Tom was smiling at her—that's what mattered. But Liza, Liza was grinning like a damn fool. "I love it, I love it, I love it!" Liza said. "I'm in. I'll answer telephones. I don't care."

"Actually, Liza," Tom said, "we'd like you to be the art director." Liza beamed. "Which means you'll be dealing very closely with Veronica, if you're both willing . . ."

"Are you kidding?" Veronica practically yelled. Tom, Liza, and Sam beamed. Only R.J. and Andrew's looks were unreadable.

"R.J.?" Sam asked.

"Well . . . I think it's great. I mean, I think it's really great. And once we get a little of my sexpertise in there, I think it'll be a magazine even I'll want to read." Tom explained that R.J. would be doing a sex column.

"Alright then," Sam said with a smile. "Now, you may have to temper yourself occasionally."

R.J. threw her a look of feigned disbelief.

"Occasionally," Sam said with a laugh.

"Look, R.J., you talk about things even I've never heard of," Tom said. "But we want you to be you, we promise. Since you can't imagine there are things the rest of us don't know, we'll feed you the questions for the first few months, until readers start writing in."

"You got it," R.J. said, looking pleased despite himself.

Everyone nodded, and then there was a moment of silence.

"Okay, so . . ." Sam said to the room. "That's the basic premise. I'm sure you guys have tons of questions—we do too—but if we haven't answered them tonight, that means we don't have the answers. Obviously, we'll all be staying in close touch, and we'll meet again next week." Sam looked around, suddenly looking up and catching Andrew's eye. He hadn't said a word. And Goddamn it, he was still sitting in the wing chair—why had she taken it from her grandmother's attic?—legs crossed, that corporate, corporate, corporate . . . smirk on his face.

She looked at Tom. This was his business. If Andrew was about to have some kind of buzzkill effect on the room, Tom was going to have to deal with it. Plus, she didn't think she had an ounce of charm left in her. "Andrew?" Tom immediately took up the slack. "What do you think? I know you're on board with being the food columnist, but Sam and I don't know anything beyond the basic numbers, and while we'll respect any parameters you set for us, we'd rather not have to think about it."

Andrew exhaled slowly, and Sam saw that what she thought was Andrew being high-and-mighty, was just him thinking . . . quietly. *I wish I could not always think out loud,* she thought. There was so much power to actually having an internal conversation and not saying everything out loud—people actually paid attention to you. *New Year's Resolution Number Three,* she said to herself.

"I think it's very ambitious," Andrew said slowly. "And I think it's a novel idea. I think you have the energy, and I think you've certainly assembled a great group of people." He nodded at the group. "But I worry that you're flying a little blind. Have you considered how much money this takes? For God's sake, Tina Brown had to fold *Talk* after losing $50 million—and that was with Disney behind her. No insult to your parents, Samantha, but I doubt they're worth quite that much."

"Look, Andrew," Tom said, "I know this is a big risk. But we want to take it. Veronica and I can stay on at our jobs while we work on the prototype. Sam is out of a job, so she doesn't have anything else. Liza's rich, so she doesn't have anything better to do," he said with smile in Liza's direction. "We don't think it's going to be easy, but we think it could be fun. And I think we could all use a little fun now, don't you? Will you work with us through the prototype, and then we can go from there?"

Sam almost yelped with happiness. Tom was so amazing at being able to talk people into things, for all of the right reasons. He didn't get that nervous, overeager thing she did. Sam thought back to a conversation she'd had with her dad that afternoon, who told her the best thing about her was also the worst—for such a small person, she took up so much *room*. Tom had a grace and reserve she'd like to learn, and sitting there watching him, she realized how excited she was to get the chance to work with him on a daily basis. They both felt they weren't learning anymore in their jobs, but how fun it would be to learn from each other, and the others sitting here. If Andrew wouldn't do it, they'd find someone else, she thought, as a silence lingered over the room. Veronica bit her nails, while Liza busied herself playing with her cell phone.

"We work within the budget Samantha's parents give us," Andrew said slowly. "Everyone else keeps their day jobs, and commits to a weekly, four-hour meeting." Andrew surveyed the room, where everyone was nodding like docile puppies. "If it doesn't fly, no loss, we've had fun. But we throw everything we can into this, so that if it can work, we're the ones that make it work." Sam couldn't help it. She flew out of her chair, ran over to Andrew, and threw her arms around him. Tomorrow, she thought as she hugged him tightly, tomorrow she'd learn to be more reserved.

Chapter 21

Sam woke up late the next morning, still feeling triumphant. She couldn't believe how everything could go so bad, so fast, and then get so good again. She sent her gratitude up into the universe, and got a cup of coffee from the kitchen before checking her email.

"Woo hoo!" There it was, from "Dirtdigger." She called Jennifer without even opening it, determined to prove her point.

"Ha!" she said when Jennifer answered her phone.

"What are you so pleased about, Madame?" Jen asked. "But make it quick—I'm late for AA."

"You know, sometimes I think you were more interesting when you weren't sober," Sam teased, knowing full well that Jennifer didn't believe her for a second.

"I wasn't more interesting, I was just more available," Jennifer said. "But I wouldn't have remembered anything you told me, anyway."

"Good point," Sam said. "Now, can we get on with it? I have an email here, ready to prove you wrong . . ."

"From Chris?"

"Yes, from Chris. Like I would bother you on a Saturday morning otherwise? I mean, I would, but I wouldn't have this tone in my voice. Anyway, it says . . ." Sam pulled it up. And then she was quiet.

"It says . . . what?"

"Blech."

Sam heard Jen sigh on the other end of the phone. "I'm sure he's really great, Sam. I didn't mean to tease you about him."

"No, he *is* really great," Sam said. "It just says that his trip has been delayed, and he's not sure when he's coming now. But he promises me a nice dinner when he does come."

"Well that's good!" Jen said. "I mean, he still wants to take you out . . ."

"I know, it's just that I'd really been looking forward to seeing him." Sam rolled her eyes. That was like saying Anna Nicole Smith was really looking forward to lunch. It was *all* she'd been looking forward to.

"Think of it this way, Sam. You can pour yourself into *Bite.* What's another six months of celibacy?"

"I'd been hoping not to have to find out."

"There's always Jack. . . ."

"No. No. No. I don't know why I have to keep saying that to you."

"I don't know why you have to keep saying that to yourself," Jen teased. "Now I'm off to my meeting. Feel free to join me, should you decide to repent your sinful ways."

"If only. I'll talk to you later."

Sam hung up and let out a mock scream. Well, she'd been in love with him for years. She was meant to be with him. So if this was a test of her patience, she could survive. She grabbed a Post-it out of her desk. "You can do this," she wrote on it, and stuck it on her computer. Hey, it wasn't a bad reminder, no matter what it actually meant.

Fellow Biters: Our first official meeting will be in three weeks. To reassure Andrew that we have nothing but faith in our hearts, we will demonstrate our utter devotion and seriousness by meeting not for any measly four hours, but for 36—the nights of Nov. 9 and 10. To make this slightly less grueling, I've reserved two suites at the St. Regis, which understands I'll be reviewing the joint for the hotel column

at my current—stress current—gig. Mandatory activities will include occasional breaks for spa services, wine tastings, and a complimentary dinner at Lespinasse, on the house. And when I say house, I do mean the St. Regis. Welcome to life as it could be.
Cheers—Tom

The email came Thursday afternoon. Sam couldn't believe her eyes. "Tom!" she screamed into the phone. "Are you out of your mind? Are you from heaven? How in the world did you swing this? Are we going to hell? Are we breaking every journalistic ethic there is?"

"Oh, baby, I think you did that right about the time you and Russell Crowe got down and dirty. The rest of us can only dream."

Sam laughed. It was nice to finally laugh about it. "Seriously, is this okay? I mean really okay?"

"It's totally okay, I promise," Tom reassured her. "I cleared it with the editor. I said I needed a few different people weighing in. And it's the lull before Thanksgiving, so the St. Regis is empty. It's not like we're taking up rooms that would be paid for by civilians. If we're going to do this, let's do it right."

"You're amazing," Sam said. "I'm in. As long as you'll be my roommate."

"You bet."

"But wait. Will that bother Andrew?"

"I've told you a million times, Sam, there's nothing between us. He's great, and I adore him, but he's a friend and I don't sleep with my friends."

"Breathe, baby. I was just thinking that he's a little finicky. What's going on? Why are you so uptight about this?" She chuckled. "Have you been having dirty little dreams about Andrew?"

But Tom had already hung up.

🍎 🍎 🍎

Liza, meanwhile, was busy emailing the caterer for the party she and her husband were throwing that weekend for his law partner in Zurich. She was ten seconds from ordering hash brownies for dessert—that would certainly loosen up the crowd, not that she had a clue where to get hash—when she saw the email. She felt a growing anxiety. It sounded like more fun than she'd had in ages—she *knew* it would be more fun than she'd had in ages—but the way her life was set up, she didn't know if she could excuse herself for thirty-six hours. Why? Her husband had never said anything to suggest the opposite. He was perfectly happy when she went to Canyon Ranch with his partners' wives, even if she was bored stiff. But there was something about seizing fun and joy that she felt he wouldn't like. When did this happen to her, that she even thought this way? How had she let herself become so trapped? She could go, she thought. She would make sure that Marta prepared his dinner and . . . This was *insane*. Her husband loved her. He had fallen in love with who she was. So she had conformed to whatever the two of them thought she was supposed to be as his partner, but it wasn't like she was stealing off to be with her lover. For God's sake, the only testosterone in the room wouldn't have the least interest in testosteroning with her. But still, she felt a gnawing anxiety, and that gnawing anxiety, more than the reality, bothered her. When did they get so disconnected that she would get nervous about living her own life in moments grabbed here and there? She picked up the phone to call him, and then remembered: All scheduling requests went through his secretary. Screw it. She'd talk to him that night, but she'd follow the rules for now. She dialed the phone. "Katie?" she said when the secretary answered. "Please write on the calendar that I will be out of pocket for the weekend of the ninth." Katie waited for the usual explanation, but Liza felt herself grow steely. "Thank you," she said, placing the phone back in the receiver. This was her life, and she *was* going to live it.

"Tom," Andrew whined. "You think I can just take that much time off?"

"Well . . ." Tom said. "Yes. It's a Friday and a Saturday night. Are you scared of playing with others? Are you not a good cooperator? Do you not want to have to share your toys?"

"It's just that Saturday is my day to—"

Tom interrupted. "Andrew, every Saturday for the rest of your life can be your day to do whatever you like. If you need your own room so you can play with your rubber ducky in the tub and no one will know, that's fine. But I have the feeling that if your dry cleaner doesn't see you drop off your shirts one time, and the receptionist at Equinox doesn't check you in, and your masseur doesn't rub your lats at 4 P.M., no one will think you're dead. In fact, they might wonder what glorious adventure you might finally be having."

"That's easy for you to say," Andrew said. "I know that you don't embrace a schedule, that you don't—"

"Act like a compulsive fool?" Tom interrupted again. "You're right, I don't. But Andrew, why don't you just come? You can leave, okay? I'll call you a car, I promise. You'll be twenty blocks from your house . . ."

"Twenty-seven," Andrew interjected.

"Twenty-seven. I apologize. But Andrew? This just might be fun. Let's give it a shot, okay?"

Andrew was quiet for several seconds. "Fine," he said.

Veronica emailed back that she was in, and R.J. had a business trip he couldn't cancel, but he wasn't essential anyway (plus, Tom told Sam, he might have some adventure that would be good fodder for his column). They were set.

Chapter 22

Let's just say Chester is as scary as they say he is." Sam and Liza were lounging at the end of a lunch at Ferrier, a smoke-filled Madison Avenue bistro haunted by those who had two and a half hours in the middle of the day and didn't have to worry that a glass of wine would dull their killer instincts during afternoon meetings.

"I could definitely get into this," Sam added, looking around the room at the Eurochic tables, filled with handsome men and equally beautiful women, who held themselves like their only care in the world was choosing between Gstaad and St. Moritz for their next week or two of skiing.

"Yeah, you say that, but try it five days a week, and you might feel a little differently," Liza said, tossing her hair so that her new highlights, courtesy of Frederic Fekkai himself, glimmered in the gentle overhead lights. "But tell me more about the dinner, please."

"Right," Sam said, turning back to her friend and crossing her legs under her, tucking them under the tablecloth so none of the chi-chi people around her might notice her less-than-posh manners at the moment. "And thanks again, Liza, for taking me out of my apartment. It's really a treat. Really." Liza nodded and gestured for Sam to continue. "So anyway, Tom assigned me a story on Jean Simon's new restaurant, and we decide to celebrate the Simon interview by booking a table there for dinner. Tom's boss James Chester invites himself along, which needless to say, terrifies Tom. I show up thinking Tom is being a little . . . overly sensitive. I mean, I understand that the guy is his boss and whatever, but it's not like Tom and I can't float through those things."

"I hope you didn't sit cross-legged through that meal, too," Liza teased, reaching across and patting Sam on the leg.

"Thank you very much, Miss Manners, but I was raised on the right side of the tracks, I'll have you remember. I may be lost occasionally, but I can still find my way back. So anyway . . ."

"Wait. Outfit, please?"

"Good, I think. My black Armani suit with the slightly flared legs—conservative without being too country club, with a T-shirt, strappy Manolos that I figured should he have chosen to look down would delight him, but also I figure he's not the kind of guy to look down. Anyway, I get there, and Tom's a little freaked, so I sit and just start asking Chester about how it feels to be in charge. He's a typical Texan, thinks he owns the world. I realize about halfway through that he's got this funny little smile on his face, like he knows exactly what I'm doing, and he can play the manners game exactly as well as if not better than I can, and now that I've shown him I *could* do it, it's really not interesting to him. At which point, he looks up, and says, 'This ain't my first time at the rodeo. Waiter! Three shots of tequila, please.' You should have seen the waiter, who clearly only knows the words 'Champagne' and 'Evian.' It was hilarious."

"So it went well?"

"I had a blast," said Sam, "and I think Tom did too, once he realized Chester was as gone as we were, and therefore wouldn't have any dirt on us we didn't have on him. But he's one of those men who is incredibly smart, and not only knows it, but trades on it to make other people feel stupid. And luckily, the food totally stank, so the review Tom's asked me to write now should be funny. I wouldn't say that if Simon weren't such an uptight ass, I promise."

"Do you think Chester might be willing to listen to *Bite* ideas down the road?" Liza asked, motioning the waiter over and ordering an espresso.

"Maybe," Sam nodded. "The big news is that the day before the dinner Chester was bumped upstairs—he now oversees all Worldwide Media magazines. So if he did want to help, he's in a position to do it." Sam felt like she'd been hogging the conversation. "But what's going on with you?"

"Well, I'm hating my husband these days," Liza said with a smile. "I mean, I love him, but he's never around, and I'm feeling a little pathetic, and I'm thinking maybe I need an adventure."

"That's a great idea," Sam said enthusiastically. "Once we're done with the *Bite* weekend, maybe you should take some fabulous vacation. You've got the time and the money, you lucky dog."

"Well . . . that isn't quite the kind of adventure I meant," Liza said, with a half-smile that Sam could see was meant to be neutral, waiting for Sam's response.

Sam paused. "Like . . . an affair?"

Liza smiled, but she still looked pained.

"Huh." Sam fell silent for a minute. She wanted to say the right thing to Liza, but she also wanted to be able to listen without judging her. Hardly having mastered the love thing herself, Sam was in no position to make sweeping moral dictates. "Obviously, I've never done it. I mean, I have, but not in a marriage. But I do know, from watching them around me, that I've seen affairs both save marriages and destroy them, and maybe the best thing you could do is know which one you're after."

Liza let out a deep breath. "I don't really know, and that's what scares me. I love Chandler, I do. But I've just totally lost myself, and I feel like he doesn't know me, either. I used to think he just didn't notice that I wasn't feeling very good about myself, but now I'm wondering if maybe, this sounds so awful, but if maybe he doesn't care." Liza looked up at Sam to make sure she hadn't freaked her friend out, but Sam was just listening. "I know, I know, I have to find my own center again, but it's awfully alluring when a man comes along promising to rescue you, feminism be damned. And the problem is I've got a hell of a man making extraordinary promises."

"What?" Sam started to laugh. "Details, please, young lady. Imperious moral judgment to follow, I promise, but for the moment, I'd like to know absolutely everything."

"Oh, fuck it," Liza said, as she tucked her legs up under her, too. "What's the point of privilege if you can't get comfortable with it?"

"That's my girl," Sam said, laughing.

"He teaches at the center where I volunteer teaching the English-as-a-second-language class. His class is always at the same time, so we've seen each other coming and going every week for a year or two, and always smiled at each other. Then, a few months ago, he asked if I wanted to grab some coffee, and I said fine."

"And? And? And? I'm dying here," Sam said.

"And he's amazing. He's thirty-five, widowed two years ago, with a four-year-old daughter he's raising by himself. By day, he's an environmental lawyer."

"Um, no offense," Sam said with a smile, "But he sounds more like a candidate for sainthood—or at least a good Lifetime movie—than for a thrilling roll in the hay."

"That's exactly the thing," Liza said, reaching into her Birkin bag and grabbing her platinum card to pay, waving Sam's hand away. "It's entirely the wrong sort of affair in the making—no sex, but plenty of emotion. Wouldn't it be better to be having mindless sex?"

"On that, I can most certainly counsel you," Sam said.

"And I'd have to say yes . . . and no. As I said before, it comes down to what you're missing with Chandler, and what you want. But maybe it's a chance, whether you do anything about it or not, to take a look at what you're getting from him that you're not getting from your husband. If it's only the 'new' thing, that's powerful, but I promise you it doesn't last."

"I know," Liza said, as she and Sam stood and left the restaurant. "But in the meantime, do I sleep with him, or not?"

"That's too personal for me to possibly weigh in on. But I promise you that I'm here no matter what, and I promise that if you do, and don't tell me every detail, I will come and kill you. Remember, I have the time these days to plan the perfect murder."

"Thank you so much," Liza said, folding Sam up in a big hug. "How are you doing, honey?"

"Oh, same old, same old," Sam said, holding the door open for Liza. "I was deeply miserable, now I'm less deeply miserable." Liza looked back at her to read her face. "I'm telling the truth. I mean, my personal life is kind of lacking in the . . . male variety, or at least the straight male variety, but I'm keeping my chin up."

"Really?"

"Well, I'm trying," Sam continued. "But it's not fair asking me after I've been treated to a lovely lunch. Ask me at 3 A.M., when I'm up pacing the floor, wondering how I'm ever going to pay the rent, and if it really matters anyway, since I'll die old and alone . . ."

"Sam, I want you to hear me seriously for a second," Liza said, as they stood outside the restaurant. "There's not a single one of us, married or un-, who doesn't worry—no, isn't convinced—she's going to die old and alone."

"Yeah, only one difference," Sam said. "I really will." She tried to smile as gamely as she could. Liza got it, and got that Sam wanted to change the subject.

Liza gestured for a taxi, before calling back behind her, "Sam? One more thing! What's the name of your Brazilian waxer again?"

Sam laughed and shook her head. "It's not that easy," she said. "If you want this, you'll need to do your own research!" Liza pretended to pout. "Alright, for Christ's sake. Joyce, at the J Sisters. Tell her I sent you. And may yours have a chance to be more frequently admired than mine!"

As Sam walked up Madison, checking out the windows, it occurred to her that no matter how it looked from the outside, everyone's life was more complicated than she thought—her own included. Demons were snapping at every ankle, and maybe the trick to keeping them at bay was bringing as much levity into your life as you could. Which meant that maybe, just maybe, she thought cheerfully, *Bite* really *did* have a reason for existing. And not just because she was out of work, bored, and going to die old and alone.

Chapter 23

"I am using every piece of restraint in my bones, Sam, but you haven't said a word about Chris in a few weeks, he should be coming to town any second, and if you think I don't know that you're obsessing, you would be very wrong."

Tom was sitting behind his fabulous desk, while Sam had plunked herself on his couch. "What are you talking about, you lunatic?" she asked, absentmindedly fluffing his pillow. Sometimes she couldn't decide whether Tom had the best taste in the world or the worst.

"Sam!" Ethan burst through the door and gave her a big hug. "It's been forever. Tom told me you ran into Chris at a party a couple weeks ago—what happened?"

Sam shot Tom a withering glance, but he didn't even try to look guilty. "Look, you know I don't claim to be able to keep a secret. And that's what I was just asking you about. Now you'll be forced to answer."

"It sounded too good to be true," Ethan said. "If you refuse to share him, you at least have to share the details."

"I don't know what you're talking about," Sam said, in a voice she knew was a little too high and cavalier. Tom lowered his head and stared at her.

"I'm not even going to pretend to have heard that, young lady."

"Grrr!" Sam said, throwing the pillow to the end of the couch. "Fine. Alright. I suppose I deserve it for having obsessed about him so long."

"I love the way you say that," Ethan teased. "As if that's *so* a thing of your immature past."

"It is!" Sam protested. "I'm really over him."

Tom dramatically banged his head down onto the desk. "This isn't happening," he moaned.

"I'm telling you, I'm totally over him. I don't exactly have an option, given that he sent me an email saying he isn't coming to town after all."

"That's it?" Ethan said.

"That is certainly not it," Tom said to him, knowing Sam all too well.

"Well . . ." Sam continued, wishing there was more. "Yeah."

"Um, excuse me, but you seem to think you're entitled to a private life," Tom said.

"If I must articulate this to you both, which apparently I must," Sam said, sitting up straighter, "I am trying to keep the drama low in this particular arena. I cannot spend my time and energy fixated on—"

"The most beautiful, charming, sophisticated catch in the universe?" Ethan interrupted. "Pray tell—for whom do you reserve your fixations?"

Sam shook her head. "I've been gaga over Chris for how many years now? How long have I bored you with stories about him?"

Ethan and Tom exchanged a look. "She has a point," Tom said.

"Thanks. In any case, it just seems to me that I've reached an age where I should be able to have a small crush and not immediately be imagining the Tiffany settings that will adorn our dining room table at Thanksgiving while our children and grandchildren sit staring at us adoringly."

"Well, well," Tom said. "I don't buy it, but I think you are, if nothing else, very articulate."

Sam giggled. "Get your own life in order, my friend, and then we'll talk. I'm late for lunch, so I'm outta here." Sam rose and gave Tom and Ethan a kiss. "Before I go, here's a little Page Sex for both of you: Which star doesn't seem to be too shamed by his current case of syphilis, caught on location? He sends any available crew member to the drugstore when he needs his antibiotics refilled."

"You bitch!" she heard them yelling as she left the office. "Come back here and tell us!" When she reached the elevator bank, she rolled her eyes. Would she actually ever be able to believe the crap she'd just spewed about Chris? Sure, it was a lovely fantasy. It reminded her of this great phrase Jen had taught her from AA: "fake it 'til you make it." So maybe she was faking it, but at least she wasn't encouraging her own obsessive, fixating heart. So why wasn't she allowing herself any distractions?

As soon as she and Jen were seated at Judson Grill, she decided to raise the topic. "Alright, here's what I need to know. Now, if I were asked this question in public, I know how I would answer it. Can a woman in her late twenties enjoy casual sex? In public, here's what I would say, with—I promise—the right tone of outrage. That a woman's desire for sex is no less strong than a man's. That we're entitled to satiate our sexual appetites, as well, and why the hell should it mean more to us than it means to men? But between us, I'm really starting to wonder. When I look back at my 'casual' sexual experiences, they were pretty much all messed up. Either he ended up in love with me, or I ended up offended that he wasn't, even if I didn't want anything to do with him, or I ended up thinking I was in love with him."

Sam paused and took a drink of water.

"Are you done?" Jen asked with a smile.

"For the moment."

"Okay, here's what I have to say, having experienced my own . . . casualness. First of all, what is 'casual' to you? Meaningless? With someone you don't even care about?"

"Um . . . alright, sure. For argument's sake, let's go with that."

"Then let me follow up with this: We've both done it. Now, be totally honest with me. Have you ever, ever been able to have an orgasm with someone you didn't have an intimate emotional relationship with?"

Sam's jaw dropped.

"Well, have you? Don't sit there being all goody-two-shoes with me. Every man, barring some sexual dysfunction or too many martinis, comes at the end of sex. It doesn't matter whether he's screwing a tree or a woman."

"Jen!"

"What is wrong with you, Sam? Have you gone all Puritan on me? Do you want to have this conversation or not?"

Sam nodded, a little too much like a repentant five-year-old, she thought.

"Fine. Then here's what I think: Sex is not equal. Men do not have the same issues with their bodies. You've never heard a man say, 'But she saw me naked!' Because men assume they're fabulous even if they're bald and 300 pounds. It's about conquest. Getting it, getting off, and getting out the door. Now"—Jen paused to call the waiter over and order an iced tea—"a woman, no matter how she feels or doesn't feel for a man, is bringing generations of self-loathing and lack of entitlement to her bed."

"Jesus, is this a dissertation or a friendly lunch conversation?"

Jen pointed her finger at Sam to be quiet. "We don't believe, at the end of the day, that we're entitled to the same pleasures as men, no matter what we pretend, or no matter how much we would like it to be different and untrue. And having an orgasm—the most total loss of control you could exhibit in front of someone else—is just not going to happen with someone you don't feel trust with. No sooner than a stranger telling you to wet your pants in front of him."

"This is depressing," Sam said, slumping down in her chair. "And be nice. You know I wet my pants when I laugh too hard."

"But I'm not wrong, am I? Think about it. If there is a connection, and you are able to have an orgasm, don't you feel ridiculously bonded to that man the next day, in a way that may be totally inappropriate? It's just that we always assume it's us, and nobody else. You sleep with someone, and when your friend asks you about it the next day, you say it was incredible, because you know that the sex probably was, even if you didn't experience it that way, and that if you *didn't* experience it that way, it's probably your own problem. Hell, it's not like we actually say to each other, 'Yeah, it was awesome, but I couldn't totally relax so I didn't come.' I mean, how many times have you faked it in your life?"

"I don't believe in faking it," Sam said primly.

"Good God, you have become totally impossible. It's me! Obviously we don't *believe* in faking it, but this not an interview for an article in the *New York Times.* You go home with a date. He goes down on you for more than a reasonable time. You're thinking about your dry cleaning. You're thinking about the piece you have due in three weeks. It feels nice, but you know there ain't nothing going to be happening. What do you do?"

"Well . . . alright," Sam said, squirming in her seat.

"That's my point," Jen said. "We walk around, proudly feminist, and say we don't believe in faking it. But we do all the time. And we fake it to our friends, so we all assume that we're the only ones faking it."

"Ugh," she said, taking a big gulp of water. "This is really depressing."

Jen looked carefully at Sam. "Why are you asking this question now? Are you having lots of fabulous, meaningless, unorgasmic sex? I'm so jealous I could scream."

"Yes . . ." Sam said, pretending to read the menu, "and no. I mean, I'm not sure. I feel like when I'm having casual sex, I want it to be more, and maybe if it's more, I want it to be less, because it's easier to deal with. There's Jack, as you know, but not often enough, but if it were often, that would be bad. I guess I go back to my first answer—I'm not sure."

"What's keeping you from Jack? Are you sure it's not about your own feelings?"

Sam held up her finger as if to stick it down her throat. "No. I mean yes. I'm sure. I feel like I just said this before."

"You did," Jen said. "To which I can only respond like a true friend and say the following: You are deeply, deeply fucked up."

"Yeah," Sam said, opening the menu, "I think I might be."

The solution? Focus on someone else's problems. Sam and Liza certainly didn't know each other well, but Sam realized that Liza confessing to hating her husband and considering an affair wasn't something that Liza would casually share. (Unlike herself, Sam thought, who too casually shared absolutely everything.)

She wasn't sure if Liza would want to talk about it again—in fact, she wasn't sure if she would know what to do if Liza *did*—but it had still been selfish not to follow up earlier. Sam called Liza from Scoop, a trendy boutique on Third Avenue. "Lize, it's me," she said when Liza answered. "Since your shopping days are numbered, now that we're being cruel enough to force you back into the workplace, do you want to come meet me and help me pick out my nine-thousandth perfect black dress that I can't live without?"

Chapter 24

The St. Regis is resolutely uncool. It's everything all those Ian Schrager hotels aren't: dowdy, fussy, fancy. On the other hand, it's everything you want in a hotel—perfectly unobtrusive service, large rooms, and because it was so clearly an old-school hotel, there were no distractions. If they'd gone somewhere cooler, they'd be tempted to drink away the night in the bar, or just hang out in the lobby and watch the action.

Plus, as R.J. had pointed out, the St. Regis had the best room-service bacon in New York. (R.J. had been the guest of a guest in many of the city's best hotels—as well as some of its least desirable ones.)

The kicker, actually, was that because the hotel was so unquestionably good, because there was no likelihood of Tom wanting to write anything bad about it, he had no qualms about asking the in-house PR guy, with whom he was on pretty friendly terms, if he could get two adjoining suites. It was a major violation of journalistic ethics, but Tom figured no one would ever know and no one would probably care, even if anyone did find out. (He had lied to Sam about running it by his boss.) That was a good part of being the lifestyle editor—the other editors at *Profit* thought it was fluff, and probably figured he did this sort of thing all the time anyway.

Tom and Sam arrived early on Friday afternoon to get everything set up. "Feeeee-erce!" Sam said upon entering the first suite, where she promptly flung herself onto a bed. She'd seen her share of nice hotel suites, but it was usually only to interview some celebrity who couldn't bear to be seen in public. Things were different when you were planning on holing up in one for thirty-six hours with four people you thought the world of, or figured you would soon.

"Honey," said Tom, "no one says 'fierce' anymore. You could say 'genius,' though that's always struck me as silly. Or 'brilliant,' but it risks coming off as Madonna in her British phase. I'm partial to 'hot' these days—it has a nice late seventies vibe, and it's kind of sexy . . ."

"Jesus Christ," she replied. "Get over your hot self."

"No, you have to draw it out a bit. 'Get over your hawwwwwwt self,' and it helps if you sneer just a smidge." She threw a pillow at him. "Sam! The pillow fight isn't scheduled until 11 P.M." She hoped he was kidding.

Tom leaned against the windowsill. "Since working at *Holiday,* I've never been able to lie on a hotel bedspread. I don't have a big germ phobia, but one of the editors there did. All you have to say to her is 'bedspread' and she freaks. She kept trying to get us to do an undercover story in which we sent a reporter to different hotels to scan the bedspreads with blacklights to see if there were any funky stains." Sam roared. " 'You know that's why they always have ugly patterns,' she'd say. 'To hide the stains!' "

"No!" Sam gasped. "Wait, is that true?"

"Of course she also thought the aspirin in her dopp kit was a risk to her health, because it had gone through so many x-ray machines."

Sam buried her face in a pillow, and Tom knew he could get her to pee with laughter with one more good one. Writers loved nothing more than hearing about how weird editors were.

"And then there was the time she made her assistant put five-cent toilet paper on her expense account from a public loo she went to in Bali . . ."

Sam clutched her abdomen like a woman with acute appendicitis. "Stop! You know you'll make me—" And off she ran to the suite's very fancy bathroom.

While Sam set the table with notepads and pens, only after they argued about whether to meet at the table or on the sofas, Tom got out his CDs and tried to figure out the stereo. He had called ahead to make sure the suites had CD players, since nothing would be worse than thirty-six hours without music. You never knew with these fussy hotels—the old biddies who liked to stay here probably didn't care if they had to do without listening to the new Röyksopp record. Then they argued over who would sleep where. Sam thought they should let everyone decide, but Tom figured it was better to assign. He won, only because they both agreed that he and Andrew should share one of the suites—Sam opted not to push him on his reasoning—and the women could have the other.

The PR guy had had flowers put in the room, and Tom fussed with them, then he fussed with the lights. Sam figured he was nervous, and couldn't blame him. As well as they all had got along at her apartment, this was a whole different matter. Heck, even Sam and Tom hadn't spent more than a few hours at a time together. She was about to go fuss with the draperies, just for something to do, when there was a knock at the door. She ran over.

"Liza, darling!" Two kisses to the cheeks. "Does Chandler miss you already?"

"Who cares," she said. "This weekend I'm all yours. In fact, I'm not sure he even knows where I am."

Tom shot Sam a look, which she took to mean, Is Liza moody and problematic? Behind her back, Sam shot him the okay sign with her hand. "That's the spirit," she said. "Make him wonder. Right, Tom?"

"You bet."

While Liza got settled in the girls' suite, Sam and Tom

smoked a cigarette out the window, talking gossip. "Page Sex!" Sam said. "Which billionaire couple is more than happy to accommodate each other's desires? At parties, she hits on the guys, he hits on the girls, and then, when they get home, they swap?"

Then Veronica came, followed soon after by Andrew, muttering something about how hard it was to find a cab, and why didn't Bloomberg allow there to be more cabs in the city? Sam shot Tom a look, to which he gave her the okay sign and raised his eyebrows snarkily.

"Everyone!" Tom stood in the doorway between the two suites. "Once we get settled we need to talk about what we're going to talk about. Sam and I didn't do any sort of agenda, because we wanted to be flexible. I guess what I really want to know is this: do you want to start drinking now, or later?"

The verdict was unanimous and hearty. Tom called in the drink orders to room service, and then explained that they'd be having pizzas delivered for dinner. "Roughing it," he called it, promising them tomorrow's dinner would be downstairs at the fancy dining room (and there was only so much he could legitimately expense to *Profit).*

It was clear that Liza and Veronica had no intention of leaving the sofas, at least for a while, so they moved the notepads over. And they got down to business.

"Bite," Tom started off, in a tone that made Veronica remind herself to ask him later if this was a speech he had prepared in advance. "Life is short, as we all well know, and you can buy fancy things and see good movies and have a hot apartment, but when you're older, it's my guess—and I hope yours—that what you'll remember are your experiences. What you've done, what you've learned, where you've gone. It's our magazine's goal to be a sort of guidebook for the readers. We don't want to tell them what to do, just how to go about doing it. We never want to give the impression that

we're smarter or cooler or better than the reader—we're right in there with them."

"Is this our mission statement?" asked Liza.

"Could be, but I hate the idea of a mission statement. Ideally we'll all just know what's right and what's not. If it sounds like fun, then it's right. If it sounds like a prescription for how to have fun, then it's not. We're not about a right way and a wrong way to do things—we're about letting people know what's out there and how much fun it can all be. Anyway, I think some of this stuff will be clearer once we go over the outline."

Tom went over to his bag and grabbed some handouts.

"Sam and I met a few weeks back to talk concretely about what the magazine should be like. Not the attitude of it, but the structure. This should give you some sort of idea." Everyone read over the stapled photocopies Tom handed out.

BITE

1. We'll start with a gorgeous photo spread—a dish at a fantastic new restaurant, or the view from a perfect hideaway hotel, or a new car. We'll call it "Spread," and there'll be a deep caption.
2. Contents.
3. No letter from the editor! The only reason most magazines have them is to feed the editor's ego.
4. Our front of book. Fifteen pages or so of what's new and interesting. Mixed in will be the food and sex columns both under one name: "Appetites."
5. Advice squad. Eight pages. Rather than have the advice come from writers the readers have never heard of—and have no reason to trust—we're going to get advice from experts. Examples: Prince on making the perfect Prince mix tape; a bartender on what your drink says about you; a bookie on how to

bet the horses; sex tips from a Bangkok stripper. Would love this to be on a different kind of paper, maybe something rough and unglossy, with no photos.

6. The feature well. The size depends on how many pages the magazine has, but we'll aim for thirty. Every story will be self-contained (focus groups always say they hate having to skip to the back to finish a story). Joyce Carol Oates on what it's like to take ecstasy or crystal, a group of friends who rent a yacht and cruise the Turkish coast for a week—which could also be a fashion story; a guide to renting a villa anywhere in the world; learning to ride a dirt bike at an upscale camp.
7. "Bite Back." The last page. If a reader takes our advice and does something we've recommended, they'll be encouraged to write to us about their experiences.

"This is just a start. But it should give you an idea. Now. Let's talk first about what you like."

A month later they'd all argue over whether no one spoke, or everyone did at once. In any event, it quickly became clear that "Spread" and "Advice Squad" were the favorites, and should maybe be extended. Veronica, naturally, thought "Spread" should run before every major section, since running one photo that big is a photo editor's dream. Liza worried that would be confusing to the reader, that it might look like an ad, but thought she'd need to work on it.

Sam immediately threw out a flurry of "Advice Squad" ideas, seemingly off the top of her head: a lady-in-waiting to the Queen on how to curtsy; Lauren Bacall on how to smoke; Joan Collins on how to land a husband; Robert Downey Jr. on how to barter for things in jail; Tim and Nina Zagat on how to get a reservation at a hot restaurant; Sandra Bullock on how to tango; Danielle Steel on how to write a sexy love letter; Cheech and Chong on how to roll a joint.

"Who put the 'vice' in 'advice'?" Andrew said.

"We did!"

The front-of-book got a rougher reception. "It feels unfocused," said Liza. "I'm not sure I can make a bunch of small items and several columns—though I do love the name 'Appetite'—seem like one unit."

"And the well," said Veronica. "If it's thirty pages, that's, what, five stories at the most? Because they have to by nature be longer than the items in the front of the book. Is that enough? And how many spreads will we have? Because you're going to want to open each story on a spread, I'd guess, so it feels like an event. But as you know, Tom, we don't always have the spreads we want, since every spread is a page that you're paying for, since there's no advertiser." Andrew gave her a smile, happy to know that someone was thinking about money.

They drank and talked and tried to remember to take notes. The pizzas came and went, and they talked more—there were some good ideas (Sam couldn't stop with the "Advice Squad" stuff; she'd blurt a new one out every ten minutes or so), and some that Tom had to try to explain away. Andrew, who'd been fairly quiet when it came to the idea stuff, wisely suggested that they run an editor's letter in the first issue—just to explain what *Bite* is all about.

Around 11 P.M., Sam insisted they stop for the night. "We've got a lot to talk about tomorrow—"

"And massages at 11 A.M.," Tom interjected.

"And massages! So let's cool down by talking about something else. Like sex. I want to know who's got what going on, because if we're going to work together then I have to know what you're up to in bed. Sorry, but that's just the way it is. I'll start. Currently still stuck on Chris, a man I cannot have."

"And what about Jack?" asked Tom.

Sam blushed. "Well, Tom, I actually wasn't planning on sharing that part of my life . . ."

"You made the rules."

"But he doesn't really count."

"Fine. I'll do it for you." Curling his legs up under his rear, just like all the women were doing, Tom started talking in a vaguely breathless tone. "Jack is my fuck buddy." Sam gasped, Andrew chortled, and Tom continued, falsetto: "We have this thing, I don't know, I find him irresistible once I've had a drink or two. We're friends, I guess, except it's not like we do anything together besides go to a bar, have a drink, complain about our jobs, and then go at it. Sometimes while we're still at the bar. It doesn't help that Chris lives 6,000 miles away. Or maybe it does . . ."

"Mmmm," said Veronica. "What do they look like?"

"I'll take it from here," said Sam. "Chris is tall and blond and very Aryan. He has these really strong hands that are slightly rough, in a good way. And Jack is dark, but he looks like an angel. All goodness. But boy can he get me to do whatever he wants. Still, it's nothing serious. I mean, if something was going to happen it would have happened a long time ago."

"Well," Liza said, "I'm jealous. I'm married, so you can imagine. When you're married, you trade intrigue for stability, and at times I wonder if it's a fair one." Sam thought about pushing her, but then thought better of it.

Liza turned to Veronica. "I'm a bit younger than the rest of you, as you know, so it's taken me longer to swear off bad boys."

Tom slapped himself in the head. "I've told her a million times—"

"Anyway," said Veronica, "the last guy I dated, Charles, was an actor-slash-dropout. And now there's another actor. He's a bartender at Bar 89."

"BURPWAM!" shrieked Tom. "Don't look at me like that. BURPWAM is something Ethan came up with. It stands for Bartender/Unemployed/Retail/Public Relations/Waiter/Actor/Model. Or musician if you're a straight woman, since a man who plays an instrument seems to be catnip to you ladies. It's all the professions you need to avoid in one handy acronym."

"Wait a minute," said Sam. "I'm unemployed."

"Different for women," said Andrew. "You're not expected to provide."

"I want to hear more about the Bar 89 guy," said Liza.

"Taller than me, with stringy black hair. Matt. He's half-Hawaiian, and he has the best cheekbones—like someone who does heroin, but I checked his arms. No track marks."

"That's a relief," said Sam. "What about you, Andrew?"

"I used to have a boyfriend. His name is Lachlan, and he's a little bit younger than I am."

"Obviously," said Tom. "He might even be younger than Veronica is."

Andrew scowled. "Anyway, it didn't work out. Then it did. Then it didn't again. I don't know anymore. Do you ever get the feeling that maybe your destiny is to be a little bit unhappy?"

"All the time," said Liza, laughing.

"We got along so great when it was just the two of us—we could hang out at my apartment forever, and be so happy. But we had nothing outside my apartment in common. I like to walk around, go to the gym, see art galleries, eat at new restaurants. He's happiest at home sketching. He's a fashion designer."

They all sympathized. It was funny how you could seem to roll around in a Sunday-morning way with just about anyone and be content. The hard part was finding someone who you could spend the whole day with.

"Maybe he'll grow into it," said Sam.

"That's what I thought the last time."

Tom figured it was time to spare him more of Sam's insight. "I guess I'm next. As three of you know, I've been obsessing—and that's not too strong a word—about this guy, Justin. He's my dream date. Tall, dark, funny, smart. But he's so goddamn slippery. We've gone out and it's been terrible, and he'll evade me. Then he'll flirt. I'm trying to move on. What's worst is that I've heard through the grapevine about other guys he's done the same thing to. I think I prefer to believe that I'm the only one he treats badly."

"I know I only recently met you, Tom," said Liza. "But I can tell you that I love you." The others all "awww-ed" in unison. "But I can also tell you that that's unbelievably pathetic."

"We're all kind of pathetic," Sam said, raising a glass. "But once we get this magazine running, the whole world is going to want a piece of us." And with that she stood up and ushered everyone to bed.

R.J. had been right: the bacon was superb. So were the massages, for that matter. The next day's meetings weren't as strong as the previous day's, but no one was worried. Well, Andrew was, but Tom persuaded him that magazines aren't built in a weekend, and that even if they had a long way to go, they had come a long way. Perhaps more importantly, they were all getting along fabulously, thanks in no small part to Sam's insistence each person share sex stories: the weirdest place they'd done it, the most regrettable, the absolute best. She was a walking *Book of Questions.* When she wasn't asking about their deepest secrets, she was dishing out Page Sex items. *What Italian starlet covered her bases in her one and only American box office hit? She slept with both her costar and her director.* And Sam and Tom were relieved to see that Liza and Veronica were like sisters, as both knew how much the art director and the photo editor had to get along—it simply can't be any other way.

They had come up with a strong first travel piece: barefoot travel. Rather than blow six pages on a first-person piece about one writer's trip—"It'd be like being shown someone's slides," said Tom—they decided that what everyone wanted in a trip was to go barefoot for a week. To go barefoot was to regress beautifully into childhood, to shake off civilization like the pair of shoes it was. Sam would write a short essay about the joys of being barefoot, and they follow it with boxes and sidebars galore. Ten classic barefoot resorts, five restaurants where you don't have to wear shoes, five perfect convertible road trips (a convertible being the automotive equivalent of barefootedness) . . .

"Why stop there?" Sam said. "How about a page of places where you can go naked? I don't mean cheesy nudist travel of saggy old people playing tennis naked. I mean resorts near nude beaches, houses you can rent that promise solitude, that sort of thing."

"Hot! Hot! Hot!" said Tom. "There's a resort in the Caribbean—I don't remember which one—that has a private island where they'll drop you off for the day with a picnic lunch. And you can do whatever you want."

The idea got Liza going. She saw an opening page of two footprints in the sand, maybe with a wash of sea water coming up the side. Followed by a shot of two pairs of legs—a man's and a woman's—resting on a balcony railing, overlooking the sea. "It could even be the first cover," she said.

"Love it," said Tom. "And let's mock it up. But I was also thinking of a more conceptual cover: a gorgeous red apple in the middle of the page, with a man and a woman each taking a big bite out of it."

The room paused.

"I like it," said Veronica. "But it could be too *Wallpaper.*"

"Then again, *Wallpaper* is in a sense our model," said Sam.

"If we have two good cover ideas," said Tom, "we're lucky people indeed. And we're way ahead of most magazines, which can't even get one together."

At four o'clock, the phone rang. Veronica answered it. "There is? We did? Send him up." She set down the receiver. "There's a pedicurist here."

"Shit!" said Sam. "I forgot! I figured we'd all need a treat about now. Carlos is the best—in fact, some women swear he can make them come just by the way he rubs their feet."

"A pedicure?" said Andrew. "Is this how we're going to be spending *Bite*'s money? Because if we are, I don't know, I mean—"

Sam shushed him. "This is a one-shot. Won't happen again. Now enjoy."

Carlos was as good as promised, although it remained unclear exactly how much pleasure the women got out of it. Andrew was the last to go, and when he came out of the bedroom, he beamed like a five-year-old. "Blue!" he said. "I got blue toenail polish!" Everyone gathered around for a look. "It's what I heard the snowboarders do. If only Whitford could see me now!"

They dressed for dinner, and went downstairs at 8:00. The PR guy had given them the best table in the house, a circular booth in the middle of the room, under a veritable explosion of flowers. Tom held up his glass of champagne. "A toast. To a wonderful weekend, a sure sign of good times to come. To a magazine we can all be proud of—and maybe even make a little money with. And to the best of friends."

The glasses rang. The meal was extraordinary: a parade of truffles and cream. They talked not at all about the magazine, as much as it was still on everyone's mind. Because just as the magazine's philosophy held, it was all about enjoying the experience, whatever it was, to the fullest. Then they went upstairs and passed out.

When they got up in the morning and checked out, agreeing to ponder for at least two weeks before meeting again, each felt a little bit better, and a little bit worse. The problem with progress, it seemed, was that it raised the stakes just that much more.

Chapter 25

Veronica and Tom were standing outside, smoking a quick cigarette before the 3 P.M. writers' meeting, which, for some reason they had yet to figure out, they were expected to attend, even though neither of them were writers. It was unofficially winter, and Veronica and Tom had left their coats in their offices.

"Alright, V., you have exactly ten drags of a cigarette to catch me up on the rest of your weekend before we're relegated to the conference room," Tom said. Looking back on it, Tom wished he had simply quit smoking.

At first, of course, it was just another Veronica story. Some party on Saturday night—as soon as Tom heard the word "keg" he started to tune out, he had to admit—with lots of skanky boys, and suddenly, in walks Mr. Perfect. "But then I'm thinking, *This is different,*" Veronica was saying. "I mean, this guy wasn't a skateboarder, or a bartender, or anything like that. He was a man."

"Uh huh."

"No, I mean seriously," Veronica said, in that way that only twenty-five-year-olds could insist on and actually expect to be taken seriously. "You would finally approve! I've never met someone like this before. He was maybe thirty-three—"

"Oh, we're doing a little Hugh Hefner here," Tom interrupted.

"Tom," Veronica said, taking a fake punch at his arm, "he was amazing. He grew up in New York but hasn't lived here in years. He's this amazing adventurer, who decided to leave it all behind and conquer the world. He's total *Raiders of the Lost Ark.*"

Tom felt a little weird, but he'd had one too many cups of coffee. *Must quit caffeine.* "And then?"

"Well . . ." Veronica said with a slow smile, "it became pretty clear that he should do some digging with me. I told him I had that amazing arrowhead that my great-grandfather gave me, and that he should come check it out. And he suggested now would be a good time, which I had to agree with. So we got in a cab—he hailed it *and* he opened the door—and we went to my house. And the most incredible thing is, after we fooled around, we stayed up for another three hours just talking, about what I did, what he did—"

"What you did in *bed?*"

"No, in our *lives*. How he wanted to eventually live his life, how I imagined living mine. He left this morning to go back to his job—he's working in Cairo right now—but he's coming home again soon, and promised to stay in touch until then."

"Cairo?" Tom wasn't so sure now that the hairs rising on the back of his neck could be attributed to that extra cup of coffee. "What did you say his name was again?"

"I didn't!" Veronica said giddily. "I've always wanted to use that line!"

"No, seriously," Tom said, stubbing his cigarette on the cement and wishing desperately he'd stashed an extra Marlboro in his pocket. "What's the guy's name?"

"Oh, I get it," Veronica said, tossing out her cigarette and turning with Tom to head back in the office building. "You're wondering how you should address me in the future. That would be Mrs. Christopher Foster, thank you very much."

Tom suddenly felt like he might throw up. Sam was Mrs. Chris Foster.

"You know what? I totally forgot I have to call that hotel in Lyons," Tom said in the elevator. "I'm not going to be able to make it to the meeting." Veronica groaned.

As soon as they got off the elevator, Tom beelined to his office—a little too fast, he had to admit, as he saw Veronica's surprised face—and closed the door. He sat at his desk and took a deep breath. Shit. This was exactly the kind of situation he utterly sucked at dealing with. He knew, with absolute certainty, that Sam should never have this piece of information. At least, he knew that with the certainty that came with being his age and (relative) maturity. But he also knew, with all the power of a seventh grader with information—and what was more powerful than that feeling, even at his age?—that Sam should be told. It was his job to protect Sam, he told himself, and she should know this. If she knew that Chris wasn't just seeing her when he was in town, then she'd understand him for who he was, and get over him and on with it.

But Sam had never said that she believed she was seeing him, he argued with himself. And she had said she wasn't pinning any hopes on him. Tom picked up the phone and speed-dialed her number, and then hung up, dialed again, and hung up again. Finally, he called Ethan.

"Advice please," he said when Ethan picked up.

"Coming," Ethan replied, all too happy to skip the meeting.

"Close the door," Tom commanded, and then told Ethan what had just happened.

Ethan listened carefully, and then held his finger up, gesturing for a minute to think. "Here's what I think," he said. "First of all, what Veronica told you she told you in confidence."

"I wouldn't have to tell Sam it was Veronica. God, I'd never want her to know that—that would be hideous!"

"Second of all," Ethan continued, unperturbed, "Sam is not a damsel in distress. I sat right here while she said she understood what was going on with Chris. You'd only be devastating her, even if she doesn't care about him. No one wants to feel like someone else has information about them or their private life, let alone more information than they have. You just want her to know so she has the information, but you also don't want to have to deal with feeling uncomfortable. And that shouldn't become her problem."

"I guess you're right, but . . ."

"No buts," Ethan continued. "When have you ever been grateful to a friend who thought they were telling you something you 'should know'? She's smart. She knows as much as she wants to—she may even know more than you do, as hard as that is to handle, and just isn't talking about it. But I'm telling you, if she does care more than she's letting on, she'll only be angry at you for being the one to tell her."

"The messenger?"

"Like that," Ethan said, standing and heading for the door. "This information is yours to keep."

Tom wasn't so sure. Frankly, it seemed like a lose-lose situation. As much as he hated dishonesty, he decided not to tell her, if only because that was the easiest answer. And maybe it would just go away.

Chapter 26

Goddamn December. Everyone walking around, happy to be alive, soaking up the Christmas vibe. Tom was having no such fun. He had a cold. So here he was, in his overheated apartment, looking out the window. Like many apartment buildings in the city, his used radiators, pumping out the maximum heat so the old tenants wouldn't complain. It was so bad he left the air-conditioners running all winter, but even they could only make a dent. He could go outside, sure, and maybe it wouldn't be too bad. Then again it might result in a full-fledged sneeze-a-thon—and nothing made him feel worse than looking like a snot-nosed miserable mess when everyone else was humming with joy.

Why didn't the phone ring? He wished Justin would call—maybe even bring him some chicken soup. He could call Justin, but he didn't want to. Their last date, although it probably wasn't one, was a little better than the others. They talked about how Justin was liking New York, about how he was liking his job, about everything but what Tom wanted to—his feelings. At least Justin had flirted less. When dinner was over, he said they should "hang out" again. *Face it, Tom. He's a friend.*

The phone rang, which made Tom sneeze. "Hi, Justin!" he said to the walls. "Why yes, I'd love to cuddle." He picked it up.

"Mr. T!"

"Trevor. What's up?"

"What isn't? I've got news. I've quit Goodby and I'm moving to New York."

Tom was speechless. "Wow," he croaked, then tried to make it sound more upbeat. "Wow! Why? What's happened?" He tried to imagine living in the same city as his brother, something they hadn't done since Tom was in junior high. They hadn't even lived on the same coast. He sniffled.

"Bless you, Mr. T. Got a cold? That sucks. I'm moving because I wanted a change. I'm tired of selling soap to the masses, and I'm tired of San Francisco. The quaintness wears thin after a while. And I want to be near my little brother."

"Since when?"

"Since Mom died." *That son of a bitch,* thought Tom. *How like him to trump me with that.* "Seriously. And anyway, business sucks. So here I come. In two weeks, I think. Can I crash with you while I find a place?"

"What happened to Julia?" That was her name, right? Tom was reeling. Trevor was moving here in two weeks. He wasn't sure he could handle all his friends—fags and hags alike—falling head over heels for his older brother. Plus, he was worried that it might be hard to merge his brother into his life. Trevor sure as hell wouldn't want to hang out at gay bars; then again, even Tom didn't want to do that. But he'd had other straight friends who'd moved to the city, and even if Tom loved them, it didn't mean they'd get along with his friends, who could be a tough bunch.

"It didn't work out. That was months ago—didn't I tell you?"

"Guess not." Tom said. "Sorry to hear it." Come to think of it, it was strange she hadn't come to the funeral—Tom must have really been out to lunch.

"This is going to be fun, Mr. T. I promise I won't get in your hair. I'll call you when I get the details. Later!"

Or sooner, Tom thought. "What am I worried about?" he asked the walls. "Everyone always loves Trevor." And he threw himself onto the sofa, the best position, really, to indulge in a one-man orgy of moping.

Andrew was riding his bike through Brooklyn, which he liked to do on a sunny Sunday—even a cold one like today. He liked looking at the boys there—they were all so young, so fashion-forward, so skinny. You could really get your hands around every bit of them, their fragility. He knew Tom thought he liked younger men because he was chasing his lost youth, but that wasn't exactly it; he liked their innocence, their enthusiasm (even when it was masked by a bravado of ennui). He jerked his head right to look at one on the sidewalk, and almost ran into a truck.

He stopped at his favorite restaurant on Smith Street, the one with the tasty eggs benedict and, okay, the waiter who looked like he hadn't eaten in a week. His phone rang. It was Tom, all in a dither because his brother was moving to town. Andrew didn't really get what the big deal was. Tom could be such a child, which could be part of his charm, veering from snobby sophisticate to cranky adolescent. But this was silly. He was sure Trevor was a nice enough guy who would find his own life here in the city, who Tom might actually come to like having around. He told Tom as much, then told him he had to go. Brunch was about to be served, and he wanted to get a good look at the chicken's scrawny arms.

"Andrew!" He looked up, shielding his eyes from the sun. Who was it? The guy was backlit, and all Andrew could see was shadow. He looked skinny, though. "It's me, Robbie."

"Robbie!" Robbie was a friend of Lachlan's. Not a close one, he recalled. They had chatted once or twice at parties. Andrew invited him to sit down.

What makes a man do the things he does? Andrew didn't know, but he wasn't sure the reasons were relevant. Lachlan wouldn't be happy with the fact that he had fooled around with Robbie, but it wasn't like Lachlan and he had any sort of relationship anymore, and, it turned out, neither did Lachlan and Robbie.

Leaving Robbie's little Park Slope studio, he wasn't sure what he felt. Relief, he supposed, that he was still able to have sex. It had been a while. Shame, too, tempered by the fact that he knew he wouldn't tell anyone about it. He felt guilt, because he didn't really see anything happening with Robbie, even though they had agreed to hang out next week. Sad, because sex without love really wasn't worth the trouble. He knew that before going in, but it was funny how the sight of Robbie's narrow little hips could make him forget that. And finally, he felt tired. The last thing he wanted to do was ride his bike back across the Brooklyn Bridge.

"You're still working on it?" Chandler was not happy.

Liza had become obsessed with *Bite.* She refused to tell her husband much about the project, for fear he'd ridicule it. He was remarkably good at coming up with reasons why things wouldn't work. She'd liked that no-nonsense way of his when she'd met him, and she still liked it now. But not *right* now, not when she finally had something that she could get excited about. She turned from the computer, gave him her most mysterious smile, then turned back. She hoped that would work.

"Fine," he sighed. "I'm going jogging in the park. Sure you don't want to come?"

How easy it is to invite people when you know they won't accept. She shook her head.

She had already culled a bunch of photos from the Web to use as dummy art. She'd forgotten how much she loved this—it was such a different way of thinking. Talking, shopping, running your life—these were all things you did rationally. But creating you *felt,* and it was as if a long-standing numbness was wearing off. She found a great photo of a tattooed young stud eating a pink cupcake outside Magnolia Bakery. At the far end of the photo, barely visible, an old woman was watching with what appeared to be lust, for the cupcake or the man, it wasn't clear. She put ten lines of dummy text over the guy's shirt, and the word *spread*—all caps, since she figured Tom was the kind of guy who hated lowercase letters—in the top left corner. *Not bad.* She printed it.

Chandler had insisted he buy her all this equipment, blathering on about how she had a gift and shouldn't let it die, but it had turned out that he didn't really care much if she did anything with it or not. She had let him do it, but she had never really used it beyond designing their Christmas cards. *I've been such a fool,* she thought. *This is like exercising. Once you do it, you can't stop, or you miss the rush.*

She scanned the other stock-photo service websites, but only found one good shot—and it wasn't the footprints in the sand that she'd been hoping for. It was an aerial of a sliver of a tropical beach, with a lone sunbather and, best of all, the shadow of a helicopter. She blew it up: the sunbather was a woman, and she was naked. But even if they ran it as a spread, it wouldn't be dirty—the woman was too far away. Gorgeous. This would be a perfect way to start the nudism story: the helicopter gave it a slightly shocking edge. It made the reader think about who was in the helicopter—namely, the photographer, and by extension, the reader. She could run the text in white, on the water. They can't cancel their subscriptions, she figured, if it's the first issue and they haven't even subscribed yet. She knew Tom would love it. If rule number one of magazine making was never say no to new equipment, rule number two was when in doubt, throw in a beautiful, naked woman.

Chapter 27

"So here's what I'm thinking."

"Not now, Sam, please," Tom said as nicely as he could, given how grumpy he was feeling. He dropped the phone. She could hear him grumbling. "I'm back. Listen, I'm late for a photo showing, the lawyers are up my ass about a hotel review, of all things, and Trevor keeps calling me to ask advice about the city."

"Wait! That reminds me," Sam rambled on, totally unfazed by his tone. "Which cutie pie TV actor brings his own surgical gloves to sexual encounters? His lovers should really have hash marks tattooed on their arms, so he can monitor his progress."

"I can't possibly answer a question in which you use the phrase 'cutie pie,'" Tom grumbled.

"Actually, what I'm thinking might help you with one of your problems, if you'll just be kind enough to hear me out," Sam said. "I feel like while we've had our *Bite* gatherings, we haven't really socialized outside of official business, and I have the perfect excuse. I think you should throw a welcome party for Trevor. It's Christmastime, so it could also be a holiday party. He comes in a week, so you have time to plan it. Plus, it would be fun, and we could use a little fun right now that's not all about a certain magazine."

"I don't notice you volunteering," Tom said.

"Come over this weekend and help me clean up my apartment and we can absolutely do it here," Sam said. That stopped him cold.

"Look, I have to go, but I promise to think about it, okay?"
It would have to be, since once again, he'd hung up on her.

The party idea started to grow on Tom. He'd been wanting his friends to all meet each other, which he knew was probably because he was feeling the need for a family right about now. He hadn't realized how much he'd come to depend on his weekly phone calls to his mom, even if they never dove particularly deep. Moreover, since most of his friends were positively thrilled at the idea of meeting Trevor, he could introduce everyone to him without having to go through the process one by one. And Sam and Veronica could finally meet Justin.

He hadn't thrown a party in years—the sofa still felt new to him, and if your sofa feels new you'll only worry about it all night. *Fuck the sofa,* he thought, then laughed—it hadn't come to that, yet. He bit the bullet. He left Trevor a message telling him to save the night of December 20th, then sent out an email to everyone he wanted to invite.

> Howdy, folks. Please come to a party at my apartment on Saturday, December 20th, in honor of my brother—yes, I have a brother—moving to the city. Cocktails and nibbly bits. 9 P.M. Regrets only.

"Regrets," he sang to himself, "I've had a few . . . "

Sam and Veronica immediately replied that they'd be there; it was gratuitous not only because Tom had said "Regrets only," but because if they hadn't been able to attend he'd have canceled the thing. Liza did her version of a squeal. She leaned back, smiled, and twisted a strand of her hair. She dialed the number she knew so well.

"Hi, Katie. It's Liza."

"Chandler's not here, Mrs. Boardman," came the reply. Liza hated being called Mrs. Boardman.

"That's okay," she said. "I don't need him. Right now, I mean. I lost my datebook. Can you tell me if he's going to be out of town the weekend of the 20th?"

"Lemme check. No, he's here."

"Would you put on his calendar that we're going to a party?"

Liza hadn't been to a party that sounded like fun for years. "A party!" *God, I sound like Mrs. Dalloway.* She had enjoyed her years downtown, but didn't particularly miss them much. Then why was she getting so excited about Tom's party? She went to her closet, and started throwing clothes on the bed. "I won't wear black," she said. "Too obvious. Shit. What's the new black?" It had been brown, then navy, then black again, then white. Was it red? No, never red. She tried a few things on, but when she looked in the mirror she kept seeing the women she used to sit on junior committees with. *Junior committees for juvenile diseases,* she thought. *Why was it always for juvenile diseases? Children don't even know they're suffering.*

She sat on the bed and sighed. "This is crazy," she said. "I am Mrs. Chandler Boardman, or so I'm told. It's time I started acting like it." She pulled on a pair of boots, grabbed her wallet, and headed for Madison Avenue. *Being Mrs. Chandler Boardman is good for at least one thing,* she thought as she waved to the doorman. *Mr. Boardman's credit.*

"You have a brother?" It was R.J.

"Yes, I have a brother." Jesus Christ, did everyone have to keep rubbing it in his face that he was in denial about Trevor? "And R.J., you're one of the few friends I had told about him!"

"I know. But I thought you were just indulging in some fantasy."

"Um, if I were having a fantasy, it wouldn't be about my brother," Tom pointed out, wondering if it was possible to reach through the phone and strangle someone.

"Is he gay?"

"No!"

"Too bad," R.J. said with genuine disappointment. "I'll be there anyway."

Andrew, of course, was his perfectly thoughtful self, offering to prepare some hors d'oeuvres. Now *there* was a friend. What Tom didn't know was that Andrew had also decided to bring Robbie.

Chapter 28

Sam was definitely struggling, she admitted to herself. *Bite* wasn't moving along fast enough to stop her from having to freelance here and there, and Lord knows, her heart wasn't in it. On the social front, she had one wonderful guy she didn't allow herself to speak with more than once a month, although Jack had called her and asked her out to dinner, an offer she'd accepted since her rule with him was that she wasn't supposed to call him. (She had to admit she was really looking forward to it. Then again, she hadn't been out in ages.) On the other hand, there was another wonderful guy who didn't seem to want to speak to *her*. Okay, so he was in Egypt, but didn't they have phones there? In other words, there was plenty to obsess about, but nothing to really sink her teeth into. Maybe she should start trying to date. All well and good to not be off sleeping around—*what was wrong with that, anyway?*—but a dinner now and then with someone who wasn't a woman, a gay man, or herself didn't sound all that bad. How could she meet someone? What if there was no one to meet? And what did it matter, since she was just going to die old and alone, anyway? Actually, maybe obsessing about this stupid freelance piece she was writing for *Parade* wasn't so bad, after all.

It occurred to her, as she sat in sweats and a ratty T-shirt in her makeshift "office"—still a corner in her living room—that as much as she liked to think she craved drama, even reveled in it, she really did far better when things were calm around her. In the past, she'd defined "drama" as waking up the next morning and realizing what an ass she'd made of herself the night before. Now that the rug really had been pulled out from under her, all she wanted to do was hibernate. It wasn't as much fun being a source of chaos when everything around her was chaotic, too.

Nor, she thought, as she chewed furiously on her pencil, a habit she hadn't been able to break since third grade, did it help her focus on anything when she had to have conversations like she had just had for the *Parade* piece, with a star who was a total stoner. Granted, he had built his reputation on acting the part, but it was altogether frustrating to realize he was, in fact, just showing up—no acting called for. *The next time a publicist gets mad at me,* Sam thought, *I'm going to point out to her how often we're doing them a favor for cleaning up their clients' acts, just to make it printable.* She thought about the notoriously mercurial actor who had gotten drunk and threatened to hit her when she didn't agree with what he had to say about Israel—did that make it into the story? "I think not," Sam said out loud, beginning to pace the room. Or the time the famous "sober" actor had ordered up a bottle of champagne before asking if she'd go back to his hotel room. No, no—all she'd written was the conversation they'd had about the movie he was making at the time. Then there was the actor who said he'd pick her up at her hotel, and then conducted the three-hour interview in his car. When Sam had jokingly written that she'd been "kidnapped," the star threatened to sue for defamation and refused to speak to Sam or anybody from the magazine again.

"Done, done, done, done," Sam said, sitting back at her desk. No more protecting louses who didn't need protecting—and if they did, they had helpers who were grandly paid to do just that. From now on, Sam was going to stop paying attention to this ridiculousness, so that she could pay attention to her own ridiculousness, solve it, and move on.

When her phone rang, she grimaced. The way the day was

going, no good could be on the other line. Normally, she would have just let the machine take it, but now that she was freelance, she knew she had to suck it up and pick it up. Money could be calling. "Hello?" she answered tentatively.

She heard crackling over the line. This could be interesting.

"Sam?"

This was definitely interesting.

"Yes," she answered, trying to keep her voice even, counting on the time she had just bought to calm her heart rate down. *This isn't new or interesting,* she said to herself in the nanosecond of crackling. *Well, it wasn't new, at least.*

"It's Chris. Can you hear me?"

"Oh, Chris, hi!" she said, trying to keep the "hi" somewhere south of a hysterical oh-my-God-it's-you pitch.

"Sam, are you there? It's hard to hear you. I'm calling from a dig, and it's not working so well—I don't know how long I have until I cut out."

"No, no, I'm here," Sam said, grabbing her well-worn pencil and putting it near her mouth for emergency use. "How are you?"

"Everything's good. I can't really talk, sweetie, but—"

Sweetie? *Sweetie?* Sam sat down in her chair. Did he just call her sweetie? Holy shit. This changed everything. Did this change everything? "Sweetie," she wrote on the piece of paper in front of her with the other end of the pencil. Always a reporter, even in her personal life, she never believed anything unless it was written down.

"Are you still there?" Chris's voice echoed across the line.

"Yes! I'm here! You're fading in and out," Sam said, trying to excuse herself. "What's going on?" Sam slapped her forehead with the stupidity of the question. He was six thousand miles away, he was on a cell phone, and that was the best she could come up with?

"Look, I just found out I have to come to New York to show a couple things to the museum next week—I'll be in early Saturday morning. Any chance you're free Saturday night?"

Goddamn it! If she missed Tom's party he'd be furious—especially after her impassioned monologue about how she didn't care that much about Chris. Nor should she care enough to blow off her best friend, she thought sternly to herself. She was amazed how much thinking she was doing to herself in such a short time during this phone conversation, actually.

"Sam?"

"Oh, sorry, sorry. Um, I would love to see you! The only thing is I have to go to this party for Tom's brother, and . . ."

"That's okay. I understand this is short notice," Chris answered, without sounding nearly as disappointed as he should have. This wasn't going well.

"No, wait!" Sam said, trying not to come off as desperate as she felt. "I mean, I'd love it if you'd come with me. It'll be fun. We don't have to stay for long." God, did she just say that? Tom would murder her. Sam put her hand over her face from the exertion of the nonstop thinking and talking she was doing.

"That sounds great—I'll call you from the airport. Can't wait to see you!" Chris said.

"Bye!" Sam said, and they both hung up. Sam began to sit forward, and realized she was stuck to the chair in a strip of sweat.

She was leaning forward to the phone again to call Tom, but then realized she really didn't want to talk about it. It wasn't so much that she felt like she had lied to Tom—saying the way you *wished* you felt wasn't exactly a lie—but this about-face was way too predictable and embarrassing. And, she thought hopefully, maybe it would wear off. After all, she had a date with Jack later that week. That could distract her. She hoped. Instead, she logged onto her email, and typed out a note to Tom: "got a call from chris that he might be in town for the party. told him to come by."

And then she lodged the pencil back in her mouth and resumed chewing.

Chapter 29

Sam sighed and rolled over in bed. She opened her eyes and looked at the clock. 11 A.M.! What the hell? Oh, but that was just the beginning. Because lying next to her, *holding her hand, for God's sake,* was Jack. And even if *he* was holding *her* hand, which she had to admit was usually a mutual activity, had he thrown her leg over him? Deep breath. Okay. She had been desperate for companionship, that was true, she thought, gingerly removing her leg from Jack, who was still deeply asleep. She was probably overexcited about having had the chance to put on a slinky dress last night and be taken out to dinner at Daniel, one of her favorite restaurants. Then they'd gone to the Rainbow Room for a glass of champagne, and who was she to resist that?

Who was she kidding?

They'd had the time of their lives, flirting and laughing. It was such a relief to be with him and tell him everything that had been going on with *Bite,* and she loved listening to him tell his crazy TV stories. So it was all too natural that they had ended up back here. Ended up back here having the best sex she'd ever had—besides Chris, of course. It was absolutely amazing how comfortable Jack made her while still being totally sexy—it was the first time she'd ever been in bed with someone where when he said, "Tell me what you want me to do," she'd just shrugged helplessly—not out of her usual shyness, but because whatever he came up with was always so much damn better than what she'd thought of. God, he was so gifted with his hands, she couldn't figure out what the hell he was doing down there, but it was so amazing that after he'd gone down on her, making her come four times, and then made love to her, she'd finally stopped him and said, "Please don't make me come anymore—I'll die." They both laughed at the absurdity of it all. Who had ever heard of a woman pleading for mercy like that?

Only one thing had taken her out of the moment—she could have sworn that Jack, after flipping her over onto her knees and taking her from behind, had said "I love you" as he exploded into her. Sam wasn't sure what frightened her more: That he had said it, or that she thought he had. Either way, it added a tinge of sadness to the situation for her, because it was becoming so much clearer to her that things were far more complicated than she thought. *Oh, God.* Things were about to get more complicated, Sam realized with a surging hot flash, as she gingerly got out of bed and reached for her robe. She had mentioned Tom's party, and Jack had asked if he could stop by to meet the *Bite* crew. And Sam had said yes.

Why the hell did you say yes? Well, she hadn't known what else to say, she explained to herself as she walked into the kitchen. And come on, they weren't in a relationship. Neither one of them thought they were. As much as she had tried to "protect" Jack's feelings, she also knew that much of that motivation came from her just getting more and more confused when they spent time together. And he was clearly a big boy, since (1) he'd never objected; and (2) he continued to call her whenever he wanted. And, she added, he got lucky every time he called her. Maybe he only called her to get lucky. *Maybe,* she thought, getting into a scalding hot shower, *this was all ridiculous.* Jack and Sam were dear friends. They enjoyed each other's company. And for Lord's sake, all the man wanted to do, if he even could make it at all, was stop by the party. Say hello, meet everyone, and go on his merry way. No big deal.

"Sam?" Jack called groggily from the bedroom.

"In here," she answered, trying to breathe deeply.

"Hi, sweetie," he said, and climbed in behind her, kissing her on the neck and enclosing her in an embrace.

Trevor looked out of the grungy cab window at the New York skyline. So here he was, on a gray, December afternoon, changing his entire life. *Well alright then,* he thought. It was time. He was thirty-six years old. And while he had made everything *look* easy, he knew it should be a little bit harder than he made it appear. A job he was good at but didn't love. A series of relationships with lovely, caring women that didn't, at the end of the day, move him to passion.

It was a life he would probably have continued living if it hadn't been for the death of his mother. The first shock he felt was when Tom had walked in the door of the house they had grown up in. He loved Tom, had faithfully called him once a week since they had both settled into their "grown-up" lives. But when he saw Tom standing there, he was hit by the fact that he hardly knew his kid brother as an adult. In fact, he didn't know him at all. Not his friends, not what he liked to do when he wasn't working, not anything above where he went on vacation and what he did at work. And that suddenly scared him, as he hugged Tom and realized they were the last two members of their immediate family.

When he had gone back to work at Goodby, a colleague had asked him out to lunch. "Look, I just want to warn you about the next year," he'd said to Trevor, in a disconcertingly honest tone—hardly the kind of tone anyone at their level was encouraged to adopt. "I won't get into my personal life, but let me tell you about what happened when my friend's mother died. In six months, she'd left her husband and become a lesbian. In eight months, her sister had quit her job as a broker and moved to Africa. I know it sounds crazy," he added, when Trevor looked stupefied, "but a parent's death does more than turn your world upside down. It sometimes gives you the permission you secretly wanted to turn it a little *further* upside down."

So here he was, driving over the 59th Street bridge, about to move into an apartment he'd leased based on pictures on the Web. A one-bedroom on Sutton Place with a fireplace and a view of the river. A one-bedroom where he'd blindly shipped all of his belongings the week before, determined to make a new life.

It was, Trevor had to admit, a little bit scary. Well, maybe not scary, but for a man who had experienced life only when it was handed to him, enough to put him off-kilter. Which was exactly what he wanted. To redefine his life, and find something he hadn't even known he was looking for. And that meant finding excitement. In a job, in a relationship, in a new place. And it meant finding his brother—and finding out who, exactly, his brother had become. If only the twerp would let him.

Chapter 30

Tom, I know I said I'd come over early, and please don't kill me, but something's come up and I'm not going to be able to make it." Tom was listening to the message from Veronica on his answering machine, and he wanted to scream. "But I'll make it to the party, I swear."

"Damn straight!" he yelled. What in the world could have come up? She didn't sound upset in the least, so it wasn't another boy crisis. And if it had been something at work, she wouldn't have been able to wait to tell him every detail. Not to mention that she had left the message for him at home without even bothering to call his cell phone . . . Screw it. He had enough to worry about, like cleaning up the apartment. Plus, he hadn't been sure he could count on Veronica anyway, so he'd already asked Sam to come over half an hour earlier than planned to help calm his nerves. The machine beeped again: "Honey, it's Sam. I'm running late, so I won't be there exactly when you wanted me, but I promise I'll be there." What was it with these people? It wasn't as if they didn't know what a wreck he was about Trevor coming, and throwing a party in his honor. Well, maybe they didn't, he admitted, as he began to rearrange the furniture—an odd habit he'd picked up several years ago when he got anxious. Something about the combination of heavy lifting and rearranging the landscape quelled his anxiety. He hadn't been totally forthcoming with them, and it was possible they thought he was making a bigger deal out of it than he actually felt. If only they knew.

An hour later, Tom was showered and shaved, dressed—

after three costume changes—in a simple blue cashmere sweater and black Paul Smith pants. He'd started with a black sweater as well, but decided Trevor might think he'd arrived at a funeral, rather than a party in his honor, if he opened the door and saw forty people dressed in black. It was weird what one became used to in New York. Tom tried Andrew again. Again, he got his voice mail. "Where are you? Oh, well, just wanted to catch up before the party if possible. I'll see you later, then. Tell me if you need any last-minute help with the food."

"Hello?" Tom heard Sam's voice from the foyer. "Help me!" Sam stumbled into the living room, struggling under dozens of French tulips that she'd gotten from her connection in the flower district. Tom began taking them from her, until finally he was holding them all and she was free to pirouette. "Do you like?"

Tom nodded. Sam had splurged on an Armani sheath that was the color of lilacs, fitted to her frame perfectly. On her feet, she wore Christian Louboutin purple silk mules with lavender flowers on the toe. "You look hot," he assured her.

"That's what we're after," she said, following him into the kitchen and nodding to the caterers. "How you holding up?"

"I'm fine," Tom said. "I mean, I'm never having another party again as long as I live, so I figure I can be a good sport about this one." He smiled wanly. "All I want is to do tequila shots, but I think everything might end badly that way. Or end before it began for me, anyway."

"One shot never hurt anyone," Sam said. "At least I think not. I haven't done one since college, that I can remember, anyway." With that, she reached under his sink to where he kept the liquor and poured them out two hits of the special mezcal he'd brought back from a trip to Mexico. She grimaced when she saw the worm. "I always think I'm drinking worm skin when I see that," she said, having gulped the shot without the help of a lemon or salt; Tom followed suit. "Does it really cause hallucinations?"

Tom shrugged. As the warmth of the mezcal filled his body, Tom instantly felt better. "I think one more," he said, wondering if this would be the sentence he would regret the most in the evening.

"No problem," Sam said, filling their glasses one more time. "To . . . to . . . oh, I don't know. To the best party we'll ever have."

"By the way," Tom said, "I'm delighted Jack will be stopping by this evening. Finally, a little quality time with the man, so maybe I can understand what exactly the problem is." He led Sam into the living room and dropped onto the couch.

"So you really think it'll be okay?"

"Of course, honey! Why wouldn't it be? He'll come, he'll say hi, he'll go, we'll continue on in our debauched ways."

"I'm so relieved to hear you say that," Sam said, sitting more gently than usual as she tried to make it through at least the first hour in the dress before she ripped it or spilled on it. "I was literally up all night obsessing about having him and Chris in the same room, but then I figured I was just being silly, and now you've made me realize I was."

Tom's jaw dropped. "Excuse me?"

"What?" Sam said, reaching for an olive.

"Excuse me that Tom and Chris are going to be in the same room?" Tom poked his side. He'd never had his appendix out. Tonight seemed like as good a night as any.

"Didn't you get my email?" Sam asked, looking up at him. "You didn't get my email."

"What email?" Tom asked, hearing that his voice had risen to a higher pitch than it had since he was thirteen.

"That Chris is in town? And coming?"

"No," Tom said, poking his side a little harder. "No, I most certainly did not get your email."

"Oh God, so this is absolutely awful, isn't it? I knew it was, I just knew it was. But I hoped maybe, oh, this is just terrible. Talk me down, please talk me down. Maybe I should call Jack and tell him not to come? Tell him I'm sick? You're sick? We're all sick?"

Tom thought as quickly as he could. How to be honest, how to calm her down, how to calm himself down, how to get himself to the emergency room as fast as possible, how not to lie . . .

"I don't think Jack and Chris being in the same room is as awful as you think." There. He hadn't lied. It was going to be even more awful than Sam thought. This was getting set to be the worst party in the universe.

"Are you sure?" Sam asked quietly.

"Look, I don't think it's great. It will make you uncomfortable. But the important thing is that Jack's feelings don't need to be hurt. You're hardly going to be all over Chris, right?"

Please God, don't let her be all over Chris. Don't let anyone be all over Chris. Don't let this be happening to him. This couldn't be happening to him. Wait. That was *definitely* a pain in his side. His appendix had probably already burst. Now he was going to die from it. Which wouldn't be entirely bad.

"Uh, any chance you could reach Chris and just tell him you'll meet him afterward? That would sort of solve everything, right?" *If only she knew. If only she knew how that would just solve everything so quickly and easily, please let her say yes . . .*

"Actually, I don't know how to reach him," Sam said miserably. "I don't have his U.S. cell phone number. He originally had said he was going to come early with me, but then I got a message that he was running late and would just meet me here. Not sure what he's up to, but it's probably just as well. Maybe Jack will have come and gone by then, and . . ."

Whatever Sam said after that Tom didn't hear, because he was suddenly having a thought that he didn't like one bit. He hoped it was just the mezcal numbing his brain, but how weird was it that Veronica had called to say she couldn't make it early but hadn't offered even the smallest excuse? And then Chris, newly back in town, had blown off Sam with no explanation, either? Shit.

Shit.

Shit. Shit, shit, shit.

Well, if appendicitis wasn't going to kill him, he'd just have to take it into his own hands. "You know what, Sam?" He reached for the mezcal. "Three's my lucky number."

Chapter 31

"Mr. T!" said Trevor, looking better than he had any business to in old jeans and a navy dress shirt that appeared to have been cut to fit. He looked around. "You call this a party?"

"I call this New York," said Tom. "No one arrives until an hour after the party is called. Even Andrew, who's bringing the food, won't be here for a while. Trevor, this is Sam, who you've—"

"Already met. On the phone anyway. It's great to finally see you, Sam." Tom had never seen Sam blush before.

"Likewise," she said, doing that thing women do when they tuck their chins down as they shake an attractive man's hand. Tom went to get drinks.

If Sam didn't already have a full plate—two full plates—she would have seriously considered ruining her friendship with Tom, just to make a move on Trevor. *Not really.* But it would be the best of both worlds—everything she liked about Tom, but Trevor was even cuter, and more to the point, straight. Maybe, she thought, as they chatted about his move to New York, it could happen. After all, as of this moment she didn't seem to have any plates at all. It had been an hour, and neither Chris nor Jack had showed up. But of course she would never. "So," she said. "When are you going to have us all over to see the view?" She wasn't flirting, she rationalized. She was being friendly.

The buzzer rang again. Tom had put R.J. on door duty, not the best decision—he was nowhere to be seen. "Excuse me," she said to Trevor. "I should get that." It was rude to make people wait outside, especially on a chilly night. Tom went to the buzzer at the same time.

"Tom," she said, "where's Chris? I can't believe he won't show. He's not like that." If she had managed not to freak out about Chris and Jack both showing up, it was only because Trevor had distracted her.

"What's the worry?" Tom replied. "I thought you were marrying my brother."

"Don't be a dork. I'm being friendly. He's a doll."

Tom opened the door. It was Veronica, looking very sexy in a red halter dress. "Wow! You look—" Sam noticed that Tom had turned white.

"Finish it, bitch!" Veronica did a little twirl.

"H-h-hot," he stammered.

"Gee, thanks," Veronica said, giving him a strange look, at which point Sam saw that Chris was standing right behind her. And way too close.

"Chris!" she said.

"Hey, Sam." He gave her a peck on the cheek.

Veronica looked perplexed. "You two know each other?"

"I invited him!"

"Have you heard the new N.E.R.D. record?" Tom said, and bolted.

Chris told some story about how he had met Veronica awhile back, and only on the way to Tom's had he realized that she was taking him to the same party Sam had invited him to. Sam's bullshit detector was shooting sparks—not least of all because this was clearly the first Veronica had heard of it. Sam couldn't believe her eyes. Could. Not. Believe. It was enough to make her very angry. But first it made her cry. "Excuse me," she said. "I have to . . . I have to . . . I have to find Tom. The music." She walked as gracefully as she could to the bathroom and locked herself inside.

🍎 🍎 🍎

Liza was deeply peeved at Chandler. He had some business that kept them waiting to leave for the party until it was a good forty-five minutes under way. What kind of documents were that important? And couldn't the doorman just take them? But when she walked into the party, she sensed something was wrong. Veronica was there, standing next to a very handsome man, but she didn't seem thrilled about it. *Best to avoid.* She gave a little wave, and headed for the bar.

Things were better by the bar. She and Chandler met Trevor, and Chandler was clearly relieved that there was at least one other straight man in the house. Leaving them to talk business, she took her glass of tonic over to the sofa. "R.J.!" she said. He was always good for a laugh.

"Hi, Liza. How's it hanging?"

"Quite well, thanks." She liked R.J. He didn't try to flirt or impress you. He just was. "Did you bring a date tonight?"

He shook his head. "I was hoping to scrounge something up here. Should've known better. It's Tom's, after all. Hey, let's play a game. It's one that comes in handy when you're bored. Who in here would you sleep with?"

Liza scanned the room. "Well, that one's my husband, so I guess I have to say him."

"Cop-out," R.J. said. "My turn. I'd say Trevor."

Liza nodded. "He looks just like Tom!"

R.J. hacked as if he had a fur ball. "I revoke my choice. Pick another."

Liza held her finger up to her lips and scanned the room again. She pointed at a man alone in the corner. "That one. He looks sweet."

R.J. followed her glance. "The dark one? I don't know who he is, but he's been standing there for a while." Probably because the two of them were looking at him, the man walked over. "Shit! Look away!"

"Don't be silly."

The man sat on the arm of the sofa. "Hi, I'm Jack. I was hoping you two might take pity on me and let me join you. The friend who invited me hasn't shown up yet."

"Don't be silly," Liza said just a little flirtatiously this time, then introduced herself and R.J. "We'll be your friends. But who are you waiting for?"

"Samantha Leighton," he said.

"We know Sam!" She turned to R.J. "Where *is* Sam?"

R.J. fluttered his arms around. He was clearly excited. "This is good! She threw a hissyfit because Veronica brought some guy who Sam was totally and completely obsessed with. She's locked herself in the bathroom. I had to piss off the fire escape!"

Liza paled. Wait, was this Sam's Jack? Was it Chris that Veronica had brought? As she turned to look at Jack, R.J. said, "That's him over there—the blond one. His name's Chris Something."

Jack stood up. "You know, it's getting late," he said. "I guess I should go. It was really nice meeting you." He went for his coat.

"Jesus," R.J. said. "Was it something I said?"

Sam sat on the bathroom floor, slowly pulling sheets from the roll of toilet paper, wadding them up, and throwing them in the trash. Every now and then she used one to dry her eyes. Chris was sleeping with Veronica, there was no doubt about it. Or at least dating. But probably screwing. There was an ease between them, the kind of shared body language that only two lovers had. The kind of shared body language she didn't have with anyone. Except maybe Jack. It hit her like a punch in the gut. Was he actually going to come? That would be the coup de grace.

She struggled to her feet—what Tom needed, she decided, was one of those rails they have next to handicapped toilets. Where *was* Tom? Why wasn't he banging on the door? Begging her to come out? Telling her everything would be okay?

She looked at herself in the mirror. Under no circumstances could she leave this room.

Someone knocked. Finally!

"Sam? It's Liza. Let me in."

Sam sighed, and unlocked the door.

"Are you okay? I heard what happened. Oh, honey!" She enveloped Sam in a big hug. "I'm sure Veronica didn't know—"

"That's not the point," Sam said, thinking maybe it wasn't time to reapply mascara just yet. What was wrong with her? Was Veronica more appealing? Sam was older, sure, but it wasn't showing, was it? And Chris was even older than Sam was, so he really had no business with Veronica.

"I know, I know." Liza patted her back. "But—I know this sounds trite—but maybe it wasn't meant to happen, you know?"

Was she kidding? Now Sam had no way to pretend otherwise, no choice but to move on. "Hey," she said, trying to get back some of her bravado. "There's always Jack, right?"

Liza stopped breathing. She pulled free of Sam. "Maybe we should sit down."

So Andrew was dating Robbie. Huh. Back when Andrew was with Lachlan, and they'd all be at a party or something, Tom would tease Andrew that he was only with Lachlan to get to Robbie. Maybe Andrew had been lusting the whole time. This was too much for Tom to handle. He'd been out of his mind to think, or not think, not really, but to allow to creep into the back of his mind, to some corner, that he and

Andrew could have had something. It was crazy. They were friends, the best of friends, and Tom was just confused. And lonely. Besides, he was in love with Justin. Or not, that's right, but maybe all this Justin stupidity had driven Andrew away? Where was Justin? He had been here a minute ago. God he was sick of this party.

"I think I calmed Sam down." Liza gave him a squeeze. "I got her out of the bathroom—okay, so she went into the closet instead. At least now people can pee."

"Great," Tom said. "Is she speaking to me?"

"Why wouldn't she be?" It dawned on her. "Wait, you knew?"

"Not officially. No, that's a lie. Yes, I knew. But I didn't think it was my place to tell."

Liza exhaled. "You're going to have one hell of a mess to clean up when Sam finds out."

"Maybe she doesn't have to know?"

"Too late." It was Veronica. Tom and Liza listened in horror as she explained that she went to talk to Sam, to tell her that Chris had left. Desperate to make Sam understand her side of the story, she had let slip that she had told Tom about meeting Chris. "I don't think she's ever coming out now."

Tom put his head in his hands. "Hey," he said with mock chipperness. "Do you think I can make her pay rent?"

Justin approached, and the others scattered. "Hey, Mr. T. Can I call you that? Your brother did." Justin was talking a mile a minute, and standing way too close. He reached out and messed Tom's hair. "By the way, your brother's a fox. Are you sure he's straight?"

"Yes." If Tom didn't know better, he'd say that Justin was coked up.

Justin looked over at Trevor and leered. "Because sometimes it runs in the family."

That did it. First Justin flirted, then pushed this fantasy

about Trevor? Tom snapped. "Well, sometimes he and I go at it. You know, the way brothers do. Naturally, he's the top, because he's older. And I don't call him my big brother for nothing!"

He went to the bar. *Fuck Justin.* He didn't need another friend that badly. He grabbed a beer, popped off the lid, and took a big swig. With that came a lull in the room, and Tom hoped—but was sure he was wrong—that he did not hear R.J. say the word "buttplug."

Jennifer tugged on his shirt. "I need the phone?" Tom figured it was the tears that made her turn it into a question. He pointed to the kitchen.

"Are you okay?" he asked, but he was already talking to her back. Tom clicked his heels three times. *Fuck,* he thought. *I'm already home.*

Liza could feel her pulse race. Chandler didn't smoke, and she knew there was only one reason he'd be outside, especially on a winter night. She stood up and went to the window. "Chandler."

He turned away from the view. "Hey, baby! How's it going? Where've you been?"

"Aren't you cold? You're not wearing a coat."

He looked around, as if realizing for the first time that, yes, it was cold outside. "Not really. Isn't that funny?"

"Come inside."

He walked toward the window, and as soon as he got near the light, Liza knew. She could tell by the look in his eyes—rather, the look *of* his eyes. His pupils were tiny. "You bastard," she said. "How could you do this?" She turned and fled—to the bathroom, which conveniently enough was empty.

Chapter 32

Finally, just when it seemed like it would never happen, everyone left. Trevor, who had been the last to go, had patted him on the shoulder and said he'd call tomorrow.

It occurred to Tom that his mistake had been not just downing the bottle, worm and all. No hallucination could have been worse than the reality. *Fuck, I should've broken the bottle and eaten the glass.*

He paused, looking at the mess in the apartment, and wondering if he was judging himself too harshly. After all, you never had a sense of how your own party went. Nope, no chance of that. It was definitely the worst party in the history of the universe.

Tom grabbed the rest of the mezcal and another shot glass. Then he put the glass back down. He went into the bedroom and propped up some pillows, and threw himself onto the bed. The good news was . . . The good news was the party was over. The other good news was that he lived in New York, so even though he would have to find totally new friends, it probably wouldn't take that long, with so many people to choose from. There were worse things than fresh starts.

He heard a noise from the closet. Maybe it was Andrew and Robbie. Or Justin and R.J. Or Chris and Veronica. Or an intruder. That would just be perfect. "Go ahead!" he yelled. "Take it all!"

Sam opened the door and poked her head out. She looked like a mess—could anyone really cry that much? "Is it safe?"

"How long have you been in there?"

Sam wailed again. "Not long enough! Which formerly

high-flying Hollywood reporter is having a total meltdown because the man she loves is humping her new friend?"

"You're having a meltdown? *You* are having a meltdown? Did you just throw the worst party in history? Remember, I'm gay. Throwing parties is what we're supposed to do!" Jesus Christ. Pol Pot left more people standing.

"Um, no," Sam said slowly, crawling onto the bed. "But I did realize that the man I thought was the love of my life was sleeping with someone else, who happens to be your close friend, and my new friend, or so I thought, and that you knew about it and didn't tell me, which makes me a fool on top of being heartbroken. And that's not even getting into the Jack debacle."

"You're right. I'm sorry. I didn't tell you because I thought it would only muck things up, and that maybe you'd get over it without ever knowing. And I swear, I had no idea they had seen each other again. The way Veronica described it to me, it was a once-only kind of thing."

"I just can't believe it," Sam said. "I never thought he'd be capable of cruelty, for God's sake. And you of, of—"

"The guy is, above all else, a man. I'm sure he didn't mean to be cruel, it just never occurred to him that you would put two and two together, and that even if you did, that you would care. You have to admit that you've always acted calm and cool around him, even if you didn't feel that way. As for me, I'm truly sorry. I didn't know what to do. Ethan was the one who said I should—"

"Ethan knew too?" Sam started bawling again. Tom pulled her over to his side and handed her a Kleenex. "At least I didn't lose it in front of them."

"And locking yourself in the bathroom would have been what, exactly?"

"Oh, fine, if you're determined to be honest about it." Sam sniffed. "It's just too bad that we're going to have to fire

Veronica, or I'm going to have to quit, because I obviously can never face her again."

"Honey, I don't think we can face anyone again." Tom told her about Andrew, Robbie, and Justin.

Sam was distraught. "I missed Justin!"

"I think I might be getting over it, actually," Tom said. "All of it. Justin's not for me. He's fucked up. And I think I was liking Andrew because I love him as a friend, and hoped it could be as easy as falling for your best friend. God, maybe I was just thinking of him as a backup. But that was obviously wrong on my part. Anyone who could date a boy like Robbie is certainly not man enough for me," Tom added with a laugh.

"So what was the worst part for you?" Sam asked. Even if you were the frog, the dissection was part of the fun.

"I'm going to go with the moment that Chandler pulled Jennifer over to the corner, offered her coke, Jennifer freaked out, and spent the next thirty minutes on the phone with her sponsor. I can't tell you how close I was to ripping the phone away so her sponsor could talk *me* down."

"I feel so bad for Liza," Sam said. "I mean, Chris and Veronica, that sucked. But Liza and Chandler have been having a hard time of it, and that was so damn stupid. His own wife is sober, for God's sake, and the man is not only doing blow, but offering it to someone else?"

"Not just someone," Tom said. "He offered it to the one person who can't handle it. Besides Liza, I guess."

"Did R.J. really offer to tell them how to make a booty bump?"

"Oh, God," Tom said. "Did you talk to Liza? What's she going to do?"

"Leave the son of a bitch, I hope. At least this might get her out of limbo. And I've never gotten a great vibe from Chandler. We had this weird evening once where I felt like he was a little inappropriate toward me. I wrote it off thinking maybe it was in my head."

"I'd say the question of Chandler and his inappropriateness was pretty much settled today."

Sam started to giggle. "What the hell do you think Trevor thought? Me locked in the bathroom, totally missing that Jack came and went, Jennifer in the kitchen, Liza freaking out . . ."

"I can't go there. That's tomorrow's problem—one of them. Hey, at least you and I are still talking."

"That's just because I can't handle going home. I guess I'll have to forgive you. After all, if we can never talk to any of those people again, we're facing slim pickings."

"It would be nice," Tom said, "if not everyone's relationship was ruined this evening at Chez Tom's, the most cursed home in all Manhattan."

"I wouldn't worry about it—Andrew and Robbie seemed just fine," Sam said with a laugh. "I guess we should try to go to sleep. God knows we'll have a lot of damage control to do tomorrow."

"Not if we never speak to anyone again," Tom replied, finishing the last of the mezcal. And he reached over and turned off the light.

Chapter 33

Sam finally gave up around 7 A.M. and left Tom snoring beside her. She was way too wound up to sleep, and besides, he was a lousy cuddler. What she needed was a hot shower and her own bed.

Which, she realized as she got off the elevator, were going to have to come a little later than anticipated. Sitting in front of her door were three enormous suitcases and one wrecked-looking person. "Lize?" she whispered gently, nudging her awake.

"Hi," Liza said, opening her eyes. Or at least trying to open them, since they were pretty much swollen shut from crying. It looked like Liza had traveled much farther than the few blocks from her Park Avenue apartment to Sam's place. "I hate to ask, Sam, but . . ."

Sam hadn't made her continue, but led her in, made up the sofa with sheets, a pillow, and an extra duvet she had stored in her closet.

"It was the last straw," Liza said, pulling the covers up around her and curling into a fetal position. "I'm totally terrified about being on my own, but I think I'm more terrified of staying in a situation that's so wrong. I mean, it's got to be less lonely being alone than being with someone who makes me lonely when I'm with him, right?"

Sam nodded. "I think I'm following you," she said with a smile, "and I think you're right. And I think what you're doing is very, very brave."

Liza smiled weakly. "Thanks. I think I know the answer to this by looking at you, but how are you feeling?"

"Like total shit. But my biggest concern right now is Jack. I can't imagine what an ass he must think I am."

"Well . . ." Liza said gently, unsure of how to continue.

"I absolutely know," she said miserably. "He's the last person in the world who deserved to be hurt, let alone by me. I'm not sure how to make it up to him, or if maybe the way to make it up to him is just to get out of his life forever, or if there's even an option to *have* him in my life anymore. If I were him, I'd never want to talk to me again."

"I think you should deal with this when you've had some sleep," Liza said, squeezing Sam's hand. They were silent for a moment. "Sam? I'm terrified."

Sam nodded. "Of course you are. But you're going to be great, I promise. You're the only person who doubts that. And anyway, weren't you the person who told me that being brave isn't about not being scared, but about being scared and doing it anyway?"

"I doubt I'd say anything that wise," Liza said.

"I disagree. Try to get some sleep. And I know this goes without saying," Sam added, "but you're welcome to my couch as long as you can bear it."

"Only until I can figure things out," Liza said, as she started to drift off to sleep.

"It wasn't that bad," Trevor was saying to Tom, but they both knew he was full of shit.

"I wish you were here so I could call you a liar to your face," said Tom.

"Hey, I'm the one person who doesn't hate you!"

Silence.

"I guess Andrew doesn't hate you, right? He seems like a good guy—"

"I'm not dating him, Trevor. We're friends. Can't people get their heads around the fact that two gay men can have a close friendship that isn't also sexual? Just because we're gay doesn't mean—"

"Oh, shut up." There were times when being the older brother sucked. "I just meant he was a good guy. He was telling me about your magazine, which sounds fantastic. Why didn't you tell me about it? It's great! And Sam's parents are really going to back it? It sounds like a good investment—at Goodby we had tons of clients who wanted a young audience eager to get out there and spend."

Tom was grateful for the chance to talk about something besides last night. He told Trevor the whole story, from how he met Sam to their many nights drinking and talking, to Sam getting fired for giving a blow job—Trevor particularly liked that part—to Sam's parents offering to bankroll them. He explained the premise behind the magazine, pointed out that no one was doing anything similar, but also explaining that starting an independent magazine was pretty much unheard of these days. He said Andrew was running numbers for them, but they needed a publisher, someone to oversee the selling of the ads that would pay for the whole thing and hopefully make them all gobs of money. "If you know of anyone . . ."

"I'll think about it." In the meantime, Trevor gave him one piece of advice: "You need to get your team together pronto, Mr. T. Because if they're not speaking to each other, they sure as hell aren't going to make a magazine."

Chapter 34

Veronica checked her shirt for sweat stains. She wasn't used to feeling this anxious. On the other hand, she wasn't exactly used to finding out that she was sleeping with her future boss's dream guy, being lied to by Tom, segueing into a new job, and dealing with the lunacy that had been Tom's party.

And now they all had to *talk* about it. Veronica hailed a taxi and gave the driver the address of El Quijote. She wasn't sure how she would react, or what she should say. She definitely owed Sam an apology. True, she hadn't done anything intentionally hurtful—she would have run the opposite way had she had any idea—but she couldn't imagine how she would feel if she was in Sam's place. And while she could imagine what that apology would be to a friend, the reality was she and Sam were just starting to get to know each other, and Sam was not only above her at the magazine, her parents were responsible for funding it, for God's sake. Even more pressing for Veronica was how to deal with Tom. If he'd just been straight with her, none of this would ever have happened in the first place. Well, the party would have still *sucked,* but maybe not for her.

Veronica took a deep breath and opened the door to El Quijote. Dusty and falling apart at the seams, El Quijote served cheap, mediocre Spanish food. But it was next to the ghost-ridden Chelsea Hotel, and it was comfortable. At least, it had been until now.

She was the last to arrive. Sam, Tom, R.J., and Andrew all looked up at her, and, Veronica noted with a breath of relief,

Sam was the first to smile. "Hey, V.," Sam said, standing and giving her a hug. "Thanks for coming."

"I'm so sorry," Veronica whispered in her ear. Maybe it wasn't the best presentation, but she couldn't help it.

Sam smiled and gestured for Veronica to sit in the empty seat at the head of the table.

"Hey." Tom looked up at her mournfully.

"Say you're sorry," Veronica said.

"Beyond. I'm sorry beyond, I swear it. To you *and* Sam."

Sam and Veronica both nodded.

R.J. made a caustic "aww" sound.

"Shut up," Tom said.

"Don't start again," Andrew said.

"Don't *you* start," Tom snapped back.

"I didn't start anything!" Andrew yelped.

"Stop!" Veronica yelled across the table. And she was the youngest here? This was absurd. "Look, everyone's sorry, okay? Or they're not. Whatever. Clearly we're all important enough to each other to have come here, humiliated or angry or sorry or whatever we each are."

Tom cleared his throat. Sometimes a little throat-clear could change everything. "Exactly my point," Tom said. "I wanted to get together because I wanted to know if we can put this behind us and do something more important like, oh, run a magazine."

"I wouldn't be here if I weren't," Andrew said, sounding a little hurt.

"Let's do it already," Sam said.

"Here? Now? An orgy?" R.J. said.

Everyone glared at him.

"If Sam will still have me, I'm in," Veronica said.

"We couldn't do it without all of you," Sam responded, trying not to sound as sticky-sweet as she felt. "Let's just all acknowledge that Tom's an awful person, and move on from there."

"I'm not an awful person," Tom joked back, "just the worst party thrower in the world. And it's not like the party was my idea." He shot Sam a so-there look.

"Alright then," Andrew said. "How about this? Tom doesn't get to have any more parties, which is just as well, because it's time to get to work."

Veronica felt relief, and even a flutter of excitement.

"So one more time," she said, pouring everyone a glass of sangria, "to *Bite!*"

And finally, everyone was in agreement.

"By the way," Tom asked. "How's Liza?"

"And I guess that's why they call it the blues . . ."

Liza was singing along to Elton John when Sam walked into the apartment. "Lize?" She spun around and blushed. "You hate Elton John."

"Utterly," Liza said, collapsing on Sam's couch, which was still serving as her bed. "But sad songs say so much." Neither of them was yet in a place where they wanted to be alone—even if that meant living on top of each other.

"I just had one of those fall-to-my-knees terror moments," Liza continued, while Sam dropped her bag and curled up on the club chair next to her. "What if I never get the hang of this life thing?"

"Well, at least then you won't, in fact, die old and alone, because I'll be there keeping you company," Sam said with a smile. "I totally understand what you're saying—I just passed this elderly man being pushed in a wheelchair, and I thought, 'That's going to be me. No friends, no family, and I won't even be able to afford a nurse.' "

Liza cocked an eyebrow. "Sam, your family is loaded."

"There you go again, ruining my fantasies. Alright, let's change this music and see if we can change our moods."

"Ah, Coldplay," Liza said sarcastically of Sam's next pick.

"Yeah, that'll help. I know the answer is obvious, but I just need you to say it to me one more time, okay?"

Sam nodded.

"Did I do the wrong thing? I mean, was there a possibility that we could have worked things out? What if I'm just too scared of being intimate with someone, and used it as an excuse to run?"

"I'm sure you're scared of being intimate with someone," Sam said slowly, "because who isn't? But I'll remind you that (a) you had good reasons to run, and (b) you weren't happy for a long time before that."

"Because now I can't remember. Now I'm thinking my life wasn't all that bad, and I just didn't see the good stuff."

"Promise," Sam said with a smile. "Cross my fingers, swear to God, needle through my eye, the whole thing."

Chapter 35

Tom and Andrew were back at the Red Cat, having one of what Andrew called their dividend dinners. Andrew owned stock in Worldwide Media, *Profit's* parent company, but the stock only went down—so Tom gladly expensed dinner, saying Andrew had it coming.

"Trevor has been kind of great," Tom said. "I mean, sometimes the very thought of him drives me nuts, but I think that's just because he's my older brother and it wouldn't matter who my older brother was. If Gandhi were my older brother—"

"And alive—"

"And yes, if Gandhi were alive—well, I'd probably hate him too." Tom dipped a radish in salt and popped it in his mouth. When he finished chewing, he told Andrew how it had been Trevor's idea to get the team together, and how Trevor was going to see if he knew someone from his advertising days who would make a good publisher. "Because we need one. Someone has to sell the ads! I think it should be a woman. A fierce Latina. We need diversity, and it would just be so hot!"

Andrew sighed. Tom was being more stupid than usual. "Tom," Andrew had said gingerly, "don't freak out."

Tom furrowed his brow. "No promises."

"Okay. Here it is. I think you should think about—and all I'm saying is that you should think about it—asking Trevor to be the publisher of *Bite.*"

Tom ate another radish—it would give him at least ten seconds, fifteen if he really worked that radish over, to think before he spoke. First, the review: Trevor? Publisher? *Bite?* Then, the reaction: No. Then, the re-reaction: Maybe. *Pretend he's not your brother.* Trevor had the sales skills the publisher would need, he didn't have a job, and didn't even seem to particularly want one. At the very least he'd agree to help start the magazine out of a sense of family obligation. Lord knows how he was always going on about that. It was perfect—except that he was Tom's brother.

"Maybe," Tom said, taking a swig of his gimlet, "I can find some formal way to de-siblingize him."

Andrew had had enough. "Grow up."

"Easy for an only child to say." Tom laughed—there was nothing only children hated more than having their only-childness held against them.

Sam got Tom's message about lunch at 11:30, right about the time Tom generally liked to be eating said lunch. She knew something big must be up, since Tom hated to go out for lunch. She called him up.

"Finally!"

"Look, the one benefit of not having a job is not having to get up early."

"Meet me at noon at Corner Bistro for a big burger."

"Half-past."

"Fine."

Tom was hoping they could ease into the conversation, but she was having none of it. "I am not a patient woman," she said.

"Okay. Well, you know I'm a big fan of nepotism."

"You and me both."

"Well, it was Andrew's idea. He thinks Trevor should be our publisher."

Sam's jaw dropped. Sometimes Tom confused her no end. All he had done since Trevor had said he was moving to

New York was bitch about how much he dreaded being in his brother's shadow, how his brother always trumped everything he did. She would have sworn that Tom wouldn't want Trevor anywhere near *Bite*. "If you don't like the idea we can just drop it."

"But Tom—"

"I mean, I can see why you would think it was weird."

"Tom—"

"You just met him, he has no magazine sales experience, he's my brother, which could leave you feeling outmaneuvered."

"Would you freakin' shut up already?"

"*Freakin'?*" They both laughed.

"Well, I had to do something to get your attention, and I don't like to flash my breasts before happy hour. I think it's a fantastic idea. He's slick enough to be a publisher, and his lack of experience means he'd come cheaper than most. And I'm not even going to acknowledge the outmaneuvering part. That's ridiculous."

"And you'd like to get into his pants."

"If that's what it takes, I suppose I could be persuaded. Kidding. Rest assured I wouldn't go near him that way if he comes on board. I am a professional. Or I was, anyway, back when I had a job."

They spent the rest of the lunch getting up to speed on what the other had been doing to move *Bite* forward. Now that the party scars were finally starting to heal, they needed to start moving. Tom said he'd pitch the publisher job to Trevor, and he promised to talk to Andrew about his food column.

"Someone has to deal with R.J.," Tom said. "And I just don't think I can handle it."

"No problem, sweetie. It'll be my pleasure. With our combined sexpertise, we'll make the whole world wet."

🍎 🍎 🍎

Trevor was liking New York, and New York was liking Trevor back. It was one of those late winter days when the sun hits the back of the neck and sends the opposite of chills down the spine. He walked around Tribeca and looked at the furniture. Or more to the point, he looked at the women looking at the furniture.

He had been to New York before, obviously, and had certainly noticed that the city had no shortage of beautiful women. For all San Francisco's charms, the women there were sort of the same. He wasn't sure how to describe it, not that he had ever tried, but what it came down to was this: most women in San Francisco seemed as if he slapped them, they wouldn't slap him back. He liked women who would slap back—not that he'd ever. This was all a theory.

He followed a tall black woman in a tan pantsuit into yet another furniture store. She went straight to the back; so as not to appear to be stalking her, he lingered up front, where the gay salesguy scrambled right up to him, like a dog, if dogs could ask if you needed any help.

"Just looking, thanks." The black woman came back toward the front. "Actually, I'm looking for a chair for my brother. Sort of a thank-you gift. I just moved here and he's helping me get settled." He wanted the woman to know something about him. "How much is this one?" he pointed at the nearest chair.

"Five thousand, give or take, depending on the fabric."

"Right." He watched the woman while the salesguy watched him. As she started to pass by, he stopped her. "Excuse me, but I was wondering if you could help me. I want to buy my brother something to thank him, and I know he needs a chair. What do you think about this one?"

"It's shaped like lips," she said. She had a British accent, and he liked that.

"And that's bad?" he said, smiling. "Lips are . . . bad?" He could see the salesguy rolling his eyes.

"Lips," she said, drawing her own into a smirk, "are for kissing."

Chapter 36

"You're *luscious,*" R.J. said, making smacking noises with his lips.

Sam sat down beside him at the bar at the Four Seasons. She knew that inserting R.J. into this kind of sophisticated atmosphere was going to be a disaster, but then he did too—that's why he insisted they come here in the first place.

"Is everything sexual to you?" Sam asked, ordering a dirty martini.

"Thanks to my new gig as your columnist, I think it's fair to say that yes, it is. It's a wonderful thing," R.J. said with a deep sigh. "A wet dream come true." He picked an olive out of Sam's glass before she even had a chance to touch it, and pretended to rim it.

"Good God," Sam whispered, watching the bartender hightail it away from them with record speed.

"Oh, get over it," R.J. said, putting the olive back in her glass. Sam grimaced. Leave it to R.J. to redefine the dirty martini. "I'm just teasing. But clearly, you can't take it. How are you going to take my copy?"

"I hope seriously," Sam said, "but not too seriously. Let's talk about how you see it."

"Fisting! How far can you actually go, that's what I want to know!" R.J. yelled. This time, the whole bar looked up.

"Okay," Sam whispered, as if her low decibels could make up for his high ones. "I'm gonna go with . . . no. Not right away, anyway. This has to appeal to men and women, and frankly, not every man is interested in fisting, anyway."

"Oh, they are, my dear, you just don't know it. Speaking

of which, since you seem so deeply ignorant in the ways of pleasing men, I have to ask: When was the last time you got laid?"

Sam winced. She'd been trying to put both Chris and Jack out of her mind, and had managed not to think about either or both of them for stretches that lasted up to, oh, three minutes at a time now. Which was definitely progress.

"Let's just say I'm not any better at pleasing men out of bed than in it, it would seem," she said.

"More, please."

Sam felt her face flush with shame about the way she had treated Jack again. She'd sent him an email with just the words "I'm so sorry," but he hadn't responded. And it had become clear, as she'd run out of excuses ("Maybe he's hiking in Tibet!" "Maybe he's dead!"), that he wasn't going to. Anyway, she knew he wasn't dead—she called his work machine late at night a few times, and his message didn't even say he was out of the office.

"I haven't had a regular sex life in a long time, R.J.," Sam said, trying to sound firm that the conversation was going to end there, no matter what he wanted. "And I may not for a while. But I do have some recollection of it from years past, so I think we'll be okay." She told him *her* idea, which was that sequined bikini wax Elizabeth had told her about months ago. Sam started to laugh. "In fact," she whispered, "I've got them right now."

"What a waste of a good sequin."

"Well, they cheer me up," Sam said, "Even if they're itchy. But I doubt a lot of people outside of Manhattan have considered it might be possible. In fact, I wouldn't have considered it possible only a couple weeks ago. So maybe you could do something about the logistics—how long they stay on. Maybe a little is-it-safe thing to make it sound serious. Or not. What do you think?"

"I love it," R.J. said. "I can't believe you're teaching me things I don't know."

"That makes two of us."

R.J. then gave Sam an idea he had: He'd heard from a straight male friend—"I have a few, actually"—that his last girlfriend could ejaculate out of her clitoris, like a man. Sam laughed. It was gross, and the rest of the staff might not be up for it, but why not try?

"Will you talk to a gynecologist?" Sam asked. "I think we can be totally out there on this page, but it will need some authenticity."

"No prob," R.J. said. "I have hundreds of them on speed dial."

"I'll give you the number of mine. Anything less . . . vivid?"

"It's not less 'vivid,' as you so primly put it." R.J. said, "but I definitely want to do something on the difference between giving the perfect blow job to a circumcised man and an uncircumcised one."

Sam practically spat out her drink. "Oh my God. But I'm interested. And if I'm interested, I bet a lot of other people are, even if they wouldn't admit it."

"Then we're set," R.J. said.

"I don't know who's going to want to advertise against this page, but I guess that's not my problem," Sam said. "By the way, what is the difference?"

"If I tell you all my secrets now," R.J. said with a smile, "you'll be bored when you read it."

"I highly doubt it." Sam gestured for the check.

"Very funny," Trevor said, sitting on Tom's sofa. Tom had just put "Jungle Fever" by the Chakachas on the CD player. "How was I to know that in New York you're never supposed to ask if a woman is a model?"

Tom told him what he had learned from countless conversations with his female friends. Ask a woman if she's a model, and she'll think you're smarmy. Ask if she's a writer, and she'll go home with you. Handing Trevor a beer, he said, "All I can say is thank God she didn't work there or I'd be sitting on a lip chair right about now."

"Actually," Trevor said, "it wouldn't be ready for four to six weeks."

While the song played on, Tom thought about how it was funny that they could easily talk about Trevor's love life, but had only rarely talked about his own. To be fair, Trevor used to ask, but he stopped because Tom's answers were so vague that he either didn't want to talk about it or had nothing going on.

"Tell me, Mr. T.," Trevor said. "Does jungle fever run in the family?"

Tom stiffened. "I don't remember if any of mom's lovers were black, if that's what you're asking."

"You know that's not what I'm asking. What's going on with you? How come you never talk about that stuff?"

"There's not much to talk about," he said. "I haven't been into getting laid lately."

"If you haven't been into getting laid lately," Trevor said, "that's simply because you haven't been getting *laid* lately."

Understatement of the year. In truth, he really had been getting bored by casual sex—with the right guy, sure, it could be great. What he really wanted was a boyfriend. Back when he had actually had boyfriends, sometime in the Paleolithic era, the relationships had always ended badly, with them in love with him and him feeling something less. Tom told himself that he hated hurting people so much that he was loath to get into a relationship, for fear he'd only end up hurting the guy. Sam and Andrew and Veronica all thought, but didn't say so, that he was simply afraid of getting hurt.

"All I'm saying," said Trevor, taking another tug on his beer, "is that it doesn't hurt to roll around every now and then. Do you have a fuck buddy? I thought all you homosexuals had fuck buddies."

"Trevor, I promise you that when I have sex you'll be the first to know. But can we change the subject?"

"Sure."

"Are you looking for a job?"

"Not yet."

"Do you want one?"

"You offering me one?" Trevor replied, laughing.

"Actually, I am."

"Bite," said Trevor.

Tom nodded. "Publisher."

"I'd read it."

"But could you sell it?"

"Let me think about it."

Walking home from her book group—she didn't care how "ironic" it was, the choice of Nora Roberts was just wrong—Veronica ran into Chris.

It was on the corner of Second Avenue and St. Mark's, and the first thing she noticed was that he looked older. Granted it was soggy late winter, and no one looked particularly good, except for possibly Christy Turlington because she always looked good, but that was another matter entirely. Veronica's mind was racing. Not, it came to her, because she was in thrall to Chris, the way she usually was with men she liked; but because she wasn't. She didn't really know what to do; she had never gotten over someone so quickly.

As usual, Chris's behavior had helped. It was no surprise to her that he was being slippery; she now knew all about Sam's history with him—a little too late for anyone's good. Sure enough, he said he'd call when he left town a few days after

Tom's fiasco of a party, and sure enough, he didn't. Evidently he was back.

But it didn't really bother her. She wouldn't have minded if he had called—he had years before he'd be anything but a snack—and yet, life went on. So when, on that crummy winter night in the East Village, he asked if she wanted to grab a drink, she said no.

"No?" he said. "Will you at least make up an excuse?"

She smiled. "We had fun, Chris. And I like you. But I get who you are, and I don't really have room for that in my life right now." Tom may have been right—maybe she did need a real man. But he wasn't it. She reached out and gave him a tug on his scarf. The least she could do is flirt a little. "I do reserve the right to change my mind, of course."

That seemed to be enough. He gave her a salute, and walked off into the night.

Tom, Ethan, and R.J. were checking out John Street, a new bar way downtown. It was famous for being completely over the top—go-go dancers, for one, who were not only completely naked (itself a relatively new phenomenon), but aroused. And patrons who had no shame in blowing said dancers.

"Why are we here?" asked Tom. "I mean, I like to stay on the cutting edge of New York nightlife as much as anyone. But this is gross."

"I agree," said Ethan. "It's demeaning." Tom wasn't sure if he meant it was demeaning to them or to the dancers, but guessed it didn't matter. He and Ethan had had a touchy relationship since the party, when Liza had told Ethan about *Bite.* They didn't talk about it; Tom had hoped that going out might help them get past it (without ever talking about it).

"I'm sorry," said R.J., gesturing at Tom's chest. "I couldn't hear you over that shirt."

"Bitch! This is very chic, I'll have you know." It was from

Paul Smith, in his signature multicolored vertical stripes. It may have been a little loud, but that was the point. "Look around. Everyone's wearing T-shirts, tucked in. They're tuckers, all of them. Five minutes here would disabuse anyone of the notion that all gay men dress well." Up on the stage, two men were busy simulating sex.

"Anyway," said R.J. "There are tons of cute guys. And when we went to Amsterdam you didn't seem to be such a prude."

"That was years ago!"

"I think I'm going to go," said Ethan. "Anyone want to join me?"

Tom would have liked nothing more, but he felt he owed it to R.J., since he had been the one to drag R.J. away from his computer. Besides, he had had enough of Ethan for one night. They couldn't really be expected to rebuild their friendship over a few drinks. "See you at the office, Foxman."

They went over to a bench and sat down. "What's Ethan's problem?" asked R.J.

"He's just not into this stuff. He lives on the Upper West Side. The air is thinner there." They watched as, on the TV hanging from the ceiling, a man got fake-raped by a group of West Hollywood thugs, all of whom seemed to have waxed their legs and chests for the occasion.

"I don't know," said R.J. "He seems to have issues."

"And you, we all know, are a famous judge of character." R.J. had dated some of the oddest specimens around—one, famously, was missing a front tooth—and never realized until way too late that they were freaks. Tom's favorite was the young Greek actor who announced he had won an Academy Award—in Greece. "Believe me, Ethan's so PC he wouldn't hurt a fly unless the fly consented."

"Whatev," said R.J., eyeing a blonde against the opposite wall. "I'm moving in."

Chapter 37

Trevor got a slight kick out of watching his little brother worry about his response, but only because Trevor knew he was going to say yes. What was there to lose? Plus, it sounded like fun, and fun was something he hadn't had in a job in a while. Once he sold a few ads he'd ask for—and get—a chunk of the business. Blood is thicker than water, but what does that have to do with money?

So he made Tom wait almost a week, and he told him it was a go. He called Andrew, got a bank account going, and didn't look back. "This is a business, Tom. You don't work for me, I know, but it's time to ramp it up. Once I get out there selling pages, we have to have a product within months. Momentum is everything." Over the next few weeks, Tom and Sam sat stunned by the quickness with which he moved. For them, it had all seemed rather distant, something they figured would get off the ground, oh, eventually. Trevor had immediately started looking for cheap office space, and sent Liza an email pointing out that before she did anything else he needed a logo, and then a few pages—including a mock cover—that he could tantalize advertisers with. He called the Harvard alumni office and placed an ad for interns. "It's the cheapest labor out there," he said to Tom, "and they'll work like dogs just for the glamour of it." One of the positions, naturally, was an assistant for himself. "As publisher, I can't be answering my own phones, you know."

Within days he had found her. He was at a Duane Reade, a chain of drugstores with legendarily unhelpful help—he had been in New York long enough to dread going to one.

But this Duane Reade was unlike the others: The cashiers were friendly, and more shocking, they were fast. He had joked to the cashier—her nametag said "Mao," which Trevor loved—that this was like a drugstore from heaven. "Thanks," she said. "I'm the assistant manager, and I'll take all the credit. The manager is a lazy cow."

He asked her to meet him for coffee—"No funny business!" she said—and told her about the magazine. She was sold; a first-generation Chinese woman, she had few options career-wise. She had a strange look: short, assymetrical hair and oddly dramatic makeup. Trevor couldn't tell if it was downtown chic or hopeless, but it seemed to suit her.

He hired her on the spot, then told her to call a meeting ASAP to get everyone on the same page. "Mao is a machine," he said in a phone call to Tom. "She's four feet two, and yet I get the impression she could lift a truck if she had to." He read the last year's worth of every magazine that could possibly be a competitor—*Wallpaper, Outside, Gourmet, Travel + Leisure, GQ, Details, Esquire, Vogue, W, Holiday, Forbes FYI, Food & Wine,* and so on—and had Mao make lists of every advertiser in those issues; she was also to call and find out who was doing the media buying for every one of those companies. It was the main rule of the publishing side of magazines: there are no new advertisers, and if you want to survive you have to poach.

Tom sat in his office cranking out a story on the latest spas to offer sacred stone massages. Did anyone actually care that the stones were left outside during the full moon cycle to be reenergized? Obviously they did, since thousands of people had declared this treatment the "new thing," but he couldn't quite believe he was having to give this his full attention.

Living in limbo between *Bite* and working full-time here was beginning to get to him. With Trevor so gung ho, his doubts about the magazine got worse. Were he and Sam totally delusional?

On the other hand, he told himself, not even pretending to edit the spa piece anymore, what didn't he have doubts about? The phone rang, and Tom looked at his watch. Who would call him at 8 P.M. at the office? The caller ID read "private."

"Tom Sanders," he said cautiously.

"Tom, hi, this is Moira McGowan. I'm sorry to call you so late, but one of the many virtues I've heard about you is that you work like a dog."

"I'm not sure it's a virtue, but thanks, I guess," Tom said, still wondering where this was going.

"I'm an editor at the *New York Times,* and your name has come up."

Tom waited. An editor who wanted to assign him a story? He was flattered, but he barely had time to brush his teeth these days, let alone write a piece for the *Times.* As prestigious as the paper was, they paid peanuts, and if Tom took on one more thing, it had to be for a paycheck that could help him take a great four-day break.

"Thanks again," Tom said cautiously. "May I ask in what connection?"

"Between us, the editor of the travel section is taking early retirement," Moira continued. "Not for another six months or so, but we're beginning to look, and as I said, your name has come up."

For years, editing the travel section of the *Times* had been Tom's dream job—but so much in his dreams that he never considered it a possibility. As confident as he was in his skills editing the lifestyle section of a business magazine, he didn't think he would ever be taken seriously enough to qualify for a job running an important section for the *Times.*

The thing about the *Times* was, as much as it frustrated

him, especially the bloated Sunday edition, everyone read it. Unlike every magazine he'd ever worked at.

"We're obviously looking at a lot of people," Moira said, "but I want you to meet with me and a couple of the other editors. Next week?"

Tom looked at his Palm, although he knew he was just buying time. No matter what was on his agenda, of course he was available. Now, if only the meeting could be far enough away so that he could go to a couple yoga classes, take up meditating, sign up for a hypnotherapist, get a prescription for Xanax . . . Instead, he said, "You tell me."

"Great!" Moira said. "Wednesday, 2 P.M." She went on to give him the address. Like he needed it.

Chapter 38

Tom was doing all he could not to think about the interview at the *Times,* which had been pushed back a week. *Why now?* he asked himself in a taxi on the way to the opening of the new Ritz-Carlton on Central Park. *Why not a year ago?* His cell phone rang.

"Hey." It was Andrew. He didn't sound good, but he often didn't. Whitford had really been getting him down.

"What's up?"

"We're going out of business. The announcement comes tomorrow."

"Man, that sucks. I'm so sorry."

"Well, it'll make my life hell for a few weeks, but then I'll be free to eat—or should I say *Bite?*—my way through New York. I'm telling you, it's the only thing keeping me going."

"You bet! That's right! Rock and roll!" Realizing how stupid he sounded, Tom shut off the phone. He could claim later it was a bad cell patch, but what he couldn't do was get excited about *Bite* at the very moment that he was sure he'd have to leave it.

The party was like all the others, filled mostly with the same hack writers who went to any event that might offer free shrimp. Ever since getting dee-runk at a James Beard dinner for the Hotel Bel-Air and openly mocking its general manager, who was a good friend of his boss at the time, Tom had a rule of not drinking at press events. No good could come of it. That said, he needed a drink, and was about to order a Dewar's on the rocks when he saw that guy from

Abercrombie & Fitch who had rested his hand too low on Tom's back one too many times. Tom moved to the other bar.

A puffy-looking man approached. "Tom Sanders!"

"Well if it isn't!" Tom replied, unsure of who it in fact was.

"What have you been up to? How's *Profit?* Your stuff looks great."

Shit, Tom thought, taking a big swig of his drink. Slightly balding, probably mid-forties. He flipped through his mental Rolodex but came up with nothing. "*Profit*'s all good," he said, "and thanks for the kind words. Lord knows they don't come often enough. What have you been up to?"

But no go. "The same. Hey, I heard you were up for the *Times* travel job. When do you meet with Moira?"

Tom didn't want to answer that question, and luckily enough right then he saw a friend from *Holiday.* "Laura!" he called, trying to get her to come over.

"Tom!" she shrieked. "You dog! Why didn't you tell me about the *Times* thing? Have you met with them yet?"

Astounded that she knew about it—and suddenly afraid that everyone, even his bosses knew about it—he answered before thinking. "No, next week."

"So good to see you, Tom," said the mystery man. "And you, too, Laura. Good luck next week!"

"See you around, Jack," called Laura.

Tom was bright red. "Oh. My. God."

"Tom! What?"

"That was Jack Keegan." Laura nodded. "Fuck me," said Tom. "And fuck the Dewar's." Keegan, as pretty much everybody else in the room knew, covered the media beat at the *New York Observer.* He famously loved nothing more than announcing to the world who was interviewing where.

Tom drained the drink—*To the damage done,* he thought, toasting the air—and headed downstairs. Now he had to tell Sam. And Andrew. And Trevor. And Veronica, don't forget Veronica. Because Keegan was sure to write about it, probably soon. He thought about it all the way home, where he found a bill from his cell phone company—$150 more than usual—and a broken air conditioner in his living room.

Chapter 39

Trevor cleared his throat. They were in Tom's apartment, having a meeting. "Okay, people. Let's get started. I don't know what everyone knows at this point, so I'll start at the beginning—well, the beginning for me, anyway." Trevor was wearing a pair of exquisitely faded Levi's and a white long-sleeved T-shirt, sleeves pulled halfway up his arms. It was safe to say that every woman in the room had noted his forearms—if they weren't too busy fanning themselves from the heat.

"I'm Trevor, Tom's older brother." Tom turned just the slightest bit pink. "I met most of you at the party Tom graciously threw, but I'm not sure you all remember me, the drama of the night being what it was." The group laughed. "And I'm the publisher of *Bite.* That doesn't mean you work for me; Tom and Sam will be running the day-to-day operations of the editorial side. It just means that I'll be the one selling the ads. Or at least hiring other people to sell the ads. But without ads we have no revenue, and without revenue, well, you know what happens. So we all have to work together."

Tom had to give it to Trevor: he knew how to lead. Trevor went on to talk about the offices he had rented, dismissing the merest hint of a complaint from Sam about it being out of the way by saying that it was going to save them a ton of money. "You may know the space—it's the Liberty Inn, that old by-the-hour motel on the West Side Highway, in the Meatpacking District. Everyone gets his or her own office. With bathroom."

Trevor could see Andrew counting the rent in his head. He slipped him a piece of paper he had prepared earlier; it said, simply, "lease with an option to buy—cheap!"

"I love it!" said Sam. "It's so down-and-out it's chic. And the check-in desk can be our reception area! But is it clean?"

"I'm having it fumigated as we speak." The room breathed a collective sigh of relief.

"Plus," continued Trevor, "and this is something I didn't tell anyone. Because it's a very small building and we have the whole thing, the owner has agreed to let us put a sign on the façade that says 'The BITE Building'." Everyone giggled. "If we're going to build a brand, let's do it right and give people something to talk about."

"What about hubris?" asked Andrew.

"No time for it," said Trevor. "We've got to make a splash, make people want to be us. I'm going to sell the culture of the place as much as I'm going to sell the editorial. A big story in the *New York Times* design section, a feature on MTV, you name it. If it works, everyone in town will want to work at *Bite.*" They cheered. Well, everyone but the three interns, who were too scared to move.

It was Tom's turn. "Okay, here's the first brainstorm of ideas." He motioned to Mao to pass them out. "It's very tentative, and will probably change thirty times before we go to press." If we go to press, he wanted to joke, but checked himself in time. *Trevor would never say that.* "We're going to try for two covers, one conceptual, with a man and a woman both taking a, yes, bite, out of an apple. And the other two pairs of barefoot legs propped up over a balcony railing, with a seascape in the background. To go with the barefoot travel story." He went on, outlining the first issue piece by piece, explaining that Sam would be in charge of the Advice Squad, and he'd take care of the front-of-book. The two of them would share the feature well.

Liza stood up, and went over to the corner, where she had her pasteboards. "I'm not good at talking to groups," she said. "So bear with me." The first one she showed was a mockup of the barefoot cover, using a photo Veronica had borrowed from a photographer friend. "We won't be able to use this photo, but you get the idea." The logo, flush left, was all capital letters, in a stark, modern, very red typeface. There were no cover lines on the photo; instead, a Day-Glo orange banner ran slightly diagonally across the page, with cover lines on it in black-and-white type. "I figure we can use the banner every time, placing it on the page wherever we want, depending on the photograph."

The other stories she had laid out were completely dummy, but they all agreed she had nailed the clean, fresh look they wanted. The Magnolia Bakery punk was there, as was the helicopter-shadowed sunbather. She used capital letters in all the display type—"to give it force," she said, to Tom's nod of approval. The Advice Squad pages had no photos, and she had indeed put them on a heavy, unglossy paper stock. "The only art on these pages will be drawings of the faces of the famous people giving the advice. That way on the beginning of the section, we can run all the faces as a group, without identifying them, simply saying The Advice Squad."

"God, it's hot!" Sam said, standing up.

"Jesus, Sam, open a window! I told you I'd get the A/C fixed just as soon as I—"

"I'll take care of it," Mao said.

"No, the magazine. It's so hot I can't stand it! I want to get to work right now!"

"Fantastic," said Trevor. "And I'm sure everyone feels the same way. We move into our offices next week, even though the renovations will still be going on, so anyone who can make it at 9 A.M. should be there. If you can't, no sweat—just get there whenever you can."

Tom whispered to Trevor. "Oh, fine," Trevor said, laughing. "Ten o'clock. Goddamn New Yorkers!"

"Mao will email you everyone's email addresses and phone numbers," said Tom. "We have a lot of work to do and not a lot of time. We're shooting for a September launch so we can be around when all the luxury-goods advertisers want to sell their fall stuff. Everyone should feel free to call anyone whenever they need help or information. Some of us have jobs, for now, but we'll just have to make it work. If you have story ideas, send them to me and Sam—and if we shoot you down, for God's sake, keep trying. This is new for all of us, and I'm convinced we can do it, and do it right."

"Now let's drink!" screamed R.J. And drink they did.

Chapter 40

Tom was taking the afternoon off from *Profit,* waiting for the air-conditioning repairman. He loved his apartment but hated being trapped there. It was funny that way: leaving the apartment in the morning, all he wanted to do was sit around and organize his life (even more than it already was, which was borderline pathologically). But when he had no choice but to be there, he couldn't remember one thing he had been hoping to get done.

As if that wasn't bad enough, it was 80 degrees in there. He paced from the living room to the bedroom and back again, wondering how in the hell he was going to deal with this *Times* thing. He hadn't even interviewed, but what if they offered him the job? If Keegan ran an item before it was decided, it wouldn't matter. His friends at *Bite* would lynch him. That the Biters were his friends was a big part of the problem: normally, he'd hash it out with Andrew or Sam or Veronica, or heck, maybe Trevor, but he couldn't talk to any of them about it.

The buzzer. "Be Cool," the voice said, pronouncing the company's name as if it were coming from the mouth of a fifties beatnik. Tom buzzed him up, having long given up on the dream of the hot repairman. It was something that, in his experience, only existed in porn.

Surprise! The guy was sex on a stick. Not tall the way Tom usually liked guys, but not unnaturally short, either, and decidedly swarthy. He wasn't stocky—or "humpy," as Ethan would call it—but there was certainly considerable muscle there. "Hey," he said, and Tom wondered immediately where he was from. He'd guess Israel or somewhere in the vicinity.

"Um, hey. Come on in." Tom led the repairman into the living room. "It's in here. I don't know what happened, it just stopped working one day, on the hottest day of the year. Well, so far, anyway. Which figures." Tom was babbling.

The repairman walked over to the air conditioner, ripped off the casing, and yanked out the central machinery. He fiddled with a few things, then went back over to his toolbox. Tom, at great pains to hide his growing arousal, shut his eyes and started thinking of dead puppies. It used to work . . .

"Hey, can you come over here?" Tom looked up to see the repairman on his knees in front of the unit, which was in a window unnaturally low near the floor. "I need you to hold this thing right here"—pointing at a coil—"and use your other hand to hold the window shut." Tom, standing above the repairman, did as he was told. The guy tightened a screw. "That should do it," he said, slowly looking up at Tom.

What happened next was something Tom was sure he'd play back in his mind for the rest of his life. Tom, hands occupied by the coil and the window, was unable to hide the bulge in his jeans. *Dead puppies, dead puppies, dead puppies* . . . The repairman looked up at Tom, gave him what was almost a sneer, and reached up and unbuttoned Tom's jeans. Then he stood up, never taking his eyes off Tom's, and stood right in front of him. He leaned in and kissed Tom's neck; since he used more tongue than lips, it would be more accurate to say he licked Tom's neck. He had one hand working Tom's dick, and with the other, he reached up to Tom's mouth, and ran a thumb along his lower lip. Then he went and stuck his thumb in Tom's mouth. Tom didn't need to be told to suck it.

Tom forgot his objections to casual sex. He also forgot about *Bite,* the *Times,* and everything else. *If opportunity sticks its thumb in your mouth . . .*

Because Tom was tall and generally sure of what he believed, he tended to be the one to call the shots in bed. He didn't mind, mostly, but if pushed to talk about it, he might admit that he had fantasies of giving up that control. Problem was, he'd argue, it was hard to find anyone he could respect enough to cede control to. Whether it was because he was caught off guard or he simply didn't know the guy, he let go. All the more out of character because it was the first time in forever that he had done anything sexual and not had at least two drinks.

The man was all hands: slow hands, soft hands, firm hands. He gave Tom a long, aggressive kiss. Then he pushed Tom back down, and ran his hands—again, those hands—through Tom's hair. It had been a while, but Tom remembered what to do. Tom grabbed hold of the repairman's thick thighs and didn't let go until he was pulled back up once again.

"Where are you from?" Tom asked.

He just smiled, and took Tom by the hand to the bedroom.

"Um," stammered Tom, "I'm not sure, I mean you should know that there are things that I don't normally . . ." But by then they were on the bed, and the man had once again stuck his thumb in Tom's mouth.

An hour later, the repairman let himself out. Tom knew better than to ask any more questions, including whether or not they might ever do it again. He went to the phone to call R.J., who upon hearing the story, hollered "Praise Jesus!" so loud his boss came over to ask him to keep it down.

Back at *Profit,* Tom leaned against Veronica's door. "Am I interrupting something?"

"Just designing a fishing net that won't hurt the dolphins."

Tom laughed. "Smoke." Veronica registered immediately that this wasn't a question, and grabbed her cigarettes.

In the elevator, she tried to get him to tell her what was going on, but all Tom would do was look at her and exhale. Outside, he told her the story, and like any good straight girl with a lot of gay friends, the first thing she said was "I damn well hope that you used protection."

"Don't be classist," he said. "And of course we did."

"Good. Now tell me everything you didn't tell me the first time."

Chapter 41

Quarter of noon. Tom was standing outside the *Times* building, waiting until it was close enough to noon to go inside. He thought about smoking, but didn't want to smell like it, and didn't want to have to go and buy gum. He thought about the air-conditioning repairman, then decided that having a boner might not make the best first impression. He wondered what Moira looked like. She was reportedly a bit crazy, but everyone in journalism was, so that didn't really offer any clues.

He went inside and up to the fourth floor. It had to be one of the crummiest offices he'd been in in a long time. Mostly cubicles, messy cubicles, with everyone yelling and phones ringing. He'd never worked at a newspaper, and even though this was the cliché, he hadn't really figured it would be true.

"So nice to meet you, Tom. Come on over." A middle-aged woman with a severe black bob, Moira looked like the kind of woman who wouldn't just eat her young, she'd serve them up as a smorgasbord for assorted passersby. Moira led Tom through the rabbit warren of cubicles, to one that was only slightly larger than the ones they had passed. He was shocked: He'd had an office of his own since 1995.

"Tell me why you want to leave *Profit.* Wendy! Coffee! Want some?" He declined. "Skim, Wendy, skim! Go on."

He took a deep breath. Okay, so she was crazy like this. "I hadn't even considered leaving until you called. I have a great gig—the editors let me do whatever I want. It's a sweet freedom, that's for sure."

"Freedom's just another word for no one watching over

you," she said. "I'm kidding. But I'm not. Do you know what I mean?" He tried to nod sagely. "This is the *Times,* Tom. We can't just have the editors wantonly doing whatever they please."

"I only behave wantonly on my own time," he joked.

"I can't wait for the movie," she said. "What would you do with the travel section if indeed you had this freedom?"

Tom didn't know one person who thought highly of the section. It made travel sound dull, a cardinal sin in his mind. "First off, I'd make it newsy. Everywhere I've worked I've tried to make the travel stories have a reason for running in the issue that they do. Sometimes it's as little as doing a Oaxaca story in October to coincide with the Day of the Dead. Or maybe it's a Death Valley story that you run in the summer because more and more tourists want the ultimate desert experience. Or maybe it's getting someone in on the first tour to Saudi Arabia, or doing an Iran story right when relations between the U.S. and Iran were starting to thaw."

She took a drink of her coffee.

"Of course, sometimes you do stories on places that people love and don't care if they never change—Paris, San Francisco, New Orleans. But I worry sometimes that the *Times* travel writers only know how to write in the *Times* voice, which can occasionally get a little . . . dull."

Her eyes widened.

"Which is what you want when you're reporting the hard news. But when I'm reading a travel story, well, a travel story isn't that different from your friend or neighbor making you look at their vacation photos. And the person who tells a funny story along with those pictures is going to keep my attention a lot longer than the person who can't."

"So you want it to be funnier."

"I want it to be something-er. Sadder, at times. Smarter, always. Funnier when appropriate. I want to hear about how it made the writer feel. Tell me if the hotel was nice, but tell me what you felt when you first opened the hotel door, tell me if the view from the balcony reminded you of the first time you got laid—sorry—tell me something!"

"I like what you're saying," she said. "Wendy! Call Jim Boggs and see if he's in. I want him to meet Tom Sanders."

They sat and looked at each other until Wendy called back.

"Is Thursday at three good for you?" He nodded. "Good for you. Tom, it was a pleasure. Wendy, help Tom find his way out." She shook his hand and turned toward her computer.

"Wait!" she yelled over the cubicle wall. "Come back here. I forgot something." Tom rounded the corner. "This little magazine you're trying to start. You do know you'd have to give that up, right?"

Tom turned bright red. He wanted nothing more than to ask her how she'd heard about it. "Of course," he said.

As he left, his mind raced—how could she have heard about *Bite?* And more important, if she knew, who else did? His boss at *Profit?*

Chapter 42

Trevor wasn't kidding about the renovations. And they were all thankful that he wasn't kidding about the fumigating, either. None of them had actually been in the Liberty Inn when it was a fleabag hotel, but they could tell that it wasn't exactly the kind of place you'd have your mother stay when she was in town.

There were twelve rooms on each of the three floors; the best offices, the ones facing the river, not the highway, went to the higher-ups. "Let the interns suffer through the noise," said Trevor, knowing full well that the kids were so excited to be there they would have put up with much more. For now, Mao was sitting in the reception area—not because they had many visitors, but because the few people who tended to come by still thought it was the Liberty Inn and were looking for a quick place to get it on. Mao was like a cold shower. Plus, they were still trying to keep the whole thing a secret—the sign wouldn't go up until Trevor gave the word—and Mao was an expert at getting rid of people without telling them what was up.

Besides having it fumigated, Trevor had had the walls painted white and the carpet redone. Beyond that, everyone was on his or her own: they each got a $2,000 allowance to buy furniture for their offices, and everyone was encouraged to bring any extra furniture of their own that they could spare.

Veronica was beside herself. She had only worked at places where the furniture was not only modular but connected to the cubicle walls, so she couldn't have moved anything even if she wanted to. She had a friend in San Francisco who worked at Design Within Reach, and he got her a fantastic deal on a simple blond wood desk and a reproduction Eames chair. If she could find a way, she decided, she'd live in her office (it all made her hovel at *Profit* so much more sad). She popped into Tom's, all spare and simple. But he was no fun; preoccupied about something and in no mood to share.

Liza, it seemed, had spent most of her money on plants. "What can I say?" she said, evidently answering her own question. "I like having living things around me. And crashing at Sam's has been great, but she's terrified of caring for plants, and I miss them." She had painted the walls a pale pink and bought, against all better judgment, a white sofa and a white Jonathan Adler rug. "Don't tell Trevor," she said, "but I used some of my own money. Or I should say, my soon-to-be-ex-husband's money."

"Must be nice," Veronica said without malice.

"I know it's wrong to say so," Liza said with a faint smile, "but you know, it really does help."

To furnish his office, Tom thought about what strings he could pull. Then it hit him: R.J. must have tricked with someone who dealt in furniture. Sure enough, there was a manager at the Terence Conran Shop who remembered his night with R.J. fondly. Tom bought a floor model charcoal sofa and a glass dining room table, which he was using as a desk. He sat at the desk now, wondering what in the hell he was supposed to do. The interview at the *Times* had gone well, and the *Observer* was probably going to break the story of his meeting with them in this week's edition. He had to figure it out. Should he stick with *Bite?* It would help if he knew what exactly he had here, besides some great furniture. An old worry came back: Was he the editor-in-chief? Was Sam the editor-in-chief? It was amazing they had gone for so long without ever discussing it—probably because in Sam's mind it was decided they'd be co-editors. His next decision was like something from the Discovery Channel: When a panicked animal is trapped, what does it do? It fights.

Dear R.J.: Last week, we saw this video clip of a woman ejaculating when she came. And we mean ejaculating. She must have come like, oh, two feet. I've sent you the tape, because we need to know. My boyfriend thinks it's awesome; I say it's impossible. What's up?—Curious about Coming

Dear Curious: Your boyfriend is wrong, and that poor fool who thinks her party trick is so neat she's taping it is actually doing nothing more glamorous than peeing in an arc. I showed the tape to the head of Urogynecology at Columbia Presbyterian, and he pretty much laughed in my face. He kindly suggested that we learn to identify our body parts—not hard to do on this tape, we might add, given the oh-so-close-up. There is the urethra, and then there is the vagina. Read my lips (and hers): This is most definitely not coming from the latter. Get out the rubber sheets.

"R.J., I admit that I'm laughing," Sam said, looking at R.J. sitting on the couch opposite her, "but can we really go with this?"

"Just because you have a fancy office is no reason to get all corporate." Sam looked around the room. Maybe it was a little fancy—Ikea's version of fancy, anyway. She was thrilled to finally have a couch in her office. Even if it barely fit, its presence suggested that she was pretty damn fancy indeed.

"And excuse me, but are you wearing a suit?"

R.J. looked Sam over with half approval, half disdain.

"Too much?" she said with a laugh. "I thought maybe if I dressed the part of editrix, I'd feel it." She was wearing a beautifully tailored suit, but it was—even she had to admit, now that she thought about it—a bit serious. With the low-cut white silk halter top, she ended up looking like a banker in a porn movie. "Tomorrow I'll go back to jeans, I promise, but can we go back to your column for a second?"

"Saved by the knock!" R.J. said, as Tom walked in.

He looked a little peaked to Sam, although he immediately began to smile, covering up whatever was going on. "What's happening in here? I'm scared to ask what I'm interrupting."

"Yes, you are indeed," Sam said.

R.J. saw the same stressed look. "I still want to talk about my expense account," he whispered as he walked out, closing the door behind him.

"Nice office, Sam," Tom said, nodding approvingly.

"What are you talking about, you goon? Yours has a much better view." Sam paused and lowered her voice. "Are you kissing up to me?"

Tom's face darkened.

"Oh, shit. What's up?"

"I just dropped by to see how things are going, and Liza told me she's starting to draft the masthead."

"God, that's great! I can't believe this is really happening," Sam said, coming to sit on the couch next to Tom. "Doesn't that make it feel like it's actually real? I mean, I never got why the people I interviewed would want to see their names up in lights, but I have to admit I'm totally turned on by seeing my name up on a masthead. And I mean up. Like at the tippy, tippy top. The tippy, tippy top suits me just fine." Sam smiled at Tom—who didn't smile back. "What? You're scaring me."

"We haven't really talked about this before, and I'm sure this isn't a thing at all, because I think it's always been assumed, but I just wanted to make sure it was okay with you . . ."

"Tom, you're breaking out in a sweat. What is going on?"

He leaned forward and pressed his hands together. "I guess I've just assumed this whole time, and I need to make sure that you've assumed it too, that my name will actually be at the top, and your name will be right below mine. We never talked about titles, but I'd like to be the editor-in-chief, with you as the executive editor."

Sam felt all the air leave her body, like she'd fallen down and knocked the wind out of herself. Then she felt nauseated. This wasn't possible. Now she was the one sweating.

"What?" That was all she managed to get out.

"Sam, this is totally our baby, but the reality is I'm the one who has editing experience, and remember, we have to sell this magazine. We have to sell it to advertisers, and eventually, we need to sell it bigger than that—to a publishing company, so we can get our big payday. And I don't know if your name at the top can carry that. You have an amazing reputation as a writer, but not as an editor. Which isn't to say you won't be a great editor"—Tom was up and pacing now—"but I don't know that it makes sense."

"You giant biggest motherfucker asshole, I can't believe this is happening," Sam said in one breath, so the whole sentence sounded like one word. "This entire thing has been about us. Our ideas. Our planning. Our dream. What the fuck are you doing trying to fuck me now?"

"Don't get dramatic, Sam. I'm not trying to fuck you."

Now Sam was standing too, and she was yelling. "You're not trying to fuck me?"

"Stop yelling," Tom said quietly.

"Stop yelling? Stop yelling when it turns out my best friend is trying to fuck me just like every other fucking man I've ever worked with? Why do you think I did this with you? So I could be fucked again? I hate you, I really do."

Shit. Tom knew that Sam lost her temper maybe once a year, but when she lost it, she lost it good.

"How could you not even offer to share the title with me?" Sam asked, still screaming. "I assumed we were sharing it! But no, you have to be the one who has the whole goddamn thing to yourself. It's no good unless you get all the glory. Well, I think not, you enormous asshole. You can go fuck yourself." She was so angry she was seeing spots, but there was still a cogent enough part of her brain to realize that yelling "fuck" every three seconds wasn't necessarily presenting the most mature of arguments.

"Sam, the thing is, something's come up, something that could give me the same title, and we haven't had a chance to talk about it, but it's a deciding factor for me, I think, in what I do, and I just want to talk about . . ."

"Fuck you!" Sam said, walking to the door. "I don't give a rat's ass what's a deciding factor for you. Get out of my office! And I don't want to have to remind you," Sam heard herself saying, as her anger mounted to a place of such intensity she was grateful for gun control, "who it is paying for your pathetic place on this pathetic masthead."

A horrible stillness came over the room.

"Shut up, Sam," Tom said coolly, heading to the door and pausing as he started to open it. "The good news is, you don't have to worry about 'reminding me' who's paying the bills. You just did."

And with that, he was gone. Sam walked over to her brand new couch, lay down, and burst into tears.

Chapter 43

What surprised Sam—even more than the episode with Tom—was what she did next. She got off the couch, she walked to her desk, and, without thinking about it for a second, she dialed a number she knew by heart. When she heard Jack's voice, she was almost as taken aback as he was.

"Hi," she said, her voice muffled a bit by sniffling.

"Sam?"

"Yes, it's me." She gave a pathetic attempt at a laugh, and wondered if this was the worst idea she'd had ever. Would he just hang up on her?

There was silence for a few seconds. "Sam, what's up?" There was definitely distance in his voice.

"I just wanted to talk, if that's alright."

More silence. Sam slouched down into her chair. This was not the comfort she was after.

"Look . . ." Jack said.

Nothing good ever followed the word "Look."

"I was just hoping we could talk."

"I was too," Jack responded, and Sam immediately knew that whatever talking it was that Jack wanted to do, it was most definitely not the kind of talking she had in mind.

"Oh. Okay," Sam said, sniffling one more time. "So?"

Jack sighed. "So why don't we meet at the Carlyle in an hour."

Sam had tried her best to repair her face, but even a heavy dose of eyedrops and mascara couldn't hide the puffiness. Thank God the Carlyle was so dark.

When she walked in, Jack was already sitting, an

untouched martini in front of him. He looked so handsome, she thought as she approached the table, every inch one of those self-confident men that any woman's eye naturally turned to.

"Hi," Sam said, standing shyly in front of him.

Jack kissed her on the cheek and gestured that she sit down beside him. Sam meekly did as he suggested, surprised that he was taking such control.

"What's going on? You don't look so hot."

"Thanks!" Sam said, with a laugh. Jack looked back at her. Breezy clearly wasn't the way to go. "I needed a friend to talk to, and you were the first one I thought of." Sam felt all pretensions drop. "I had a really bad day, and I thought seeing you would make me feel better." She paused to order a glass of champagne before turning back to him. "But you look like you need to talk, too. You first."

"It's all intertwined, Sam," Jack said, looking straight into her eyes with an intensity Sam had never noticed before. "I'm glad you think of me as the kind of friend you can call when you're having a bad day. But the truth is . . ." He paused, and Sam noticed that it clearly wasn't out of nervousness, but out of care for saying exactly what he meant. "The truth is, you're a really lousy friend back."

Sam just sat there. Her first thought was "This can't be happening." Her second thought was quite different. She had had a blowup with her closest friend in the world. And here was another person she felt she could turn to, telling her she'd been a bad friend. Somewhere, and not as far in the back of her mind as she would have liked, she had to admit that this may not have been a random pattern. She took a deep breath.

"Go on," she said, looking back at Jack with an openness that let him know it was alright to continue.

"We've never talked about our relationship, and frankly, I'm not sure there's been a reason to. I've never asked or expected anything from you. I'm not even sure I've wanted anything from you."

"Ouch," Sam said, before she realized it had come out of her mouth. Before Jack said that, she hadn't accepted quite how much she relied on him to be the ever-ready, ever-devoted lover, the lover who—even though nothing was ever discussed or demanded—obviously harbored desires for something deeper. Obviously, Sam was wrong.

"But what I don't like," Jack continued, "is that I don't think you treat me with the kind of respect I treat you with. You're an amazing friend—I see you being compassionate to a lot of people in your life. But sometimes, you take me totally for granted. Do you know that I spend every Sunday afternoon with my niece? Do you know that I play in a jazz band once a month at Smalls? Do you care that I've been up for the top producing job for the last six months?"

Sam started to defend herself, and then paused. She was tired of fighting, and tired of fighting without thinking. "You're right."

Now it was Jack's turn to sit still. He lit a cigarette and finally took a sip of his martini.

"I don't have much to say after that, but I think you might be right," Sam said quietly. "I guess I've felt like we had an arrangement that might have precluded any feelings on both of our parts."

"How would you have felt, Sam, if I'd invited you to a party that I had also invited a past-and-present lover to, without so much as a heads-up to you? I'm not saying that I want you to be my full-time lover, I'm really not. But I think I'd at least have the decency to call you and let you know. The way you behaved at Tom's party was at best unkind."

Sam felt her eyes well up again, and then they stopped. They stopped because she knew that he was right. She had treated him unkindly, without even knowing it, without even thinking about it, which was all the more unkind. And she knew, in that instant, that she had lost her way.

"I know you've been having a really hard time since you were fired"—Sam winced as Jack said the word she had been avoiding for months—"and I understood. But your self-involvement has been extraordinary. I think I understood that, too, to some degree. But it's not acceptable for you to treat me like the hired help." Jack leaned back, taking his martini in hand. For all of his composure, Sam thought, he looked relieved to be done saying what he had to say.

"I'm sorry," Sam said, with the kind of resonance that made it abundantly clear that she meant it. "I think I've been dealing by just going into myself, and that's been unfair." She was thinking out loud, talking about things that hadn't occurred to her before she said them, something that usually made her miserably uncomfortable. But at this moment, it felt right. "Everything's really unsettled, and I think I may not know what I want. And I think that you've gotten caught up in this, and I never meant you to. You deserve better." And somehow, when she said that, it didn't sound clichéd to either of them—it sounded like the truth. Because it was.

"What did you want to talk to me about?" Jack said, seeing that Sam's defenses had vanished, and she was sitting in front of him absolutely undone.

"I don't think it's important," Sam said slowly, beginning to stand. "I mean, it's important, but we can talk about it later. I think I need to go home now. Is that okay?"

Sam half expected Jack, the old Jack, to stand up and insist she stay, insist she tell him about what had happened to her, to allow her to be the egomaniac once more. Instead, he nodded. "That's fine," he said. "Call me when you want to talk."

Sam nodded slowly, gathering up her bag and preparing to

leave. She turned away, allowing the tears to finally begin to fall again.

She'd hurt Jack in part because of her feelings for Chris, who had been consistent in only one thing: letting her down. And now, she'd lost both of them. She walked up the street, keeping her head low so strangers wouldn't see her crying.

Chapter 44

The *New York Observer* operated on one principle: If you want to be talked about, you should talk about the media. The media, like any other profession but probably more so, loved hearing about itself. And so just about everyone in town—that is, in the media—read Jack Keegan's "Between the Lines" column.

It was no surprise to Tom, then, that his phone started ringing off the hook as soon as he got in to the *Profit* office on Wednesday morning. He had already read the piece—where did they get that photo?—and was expecting a very long day. He decided not to answer the phone, but he couldn't simply automatically forward all calls to voice mail because he had broken his last phone when he got annoyed with someone—he couldn't remember who—and as punishment the phone people wouldn't program his phone to do that.

And so it rang and rang. "Who'll it be?" he asked. "Sam, probably, though maybe not until later. Andrew? Trevor doesn't know to read the *Observer* yet, but Mao probably told him. Veronica, Ethan, Liza, Moira, everyone at *Profit* . . ."

Veronica poked her head in. "Am I interrupting anything?"

He smiled weakly. "Just pondering Armageddon."

"You know, I was meaning to ask you how we were going to broach the subject of *Bite* to both my boss and yours, but I guess that's on the back burner right now."

"On the back burner but about to boil over."

"Why didn't you say something, Tom?"

"I know, right? It's not like me to keep a secret. I couldn't.

I mean, I didn't go looking for that job. Sure, before *Bite* came along I had told everyone I ever met that I'd love to get my hands on the *Times* travel section. But I was completely devoted to *Bite.* Then Moira called. And what was I supposed to do, not go to meet her?"

"I don't know, but this isn't good."

"You think? Let's see. I've pissed off Sam already, and that was before this. Well, kind of. I've certainly pissed off Andrew, though I guess it's unofficial, since I haven't heard from him yet. My brother is sure to beat the shit out of me, and though I think you'll forgive me I know you think less of me. Let's not forget my boss, who is probably too angry to call. And even if Alex *isn't* angry enough to fire me, I have to turn around and tell him that, gee, I actually want to go start another magazine, one that vaguely competes with *Profit,* and continue to work here as long as I can. I am not in a happy place."

They sat there for a few minutes, looking out the window. Finally, Tom spoke. "And that photo."

"It was awful."

A few more minutes passed. "Why is Sam mad at you?" Veronica asked.

Tom told her the story, and she looked at him silently. "Tom."

"Yes?"

She dug into her pocket and pulled out a cigarette. "Here. Light it."

"In here?"

"Extenuating circumstances. Light it."

He did as he was told.

"Now. Don't talk for a second, will you? Just listen. One. The *Times* thing is a sweet deal. I'm not going to tell you what to do, but yes, I do know what I think you should do, and will tell you when you really want to know what I have to say.

Two. Are you an idiot? Share the goddamn masthead with Sam. You love her, you two get along, you'll have no problem with figuring out what will work and what won't because basically you two agree on everything. I see what you were worrying about, but have you also thought how sexy it is that you two are co-editors? No other magazine dares try it—and face it, no one will think it will work, and if I know you at all I know you love nothing more than proving everybody else wrong. Three. You're worried about *Profit?* Hello! They love what you do. You started "Dessert," and no one else here can do it, because you gave it your voice. Even without *Bite,* they wouldn't let you run off to the *Times* without a fight. So now, when you decide that *Bite* is more important than the *Times*—and I'm confident you will—you can walk into Alex's office and say, 'I want to stay here. I don't want to go to the *Times.* But here's what I do want.' It's called leverage, Tom. Get your head out of your ass and use it." She stood up and walked out.

There was a crash in the hallway. He got up and looked around the corner. Veronica had run into a messenger, and they were both on the floor. Veronica staggered up. "So much for my dramatic exit!"

"You Sanders?" said the messenger.

"Yep."

He held out a bag—it was filled with apples. Tom went back into his office, which now reeked of smoke, and read the note:

Which washed-up has-been of a magazine writer feels like a fool for the way she acted? I hate me, and I hate you, but I love you, and I don't want to lose you. This magazine means so much to both of us. It's our chance to do something big. I'm not going to beg—not yet anyway—but please, Tom. Don't run away now. I would

gladly work for you, just as long as I get to work with you.
Love, Sam

Dead puppies, dead puppies . . . Oh shit. That's not it; that's to stop an erection, not to stop crying. In fact dead puppies, really, is more of a reason to cry. He locked the door right as someone knocked at it.

"Mr. T."

Trevor? Tom stood and opened the door. "How'd you get past security?" he asked.

"What a lovely way to greet your brother. I knew you wouldn't let me up, so I called a friend at the *Weekly News* and had him get me in."

"Pretty sneaky, sis."

Trevor reached out and pushed Tom in the chest so that Tom fell onto the sofa. He stood above Tom, glaring. "You fucked with me, and I'm not happy about it. Why didn't you tell me? I am your brother first, Tom, and when you've got shit going on I wish you'd share it. I didn't move to New York to see the goddamn Empire State Building, you know. And I didn't take this job to make my millions—though I have become convinced that may yet happen. I did it to be with you. I like you. I *love* you. But you won't let me in, and it's pissing me off. This *Times* thing, yeah, I see the appeal. But I'm not half as angry about the possibility of you ditching *Bite* right after you brought me on as I am about you not talking to me about all this. So apologize."

"I'm really sorry. I—"

"That's one down. Now. Just because I'm only half as angry about the *Bite* thing doesn't mean I'm not totally pissed off. It's all just relative. I want you to tell me you'll stay at *Bite,* but I realize that could be premature. So at least apologize for fucking with me."

"I'm so sorry. When I—"

"That's two. We're right on schedule. Now. What did you say to Sam? Don't answer that. I already know. Jesus H. Christ, Tom, what were you thinking? Let me explain it to you: IT'S HER FAMILY'S MONEY. And that makes it *her* money. She has every right to want to be running the show, and frankly, I think it's pretty damn gracious of her to let you even participate—and stupid of you to presume otherwise. Anyway, the two of you can easily run this thing together."

"I know, you're right, I was just so—"

"Shut the fuck up. Here's the deal, Tom. I'm in this *Bite* thing now; people know I'm in it, and I've got too much pride to walk away. Can we do it without you? That's a question I had no idea I'd ever have to consider, but I did, before I came over here. And yes, I believe we can. So do what you have to do for yourself, and don't worry about the rest of us. We'll be fine."

Tom was silent. He hadn't really thought about everyone going on without him, making his magazine. Without him.

Trevor let himself out.

Tom stared at the shut door. "Did I tell you I got laid?"

Chapter 45

Tom managed to get out of the office for a lunch with a writer, who mercifully hadn't heard about the *Times* gig. Back in his office, he checked his voice mail.

1. Alex, his boss at *Profit.* "I imagine you knew I'd be calling. Let's talk." Scattered as Tom was, he took a second to daydream about the day when he'd be able to leave messages that made it clear without his saying so that people were to come to him.
2. Moira. "Thomas. We're not thrilled about this thing in the *Observer.* If I find it was you that leaked it to get some sort of leverage over there, the deal, such as it might have been and may yet still be, is off. Call me."
3. Andrew. "Call me right now."
4. Ethan. "Where are you? I've been looking all over for you. Why didn't you tell me? How amazing! Everything you've ever wanted! Call me, call me, call me!"
5. R.J. "Hey, it's me. I think I may be a bottom after all."

He called R.J. back first. "Mmmmmmmm!" R.J. made moaning sounds into the phone, then a few slurps for good measure. "They were twins, or so they said, but I think they may have just been brothers, or even friends. Fraternals for sure."

"Isn't that incestuous?"

"Of course it is! But it's not like we're procreating."

"Sorry, R.J., I thought I needed another distraction but I don't think I can handle it right now. Congratulations, really. But I have to talk to you later."

"Is it this *Times* thing?"

"You read the *Observer?*"

"God, no. But I happened to Google you this morning, as I sometimes do, just to see what's out there about you, and read all about it. What's the prob?"

"Everyone hates me. I'll tell you later. But for God's sake, try to stay away from brother acts. It's . . . greedy."

He figured he should talk to Alex before he called Moira, in case he was about to get fired. He walked over to his boss's office, taking the long way in the hope of avoiding everyone he worked with.

Mary, Alex's assistant, gave him a dour look. "There you are."

"Long lunch."

"He's not happy. Go on in."

"It was nice knowing you . . ." He knocked on the door. "Alex?"

"Get in here." *Great, Tom thought. Yelled at again.* Alex got up from behind his desk, walked over to the table, and motioned Tom to sit down. "I didn't know you were unhappy, Tom." Tom knew better than to respond yet. "Which is to say that I was surprised to read Keegan's column. I wish you'd talked to me before this all came out." Tom figured he'd save up all his apologies. "I can see that you might be getting a little bored, and I can see the appeal of the *Times,* but you should have said something. Now we look like we've been played." There was a long enough pause that Tom figured it was his turn.

"Moira called me, and I met with her once. I had no reason to think they were going to offer me anything, and I still don't. And I'm not sure I'd take it. I love *Profit,* and you've been amazing. I know that. I don't know how Keegan found all this out, but I can assure you it didn't come from me. I feel terrible that you heard about it this way, but please believe me when I say that everything I've told you is all there is."

Alex leaned back in his chair and looked at his hands. "That's not exactly true."

Tom turned bright red. Did he know about Tom accidentally confirming the *Times* interview with Keegan?

"We generally leave you alone, Tom, and you do great work, possibly because of it. I've been very happy with this arrangement. It means, however, that even after two years—"

"Two and a half." *Why would he choose this particular moment to correct his boss?*

"Even after two and a half years we still don't know all that much about you. I, for one, didn't know you had a brother in publishing. And, I didn't know you had aspirations to start a magazine of your own, but I suppose every pup of an editor has that dream. With each passing minute—today, anyway—I learn more and more about you."

Tom sat there, paralyzed with a sense of powerlessness. *So this is what it's like to be fired,* he thought. *Now I see why Sam felt so humiliated.*

"What do you want, Tom?"

The answer was so simple: He wanted to work at *Bite.* With his friends. He missed them already. "I'm sorry I didn't tell you about *Bite*—the name of the magazine, but I suppose you know that—but to be honest, it doesn't seem real to me even now. I hope that you believe that." *Leverage,* he thought to himself. *Use it.* "What I would like is to stay at *Profit* for at least six months while *Bite* gets off the ground. I think I can safely say this is something you should never say to your boss, but these are strange times. I can do this job in two days a week, Alex, and you won't notice a difference, I swear. And it won't make life any harder for anyone I work with. The days I'm not here I'll be on call for anyone who needs me. Let me work part-time for the next six months, in which time I can both find a replacement for me and train him or her, and let me also work on *Bite.*"

"Explain to me why there isn't a conflict of interest."

"Because *Bite* won't be half as upscale as *Profit.* I'm not saying we won't have any upscale advertisers, and we may very well end up with some of the same ones that are in *Profit.* But we're going after a younger reader, a totally different reader, and I just don't see that we'll be stealing anything from you. As for editorial, well, what with the crummy economy and the reduced size of the magazine, it's not like I have room here to do much of anything these days. If I have an idea that's better suited to *Profit* than *Bite,* I'd give it to *Profit.* I may not seem like it—today, anyway—but I am a man of honor."

"I'm not saying yes, but I'm not saying no. I'll think about it. In the meantime, if you know what's good for you you'll put out one hell of a section this issue."

Tom smiled. "Bet on it." He left the office, wiping his brow dramatically for Mary's benefit, and started walking down the hall. It hit him then that they hadn't really talked about the *Times* at all, that if his response to Alex was any indication, he'd already made his decision.

Wendy said Moira was out for the rest of the day, and Tom couldn't tell who was more relieved—him or Wendy. He left a message for Sam on her cell phone, saying nothing but "Please call me." He knew he had to call Andrew, but decided to run it all by Ethan first. He'd been neglecting their friendship. And for all Ethan's good wishes, Tom knew that Ethan would be hurt that he hadn't told him all about the *Times.*

Ethan had one of the reporters in his office, but she evidently had read the *Observer,* or at least heard about it, because she looked at Tom with new admiration and quickly ran out the door. Tom shut it behind her and sat down. They skipped the formalities, Tom telling the story backward, starting with his meeting with Alex.

"You mean you're not going after the *Times* job?" Ethan didn't seem that hurt at all. "It's just that you've always said that that was the only place you could see yourself going after *Profit.*"

"But that was before *Bite* really began to take off." Tom hadn't been telling Ethan everything about *Bite.* He didn't want to get Ethan too excited, mostly because he wasn't sure he really thought he'd ever offer Ethan a job at *Bite.* Not because Ethan wasn't talented, but because he wasn't sure Ethan would be happy working under Tom, and he knew it would be a bad idea to take an editor from *Profit.* (That Veronica was involved was bad enough. Burning a bridge was one thing; scorching the ground on the other side was something else altogether.)

"I had no idea it was so far along."

"Sometimes I can't believe it either! Trevor has really been moving on everything. And he's hired this woman Mao—did I tell you about her?—as his assistant, and I think if she had the resources she'd not only get the magazine up and running but also reduce Third World debt and solve the Mideast crisis."

"Do you think Alex is going to let you go part-time? Even if he's cool with it, what about Chester? Does he know?"

"I assume Chester knows everything. He usually does. I have no idea what will happen. But I do know that if I don't go call Andrew I'll be advertising for a new best friend." As Ethan waved him out the door, it occurred to Tom that maybe Ethan wanted the *Times* gig. *That can wait.*

He ran into Veronica—not literally—in the hall. "Sorry,

can't talk. Must call Andrew. But the *Times* can wait. Bite, baby, Bite!"

She gave him a hug. "Finally! I'm so glad. But we need to figure out what to say to Diana." Diana was her boss. "If she doesn't hear it from me, she'll eat us both as a mid-afternoon snack."

"Shit! That's right. First I need to call Andrew. Then let's smoke. I'll stop by and get you."

He called Andrew at home. "Well, well, well."

"Andrew, I feel terrible. I never meant to screw over anyone, especially you. But I've seen the light, and there's a chance, perhaps slim, that *Profit* is going to let me work here for six months while I get *Bite* off the ground. And I'll happily be a co-editor with Sam. I'd be the luckiest man in the world to get to be a co-editor with Sam. And I'm going to tell the *Times* that even though I may very well regret it in six months, my heart is with *Bite* and this is something that I just have to do."

"I wish you would have figured this out a week ago, but better late than never. Welcome back."

"Thanks. It feels good." Now where in the hell was Sam?

Chapter 46

Liza let herself into the apartment as if she were a criminal—a criminal who knew the code for the alarm, which she automatically reached out to disarm as she turned into the foyer.

Ridiculous, really, given that she had every right to still be here. In fact, if her lawyer got his way (and given who her lawyer was, he no doubt would), all this and more, she thought sarcastically, scanning the living room that had always seemed tomblike to her—would be hers.

But there had been something so liberating getting out of this place, Liza hadn't missed a thing. She had fled with one suitcase, and as she walked into her bedroom—her old bedroom, she reminded herself—and looked at her walk-in closet, the size of most women's dining rooms, she wasn't tempted for a second. It all felt like part of a past, borrowed life, one life she couldn't wait to give back.

And that, not guilt, had driven her to call the housekeeper, Marie, to make sure that Chandler would be out of town on the afternoon she wanted to come and get her computer. It might have been easier to buy a new one—and *Bite* was providing her with one at the office with the highest graphic capabilities—but she was used to her own, and it was from her own that she wanted to create *Bite*'s first cover: An image of a big juicy apple being bitten from both sides by a gorgeous man and a gorgeous woman.

Liza stepped carefully through the master bedroom into the space that she had early on taken over as an office. Officially an extra dressing room, neither she nor Chandler had needed it. Actually, Chandler had needed much more than that for all of his suits, so he had appropriated the bedroom nearby, the bedroom where any hypothetical children might have slept, had either Liza or Chandler gotten around to talking about such a thing. Liza wondered why they hadn't—what an odd marriage, she thought, as she sat down at her desk. Years of marriage, surrounded by children, and yet neither of them had ever been tempted by the idea. Liza wasn't sure, even now, whether it was the idea of Chandler, even then, that had swerved her off that possible course, or whether somewhere along the way she had just decided she didn't want them.

She booted up the computer, just to make sure it was still working before she packed it up into the boxes she had arranged Marie to leave for her. While the computer began loading, she casually opened up the desk drawers, absent-mindedly making sure that she hadn't left unpaid bills lurking in the corners. She was humming to herself—the old standard "I'll Be Around," she realized with irony—when she came across a manila envelope wedged into a corner of the bottom drawer. She pulled it out, glancing up at the computer and typing in her password while she opened the envelope, without looking.

Into her lap tumbled picture after picture. Chandler—there was no doubt it was him, despite the blindfold. She would have known his body even if it had a coat of armor on it. And kneeling before him, in different suggestive poses—and of this, there was equally no doubt—a woman she knew very well. Dressed in a leather thong, a whip held playfully between her teeth, hair tossed back in a playful pose, none other than Constance, the woman they had shared a summer house with.

Liza felt bile rise in her throat. How easily she had comforted Sam that night after Tom's party, when Veronica walked in with Chris. How grateful—how stupidly grateful—she had been that she was getting out of a marriage with no mess like that. A bad marriage, to be sure, but a marriage in which, she had thought, Chandler had respected her to the most of his limited abilities.

Blind with panic, Liza turned the photographs over, hoping for a date. Nothing. She analyzed Chandler's haircut, as if that might tell her something. Nothing. No suntan that would let her know it was right after they had returned from, say, Portofino or the Hamptons. No bags under his eyes that would let her know it was taken during a particularly brutal case. Not a single clue. As if she needed to know anything else. As if, she thought with a miserable laugh, she needed to know any of this at all.

She felt like she was riding out an earthquake. The floor wasn't where she left it. She was going to throw up. She was going to faint. Actually, she thought in a sane moment when she was able to take a breath, what she was going to do was something that had been very hard for her before, something she was working very hard on getting better at. She was going to pick up the phone and ask for help.

"Sam?" she said, her voice shaking.

"Liza! What's the matter?" Liza could hear Sam getting up and closing her door. She took a deep breath.

"I . . . I . . . I don't even know how to say this, so I'm just going to say it . . ."

"Liza, you're scaring me."

"You'd be far more scared if you were sitting here, believe me," Liza said. "I'm at home, picking up some stuff, and I just found naked pictures of Chandler with another woman."

"Oh God, Lize, I'm so sorry," Sam said. "That's awful." Still freaked out by the article in the *Observer,* Sam wished she could offer up something a little more helpful. Something more than three words long, for that matter. But given how upset she was herself at this point, she just didn't have the energy. "Can you tell when they're from?"

"Nope." Now Liza started to cry. "I feel like such a fool. I guess it doesn't matter when they're from, does it?"

"I guess not," Sam said slowly. "Nothing could make you feel better right now, and even if they were from years ago . . ."

"He's still a pig," Liza interjected. "Wait, I think I just took my first full breath in fifteen minutes. Okay. Here's what I'm going to tell myself: I'm going to feel sick as long as I feel sick, and then I won't. He, on the other hand, will be a sick fuck for the rest of his life."

"Absolutely," Sam said, rallying behind her friend. "I just wish I'd thought of that myself."

"Don't worry, honey," Liza said, shakily rising to her feet. "You hold my head while I puke for the next month, and I promise to give you full credit."

"Okay, Lize. But get out of there. I'll meet you at home."

"Here I come."

She pocketed the photos. If Chandler was stupid enough to leave them in her drawer—and it was still her drawer, goddamn it—and if he were stupid enough to test her in court, this would put an end to it.

Slowly, and in shock, she began packing up her computer, trying to make sense of the situation far faster than her brain could manage. Whatever hurt these pictures had caused her, the hurt could stop right there. She had the power to do it. She prayed, to every supreme being that she could think of, that she would have the power to keep it that way.

Liza picked up a dozen yellow deli tulips and a bottle of Krug for her roommate. As she let herself in the door, she saw Sam gesturing angrily on the phone. Sam hung up and looked at Liza, trying to smile.

It was a pathetic attempt.

"What's going on?" Liza could tell any Chandler news would have to wait.

"Nothing as bad as what you're going through, I promise," Sam said, wrapping her arms around her friend. "You okay?"

"You first, please," Liza said, handing over the champagne. "I actually need a few minutes of distraction."

"Okay," Sam said, as Liza poured a glass of champagne for Sam and opened a Diet Coke for herself. "Tom might be leaving *Bite.*"

"Oh, Sam, come on. You had a misunderstanding over the masthead, but it's over. You're being ridiculous!"

"He also got offered a job," Sam interjected. "At the *Times.* The job he's always wanted. The job that if we weren't in this magazine together, I would tell him he'd be insane not to take."

Liza nodded, the seriousness of the situation dawning on her. Sam would be devastated, surely. But almost as important—well, more important on some levels, to be honest about it—if Tom left, would *Bite* still be able to go forward? Must everything fall apart at once?

"You don't have to ask," Sam said. "I've already thought about it. I think if Tom left, we'd be okay. I mean, it's my parents' money that's getting us going, and if Trevor is willing to stay on board, I don't see why we can't make a go of it. It's just that it's so . . . it's so . . . it's so goddamn scary without him. And I feel guilty and furious at the same time."

"I suppose this would be a bad time to give you one of those AA bits of wisdom, like, 'Let go and let God'? Or 'Everything works out the way it's supposed to'?"

Sam smiled wanly. "Kind of."

"Understood," Liza said. "Then how about a nice, miserable dinner at La Goulue? My treat. We can smoke our brains out and pretend to be hating every minute of it. Although I'm not sure I can eat, with the pictures of Chandler running through my mind every two seconds. I'm so . . . humiliated. And angry. Did I mention humiliated?"

Sam gave Liza a huge hug. "I'll eat for both of us, promise, and if it helps, you can describe every detail of the horrid pictures to me. But if you don't mind, my most sober of friends, I may need to get a little drunk. Do you mind enabling?"

Liza led the way toward the door. "Not in the least."

Sam was good and drunk when she and Liza got back to the apartment, and she stripped down immediately to her bra and panties. *Why does getting drunk make you want to take off your clothes?* she thought, then laughed. *Ain't that the truth.*

She walked over to the answering machine. "Liza, it's Chandler."

"Delete!" screamed Liza from the bathroom. Sam hit the erase button, and started to turn away when the machine beeped again.

"Hey, Sam. It's me." Sam froze when she realized it was Tom. "Listen, I understand why you're ignoring me." Sam realized she hadn't checked her cell phone all day. "I've been a shit, and I'm so sorry. It's been a hell of a day, but I wanted you to know that several people have helped me see the error of my ways, including you with your beautiful apples." Liza came running into the room, toothpaste foaming out of her mouth. "I'm not sure what's happening with *Profit,* but call me and I'll explain it all. I do know that I'm fully committed to *Bite.* Let's do it, you and me, together forever at the top of the masthead!" Liza and Sam jumped up and down around the room.

The machine beeped again. "Hey, Sam. It's Chris. I'm back from Egypt for a week, and wanted to know if you wanted to get together. Call my cell."

Sam and Liza froze. "I'm terrified it's going to beep again," said Sam.

But it didn't. Sam went to bed, tomorrow's headache already starting to arrive. She was thrilled about Tom's news, even more so because she had been dreading having to tell her parents that her partner was backing out. But why did Chris have to call right then? And why wasn't she happier about it? (Because he was a liar, for one thing.) Then it hit her, and she saw it as one of those equations from the SAT test:

Chris : Sam :: Sam : Jack

Chris was to Sam as Sam was to Jack—that is, Chris was using her the same way she had been using Jack. She tried to take refuge in the fact that she really did like Jack, but she was sure Chris would say he really did like her. There was no difference, except that because Jack wasn't halfway around the world, she had used him more often. As she lay in bed, staring at the clock and waiting for the numbers to change, she thought again about the hurt look in Jack's eyes, and she started to cry. But it felt oddly good, bringing with it the realization that she would never hurt him, or anyone else if she could help it, the same way again.

Chapter 47

NEW RULES

1. No more crying
2. No more drunk dialing
3. No more crying and drunk dialing
4. No more men named Chris
5. No more men
6. No more berating self if No. 5 is broken
7. Kill self if No. 4 is broken

Sam looked proudly at the list. Alright, so it was pathetic. But certainly no more pathetic than the sliding she had done in the last few months, from being someone she would be happy to have as a friend to becoming someone she hated being with.

Only last week, Liza had invited her away to Montauk for the weekend, where Liza's parents had a house. "What a great idea," Sam said. "Can I come without myself?" When had she become the kind of woman she used to loathe?

Maybe it was a lesson in compassion. Maybe she could learn that lesson in compassion another time. For now, she needed to find her center again, and she could only do that if she followed these rules. She stapled the list onto her office bulletin board.

So Chris was out. Maybe they could be friends someday. She couldn't help but still fantasize they would be more, but after tossing all night, she had to admit that having him in her fantasy life would probably always be far more fulfilling than having him in her actual life. The only way to get there was to stop talking about him—even to stop talking about how she was over him. Because she clearly wasn't—the only person she had fooled was herself. And she was the only person who got hurt when it turned out not to be true. Actually, she *wasn't* the only person who got hurt, and that had really been her wake-up call. She had hurt Jack terribly. As for the crying, well . . . Enough. The only time she had cried in her adult life previous to the last few months was when she got angry. Embarrassing, but not unforgivable—just some weird glitch in her brain. But this had been out of control. And if she was going to be running a magazine with Tom—heck, if she wanted to keep her friends—she had to be more together. The crying was done, over, out.

So the only rule she was leaving open for negotiating was No. 5. Because try as she might, becoming a lesbian didn't seem to be in the cards for her (although she was proud, she had to admit, that she had experienced her first lesbian pass earlier that week. At a party for a hot, talentless artist in Soho, someone had placed a hand on her hip and whispered "nice dress" in her ear. She turned, only to find the designer of the dress she was wearing, a designer who intimated she'd much rather see the dress off of Sam than on her). And Sam wasn't quite ready to face a life alone, just because she'd made some stupid list of rules. "A *good* list of rules," she reprimanded herself.

As much chaos as she'd been in, she missed having a partner. She couldn't even remember, come to think of it, having a partner. A real, grown-up partner who would support her. Whom she could support. Maybe, she thought, staring out her window, she had never had that. Had never expected it, hadn't known how to have it. And maybe she was getting closer to it. Now, if only the person would present himself. She had wrecked things with Jack. It was better not to think about it. She had learned her lesson.

Sam felt a twinge in her heart, and stopped mid-thought.

Weird, this. Every time she thought of Jack recently, she had felt this kind of sadness, a kind of sadness she was unfamiliar with. It was something more than regret. Was it possible that she had never given Jack the chance he deserved because she was so damn obsessed with Chris? She tried to reason that it wouldn't have worked with Jack anyway—and it certainly wasn't going to work in the future.

After all, she had tried to call him a couple of times—thus the importance of Rule No. 2 and No. 3. In the last couple of weeks, she called him sober, as well, and even left a few messages at work, just checking in, wondering how he was doing, coming as close to groveling as she could while keeping the message light. God, she suddenly thought, *I hope I didn't leave him messages when I was drunk.* Anyway, he hadn't called back. Who could blame him? *Oh God, I probably left him drunk messages.* Stop. None of this was important. What was important, she reminded herself sternly, were the rules. If there could be a best-selling book on the subject, the least she could do was pathetically try to follow her own.

There was a knock on the door, and in walked a delivery man, holding two dozen three-foot-long French tulips, in saffron yellow, just touched with red. Sam carefully unwrapped the flowers and read the card. It said, quite simply, "I miss you." Who on earth were they from?

Sam stared at her set of rules. This was going to be tricky.

"Don't be an idiot!" Liza said, having plopped herself on Sam's couch. "Don't you remember the first thing about being a reporter?"

"Um . . . Don't give a blow job to a celebrity you never met?"

"Very funny," Liza said.

"Excuse me, but that's my $200 ABC pillow you're smushing."

Liza examined the red satin object, which looked like it belonged in the home of a Vegas showgirl. "You paid $200 for *this* pillow?"

"Okay, it was on sale," Sam admitted. "But it did at one time cost $200."

"Can't imagine why it was on sale."

"Are you here to attack my pillow taste, or do you have something helpful to contribute?" Sam took on her sternest tone. "Because, as if I need to remind you, we have quite a bit of work to do . . . And who is it you think is paying your rent?"

Sam and Liza started to laugh. No question there: Sam was paying the rent, ever since Liza had taken up residence on the couch.

"You know I owe you," Liza said seriously.

"I'm just waiting for that divorce settlement, darling. Then believe me, I'll milk it for all it's worth. Maybe a long weekend in Venice, at the Gritti . . ."

"Make it a week."

"Fine. Anyway, I think you were trying to offer me some advice. Some priceless advice?"

"Call the florist, you goon. I can't believe you've never done this before."

"Oh, I'm sorry, Miss Fancypants, but I'm not exactly used to getting flowers from an anonymous suitor."

"What a pathetic life you've been living."

"Actually," Sam said, sitting up straighter in her chair, "I'm used to dating men who have the balls to leave their names on the card."

Liza giggled. "Watch this."

Liza rolled Sam's chair out of the way and picked up the phone. "Yes, Renny? I'm calling from the office of Samantha Leighton. We've just received a beautiful bouquet of flowers but I'm afraid I've lost the card. And I know my boss will just kill me if I have to tell her that happened. Can you please tell me who they're from?"

Sam covered her face to stifle her laugh, just as she watched a look of disbelief cross Liza's face. "Are you sure?" she said into the phone. There was a pause, followed by, "Okay, then. Well, thank you."

Liza shook her head. "Well, my dear," she said to Sam, "The person who sent the flowers left a message, if you called, to tell you that you'll have to work harder than that if you want to know who they're from."

"What!" Sam squealed.

"Sam?"

"What?" Sam replied, still laughing with glee.

"Do I need to tattoo rule No. 5 on your ass?"

"At least I wouldn't ever have to see it."

Chapter 48

By the way, when I was leaving your office I did hear you say you'd gotten laid." Trevor, sitting on the sofa in Tom's apartment, waited patiently.

"I don't want to talk about it," Tom replied.

Trevor didn't move. He knew this was awkward stuff for Tom, but he didn't care. He saw the way Tom interacted with Sam and Andrew, and hated that he was treated like some kind of second-class citizen. "I hate the way you treat me like a second-class citizen," he said. "You tell everyone else this stuff. I hear you with Sam, with Veronica, with Andrew."

All Tom could think about were the moments when Trevor, a teenager at the time, would call Tom a fag because he wasn't interested in football. It wasn't fair to hold it against him—they were kids, and he didn't mean what he was saying—but it was there just the same. "It's about time your straight white male self felt second-class."

"Where are we, back at college? Come on, Mr. T. Hit me. I can handle it."

They sat and looked at each other. Then Tom looked at the TV, even though it wasn't on. Trevor sighed, got up, and started walking toward the kitchen. As soon as he was past Tom's line of vision, he came back around and lunged at him. He grabbed Tom's arms and quickly pulled them behind his back.

"We have ways of making you talk."

"Jesus Christ, Trevor! Ow! Stop it!"

Trevor pulled Tom's arms a little higher.

"You fucking sadist!"

"Talk."

"Ow! Fine! Fine! Just let me go." Trevor relaxed his grip, but only halfway. "All the way."

"Promise me."

"Fine! I promise!" Trevor let go of Tom's arms and walked back to the sofa and sat down. "I'm not exactly proud of it, and wouldn't have even mentioned it if I hadn't been in a very bad place."

"This is going to be good."

"Yes," Tom said with a sigh. "It is. My air conditioner was broke, so I had a repairman come, and, well . . ."

Trevor burst out laughing. "Did he . . ." He couldn't talk for the laughing. "Did he . . ." More laughing, at which point even Tom started to smile. "Did he have the right tools?" And with that Trevor laughed harder, doubling over. Tom stood up as if to walk away, but started laughing, too.

"You have no idea."

Trevor looked up, and got serious. "Tell me," he said. "Was it hot? So hot you needed some help . . . *cooling* down?"

"Don't make me put 'Jungle Love' on again." Tom hated this. Then he thought of a better idea. "You want to know how it was? It was electric. The fact that he was a stranger—blue-collar to boot—the fact that he was totally in control, the fact that he was uncut—"

"Uncle!" Trevor put his hands over his ears, laughing. "I give in!"

"You asked."

Trevor couldn't tell if Tom was annoyed or not, but guessed he was. "For Pete's sake, Tom, relax. If you can't laugh at yourself . . ."

"I know, I know. You have no business living."

They both got quiet. It was something their mom always said to them when they took their adolescent selves too seriously. The thing about family, Tom realized, is that you could have a moment like that and not have to talk about it, you shared it implicitly.

Tom and Trevor had discussed what went down at *Profit,* but they started again, trying to figure out what to do if various things happened. If Tom was fired, he could work full-time on *Bite. Bite* would pay him a salary that would pale in comparison to what he made at *Profit,* but Trevor said he'd more than happily help him out. Plus, their mom's estate should be just about wrapped up. If Tom got sixth months at *Profit,* he could work at *Bite* part-time, which wouldn't be the greatest thing for *Bite,* they both knew, but would keep money coming in (and take less money from *Bite).* Neither Tom nor Trevor knew Sam's parents well enough to be positive that they'd come through with as much money as they had said they would, and were trying to keep a healthy eye on the budget.

"Maybe you should just ditch *Profit,"* Trevor said.

"I think that sometimes, but it feels wrong. One, I'd be leaving them in the lurch. Two, I really don't want to burn any bridges. Worldwide Media owns a lot of magazines, and if *Bite* doesn't work out I may have to crawl back. Three, when I worry about not being around to lead the team at *Bite,* I remind myself that Sam is my partner and more than capable of holding the reins. Four, as we both know, the money is good, and I can put that section out with so little facetime at the office it's scary. I never really let them know how easy it was for me, because I wanted them to believe I was working hard."

"When do you think you'll hear back from Alex?"

"This week, for sure."

"Good. We need to get moving on going public with *Bite."*

"You have no idea how this city reacts when someone tries to start a magazine."

"I can guess. And we need to own that moment. Not have it leak awkwardly out like, like . . ."

"Like the *Times* thing."

"Exactly."

They looked at each other, the unpleasantness of the meeting in Tom's office coming back briefly. "Tom," Trevor said flatly.

Tom raised his eyebrows.

"It's a little"—he pulled at his collar—"*warm* in here. Do you think your air conditioner could be broken again?"

The next day, Alex called Tom into his office.

"I've talked to Chester, and we'd like you to stay on for three months, not six. That should be long enough for you to find someone else and train him, and to be honest, even though you say it won't happen, I know that you're going to be less interested in *Profit* than in your project. But you've done great stuff for *Profit,* and we want to do right by you."

"Three months would be perfect."

"I hope you know what you're doing, Tom."

"I don't have a clue. But it feels right, Alex, and I have to respect that. My career isn't your problem, but as much as I've loved working here, I feel like I could do it for the rest of my life. And that scares me. If life offers you a big tasty sandwich, sometimes you just have to close your eyes and bite it."

"Is that your slogan?"

"Hadn't thought about it, but maybe."

Alex stood up, and Tom followed. "By the way, Chester wants to see you. Call Nora to make an appointment."

Back in his office, he sat down to email Nora. Procrastinating, he sent out a bunch of emails.

To: Samantha@bite.com, Trevor@bite.com,
Andrew@bite.com, Veronica@bite.com,
Liza@bite.com
From: Tom_sanders@profit.com

Subject: T minus three months
just got the news: profit wants me to stay for three more months, which seems ideal. chester apparently wants to scold me, but i guess that won't happen until next week. soon it'll be Bite full-time!

To: Ethan_foxman@profit.com
From: Tom_sanders@profit.com
Subject: End of an era
i'd come by to tell you in person, but i think i'd cry. alex gave me three months (which is more than fair, obviously). we've had so much fun, and i could never have worked here without you. i don't know if Bite is going to fly, but i do hope we'll work together again sometime (not that we won't be friends, obviously)

Then he got one.

To: Tom_Sanders@profit.com
From: Justin.miller@KPLV.com
Subject: long time no nothing
what have you been up to, T? haven't heard hide nor hair from you

Tom spun around in his chair. How is it that some people know exactly the wrong moment to jump back into your life? Why did Justin even bother? He probably wanted to see another goddamn movie. So they could continue not getting to know each other better.

If Justin would get his act together and be worthy of the trouble, Tom felt like he could finally be friends with him. Did he want to see Justin? Absolutely, always, forever. Did he want to see a movie? Nope. Did he want to keep feeling this way? Not remotely. Was it fair to blame Justin for jerking him around when in all reality he probably had no idea that Tom felt the way he did? Well, probably not. And so Tom resolved to tell Justin exactly how he felt.

To: Justin.miller@KPLV.com
From: Tom_Sanders@profit.com
Subject: long time no nothing
hey, justin. things have been kuh-ray-zee. sort of starting a new magazine, getting fired from my old one, etc. (from now on, email me at tom@bite.com.) dinner next week?

He was about to call Sam and tell her what he was going to do, but he stopped. This was something he needed to do on his own, without parsing it all before it had even happened. That, and one other thing: if he pussied out, at least no one would know.

Chapter 49

Usually, the Wednesday night AA meetings were Liza's favorites—she had an odd crew of AA friends there whom she never saw outside of that space, and she looked forward to seeing them. She was in the middle of listening to the speaker talk about how he had come to be sober three years ago when she looked up across the room and saw Chandler sitting there. She had thought that Chandler couldn't go any lower, but this was really amazing. Coming to an AA meeting when he had no desire to be sober—just to meet up with her. It was a total intrusion of her personal space, and another example (like she needed another example) that he was, at best, completely out to lunch when it came to knowing what would make her happy.

She walked briskly down the street and turned the corner onto First Avenue when she heard his voice. She knew the fucker would follow her. Damn. "Liza, wait up!" Chandler grabbed her shoulder to spin her around.

Liza looked up at him. She took in his warm smile, the suit he had had made on their last trip to Hong Kong. And then she waited. She waited for the ambivalence she'd been filled with lately. She waited to look at his face and realize that she had made a terrible mistake, that they should try again. And she almost jumped for joy that all she felt was . . . nothing.

A grin spread over her face. Chandler, of course, assumed it was for him, and he lit up.

"I've missed you so much," he said smoothly. "Could I take you out for a cup of coffee?"

"Actually," she said, looking him straight in his eyes and

feeling more powerful than she had in years, "this isn't a good time."

"Oh." He looked momentarily disappointed, but then said, "Well, okay. When would be a good time?"

Liza felt herself about to smile, but tried to control it. "Gosh, Chandler, I don't know. Have Katie call me. Maybe you, Constance, and I can get together." And she turned, leaving him stunned and standing still, to continue her walk home.

"Yes!" she said, practically skipping her way to Sam's. She couldn't wait to tell Sam what she had done.

Liza had been surprised how much the years in her rambling Park Avenue apartment had left her lonely—something she hadn't been aware of until she realized how quickly she had come to rely on seeing Sam when she walked in the door. It felt like she was twenty-two again, bunking up with her college roommate in a studio apartment in Chelsea, when they were too poor to afford any other place in New York. Sam said she loved having Liza there, but the space was tight. It was time to start looking for an apartment—especially now that Liza was about to begin working in the *Bite* offices full-time. Working together and living together was most definitely not what Sam had signed up for when she offered Liza a job and then her couch.

Veronica and one of her best friends, Erin, were at Happy Ending, a Lower East Side bar that was once a bathhouse. Erin had warned her that some people from her work would be meeting them—if cell phones did anything, they made sure you were never alone with anyone for long—but she didn't say anything about what a spoonful of sugar one of them would be.

His name was Dael. He was Israeli but raised in Brazil, and he was perhaps the most attractive man Veronica had ever spoken to (when they talked about it later, she and Erin agreed that Dael was objectively, as opposed to subjectively, beautiful—that is, there wasn't anyone in the world who wouldn't find him sexy). Dark, curly hair, cut close to the scalp, and light brown eyes. Plus, he was smart, as he proved immediately when he caught an obscure reference Veronica made to her favorite author, Geoff Dyer.

"How do you know him?" she asked.

"I am a writer," he said. "How could anyone who cares about good writing not have read *But Beautiful?*"

"I love that book!" she said. "The part about Thelonious Monk, and New York . . ."

He quoted, in a reverie: " 'A time of the day when it is possible to regret everything and nothing in the same breath, when the only wish of all bachelors is that there was someone who loved them, who was thinking of them even if she was on the other side of the world.' "

Veronica's mind raced. Was this really happening? Could any man be this perfect? Was it a problem that she wasn't Jewish? Or Catholic? Her friends all thought she was an ice queen, but she felt like Jane Eyre right about now. No, wait. The one from *Wuthering Heights.* Emily. No, it was Cathy. Someone fluttery, anyway. "Isn't there a part about women, too?"

Again, the reverie. " 'When a woman, feeling the city falling damp around her, hearing music from a radio somewhere, looks up and imagines the lives being led behind the yellow-lighted windows: a man at his sink, a family crowded together around a television, lovers drawing curtains, someone at his desk, hearing the same tune on the radio, writing these words.' "

She pulled her hair back, and tied it behind her head. "We have a saying in Brazil," Dael said. "Redheads get lucky."

"What?"

He blushed. "Sorry, I think I mean 'Redheads *are* lucky.' "

🍎 🍎 🍎

Trevor, Sam, Andrew, Veronica, Liza, and Tom sat down in the *Bite* conference room—two of the old Liberty Inn's rooms with the wall torn down—to talk about a timetable.

"Before we start," said Veronica, "I just need to say something. I met the most amazing guy last night."

Tom faked a yawn.

"No," she said. 'Seriously. He's half-Brazilian, half-Israeli, and he's one hundred percent gorgeous."

"Now I'm paying attention," Tom said. "But what does he do?"

"He doesn't really have a job," said Veronica. "He's a writer."

She had Tom there. He could hold artists, actors, and musicians against her, but there was no way he couldn't call writing legit. "Well," he said, "when we're done I can talk to you about 'the Latin phase.' "

"Name?" Liza asked.

"Dael. Die-ell." She spelled it for them.

"Okay, people," said Trevor. "Time to move on." Sam looked at Veronica and made the call-me gesture. "It's June. If we want to launch in the fall, we have a ton of work to do, fast."

"I'll say," said Liza. "We have to start shipping pages at the beginning of next month."

"Which means we have to start shooting right now," said Veronica.

"Which means we need a concrete lineup of stories right now," said Sam.

"Which means we shouldn't spend too much time sitting around here yammering," said Tom.

Everyone shot him variations on the same dirty look.

"Sorry," he said. "I've never liked meetings. Okay. Sam and

I will sit down tonight and come up with a concrete story list, even if we have to drink this island dry to get it done. Right after we're done here, we'll make sure R.J. and Andrew are ready with their columns."

"Haven't started yet," said Andrew. "Tonight, tonight, tonight."

With pretty much everything editorial postponed until that night, they skipped to matters of production. Liza said she felt more than ready to design whatever needed to be designed, but she had no confidence in her abilities to see the pages all the way through production (plus, she had no interest in the task). She said they really had to hire a head of production, someone to deal with the printers—and that she might know someone she had worked with years ago.

"Do what it takes," said Trevor. "We don't have time. Call him or her right now."

They also realized they'd need a copy editor, someone to make sure everything was grammatically correct. Both Sam and Tom knew people who were good and out of work.

"Get them," said Trevor. "Don't be afraid of spending money. It's time."

Tom pointed out that they didn't need fact checkers, as the interns could check the stuff written by freelancers; staffers would be responsible for checking their own facts. "Sorry, Sam," he said, knowing she'd dread fact checking. "That's the way we do it at *Profit,* and it makes sense here."

"How banal," she replied.

Chapter 50

"Is this a date?"

Damn the young ones, thought Andrew. They couldn't just let things happen; they always had to make sure everything was out on the table. He wasn't sure if it was a date. He had to go to dinner so he'd have something to write about in his column, and Tom was busy powwowing with Sam. So he asked Robbie to accompany him to Eileen's, a Williamsburg seafood restaurant he'd been to many times but he figured he was allowed to refresh his memory. Eileen had previously been a co-owner of the Clam Hut with her lesbian lover. They broke up and Eileen opened a restaurant nearby with a similar menu. It was such a bitchy thing to do, Andrew thought, and he figured it was just the kind of drama that would play well in *Bite.* The Lesbian Lobster War!

"Do you want it to be?" Andrew asked.

Robbie shrugged his shoulders, which could mean anything.

As the waitress brought over the lobster roll for Andrew—it was the Clam Hut's signature dish—and the salmon for Robbie, Andrew noticed someone watching him. He looked up at the counter, where he saw Lachlan. *What the fuck?* It was bad enough that Lachlan had seen him and Robbie out on a date—or whatever—but it was positively unbelievable that he'd be in a restaurant when all the time they were together he never wanted to do anything but order in food and work on his sketches. And that it was a fish restaurant was beyond the pale. Lachlan hated fish! "I think we should go say hi," said Robbie.

But when they walked over, "hi" wasn't what came out Andrew's mouth. "You hate fish!"

"Hi, Andrew. Hi, Robbie. How's it going?" Lachlan seemed to operate at a cooler temperature than most human beings, and Andrew had only seen him get really angry once, when Andrew insisted on getting a share on Fire Island one summer because he just couldn't stand the heat of New York.

"Not bad," Robbie said. "You?"

This doesn't have to be awkward, Andrew thought. Neither of them was friends with Lachlan anymore; even if Lachlan did care, that was just too bad. And anyway, Lachlan was with someone.

"This is John," Lachlan said, introducing the guy to his right. "John insisted that I at least try a lobster roll before swearing never to eat one, so here we are." Andrew was dumbfounded, and he and Robbie took their leave.

That didn't have to be awkward, Andrew thought again. *But it was.* And it hit him: It was awkward because at that moment he knew that he and Robbie would never work out, that Robbie and Lachlan were too similar, that Andrew had been down that road before and had no desire to go down it again.

It amazed Sam and Tom both that they had been able to avoid coming up with a final lineup until now, and made them more than a little nervous that neither was able to stop the other's procrastination. They were sitting in a corner at Casa di Pre, a random Italian restaurant in the West Village. It was precisely the kind of place no one who might want to eavesdrop would ever go to.

They went over what they already had. The barefoot travel piece, obviously, but also the Advice Squad. Sam was ready to get the interns started on calling the celebs. Tom wanted to do a story on learning how to climb trees—not like kids do, but like mountain climbers would. There was a group near Atlanta that had two-day workshops. "What could be more fun than climbing a tree?" he said. "It's the perfect example of the kind of fun thing adults forget they once loved to do."

Sam started shaking. "That's it! I know you hate theme issues—"

"I hate theme issues!"

"Yeah, I *know* that." She shot him her shut-up look. "But, but, but! Why don't we make the theme"—she whispered the word—"of the issue, or at least of the well, since we do have a sex columnist—childhood pleasures. Going barefoot, climbing trees . . ."

Tom didn't move, but his scowl slowly disappeared. Suddenly he came alive, reeling off five great ones in a row: A profile of the world champion of miniature golf ("There's a tournament," he said. "If it's this month, and it might be, we could send someone to report on it."). Lessons in table tennis with an expert. A quick list of companies that sell old-fashioned candy—Abba Zabbas! Pop Rocks!—over the Web. A page of fun, cheap outdoor toys you can buy at a drugstore or a toy store: Frisbees, Track Ball, Whiffle Ball. A shopping story on where to find the world's best kites. A photo portfolio of people who've built amazing treehouses—not for their kids necessarily, but for themselves.

They briefly worried whether it would be too downmarket, but decided the barefoot story would have lots of expensive, if casual, hotels, and the treehouses would look like they cost a lot of money. Tom pointed out that there were a few hotels—he knew of some in Costa Rica and Nepal—where the rooms were in trees; they could do a sidebar listing the hotels for people who weren't about to build a treehouse. "And," he said, "to go with the kite story we can do another sidebar on the new sport of kite surfing—you use a kite to power your way over the ocean."

"Why do all editors love sidebars?" said Sam. "They're so much work." She took another sip of wine.

All they had to do was come up with a front section of newsy stuff. "Tom," Sam said. "I hate to compare *Bite* to *Wallpaper,* but it doesn't have a front-of-book, not really. It divides the magazine into interiors and fashion and travel. Maybe we could just—"

He leaned over and kissed her right on the lips. "You're a genius. Let's drop the front-of-book. No one likes what we've come up with. After the Spread and the Contents, we'll just launch right into the stories, and some will be big and some will be small. And we can have "Advice Squad" at the back, followed by the columns."

"Shit!" Sam barked. "If we don't get fashion in there Trevor is going to kill us. We both know he's hoping to get lots of fashion advertisers—it is for the September issue, after all, and designers want to sell their fall lines."

Tom pointed out that with more wine they could certainly come up with something. And they did: get celebrities to share pictures of themselves as kids, "and we can style them," he said, "in clothes that approximate the same things they were wearing way back when. Not exactly, of course, and we don't want them to look like overgrown children, but face it—everything Marc Jacobs designs looks like it was ripped off the back of someone you went to junior high school with!"

Tom leaned in, but Sam pushed him away. "One kiss a night, sweetie. Remember, I've sworn off men."

Chapter 51

After initial reservations that the child's play theme was indeed too downmarket, Trevor got on board. And anyway, Tom didn't care if he didn't. Even if *Bite* was simply about the good things in life, there was no reason the church/state divide shouldn't exist between editorial and advertising. Trevor could suggest but never insist.

As soon as Tom and Sam announced the lineup to the staff, Veronica and Liza disappeared into Liza's office to figure out how to make all the stories look different from each other but part of the same magazine. Andrew, Tom, and Sam stayed behind.

"How's your column coming?" Tom asked.

"Oy." Andrew went on to explain the Robbie and Lachlan situation at Eileen's. Andrew told the story with so many funny asides that by the end—when he turned around to wave good-bye to Lachlan and ran into the glass door—they gave up and put their heads on the table and laughed.

"Hey," Tom finally said. "While I'd love it if you'd simply review the restaurants and tell us what the food was like, why not include all the romantic intrigue? You don't have to name names, or you can change Robbie and Lachlan's names, if you want. It'd make a great counterpoint to the lesbian saga."

Andrew scowled.

"Don't be a prig," Tom said. "It'll be much funnier!"

Sam piped in. "Do it, Andrew. No offense, but you're not a writer, and it'll be easier if you write it like you tell it—that's what I always tell people who are trying to learn how to write for magazines: Write it like you'd tell it at a cocktail party."

"And it'll fit perfectly in the Appetites section," said Tom. "You can always write about your love life. Think about it: Next issue you can take, I don't know, Josh Hartnett to dinner to see what he thinks about good food."

"He likes it a bit too much, if you ask me," muttered Andrew, still disappointed that Hartnett had graduated into a man's body.

"So you'll at least try it?" When Sam and Tom were tag-teaming in an argument, it was almost impossible to escape.

"Fine," he said. "I was planning on firing Robbie—I guess I'll have to do it before the piece comes out."

R.J. walked in. "Oh my God," he said. "You will not believe what happened to me last night." Yes, they nodded, he was probably right. "I was walking from the cab to my apartment, and this guy came up to me. He was cute, and gave me the look. So I gave him the look. We started chatting, and I invited him up for a beer. Anyway, we moved it to the bedroom, and I went to the bathroom. I came back into the bedroom, and as I was opening the door, I said, 'I hope you've got those clothes off.' Or something stupid like that. Anyway, the lights are off, and when my eyes got used to the dark I realized that he was crouched next to the bed. 'I'll just be a second,' he said. 'I'm in the middle of saying my prayers.' "

Tom, Andrew, and Sam completely broke down.

"I know! I'm standing there, wondering if I should leave or take my clothes off or what. He wasn't saying them out loud, thank God. So to speak."

"Then what happened?" asked Sam.

"After about thirty seconds he said, 'Okay, I'm done.' And we got down to it."

"Was it good?" asked Andrew.

"It didn't shake my faith or anything," said R.J. "But it got the job done. He was young and cute and the young ones smell so good. And they kiss like it means so much."

"You said a mouthful," said Andrew.

"That's not all I got a mouthful of! He had this—"

"Whoa!" cried Sam. R.J. never knew when to stop.

Veronica and Tom took a cab up to *Profit* together. It didn't really matter when Tom got into the office, even before he had started his three-month exit, and especially not now. But Veronica had to be there by 11:30 at the latest or her boss, Diana, would dress her way down. Diana protected her photo editors like a mother hawk, but she could be just as tough on them. It was part of the reason that Veronica wanted to talk to her about *Bite* sooner than later.

"I think it's time," she said to Tom. "If she finds out I've been working on it at all, she'll explode. And it's got to come out any second."

"Are you ready to come on full-time?"

She didn't need to answer. While *Profit* was actually a great place for photo editors—there was more freedom to use a wide range of interesting photographers than at most other magazines—she couldn't wait to be in charge. All she had to do was tell Diana, no small thing. "She's Sicilian," Veronica reminded Tom. "Everything's a betrayal."

"I'd offer to do it for you, or come help, but I think it would only make her feel ambushed. Just talk to her. I think she'll be cooler than you think. Unfortunately, she's going to hate me, and probably get Alex to hate me as well."

"Don't be so sure," Veronica said. "As good as I am, I'm one more photo editor they don't have to pay, and since the magazine doesn't seem to be getting any bigger, maybe they'll actually be fine with it."

The thing about maybes is that they sometimes turn out right: Diana's eyes welled up, and she gave Veronica a hug and welcomed her to the big leagues. If Veronica wasn't completely convinced that Diana didn't also have one teary eye on her budget, well, so what. She got what she wanted. Part of being an adult, she thought to herself while smoking a cigarette solo afterward, was realizing that just because you got what you wanted didn't mean someone else couldn't get what she wanted too.

Sam had to run to her parents after work, just to comfort them quickly that they really were putting their money to good use—or use, anyway. Afterward, she met Liza and Jen at Rosa Mexicana, where they were standing at the bar.

Sam noticed that ever since Liza had moved out of Chandler's, not only had she seemed lighter and more relaxed, but her whole wardrobe had relaxed, too. Sam had never realized how amazing Liza's body was until she had ditched the designer suits for tight-fitting Levi's and little T-shirts. In fact, Sam thought with a smile as she approached the women, she was pretty sure those were *her* jeans and T-shirt. Well, she'd never look as good in them.

"Hello, glamour girls," Sam said. Liza and Jennifer gave her big smiles, and pulled a stool over for Sam. "What are you both so busy laughing about?"

"Jennifer was just telling me what she's been doing instead of drugs," Liza said. "It gives replacement therapy a good name!"

"Like what?" Sam said, taking a sip out of Liza's Diet Coke while she gestured at the bartender for a margarita with her other hand.

"Well . . ." Jennifer said, with a sly smile. "The joke was really on me for this one, but I was riding home in a taxi with George the other day . . ."

"Are you seeing him?" Sam interrupted. "I didn't realize you guys were going out regularly."

Jennifer broke into a smile. "Yeah, I'm really happy. I know you guys never imagined me settled down with a nice doctor, but I'm starting to think well, maybe . . ." She raised an eyebrow at Sam. "What about you?"

"Nope, not me," Sam said, taking a swig of her margarita.

Liza rolled her eyes at Jennifer. "Sam's on the wagon," she explained. "No men."

"You guys are a ball of laughs," Jennifer said with a smile. "One of you doesn't drink, one of you doesn't have sex. Actually, Liza, do you not have sex either?"

Liza didn't answer immediately. It was a long enough pause that Sam put her drink down and stared at her. "Liza? I've been living with you, working with you—you're wearing my clothes, for Christ's sake, and you forget to mention this to me?"

"Oh, hold your horses," Liza said. "Nothing has happened. I would share immediately, I promise. However . . ." Liza ran her fingers through her hair, enjoying drawing the moment out. "However . . . remember how I told you, Sam, about that guy I met at the place I was volunteering as a teacher?"

"Yeah . . ." Sam said slowly.

"Well, this afternoon we went out for coffee. And sadly there's no chemistry. But, while this may sound small to you, I just can't believe I went on a date. Even if it was coffee, even if it didn't work, I just feel like I'm finally making some movement."

Sam high-fived Jennifer.

"Are we growing up? Because we're starting to sound more like the Golden Girls than the Glamour Girls." Sam grabbed Jennifer's hand. "Wait! We totally forgot that you were about to tell me a funny story!"

Jennifer lowered her voice to a conspiratorial whisper. "We're in a taxi on the way home from the theater, and I think, 'Here's an original idea,' so down I go and . . . well, you guys know the rest."

"All too well," Sam said. "Although I have to say, that

whole thing has always grossed me out because I feel like the cab driver has to know what's going on, and has to be uncomfortable."

"Sam, that's so Upper East Side of you," Liza said.

"Hold on!" Jennifer said. "Sam is totally right! So George drops me off at the house—and please believe me when I say we were so, so quiet, and in fact, the driver was talking on his phone the whole time—and the driver turns around to him when I get out and says, 'Smooth ride?' "

They burst into laughter. "Busted!" Liza said.

Chapter 52

When Tom called Justin to make a plan, he had no qualms saying he didn't want to see a movie; there was no point in pussyfooting around it. Tom needed to do this, even if it was going to be painful.

They met at Roc, a place in Tribeca where Tom knew there'd be enough space between tables to avoid being overheard. They ordered their meals—and at Tom's insistence, a bottle of wine. "A little anesthesia," he said.

"What's hurting?"

You couldn't ask for a better segue than that. Tom hemmed and hawed for a few seconds, then realized that he could say what he had to say, but not if he was looking Justin in the face. He looked down. "I need to talk to you about something. I don't know if you have ever realized this, but when I met you I really liked you. Really. And I guess you didn't like me, because you were, frankly, a schmuck. But I kept coming back, because I like you—I like the way you think, I like the way you talk, I like the way you look. I never thought you were anything but a genuinely good person, and yet all the evidence pointed elsewhere. Justin"—Tom looked up, just to make sure he was still there—"I *really* liked you. You're an incredibly odd combination of arrogance and insecurity; I hadn't realized that those attributes weren't at opposite ends of a spectrum. In your case, anyway, they formed a circle. And I don't know what on earth you have to be insecure about." Tom hoped Justin would realize what a huge compliment he'd just given him.

Justin inhaled. "No," said Tom, "I need to keep going.

Everyone I know told me to stay away from you, but I couldn't. I understood, eventually, that you wanted to only be friends. But you kept flirting with me. It was only later that I realized you flirt with anyone. It's like you're running for office." Tom looked up again, and smiled this time. "Sorry. Anyway, I do want to be friends with you, but if we're going to be friends, then I need to be totally honest with you—which is why I have to tell you this. And I'm going to hold you to a higher standard. You need to stop flirting with me. Forever. If you don't show me that respect, I'll give up. Because you made me feel things I'd never felt before. I'd never been the one on the wrong side of unrequited love, and no one had ever put me through the wringer like that. I wouldn't wish it on anyone, but I'm glad I went through it. I needed it. To know what I could feel, to know what I want to feel. Perverse as it sounds, I'll always be grateful for that. But it's time for me to start feeling something else."

Tom took a sip of wine. He had done it. He had been more honest with another person than he had ever been. And now he wanted to leave. But first Justin had to say something, anything.

Justin wasn't saying anything back. *Why wasn't he speaking?* Tom looked at him, but Justin was looking elsewhere—up at the ceiling, to be precise. "I'm sorry, I know I should be saying something. I didn't know, I mean, I wasn't prepared . . ."

"Look, it's cool," Tom said. "We can just bail, or talk about someth—"

"No." Justin looked straight at him. "I'm glad you brought it up. I was a jerk when we met. I got that you liked me—not immediately, but soon. And I couldn't deal. I had just moved here, just broken up with my boyfriend, and I liked knowing someone like you was around. I like talking to you as much, I think, as you like talking to me. But you never forced the issue, so I just kept on keeping on. Was I flirting? I guess I was, and that was mean. I didn't realize you felt as strongly as you did." He chewed on a nail. "You don't give much of yourself, Tom."

Tom nodded. Justin continued. "I had started doing coke, and not long after your party I realized I needed to stop. I've been working on being a better person. I know how stupid that sounds, but it's true. It means a lot to me that you still want to be friends. I'm not sure if I were you I'd feel the same way."

"I'm serious," Tom said. "No flirting."

Justin raised his glass. "To a new us."

They spent the rest of the meal talking about the usual other things. After the meal, they walked back to Justin's apartment and sat outside on a ledge. Tom said he had to go. They hugged. Tom walked home, finally facing the fact that Justin had never said he wasn't interested in having more than a friendship, but he didn't have to. And that was okay.

Chapter 53

One by one Tom's cohorts came in. Trevor was first, complaining that they really had to sit down and figure out when they were going to announce this thing, and decide who to give it to—Keegan at the *Observer*, Keith Kelly at the *Post*, the *Times*, or the *Wall Street Journal*. He was itching to sell, sell, sell, but Tom thought (to himself) that the more itchy Trevor got the faster he'd fly out of the gate.

"I want to get going," said Trevor for the fifth time that morning. "Mao has a contact at MTV—I think we can get them interested in doing a reality series on the *Bite* offices. I wish we had someone punky and annoying to flaunt, though. It seems to help."

"Maybe Mao can dye her hair blue," Tom joked. Trevor thought about it. "I was joking."

Then came Sam with an update on how the interns were progressing with the "Advice Squad." Ben already had good stuff from Robert Downey Jr. on how to barter in jail and from milliner Philip Treacy on how to wear a hat, and had Joan Collins' PR guy promising she'd talk to him that week—Joan was going to share her secrets on how to get a younger man. Eleanor had the Zagats on how to nail a hot reservation even if you're not one of the Zagats, and was getting her dad, a literary agent, to talk to Alain de Botton about how to write a sexy love letter. Gavin knew someone who knew Cheech of Cheech and Chong, and was sure they'd explain how to roll a joint. Sam thought she could get Jennifer Aniston to do a quick list of ways to keep Brad Pitt happy as long as *Bite* swore to have her item run first.

"Two thoughts," said Tom. "One, we need more celebs like Aniston. Love the weird ones like Joan Collins and Cheech and Chong, but is there anyone else big we can get? And we need something for the homos."

"Excuse me," said Sam, "but what is Joan Collins if not for the homos?"

They brainstormed. Karl Lagerfeld on how to keep the weight off, Christopher Hitchens on how to pick a fight, Donatella Versace on how to throw a party, Julia Roberts on how to leave a lover—"Dream on," said Sam—and so on. They got enough to keep the interns busy; the best thing about these items, they agreed, was that they could hold the ones that didn't work and run them later, and they wouldn't get old.

"Music," said Tom. "What about musicians? Gwen Stefani on how to do your makeup, Moby's choices for the best chill-out mix tape, Al Green on five Sunday morning CDs . . ."

"How long do you think we can get away without paying the interns?" asked Sam.

"Indefinitely," said Tom. "They're getting experience they could never get anywhere else, and once we get this thing announced they'll be beating down the door."

Then Veronica. "Am I interrupting anything?"

He scrambled to come up with something—all he was thinking about was *Bite.* "Just thinking about Palestine."

"Me too!" she said. "Dael has family in Israel and he's worried about them, so I'm worried about him."

"Wow," he said. "You've got it bad. I don't think we've ever had a conversation that actually related to one of those jokes." It was good to see her happy. And it was funny how accustomed he had become to her being disappointed by some man. What he had thought of as her dignity was more of a reserve; clearly, the Brazilian was knocking it down.

That snapped her back to business. About the tree-climbing course: They'd obviously want pictures of the writer up in the trees. Did Tom have any idea who might be writing the piece?

"Nope!" he said. "But I did get my friend Laura from *Holiday* to agree to write the Barefoot Travel roundup, and she's emailing a list of resorts today. So at least you can start calling in publicity shots of the hotels. I think we need to show each one we mention—there's nothing more annoying to the reader than hearing about some sweet hideaway and not being able to see it."

"Okay, so you want lots of crappy photography."

"Is that what you got out of that? Let me try again. It's a good thing you're so good at what you do, or this story could really be a problem."

"Does that really work?"

"More than you think. And let's see, I do have some other stuff for you. We need to shoot the women who run the Clam Hut and Eileen's, although don't tell them we're shooting the other, or they'll flip. Lie if you have to. And let's sit down this afternoon and look at the old candy websites, order a bunch of candy, and figure out how to shoot it."

"Shit! I forgot to tell you! I looked up the U.S. Open of Putt-Putt Golf, and it's two weeks. In South Carolina."

"I completely forgot about that! Sweet! Who can we get to write it? It should be someone who knows golf." He called Sam in and told her the news.

"Golf, golf, golf," she said. "The dead man's sport." They watched her think. "Got it! My Star Fucker colleague Brian lives for golf, and would kill to write about something besides Matt Damon. I'll call him."

"No more than a dollar a word!" he called out as she left the room. "Tell him it's running in the launch issue so he'll make up for it in exposure."

While Veronica and Tom were revisiting the topic of

falling for the wrong guy, Liza came in and sat cross-legged on the floor. "R.J.'s column," she said.

"What about it?" Tom said.

"Well, how do you want to illustrate it? We need something to sex it up."

Veronica suggested they take a series of sexy-silly photos of R.J. in provocative outfits and scenarios, never showing his face. As a porn star cowboy, or Rudolph Valentino, or in a black-and-white orgy scene reminiscent of an old Calvin Klein ad.

"It's brilliant," said Tom. "A greatest hits of soft-core imagery through the years. But I don't want the picture to run too big, since it's really just art, if you know what I mean. It serves no real purpose." This was met with silence. He immediately realized his error, and the two women were sure to start getting riled up. "No, I mean of course every page needs to look hot or no one's even going to think about reading it, I understand that. But do you agree it shouldn't be more than"—he had been thinking one-eighth of a page but bumped it up—"more than one-sixth of a page?"

Veronica looked at Liza, who chewed on a pen. "Works for me," she said. "Will R.J. agree to it?"

"To dressing up in fun outfits and having his picture taken? Have you never met him?"

They all laughed. "I suppose if our sex columnist isn't up for anything . . . ," Veronica said.

"Then we need a new one," said Tom.

Trevor was in Liza's office, leaning over her shoulder as they looked at her computer screen. They needed to figure out how the blow-in cards—the annoying cards readers would mail in to subscribe—would look.

"I hate that we have to do these," Liza said.

"I'm sorry," he replied. "One day we'll have a marketing

department that'll take care of them, and you can spend all your time on the edit, but—"

"No," she said, noticing that he had the nicest hands, with blondish hair that tapered from the wrist up to the pinkie. "I mean, I hate that we have to use them at all." She pulled her hair back over her left ear.

He turned his head and smiled at her. "We could just print a small 800 number on the contents page, but that might be a little too discreet."

"What's wrong with discretion?"

Did he blush? She couldn't tell. She wasn't trying to be flirty at all—she simply happened to think the world could afford to be a bit more subtle. "Nothing," he said. "But it's less impressive in a salesman, which is what I essentially have to be."

"And you're doing a marvelous job," she said, turning back to the screen.

Chapter 54

Liza, Veronica, and Sam ordered sushi into the offices and were curled up on Sam's couch, eating off the newly delivered coffee table. Outside, barges were passing by—a truly beautiful scene as far as beautiful scenes went in New York, as long as the windows were shut so the smell from the meat packers didn't come wafting in at the first shift in the breeze.

Liza wrinkled her nose. "I think the couch has become infused with the smell of dead cow," she said. "But maybe it's just the excuse I need to switch to a macrobiotic diet."

"You are such a snob!" Veronica popped another piece of tuna in her mouth. "If you think the smell here is bad, you should move out of Sam's for a night and come to my house."

"And I'm going to have to ask you to move out if you switch to a macrobiotic diet anyway," Sam said. "That stuff is so disgusting."

"Gwyneth Paltrow swears by it," Liza said defensively.

"Yeah," Veronica cut in, "but she swore by Ben Affleck, too, and look where that got her."

"Um, he's gorgeous!" Sam and Liza said together.

"So not," Veronica said with a grimace. "He's way too cool for school. If you want gorgeous, may I suggest that you walk down the hall to where the interns are sitting? The tall, Columbia grad student?"

"Two problems," Liza said. "First of all, he's ten years old. Second of all, he looks like he hasn't had a bath since his mother got him out of diapers."

"Hmm," Veronica said, smacking her lips, "I used to love 'em like that. The dirty young ones are always the most adventurous. Obviously that's something you'll never tell Dael. When you meet him. Which I hope is soon." She sighed. "Then again, I'm not sure I'll be seeing him soon." She told them how Dael had suddenly become hard to reach. His cell phone would ring, so it was definitely on, but he wouldn't answer.

Liza spoke first. "Do you think he's giving you the brush-off?"

She sighed. "I don't know. I honestly don't think it's some-one else."

Sam put her hand on Veronica's arm. "How long has it been since you spoke to him?"

Veronica sighed again. "Three days." Sam and Liza couldn't hide their giggling. "What? I know it's not long, but we're in a crucial period! And three days seems like forever!" They laughed harder.

"We're sorry, sweetie, and you're right," Sam said. "And anyway, you shouldn't listen to me. I'm never allowed to speak to another man again." She pointed to the list of rules.

"Yeah, I noticed that but wasn't sure what to say," Veronica said. "It seems kind of . . . fatalistic."

Liza laughed. "Believe me, honey, a few more years of men under your belt, and you'll be begging for a Xerox." Veronica laughed.

All this talk about men was making Sam want to talk about—well, anything else. "Hey, Liza, when do you think we can see some cover options?"

Liza groaned. "Work, work, work, that's all you ever think about."

Liza and Veronica stood and started cleaning up the lunch. "I'd actually like to get you the first designs later this week, if that's alright."

"Perfect," Veronica said. "I should have the photos in by then—the shoot is tomorrow."

Sam's phone rang just as the women exited. "Hello?"

"Hey, Sam, it's me. Jack."

Sam sat down, stunned. She looked up at the list of rules. She hoped she wasn't going to have to resort to the last one. That would be a real bummer.

"Hi! It's good to hear your voice." And it *was* good to hear his voice.

"I would have thought a fancy-pants editor like you would have some assistant answering your phone," Jack continued. He sounded so . . . friendly.

"I still can't quite get used to the whole gig," Sam admitted, hearing herself sounding—and feeling—as comfortable relating the daily details of her life to him as ever. "Tom and Trevor have a great assistant who, if she didn't scare me so much, they'd be happy to share, but I'm still hung up on my old ways, I guess."

"That's too bad."

Sam's stomach tightened. She hadn't meant anything by it. Had he?

"So," she said quickly, "what's up?"

"I have to go the Daytime Emmys next week, and I was wondering if you might want to be my date. A couple stories I did were nominated, so I've got to go."

Her? He wanted to know if she would go with him? Why?

"That's great . . ." Sam said slowly.

"You don't sound too happy for me."

"Oh, Jack, you so deserve this!" Sam said immediately. *And so much more,* she wanted to add. "Congratulations."

"Not so fast," Jack said. "I still haven't gotten them. But it would give us an excuse to wear black tie and eat really bad hotel food."

"When is it?" Sam opened her Filofax.

"Next Tuesday."

"Shit." The Relais & Chateaux people were coming to

town, and Sam had a meeting with them. It was important not only to hear what they were pitching, but to pitch the magazine to them, as well, since they'd be perfect advertisers. It was bad enough she was thinking about going out with a man so soon after swearing them off, but she wasn't about to cancel a work appointment just to screw up her life even more than she already had. Sam told Jack about the conflict.

"Well, how long do you think it will last?"

"We're meeting at 6:30 at the Peninsula, so I'd say an hour."

"Perfect! Just do one of your Superwoman tricks, change in the bathroom, and come meet me when you're done. The only thing you'll have missed is the first inedible course."

"All right," Sam said slowly. "That sounds really nice."

"Good."

"So I'll see you next week."

"Um, Jack?"

"Yes?"

But Sam changed her mind. Whatever course he wanted the evening to take—even if he planned to humiliate her right back, or yell at her—that was a risk she was willing to take. And she should apologize again in person, not over the phone.

"Never mind. I can't wait."

Sam hung up and let out a little whoop. Was it possible she might have a second chance to see how she felt about him? Well, it sure beat nothing.

Sam hung up and immediately called Liza. "You know how you were going to tattoo rule No. 5 on my ass?" she said when Liza picked up. "Would you mind designing that for me this week, too?"

Chapter 55

At about ten o'clock, Andrew and Tom walked up to the Red Cat to get something to eat.

"No more expensed dinners, at least for a while," said Andrew.

"Excuse me? The publisher is my brother! Anyway, this one's on *Profit.* I still have a few months there. Let's milk the monster!"

They sat at the bar, as usual. Andrew ordered a gin and tonic (you knew it was officially summer when . . .). Tom, however, asked for a Manhattan.

"Fancy!" said Andrew.

"I'm tired of drinking vodka," he said. "It's for coeds. And scotch seems so pretentious. Like I give a shit if it came from one barrel, or from Scotland, or was aged in the oak tree that Robert Burns sat under as a wee child."

They sat for a few minutes, not talking, dipping into the bowl of radishes and sprinkling a bit of the sea salt on them. "What are we doing?" Tom asked.

"Sitting at a bar, eating radishes."

"Right. Aren't you freaked out about this *Bite* thing?"

Andrew didn't answer for a second. "No, I'm not. This is a lot of fun for me, and I'm taking it very seriously, but it's different for me. I don't need the money like you do, and I can go back to business proper and no one will ever even ask me about this. It's a chance to do something different, for which I'm grateful, but I don't really have anything on the line. God, that must sound cavalier."

"No, it doesn't. Well, yes it does. But it's okay. I guess I need everything to be on the line to do it at all."

More radishes. "What's up with Robbie and Lachlan?"

"Have you heard anything? Have they run off together?" They laughed. "Though that would make sense."

"What happened?"

"I don't know. I like Robbie, but not enough, so I ended it. There isn't much more to it than that." He bummed a cigarette from Tom, a rare occurrence, and they stepped outside. "My turn. You never said what happened with Justin."

A light went on in Tom's head. Something had felt different all day, and that was it: He was officially over Justin. He wasn't clooney for Justin, not for anyone. He told Andrew about the dinner, and couldn't blame Andrew for not believing him. But he was as sure of it as of anything. That part of his life was over. And it felt for the first time like they could be friends.

The rest of the meal was uneventful—although there was one great moment when a woman poked her head inside the restaurant and yelled out, "Do you allow dogs in here?"

"Honey," Andrew said under his breath, "you're not that ugly." Tom could have hugged him.

On the way home, Tom was walking on air. The moon was full, the air was sweet, the world was alive. He felt almost as if he was in love; how ironic that it was the opposite. *Welcome back,* he thought to himself. *It's fucking great to be here.*

Sam was tearing through her closet, looking for something, anything, she could wear to the Emmys next week.

Jennifer, lying prone on the bed with her head propped on a pillow, looked up. "Are you actually thinking you have a chance with him?"

"I don't know," Sam said, "and if I do, I don't even know that I want it. But I *do* know that if I'm not dressed to kill I won't have a shot in hell at either of those things. Now could you *please* help me?"

Jennifer rolled over and flipped herself around in a motion that Sam made a note to herself to remember. How come some people just seemed to know everything about sex? It's like there was a high school elective she had missed because she was busy taking advanced placement English.

"Okay. You want to look sexy but not trampy. Then again, it is the Emmys, and the daytime ones to boot, and not the Oscars. So it's not that big a deal. But it's Jack, so it is a big deal. But you can't have it look like it's a big deal."

Sam rolled her eyes. "I asked for *help.*"

"No question about it," Jen said. "It's got to be Versace."

"What a fabulous idea!" Sam said with all the sarcasm she knew how to muster. "I'll just ring up Donatella tomorrow and have her send something over. No, I know, I'll just call her right now on her cell. 'Hi, Donatella! It's Sam. Listen, I need something precious for next week and you're the only one who can help me . . .' "

Jennifer crawled back on the bed, supine this time. "Drop it, Sam, and pull your head out of your ass. You're the editor of what is soon to be a major magazine. You are finally in a position"—and with that she lifted her legs in the air and pinned her ankles behind her head—"to, yes, call Versace and order something in."

Sam burst out giggling. "I am, aren't I? Holy shit!"

Chapter 56

When Tom agreed to stay on at *Profit* for three months, he forgot the cardinal rule of giving notice: never give more than two weeks. Once the others got past the shock of you leaving, you began to smell like yesterday's trash.

He moped around his office, checking his email every thirty seconds. He had come in way too early for his meeting with Chester, and had nothing to do. The lineups for the next three issues were in good shape, the stories assigned, the photography in the works. He called Ethan.

"I'm bored."

"What time's your meeting?"

"Three."

"Come by. I'm killing time waiting for galleys."

Tom and Ethan hadn't been spending so much time together, mostly because Tom hadn't been around. But it wasn't so long that Tom didn't notice the band on Ethan's right ring finger.

"Wait. Stop." He pointed. "What is that?"

"Patrick gave it to me." Patrick was a guy Ethan had mentioned what seemed like months ago; Tom had no idea it had gotten serious. Back then, they called him "the Asian" if only to keep him straight from the two other men Ethan was seeing.

"Mazel tov! Did you give him one?"

"I did."

"When's the commitment ceremony?" Ethan threw a pen at Tom. They had long decided that if the other had a commitment ceremony he would have to be shot, preferably before the ceremony but during was acceptable too. Really, once you've broken the big rule—sleeping with men—why bother with the little rules of society, like getting married?

"No ceremony, obviously," Ethan said. "It's just something we wanted to do."

"I think it's nice," Tom said. "Really. I'm thrilled for you. But I'm embarrassed that I haven't ever met the man you're going steady with."

"Well, you've been busy."

Tom wasn't sure if the statement was loaded or not. He figured it probably was, and had to choose: acknowledge it and risk a big discussion, which he did not want ever but especially right then, or let it go and risk being even less thoughtful. He took the middle road. "I have, I have," he said. "Too busy, obviously to keep up with the lives of my friends, and I'm sorry." Maybe that would be enough. No, wait—it wasn't. "And let's figure out when we can all go out."

Tom then went upstairs to see Chester, who in the months since he'd been promoted upstairs had freaked out everyone at Worldwide Media by moving anyone he wanted to anywhere he wanted. Worldwide had always been a place where things moved slowly, if at all. Chester hadn't just shaken it up—he'd shaken it up and let it fizz all over. Naturally, with all the chess moves came an aura of invincibility. His assistant waved Tom right in.

"Hello, Sanders," he said. Chester was looking unnervingly thin, perhaps even gaunt. And yet he still filled the room. His pinstriped suit made Tom think that perhaps he should have dressed up a little for this meeting, even if he was leaving the company.

"Hello. That's a beautiful tie."

"Thanks," Chester said, motioning toward the sofa. "You can borrow it sometime." Tom had the good sense to laugh. If he knew one thing about Chester it was that Chester hated weakness, and if he found it in you he'd go after it. "I hear you're moving on."

"Indeed. To what, I'm not sure."

"I hope you won't be offended when I say I don't believe you. I hired you at *Profit* because I liked your talent, sure, but even more because I liked your ambition. Most people only want the job they're interviewing for. You clearly wanted more."

"I think you're probably right," Tom said.

"Yes," he said. "I am. But I didn't call you up here to confirm what I already know. I wish you luck, Sanders, but I have to tell you, I think you're going to need it. I probably shouldn't even say this, but I feel an obligation. We're starting a magazine similar to your *Bite,* at least as far as I can tell. Ways for cool people of all ages to spend their time and money in the pursuit of a good time. I can't tell you much more, but I wanted you to hear it from me, and I also wanted you to hear from me that I can assure you the idea came about long before we heard of your magazine."

Tom couldn't move. They didn't stand a chance against Worldwide Media. *Shit,* he thought to himself. *Shit, shit, shit, shit, shit, shit, shit.* And then: *I must call Sam.*

But first: "Who's working on it?"

"The details don't matter, Sanders."

"When's it launching?"

"I'm afraid that's an internal issue."

Tom got the hint. Chester had done him one favor by telling him, now get out. "I can't say I'm thrilled," Tom said, standing up. "But I appreciate your being forthright with me. And if nothing else, I'm glad I had the opportunity to thank you in person for hiring me at *Profit.* It was an amazing ride."

Chester, who had remained seated, smoothed out the fabric of his pants. "Sanders," he said, "I love being flattered. But it doesn't suit you at all. Now go. And good luck."

"Thanks," Tom said, heading for the door. He turned and gave Chester a smile. "You too."

He went straight to the lobby to buy cigarettes. He had to tell Sam, but how? And when to tell Trevor? Better to tell Sam and let her decide whether to tell Trevor. Not to mention everyone else.

"Have I told you how much I love answering the phone, *'Bite!'* "

Tom told her to shut her door. Then he told her not to scream. Then he told her. She screamed. "Now you see why I told you to shut the door." He could hear someone asking from the hall if Sam was okay.

"Just a particularly good epiphany!" she said with false gaiety. "You know me! Whoo-hoo!" She came back to Tom. "What the fuck?"

"I know! How could this happen? What do we do?" They resolved to meet at Zinc Bar in thirty minutes.

Settling at least one issue, Sam brought Trevor, who looked like he had seen a ghost—a ghost with a $50 billion market cap. They chewed their nails, pulled at their hair, did everything but bang their heads against the wall.

"What are we going to do?"

"How can we even compete with them, let alone beat them?"

"Is it really possible they didn't steal the idea?"

"How is it possible everyone knows about us and we don't know anything about this?"

"These are questions without answers," Trevor said.

Tom sipped his drink. *We can't know what we're up against unless we know who's working on it.* But how to find that out? He was remarkably unconnected to anyone at the corporate level at Worldwide Media. *There must be some way to find out . . . Wait. Maybe . . .*

"Seduction," he said. "So far as I can tell, it's the only way."

"I thought Chester was straight," said Trevor.

"Oh God," said Tom. "Not him." And then he went on, in a fairly roundabout way, to outline his plan. As at most places he'd worked, the tech support guys at *Profit* were social misfits, having spent way too much time reading science fiction and playing Dungeons & Dragons or whatever the computerized equivalent was. But there was one, Billy, who tended to give Tom long, soulful looks whenever they ran into each other in the hall—or worse, in the bathroom. And at the last Christmas party, he had spent far too much time dancing behind Tom, bumping into him too many times to be ruled accidental. It had been a while since Tom had seduced anyone, but he figured he was already halfway there with Billy. "And I think I can get him to poke around the email until we find out who's behind their magazine."

Sam sat with her mouth dropped to the floor. "You've got to be kidding," she said. "I mean I don't doubt that you can get him in the sack—most tech guys, let's face it, don't get laid that often. But in my experience they tend to be a fairly moral bunch. They believe things like the Internet work because there are rules that everyone obeys. It's some sort of socialist etiquette."

Trevor agreed. "Points for effort, for sure. And it's great you'd whore yourself out for the cause." He drained his glass. "Though I never thought I'd think of my brother as a whore. But I'm not sure how you'll get from here to there, if you catch *el drifto mio.*"

Tom couldn't explain. He recognized something in Billy's eyes. "I'm not saying he's going to give it up that easy," Tom said. "But trust me. Ultimately, the kid's a goner."

"What does it say about us," asked Sam, "that we have never even questioned whether it was right or wrong, but only whether it would work?"

The next day, Tom went into *Profit* with more motivation than he'd felt in months. He quickly disabled his email and dialed the tech hotline—then hung up when he realized there was no guarantee Billy would answer the call. He walked over to their communal office, and poked his head in. Billy and one of the other guys—Jed?—were arguing the merits of the new Moby album. "Howdy," Tom said, getting an immediate blush from Billy. Staring only at his quarry, he said, "My email is broken. Can one of you help me?"

"You're supposed to call the hotline," said Jed.

Tom had learned back at school down south that the best way to get people to do what you want was to affect a slight twang. "Don't you all like visitors?"

"I'll help," Billy said. "Rules are made to be broken, right?"

Rules and beds, Tom thought, but managed to stop himself from saying it. *Slow down,* he thought. *Rome wasn't deflowered in a day.*

To: Samantha@bite.com, Trevor@bite.com
From: Tom_sanders@profit.com
Subject: Phase one
the Eagle has, if not landed, made preparations. we're grabbing a beer tonight.

Sam's reply:

To: Tom_sanders@profit.com
From: Samantha@bite.com
Re: Phase one
Page Sex! Which hotshot magazine editor isn't just starting a magazine—he's also starting a new career as a whore?

Tom put in a call to R.J. "I bought a new cock ring," was the first thing out of R.J.'s mouth.

"How special."

"It is. Made to order. I went down to the Leatherman and dropped trou, and the guy took a tape measure and wrapped it around my cock and balls. Do you want to know my measurements?"

"No."

"Prude. Anyway, it's lovely. I wore it to work." R.J. was only moonlighting as the sex columnist, and Tom feared the line between his two jobs would blur.

"What? Didn't you learn anything from the butt-plug incident?"

"I did think about that when I walked across the marble floor of our lobby"—they paused a second to imagine the clang of metal on marble—"but to be honest it only turned me on more."

It never ceased to amaze Tom that he could still be shocked—by R.J., no less.

R.J. yawned. "Isn't your birthday coming up?"

"Don't you dare," Tom said. "And anyway, I don't believe in man jewelry. Now listen . . ." He explained his plan to R.J. without getting too much into the why—and R.J. didn't ask—then quizzed him for tips.

Tom immediately saw how R.J. might just be brilliant at his day job, if indeed he put his mind to it the way he put it toward sex. "First, alcohol. But you seem to have that covered. Second, don't forget to look into his eyes—a lot. You're not very good at that, you know—and I don't *think* you even want to sleep with me. Then, get caught looking at his crotch, or at least his chest, if you can't handle going further south. Compliment him. Then, when you say something funny—or even better, when *he* says something funny, touch him. It doesn't matter where—the leg, the arm, anywhere. It's crucial.

The way we, as animals, communicate. Most guys want to give in."

"How do I make sure to get the information I need?"

"You either date him for weeks, then spring it on him—"

"No time."

"Or you just spring it on him."

"So it's like this: 'Here's your beer, Billy. You have such pretty eyes. Ha!'—pat the leg—'You're so funny. Do you want to go home with me? Great, but first I need your help.' "

"His name is Billy?"

"Yep."

Tom could hear R.J. typing. "Is his last name Becker, Thompson, or Chu?"

"Nope."

"Haven't done him then, unless he gave me a fake name."

Tom was shocked again. "You have a *database?*"

"It's called iTrick. It's fabulous! I'll send you the link!"

Chapter 57

"I think we can win if we get out first."

Mao and Trevor sat in Trevor's office, trying to come up with a plan on how to announce *Bite.* Actually, the plan was for Trevor to brainstorm ideas and Mao to write them down, but she wasn't playing along. In fact, Trevor noticed, she wasn't even taking notes.

"Did you get that?" she asked.

"Oh, yeah. Sure." He was going to have to figure out a way to remind her that she was his assistant and not his partner, but maybe not until after she was done brainstorming. He had to hand it to her: she was good.

"From the top," she said. "We give a small interview to Keith Kelly at the *Post,* because everyone in the media reads him and if we don't give him something exclusive he'll get pissy. Then we'll follow it with a big interview to the *Times,* because they don't mind if they're not first, and they're better than the *Wall Street Journal* because half of New York won't read a paper without pictures."

"And the *Observer?*" Trevor asked.

"I thought you got that down," she said, smiling. "Sorry. They don't matter, not really. If it's not about how things are going wrong, they don't care and won't give it big play. If we can get the MTV show moving, we can leak it to them: they'll make it page one, for sure."

"Tell me again how you know all this," said Trevor.

"We Asians are wily," she replied. "Everyone knows that."

He knew she was mocking the stereotype, but wasn't sure she wasn't wily just the same. "Are you angling for my job?"

"Absolutely," she said. "But not until you're ready to give it to me."

Looking to clear his head, Trevor took a walk. This sucked. Starting a magazine was one thing—as seriously as he took it, he felt like it was manageable. But going up against Worldwide Media . . . *Oy.*

"Ha!" he said. "I must be a New Yorker if I'm thinking in Yiddish." He walked down Hudson Street, hands in pockets. Did Tom really think he could solve the problem by sleeping with a tech guy? One moment he thought he understood his younger brother, and the next moment Tom was whoring himself out. While he hoped his mother was in heaven, he hoped even more she was doing something right now besides watching what her sons were up to.

And it had been going so well. Tom and Sam seemed clear on their editorial mission, Mao was a force of nature, the few pictures Veronica had allowed him to see were really fun, and Liza . . . He smiled. He really liked Liza. Did he *like* Liza? Liza was hot, no doubt. When she wore jeans it was all he could do not to follow her ass down the hall, like a puppy. But she was total rebound material, and he didn't need that right now—or ever, really. Anyway, it wasn't like she liked him. Right? It was hard to tell with her.

He poked into Myers of Keswick, a store that sells all kinds of British food. She had mentioned that she loved British Kit-Kats; he didn't know there was a difference, but she swore that the chocolate was better than in American ones. He picked one up. Wait. Would it be weird? He didn't want to be the creepy office guy hitting on the new divorcée. He put it down.

He left the store, and headed back to the office. *I should have bought it,* he thought. *It would have been the nice thing to do.* And if she took it the wrong way, well, that was her problem. He could always deny it. But did he want to?

As he entered the *Bite* building, he resolved to buy her something, something friendly. What harm could it do?

Tom and Billy sat on bar stools against the wall at Chase, a midtown gay bar named after the bank in the hope that young homos might actually think that financial types would show up. It reminded Tom of when he was twenty-two, and how he figured he'd have years to find a rich husband. It was one of his biggest regrets that he hadn't worked harder at that. Money couldn't buy happiness, but it could certainly rent it.

Back to the matter at hand. Billy was cute, really: like a cross between an American Indian and a Long Island Jew. Thick black hair down to his shoulders, a sturdy build . . . and yet something about him didn't grab Tom's attention. They had gotten along well enough on the walk to the bar—Tom had learned to be able to talk to anybody, even the most reticent of techsters—but he wasn't sure he would indeed be able to seal the deal. *Think of England,* he muttered to himself.

Or not. "What?" Billy asked.

"Nothing. You have beautiful hair."

"Er, thanks."

It was going to be awfully hard to get this moving if Billy didn't start talking soon. Tom really didn't relish the alternative, which was waiting until Billy was good and drunk—at which point he might not be able to do the necessary email work. "Do you like *Profit?*" he asked.

"It's fine."

"The guys you work with?"

"What about them?"

"Do you like them?"

"Sure."

Jesus. Tom was going to lose his mind. Billy had hardly

spoken, and yet he still seemed antsy. Time for Plan B. "Do you want another beer? I'm going to—"

"No." Billy grabbed Tom's arm and forcibly pulled him back down to the banquette. "Listen. I like you, I've liked you for a while. I guess you knew that. But you don't like me, not really. I get that. So why are we here? I can handle a lot of things, but not bullshit."

"What do you mean? I just thought it would—"

"Jesus Christ. You mean to tell me that after two years of not paying me any attention you've finally seen the light? That's not the way it works, Tom, and we both know it. If you're not in touch with why you've invited me here, then whatever. But if you know and won't tell me, I'm out of here."

Tom weighed his options. "I need your help."

"What?"

Tom explained. The magazine he was starting, that Worldwide Media was doing something similar, that he needed to know who was working on it.

"So you thought you'd seduce me? And then I'd just hand you the keys to the email and let you poke around? Are you nuts? It's like a bad novel."

Tom had to laugh. "My whole life is like a bad novel," he said. "It's like there is a God, and it's Jacqueline Susann."

That got Billy going: He loved Jackie Susann, had read *The Love Machine* at way too early an age. Tom had always preferred *Valley of the Dolls,* even if it was a cliché, or maybe *Once Is Not Enough*. Either way, they let the email snooping idea go away. They compared the different books they had read to learn about sex—Sidney Sheldon, Harold Robbins—and how little they had in common with reality. Sex in real life, Billy pointed out, was usually so much weirder, and certainly funnier.

"Tell me about it!" Tom said, and went on to tell the story of R.J.'s prayer boy, much to Billy's amusement.

"No wonder you're a writer," he said. "You tell a really funny story."

Tom blushed a little; it was a point of pride for him that he considered himself funny, and he wondered if other people agreed. A boyfriend had once told him he "tried too hard," which pretty much ended the relationship right there. "Shucks," he said.

Billy stood up. "Should we have one more?" he asked, touching Tom gently on the lower shoulder. "I'll buy."

"Why not?" said Tom. "I promise, I'm over the email thing."

"Don't sweat it," he said. "I'm honored, in a stupid sort of way." He gave Tom a smile. "And a little disappointed I didn't just give in."

When Billy came back, Tom had given it some thought. Maybe he should sleep with Billy. Not because he thought he'd get info out of him, but because he'd probably enjoy it. Billy was looking more and more like he'd be a good roll in the hay. And let's face it: Tom hadn't had one of those since his air conditioner broke. "Listen to this story," he said, trying to maintain eye contact with Billy, but it was hard—so hard—when all he wanted to do was look down at Billy's hand, which had come to rest ever so lightly on Tom's thigh.

Beer is for children, thought Tom upon waking up in Billy's bed. The older he'd gotten the less he'd been able to drink of it. Then again, it could be the lack of sleep: Billy sure could get it on. Tom felt a twinge of guilt—he knew better than to sleep with someone he worked with, even if it wasn't for long—and dreaded having to tell Sam and Trevor that he'd slept with Billy but not persuaded him to help them. *Oy,* he thought.

Billy came in from the shower, towel wrapped around his waist, wet hair pulled back into a short ponytail. Who knew he was going to have such a body? Tom was old enough to remember when the geekier guys were the ones least likely to work out; times had obviously changed. He had thought Billy would be a little porky, what with the oversized clothes he tended to wear. But he wasn't, he was perfectly meaty. Maybe that was when you truly became old, Tom thought: when you started wearing clothes that fit because you really have to make the most of every asset.

"I don't drink coffee," Billy said. "But I do have a gift certificate to Starbucks that I can give you."

"You keep them for your tricks?"

"Just the special ones," he said, leaning down for a kiss.

Tom got up, accepted the gift certificate—tacky, he figured, but rather efficient—and started to put his clothes on.

"I should tell you something," Billy said as he pulled on his underwear.

"You really do drink coffee?"

Billy laughed. "Nope. But I know . . . Shit, I don't want to be the one who tells you this." He paused. "I know who's behind Worldwide's magazine."

Tom stopped in the middle of tying his shoe, and looked up. "Are you going to tell me?"

"I guess I am. My friend Patrick is dating Ethan, and it's all Ethan can talk about, apparently—though apparently not to you. He's leaving *Profit* in a few months to head it up full-time."

"Are you positive?"

"You really should have asked me before you came home with me."

"Bad joke, Billy, and bad timing. Are you serious?"

"Yep."

"When's it coming out?"

Billy used his fingers to zip his lips.

"But Ethan's leaving *Profit* in a few months?"

Billy unzipped his lips and nodded.

"I'm sorry," Tom said, standing up. "But I have to go. Like right now. I had a lot of fun"—and he tried to give Billy a smile, but all Billy could see was the anger—"and I thank you for telling me. But I have to go. Like right now." He walked out the door, tripped over his shoelace in the hall, said "fucking asshole" about fifty times, then headed for the subway. But first he went to Starbucks and redeemed his gift certificate. He'd need caffeine if he was going to make that motherfucker pay.

Chapter 58

Tom seethed all the way to *Bite*'s offices, seethed up the stairs, and sat in his office for five minutes, seething. Then he called Sam, and told her to get her ass in his office pronto.

She threw herself on his sofa. "If you think you can talk to me like that when we're not even sleeping together, you can just—"

"It's Ethan. Ethan's the one behind Worldwide's magazine."

What followed was one of those wordless conversations. With her eyes, Sam basically said, "What the fuck?" To which Tom replied, "I know, I can't believe it." Sam: "How could he?" Tom: "I don't know." Sam: "I thought you were friends." Tom: "I thought so too." Sam: "What are we going to do?" Tom: "I don't know."

Then, Sam, aloud: "Kill him?"

Tom tended, when disappointed by someone, to simply want to note his disgust and move on. Why waste time pointing out how someone had wronged you, when you knew in your heart you weren't going to have anything to do with him ever again? And yet, he knew this was different: he was going to have to confront Ethan, or at least the problem. "I guess I should call Trevor," Tom said, and did just that.

"It all makes sense, now," Sam said. "Why he wanted you to take the *Times* job, why Chester wouldn't tell you who it was, and why Chester really wanted you to believe they had already had the idea before you mentioned yours."

Trevor entered, and they briefed him. "Ethan?" was all he could say.

"What I don't get," Tom said, "besides why on earth Ethan would mess with me when he knows how vicious I can be, if pushed, is why, if they did have the idea, and drafted Ethan to work on it, well, why didn't they draft me? It has so much more with what I do than what he does. He's never done anything lifestyle-related!"

Trevor sat on that for a minute. "I understand," he said. "But you have to move on. We have to move on. Be glad you got out: If they didn't think you were right for that, what would they have thought you were right for? And we have to do something. Ethan deserves to pay, even if he didn't steal our idea. Which I'm not sure I believe."

"I need to think about something else for a few minutes," Tom said. "How's the magazine coming?"

Sam was more than happy to detail their progress. Laura had delivered her barefoot travel copy, Brian was leaving that day for the U.S. Open of mini golf, the shoot for R.J.'s first sex column was taking place Monday—with R.J. dressed as Casanova—and the Advice Squad was basically done, but Sam was having the interns keep going, because if they got better stuff they'd happily sub it in.

"I have to say," Tom said, "it sounds good."

"I know! I still can't believe it. I mean—"

"When do you think Worldwide's magazine comes out?" Trevor asked.

"Can you ask Billy? And by the way, you were right—you got him just like you said you would."

"Not exactly. *He* seduced *me*—"

"Like that's so hard!" Trevor winked at Sam.

"—and he won't tell me anything else. I mean, we had fun fooling around, but he already regrets telling me as much as he did."

"Speaking of which," said Sam, "what do we do?" They sat and stewed. Finally, they came up with a plan—which was, basically, to come up with a plan.

"I'm tired of coming up with plans," Tom said. "I just want to work."

"Welcome to management," Trevor said.

The plan was this: Get together the smartest, most manipulative people they knew, explain the situation—leaving out the Billy part, at Tom's insistence—and see what they could come up with. Tom's feeling was that this wasn't something he, Sam, and Trevor could figure out on their own. They needed a cabal. A machine of malicious intent. They needed to essentially shut down the competition before it even had a chance to start. If that meant totally screwing over someone he had only yesterday considered a good friend, so be it.

They drew up a list: Sam, Tom, Trevor, and Andrew, Liza and Veronica, Mao, obviously, R.J., and Jennifer. "And I want to invite Justin," Tom said.

Sam looked askance at him. "Are you sure?"

"Absolutely. Trust me, I'm over him. And it might help to have a lawyer around."

"I wish I could invite Jack," she said.

"Wait, he's a lawyer?" Tom asked.

Sam looked up, suddenly snapping back. "What? No, he's a producer."

"So why did you say you wanted him around?"

"God, I did, didn't I?" Sam said, blushing. "That's so weird. I guess it's that I just really trust him, that's all."

Tom raised his eyebrows.

"I don't know," Sam said, "But for some reason, that's meaning more and more to me, at the end of the day. Trust may be more important than anything. And I have to admit," she said, taking a deep breath of courage, "now that I can't have him, Jack seems like the greatest mistake I . . . never . . . made."

Tom looked at her softly. She really had seemed to grow up lately. He wondered if the same could be said of him.

Chapter 59

Sam sat on the rooftop bar of the Peninsula, overlooking midtown, and glanced discreetly at her watch. It was already 8:15, and the two Relais & Chateaux people were talking to her about a new property they had opened in the Loire valley, and wondering if she would like to come for a week in July to spend some time there.

"That sounds absolutely wonderful," said Sam. "We're still figuring out what the magazine's policy is going to be in terms of accepting comp rates, but let me talk about it with my partner. I'm sure we can work something out—even if it's at a media rate."

The reps seemed pleased with that, and Sam decided it was better to leave with them pleased than risk any further conversation. Well, that, and she was running hideously late. "I'm sorry to do this, but I have to run—I have a previously scheduled engagement."

They said their good-byes, and Sam headed for the bathroom. "Previously scheduled engagement?" she muttered to herself as she made a run for it. "I'm starting to sound like my mother."

Although Sam's mother had probably never changed for a black-tie event in the bathroom. For good reason—she was having a terrible time trying to rip off her suit and put on the Versace gown that *Bite* had managed to borrow for her for the evening. She hadn't tried it on—hell, she hadn't even seen it. She'd just had Mao throw it in her bag as she had run out the door.

"Jesus," Sam said. The dress was a dress in name only, with

barely enough material to cover a two-year-old. It was a stunning deep eggplant, with a halter top and a neckline that plunged to her navel. The slits on the side rose to the top of Sam's thigh. Why had she stopped taking yoga classes? And why had she never learned how to tape her breasts? This was just embarrassing. Sam shoved her suit back in her bag and exited the stall. She looked at herself in the mirror. This was just not going to succeed—not at a work function for Jack. The top was totally see-through, where there was any material at all, and her breasts were totally and completely visible. On top of which, Sam noted with a small twinge of dread, they were most definitely not where she left them six months ago.

Sam scurried to find her cell phone in the bottom of her bag. "Jennifer?" she sighed with relief when Jennifer picked up her cell phone. "I know this is a little last-minute, but I need you to teach me how to tape my breasts."

"What?"

"You heard me," Sam said, trying to not speak at more than a whisper. "You know, the J. Lo thing. I'm in trouble."

"Where are you?"

"The Peninsula. In the bathroom. Don't ask."

"Okay. You'll need to go to the concierge and ask to borrow some tape."

God bless Jennifer for not asking any questions. "Won't they know why I'm asking, when I walk up in this dress?"

"And your options would be what? Besides, I'm sure they've had to deal with far tawdrier things than imagining what it is you're doing with their tape."

"Right. Can you hang on while I go get it?"

"Absolutely."

Sam left her bag in the bathroom—if someone wanted to steal her sweaty suit, let them—and jogged as fast as she could on her Jimmy Choo stilettos across the lobby. This can't be pretty, she thought, feeling her breasts swing. "Hi," she said to the concierge, who, to her relief, was a woman. "Could I borrow your Scotch tape for a moment?"

The concierge handed it over, no questions asked.

"Got the tape," Sam said into the cell phone, running back to the bathroom.

"Good girl. Now, if you can do this and balance the phone at the same time, I want you to lean over so your breasts hang forward. Then, you're going to take the tape, and put it under your breast like underwire. Keep layering it, like three or four times, and go up as high as you need to so you're not totally exposed."

"Okay," Sam said, following Jennifer's directions. Sam looked over in horror when a woman walked into the bathroom and stared at her before heading for the stall. "Shit. Someone just walked in."

"Think of what a good story she'll have to tell her friends back in Boca Raton."

"Alright. You're right." Sam kept tearing off the tape and applying it to herself. Finally, she stood up and surveyed her work. Amazingly enough, it had done the trick.

"I can't believe it!" she whispered to Jennifer. "It actually worked! I'm perkier and definitely less see-through."

"Great! Oh, and Sam, I just have to warn you about one thing."

"What now?" Sam said, grabbing her bag and heading for the exit.

"It's really going to hurt coming off."

"Well, it will just keep me from even being tempted by the possibility of having anybody else do it for me," Sam said, handing the tape back to the concierge. "Thanks, honey. I owe you one."

The Emmys were a madhouse, but Sam was relieved that by getting there two hours late, she'd missed the arrivals.

Now, the paparazzi frenzy had died to a minimum—the photographers were standing lazily around, smoking cigarettes and waiting for someone famous to wander in. Much to Sam's surprise, a couple of photographers jumped to attention as she walked by.

"No, no," she laughed. "I promise you, I'm nobody."

"You're one of the hottest nobodies I've ever seen!" one photographer shot back.

"Thanks," Sam said, blushing. Praise Versace.

In the ballroom, three thousand people were sitting at banquet tables, chattering away while Ellen DeGeneres presented Merv Griffin with a lifetime achievement award. Amazingly, Sam found Jack's table quickly, and walked over. Jack looked up and—Sam had to smile—his mouth dropped. So much for his reserve.

"Sam," Jack said, standing as she approached and sat beside him. "You look simply amazing. I can't believe that dress. I can't believe you in that dress."

"Thank you," she said, feeling suddenly shy.

"Thank you for coming," Jack said, reaching under the table and squeezing her hand.

And in that moment, Sam finally understood that old cliché of what it felt like to think your heart was going to burst.

After the show—Jack lost—they went to the King Cole Bar at the St. Regis, and sat side by side on one of the burgundy leather banquettes. Sam had placed her duffle bag—still holding her suit from the bathroom change—between them. Then she ordered a Diet Coke.

Jack merely raised his eyebrows at both gestures, but once they had their drinks—a bourbon for him, she noted (no problem with self-restraint there)—he turned to her.

"What's with the defensive maneuvers? I promise I don't

mean any harm," he said gently, clinking his glass to hers.

"It's not you I'm worried about, Jack," Sam said. She had decided, when she accepted his drink offer, that she would be honest with him if he asked her any questions.

"What does that mean?" Jack fiddled with a cufflink. Man, was he handsome. She'd always known it as a fact, but she was usually too frantic running from somewhere and then trying to hurry him to bed to have really noticed before.

"I'm just really grateful that you're willing to see me after everything," Sam said slowly, "and if you're willing to give me a chance, even for an evening, I don't want to screw it up like I have in the past. I know I've been really thoughtless, and I don't want to muck things up by suddenly trying to turn this into a seduction just so I can feel more secure. Not that you'd have me," she added with a nervous laugh. (And not, she thought, that she'd actually do it—the Scotch tape was beginning to poke into her skin, and the feeling was the opposite of sexy. Still, she could always go downstairs to the bathroom and rip it off . . . No, she reminded herself. That was *not* what the plan was. Not anymore. And she had a Post-it tucked inside her wallet saying "Don't be an ass" if she needed affirmation. Which she wouldn't.)

"Actually," he said, "I've come to the conclusion that we probably can't be friends."

Sam felt disappointment move from her stomach up to her face. She blushed—not with embarrassment, but with sadness. She knew Jack wouldn't be able to make it this easy—not after what they'd been through together. Not after what she'd put him through.

"Oh," Sam managed to say. "I think I knew that in the back of my brain. Well," she continued, trying to put a little perkiness back in her voice so that the evening wasn't a total dismal failure. "Well, you can't blame a girl for hoping—anyone would be lucky to have you as a friend."

"But," Jack continued, "I wanted to talk to you about seeing if maybe we could be more than friends."

Sam looked around. Was she hallucinating? Was he talking to someone behind her? Was this his way of getting revenge?

"I think," he said, "that we've both spent a lot of time blaming you for this not going any further than it has. But the reality is, I've been just as frightened as you. At least you called me when you wanted to talk. But I've tended just to run away. So what I've been thinking about lately is that maybe we should both try to be brave and see this through. Maybe," he continued, taking a deep breath, "we both need to really try this. And if it doesn't work out, at least we gave it a shot."

Sam felt disoriented, like she was in a dream and the room or the cast of characters had just changed, in that seamless way where it all makes sense because you know, somewhere in the back of your mind, that it's alright because you're dreaming. But Sam was most definitely not dreaming—no dream would be punctuated by the feeling of tape beginning to tear off her side. She wanted to yell "Yes!" but she was still scared he might be joking.

"Why?" This is what came out of Sam's mouth. Screw it. She decided to roll with it. Hard to go wrong with such a simple question. Put it back in Jack's court, watch his face, try to breathe deeply and gather her wits before she had to say anything again. She wished she could call a time-out so she could run home, throw on jeans and a sweatshirt, and think about this some more. Instead, she rummaged for a cigarette and let Jack light it, both of them buying a moment or two.

Jack sighed. He took a deep sip of his bourbon, and then reached out to hold Sam's hand. Immediately, she (and her hand) began to sweat. Jack's hands had always been her downfall, and this was too much. She began to sweat so much, in fact, that she felt one piece of the tape around her right breast loosen and curl off.

Jack, on the other hand, was registering not the slightest flicker of anxiety. Sam looked longingly at his bourbon. Maybe that's why. She reached over with the hand he wasn't holding and drank quickly from his glass.

"Last month, when we weren't speaking, I went on vacation to Santorini."

So he had been away, Sam thought with a moment of relief. But then, she immediately imagined him in some perfect cliff-top villa overlooking the Aegean, drinking white wine with some fabulous woman who would never, ever have to tape her breasts, so high and mighty were they still. She forced herself back into the present and focused on looking at Jack. Not at his eyes—they made her stomach flit too much—but at his lips. Not that his lips weren't fabulous too. *Listen to him.*

"It was as amazing as it sounds, Sam, it really was," he said. "Except that I kept feeling like something was missing. That's why I sent you the flowers when I got back."

"You?" Sam couldn't believe it.

"Yes, me," Jack said with a smile. "I couldn't figure out what was wrong on the trip. I was having a good time, I was getting rest and reading good books, but something kept nagging at me. And then I realized—I know it's amazing it took me this long to realize—that what I was missing was you. It's not just the sex—" He held up his hand to cut her off as she opened her mouth to protest. "Although you and I both know two people have never had a more amazing sex life. It was your companionship. Because in between the sex, even though you or I would try to race out as fast as possible, we actually laughed a lot, and talked a lot, and had wonderful moments together. And I wondered if it wasn't time to see if we could actually make it work."

Sam definitely wasn't feeling good now. In fact, her sweat had turned cold. "But I was awful to you, Jack," she said. "I really was. And I see it, but—"

"But you'd have to change a little," Jack interrupted. He let out a laugh. "I'm not saying I want you to be a different person, because I really love you the way you are." *(Did he say love?* Sam wondered. *Where was her notepad?)* "But when it comes to your friends, there's no one more giving than you. It's just that—well, I've known you long enough to say it: You don't always take those traits into a relationship with a man."

Sam snorted. It was a welcome comic break for a moment, even if it was at her expense. "Try never," she said with a nod. "I definitely don't. I don't know whether I get scared, or more like terrified, but it's almost impossible for me to believe that someone could really love me at the end of the day—at least someone I'm sleeping with."

"That's something we both would really need to think about," Jack said with a nod. "And I don't know if you even want to try. I certainly don't know if it could work. But I do know that I'll regret not giving it a chance."

"Okay," Sam said weakly. The two of them looked at each other, and then were silent for a minute.

"So . . . okay, what?" Jack asked, squeezing her hand and actually looking nervous for the first time.

"Okay, as in yes," Sam said, a smile spreading across her face as she realized how happy saying that—and saying that to Jack—made her feel. "Okay, yes," she said again, this time more slowly.

Jack looked at her and raised his free hand to the back of her neck, slowly pulling her face toward his. When his lips touched hers, softly but insistently, she felt her body instinctively move toward him. Her body, if not her heart, knew how much she had missed him. And then, after a long, lingering kiss, that made her want to grab him right there, he gently pulled away. "What would you like to do now?" he asked seductively.

"Actually," Sam said, feeling clearer than she had in years, "what I'd like to do is go home."

Jack let out a laugh. "Wow—you really are determined to change."

"I really am," she said seriously, saying one more prayer for the unraveling state of affairs around her chest. "And now, if you'll walk me to a cab . . ."

"Oh, honey, that's not how it works," Jack said sweetly. "We're going to do this right. I shall drop you off at your house, kiss you chastely at the door, and then be on my way."

"And then what?" Sam couldn't help asking. It had been a long time since she'd dated properly. In fact, as she scrolled back through her head at her more memorable relationships, she wasn't sure if she ever had.

"Then," Jack said, leaning in closely so he could whisper in her ear, the feeling of his breath on her almost melting the last of her resolve, "you will sit by the phone and wait for me to call. And just when you have almost given up, and replayed the conversation eight thousand times in your head to figure out where, exactly, it is that you have gone wrong, I will call, and I will ask you out to dinner, and you—well, you . . ." Jack said, still an inch from her. "You will say yes."

"Okay," Sam said weakly.

"Okay, as in . . . ?" Jack's voice, still low, was unbelievably seductive and playful, all at the same time.

"Okay," Sam said quietly, with a deep breath. It was amazing how far a vocabulary limited to "okay" and "yes" could go.

And then Jack made a fateful move: He grabbed her back and slipped his hand along her side to pull her closer. As he embraced her, her knees grew weak, and she knew she was a goner. And then, as Jack's hand moved along her side, they both heard the sound of crinkling tape.

"What was that?" Jack asked.

It was just the break Sam needed to make a clean getaway. "Um, it must have been the lining of my dress," she said, slowly getting up and giving him a very sweet smile. "Shall we go?"

Chapter 60

The machine of malicious intent gathered in Tom's living room. He quickly detailed the situation, ignoring all interruptions and questions. He explained his relationship to Ethan, the extent to which they'd been screwed, even how he got the scoop—he hadn't wanted to, especially in front of Justin, but he figured the cabal needed to have all information at hand.

Jennifer summarized it neatly: "So what you're saying is that we need to completely ruin him."

"It appears so," Tom replied. "From what I've gathered"—he ignored the snickering—"Ethan's the main force behind Worldwide's magazine. If we can get them to doubt his ability, then maybe we have a chance to at least delay their launch."

"I can't believe Ethan would do this," said Veronica. "He's so . . . nice. He's one of the nicest people at *Profit.*"

"Maybe he's tired of being nice," said Trevor. "It happens. And anyway, it's not the point. He's fucked with us. We have to go after him."

They sat and looked at each other, realizing that they really had no idea how to work in a Machiavellian manner. They'd all been successful by being decent, hardworking people. Even in their love lives they were more or less upstanding. How do you suddenly switch gears?

"If Worldwide leans on us," said Trevor, "we're screwed. They can insist that newsstands and supermarkets shove *Bite* to the back of the racks. They can force us to use a minor distributor who doesn't have the reach we want."

"Maybe the fact that we haven't heard of it means it's not that far along," said Veronica.

"I don't know," said Tom. "If Worldwide wants to, it can be sneaky."

Justin stood up. "The crucial relationship here, from what I can tell, is between Ethan and Chester."

"Duh," said Mao.

Justin held up a hand to silence her. "Follow me for a second. We don't have the power to force them to stop their magazine, but we can come up with a wrench to throw into the works." Tom was loving the way Justin said "we"—he was over him, but still . . . "What if we found a way for Chester to question Ethan, to make him think Ethan's screwing up. Do we have anyone on the inside?"

Heads were shaking everywhere.

"I get it," said Trevor. "Mess with their lines of communication."

"Exactly," said Justin. He turned to Tom. "Can you get your tech lover to screw with the email?"

Tom winced. "Negative. The guy's got a moral streak as big as his . . . well, you know." When in doubt, retaliate.

Trevor pointed out that they absolutely had to get *Bite* out before Worldwide's magazine launched. Then he wondered if they couldn't try to poison the thing from the outside, through the press.

"Major backfire potential," said Mao. "And most of the media won't go after Worldwide because they want the option of working there someday."

Trevor looked down at his hands. "I hate to even broach the subject, but we could talk to them about a merger . . ."

"No!" screamed Sam. "Sorry. What I meant was, 'I'd really rather not.' Let's keep thinking—and drinking." She got up and went into the kitchen.

"I hope she doesn't lock herself in this time," whispered R.J.

The conversation splintered. Mao paced the room, wondering out loud if she knew anyone who would break Ethan's knees; Andrew said it wasn't in the budget. Veronica asked Jennifer to get on the PR grapevine and listen for news about Ethan's magazine. Trevor and Liza were whispering in a corner, and Justin peppered Tom with questions about Billy. Tom tried to take it like a man—this was what friends did, tease each other about their sex lives. R.J. went to the fridge to get more ice.

After a few minutes, it began to feel like a cocktail party—one with a dark undercurrent of revenge. And so, when Sam could be heard laughing maniacally from the kitchen, no one thought much of it. R.J. came out into the living room looking perplexed. "What?" said Tom.

"I was doing my impression of you, and she started laughing hysterically—"

"You do an impression of me?"

"Um, like since the day after I met you: 'All I do is tell rich people how to spend their money. I want to make it on my own.' "

"Get to the point, R.J." Tom was worried R.J. was about to mock his obsession with Justin.

"Anyway, then I did Ethan. You know, 'I want a boyfriend who doesn't want me because I look Latino. I want a Backstreet Boy . . .' And she just lost it."

Sam came out of the kitchen. "Is something wrong?" Trevor asked.

"Au contraire," she said, beaming. "Something is very, very right."

"Foxman, this is Chester. What about Post-its? They're brilliant. Do something on them."

It was R.J., doing an impression of Chester that would have had Sam and Tom fooled. Sam had called in a tape of

Chester on the Charlie Rose show, and R.J. had nailed the accent on the first try.

Sam giggled. "You know how I feel about Post-its. This just might work."

"It's going to have to," muttered Tom.

"But we need ideas that are absurd enough to have Chester think they're stupid, but plausible enough to get Ethan side-tracked." They huddled, and thought of things they hated: children's fashion, tips for organizing your closet, editor's letters.

"Foxman, this is Chester. I've decided I want to write the editor's letter for your first issue."

"Perfect!" squealed Tom and Sam.

"And let's get some children's fashion in there—it's highly significant this year."

"Bravo!"

Chester, they both knew, was famous within the company for leaving voice mails at odd hours. All they had to do was have R.J., as Chester, leave messages giving Ethan bad advice. By the time he figured out it wasn't Chester at all, they'd have at the very least bought some time. At best, Chester would think Ethan was a raving lunatic—and a terrible editor.

"Is this illegal?" R.J. asked.

"What do you care?" asked Tom back. This was no time for R.J. to develop a conscience. "Besides, no one will ever know it was you."

"Let's do it!" said Sam.

Tom dialed the number, and eventually the voice mail picked up. R.J. cleared his throat, Tom shut his eyes, and Sam said a little prayer.

Chapter 61

Liza was working from home—her new home, that is, trying to get used to the landscape of boxes and adjust to being alone in the apartment. She had finally busted out of Sam's apartment, and as hard as it was for both of them—she felt like all she did these days was break up with people—she couldn't resist this little Tribeca one-bedroom. She hadn't been alone since . . . God, she realized, she hadn't ever been alone. She'd either lived with roommates, or with Chandler, and then with Sam. No wonder she was a little freaked out.

Still, as she scrounged through a box in the kitchen and came up with the kettle, it felt remarkably liberating, with just a few twinges of fear. She felt like she was being kind to herself and taking things slowly—not slow enough to feel paralyzed, but being as thoughtful as she could.

She had gone out again with the widower she had met at the English language class, but ultimately decided they should just be friends. The last thing she needed right now was to become a stepmother, and as a full-time parent he was hardly up to a more casual relationship.

She supposed, however, that with the divorce behind her—the proceedings had been incredibly anticlimactic, and within the office she had merely smiled at Chandler and wished him well when the court date ended—it was time to begin to think about dating again. But *Bite* was taking so much of her energy, and she figured she was getting good practice at what it was like to be a single woman again—single, but totally safe. In fact, she was surprised at how much she and Trevor were enjoying each other, and she could have sworn the other day that something had shifted in their behavior. It was subtle, but Liza was intrigued, and she couldn't deny that in the last few days she had dressed for work with a little more care than usual. Something about him made her feel secure and excited at the same time—but she was willing to bet it was just a passing office flirtation. He was charming to everyone, and she'd be nuts to misinterpret his behavior to her as anything other than the playful bantering of a colleague.

Liza shook her head, heading to a box of books in the living room. The point was to be independent and get comfortable in her own skin—since getting comfortable in this apartment, she thought, looking around at the chaos, might be a losing battle. No need to go chasing after one more thing that wasn't real.

When Liza next looked up from her unpacking, it was 6 P.M. She had meant to go to an AA meeting in her new neighborhood at 5:30, but there went that idea. She stood to stretch when the downstairs bell rang. "Hello?" Liza said, unsure if she was pressing the right buttons. "Hello?" She heard gentle laughter on the other end.

"Liza, it's Trevor. I bought you a housewarming present, if this is an okay time." Liza looked around in a panic, then imagined what she must look like, after hours of rifling through dusty books and clothes. So much for worrying about her clothes the last few days. *Actually, I'm in the middle of waxing my legs,* she thought of saying, but instead, heard herself directing him to come on up.

When she opened the door, Trevor was standing there, lilies under one arm, and an enormous crate under the other. Liza immediately forgot her shyness, and let out a giggle. "Well, look what the cat dragged in," she said, motioning Trevor into the apartment.

"How did you know?" Trevor said with a grin, and then, as if on cue, a tiny mew came from the crate.

"Oh my God," Liza said, torn between panic and glee. "What have you done?"

"As I was leaving the office, this homeless man was giving away kittens, so I thought . . . I don't know, I'm sure it was crazy. But I figured . . ." Trevor stumbled. "It was unbelievably stupid."

"No!" Liza said. "It's unbelievably wonderful!"

Trevor and Liza knelt on the floor and carefully opened the crate, which Trevor explained he'd gotten at a pet store around the corner. He'd placed a litter box and bowls and treats on hold, and if Liza decided to keep the cat, they would be delivered as soon as he made the call. But again, he said, "No pressure. Really. I'd be happy to keep her."

"Indian giver," Liza cooed, holding the tiny kitten in her arms. "I can't believe this. I never knew I wanted a cat. I don't even know if I like cats, come to think of it."

Trevor blushed. "You know what? I must have lost my mind. Give me the cat, and take the flowers instead. She can live with me until we find her another home."

"Her name is Faith, thank you very much," Liza said with mock sternness, stroking the kitten in her arms, "And she's not going anywhere. Now, would you like a cup of tea?"

Trevor grinned, looking extremely relieved and pleased. "That sounds perfect."

As they sat over tea, they talked about Liza's divorce, and how it had shaken her foundations. Trevor talked about moving to the city and trying to reestablish a relationship with Tom. And somehow, it was three hours later, and Trevor was late for a date with a college friend passing through town. Liza walked him to the door, amazed by what a lovely time they had. She suddenly wondered what it would be like to kiss him. *No,* she told herself. At least, not yet. At the door, Trevor hesitated, so Liza took charge, standing on her tiptoes and giving Trevor a kiss on the cheek and a big hug. "Thank you," she said warmly, and as he turned to go, Liza swore that neither of them wanted him to.

Sam and Tom stole half an hour to sneak outside for a bite to eat. They both realized, as they crossed the street to Florent, a famously popular diner where they could get a quick lunch before getting back for the weekly staff meeting, that they hadn't been alone together for a long time.

"God, it's been forever since we've actually had time alone, hasn't it?" Sam asked Tom. "It's odd that I saw more of you before we were actually working together. Maybe not more," she corrected herself, "but everything's been so frantic, I feel totally out of the loop on how you are and what you've been up to."

Tom laughed. "You know what I've been up to—like you, I haven't left these offices."

"I just have to say," Sam said, "I love it." She gave him the update: R.J.'s column made her laugh out loud. Andrew nailed his piece on the lesbian lobster war and his own drama with Robbie and Lachlan. It was funny as hell, in a dry way, and also a little sad.

"Watch, now he'll mope for six months," Tom said. "Happens every time."

"The shopping with Isaac Mizrahi piece is an utter disaster—humorless, serviceless, totally unfixable. But I'm going to fix it."

He smiled. "I think you're beginning to like this editing thing."

She smiled back. "I like the power. By the way, Trevor has been amazing. What's it like working for your family?"

"You tell me," Tom teased back. Officially, Trevor was higher in the rankings as publisher than even the editor-in-chief. And officially, Sam's parents were higher than any of them, simply because they controlled the purse strings.

"So far, so good," Sam said, as she dove into a plate of linguine, much to the admiring stares of the waiter who had had it up to here with the borderline anorexic Manhattan women, who always requested everything on the side and then didn't eat any of it, anyway. "They're staying totally out of it, trusting me fully, for some reason I can't begin to understand, and seem pleased at what we're doing."

Tom nodded. "I'd say the same about Trevor. He's always been the consummate professional—even at home, which I found a little off-putting as a kid. But he's grown into it or something. Even when I hated him I still loved him, because he was family. But I *like* him now."

Sam grabbed one of his fries. "Actually," she said with a smile, "I meant to ask you. Have you noticed that Trevor and Liza seem to be . . ."

"Seem to be what?" Tom said, in that distracted way a man gets when he's faced with the option of eating a cheeseburger.

"Getting friendly."

"I would hope so," Tom said. "The only problem we seem to be having is with our frisky interns.

"No!" said Sam.

"Trevor caught one with his pants down, but he won't say with whom! Speaking of which, because I haven't asked in ages: What's going on with Chris, or, I guess I should say, what's not going on with Chris?"

Sam smiled—a little wistfully, Tom noticed. "More like that. He left me a message he's coming into town next week. My feeling is that there's not a lot to be added to anything by seeing him. And you know what the odd thing is? I actually am beginning to understand what happened with you and Justin—how you can keep getting burned and going back for more and then one day, you're over it."

"Uh oh," Tom said, finishing off his burger. "I've heard that before."

"When I got his message," she said, pointing a french fry at him, "I didn't want to immediately throw up, like I used to."

Tom would have pointed out that Jack had a lot to do with it, if only Sam had told him she was going to really give it a try with him. But that she felt like keeping to herself.

That night, R.J. called again. "Foxman, this is Chester. I'm thinking about the magazine, and I'm seeing night-vision goggles. Humor me."

Chapter 62

Liza announced she was ready to show layouts for the bulk of the first issue. The group convened in the conference room.

They were speechless. The magazine had energy, humor, life. The barefoot travel feature was supremely sexy—it made them all want to head straight for JFK for the first flight to anywhere. The mini-golf story was a riot. Even Sam was amazed how funny Brian could be when given something juicy to write about. The tree-climbing piece had perfect pictures of the climbers dangling high above the air; similarly, the kites were shot in the air, from below. Veronica beamed. The fashion story had come off, against all odds; Tom had hired a stylist he had known back when they were both assistants at *Town & Country,* and she had called everyone she had ever worked with. In the end, they had a fantastic range of celebrities and interesting civilians. Best of all was the Advice Squad, the perfect mix of the weird and the useful.

"And look at R.J.!" said Tom. "He looks amazing!"

"I didn't even know he had a tattoo there," said Sam. "Talk about giving 110 percent . . ." They sat in silence. "Brain flash!" It was Sam. "I've got the perfect name for R.J.'s column: 'Sex with a Stranger.' "

Tom gave her a hug. "Have I told you lately that I love, admire, and respect you?"

"Honey," she said, ignoring everyone else in the room, "it was clear from the start."

As Liza gathered up her things, she looked up and caught

Trevor's eye. He winked at her. "Really nice job, Lize," he said, putting his arm around her as they walked out of the room. Liza was amazed how good his words felt. Not to mention his hand.

Tom had a month left at *Profit,* but he couldn't bear it. Faking niceness with Ethan was taking everything he had.

> To: Alex_richardson@profit.com
> From: Tom@bite.com
> Re: T-minus . . .
> I've said again and again how much I like working at Profit, but would you mind if I cut it short? I can close the next three issues in a week and a half, and you won't notice the difference. (And of course I'd be available for any questions my successor might have.) If it's a problem, no sweat, but I'm beginning to feel like yesterday's newspaper.

"Am I interrupting something?"

"Migrant farm workers live in appalling conditions." This joke just never got old for either of them. Maybe acknowledging all that was fucked up in the world was better than ignoring it completely.

"Would you care to step outside with me? Take a constitutional?"

"We shall stroll the piers, arm in arm."

Once they were outside, she told him about the poem. Dael hadn't been avoiding her. He had been worried that she was avoiding him, and he wanted to write her a poem to show her how much she meant to him. "It was the sweetest thing," Veronica said. "He said that it was so hard to write that he couldn't talk to me while he was trying to get it out."

"You were his muse!" said Tom. "I've always wanted to be someone's muse."

She giggled. "And it's good. A guy I was dating once wrote a song for me, but it sucked and I didn't know what to say."

"Let's hear it."

"The song? God, I don't remem—"

Tom cleared his throat. "No, Veronica. I'd like to hear the poem. I know you've memorized it."

But she couldn't. She would have loved nothing more, but this was something that needed to stay between her and Dael. Tom got it. "Thanks," she said. "As a reward, I will tell you one thing. The first line is, 'I want to walk you down Satisfaction Street.' "

Tom whistled.

When they got back, Tom had received the following email:

> To: Tom@bite.com
> From: Alex_Richardson@profit.com
> Re: T-minus
> Close 'em like you say you will and consider yourself done here. Let me know when your last day is—we may yet decide to throw you a party, Sanders.

"Hey, guys!" Tom was meeting Andrew for lunch at Pastis, but instead he found Trevor and Liza. "Fancy meeting you here."

"Hey," they said, not exactly unhappy to see him, but not exactly thrilled.

That was weird, Tom thought, over at a table at the other end of the restaurant. It wasn't like he expected a hug every time he saw his art director—or his brother—but he would almost have sworn that they were conspiring. Against him? Phooey.

Sneaking up on Tom, Andrew stuck his hand through the shrubs that hid the tables from the street and tweaked Tom's ear. Yelping, Tom raised his other hand to give the intruder a nice, firm karate chop.

"Stop! It's just me." And with that Andrew crawled through the shrubs.

"Andrew, I have to say you are behaving unnaturally sprightly. Especially for a man of ninety."

"Fuck off," he said. "I'm feeling good, fun, alive. I love working with young people. Cool people. With offices downtown. Not wearing a suit. Creating something—well, being part of a team that's creating something. What can I say? I love it!"

Jesus Christ, Tom thought. What was this, Freaky Friday? First Trevor and Liza were being chilly and now his stable friend had become visibly unhinged. Could it be drugs?

"Andrew," he said, squinting. "Did you take a Vicodin?"

"What?"

"Tell the truth."

"Oh, Tom, don't be a pill. It's a beautiful day, I'm enjoying it, just relax. And no, I didn't take a Vicodin. Hey, isn't that Trevor?" Andrew put his hand to his forehead to block out the sun and get a better view—then waved it. "Is he with Liza?"

"Don't you recognize her?"

"Let me try again. Hey, isn't that Trevor? Is he *with* Liza?"

Of course! That's what Sam was talking about the other day. That's why they were behaving oddly. It made total sense. "Don't be a gossip, Andrew. You're far too old."

Andrew chuckled. "Someone needs to get laid."

🍎 🍎 🍎

And for once, it ain't me. There was no doubt about it: what he was doing was wrong. You just weren't supposed to fool around with someone you worked with. It was rule number one. Especially if you were in charge, which of course Andrew wasn't, and didn't oversee Jonas. So maybe that made it better.

Rule number two was new, though. No more young men! It was the same thing all over again! He felt like such a hypocrite, except hypocrisy never felt so good. You could be damn sure he wasn't going to tell Tom. He'd allude to it—he couldn't help it, was he in love?—but he could hear Tom scream now. "An intern! Are you insane?" and then pull out some absurd acronym that meant nothing but an easy way out of ever getting involved with someone, someone as sweet and funny as, yes, Jonas.

Heck, Andrew could have the conversation with Tom without actually having to have it. "Which one is he?" Tom would ask, knowing full well Jonas is the tall, skinny, dark-haired beauty on loan from Emory University. The one with the lips, the eyelashes, the seemingly inexhaustible collection of vintage T-shirts. Then, getting into the spirit of things—Tom loved nothing more than hearing how people met—he'd follow it with, "How did it start?" Andrew and Jonas had both been working late one night, and Jonas walked by Andrew's office, said hello, they chatted, Andrew said he was tense, Jonas gave him a neck massage . . .

"Cliché! Cliché! Cliché! Did you do it on the conference table?" No, they hadn't, not that time anyway, though Lord knows Andrew wanted to, he hadn't had a hard-on like that in what felt like years. It wasn't just the skinny boy's body, but the way he kept up a steady stream of funny, borderline absurd conversation as they kissed (make that *necked).* And he was smart, and a little full of himself, but not so much so that he was annoying. If anything, Andrew found that kind of confidence inspiring. *Thank God Trevor didn't catch both of them.*

And obviously Tom would have one more question: "Isn't this just Lachlan and Robbie all over again?" So sue him if it was.

Chapter 63

Tom stopped by R.J.'s apartment late at night. At least R.J. was behaving normally. For him anyway. He was in his alcove office, chatting up some Argentine on his Web cam.

"Stand over there!" he hissed at Tom. "I don't want him to see you!"

The Argentine stood up and flashed his ass at R.J. "Mmmm," R.J. moaned into the microphone. "How do you say 'luscious' in Spanish?"

"Delicioso," came a voice from the other side of the Equator.

"Indeed."

Tom was impatient—and from where he stood he couldn't see the screen. "Time for another call," he whispered.

R.J. pushed the mute button. "What do I say this time?"

"What were the last two?"

Tom watched as R.J. searched his brain. "I know. The Midwest as a hot new travel destination—Kansas, I think I mentioned—and a taster's guide to bottled water."

"Excellent!" Tom said. "Excellent. Let's try something different. Why don't you say you want Ethan to come up next Friday to show you what you've got so far."

"Are you sure?" R.J. asked. "Ethan will realize that it hasn't been Chester leaving the messages."

"It's time." Tom figured that they had nothing to lose—the first issue of *Bite* was two weeks from being put to bed, and after that they might as well welcome the competition. Besides, he had a feeling that it would be a good time for Chester to seriously doubt his editor's abilities. "And then after you leave that one, you can leave a few more, over the next few days, changing your mind on various topics—and add a few hackneyed topics, like the best seafood restaurants in San Francisco and travelers' tips for the Champagne region of France. It's pure in-flight magazine stuff."

R.J. turned back to the computer. The Argentine had turned off the light. "Don't cry for me, Argentina," he cooed into the mike. "The truth is, I never left you." Tom got out just in time.

"How much did this cost?" Andrew was looking at the wall of layouts, at the fashion story in particular.

Veronica exhaled. "Someone once taught me something that I've never forgotten: They don't remember if it went over budget, but they always remember if it's good."

"Might that have been our mutual friend Tom Sanders?"

"Might have."

"Sounds like him." As Andrew was speaking, Jonas walked by and sneakily pinched him in the ass. It took everything Andrew had not to squeal—or run over, pin the intern against the wall, and lick his face. But being Andrew, he flinched only slightly.

"It wasn't that much, really," Veronica said, misreading his reaction. "And Tom said we should go all out on the first issue."

Liza approached the wall and turned toward Andrew. "Don't sweat it, Andrew. We'll be right on budget for the issue—some stories are going to be way more expensive than others, but it's nothing to worry about. We'll cut costs on others." She gave Veronica a look that the photo editor had no trouble reading: *Don't give in.*

Mao bounded in—if she could have flown, they had no doubt she would have done just that. "Big news! Trevor just called. Nautica bought an eight-page spread! We need at least four more editorial pages!"

"What are we, a news magazine?" Veronica had turned white. "We don't have time! We can't just come up with four pages like that."

Liza knew better. "Like hell we can't. You did it at *Profit.* Mao, call Tom and Sam and get them thinking about what we should add—or if they want to expand one of the stories we've already got." Mao took off. "V., call your friend at *Blue.* I heard they're about to go out of business—they might have a story we can buy." She looked at Andrew. "Cheap." Veronica took off.

"Speaking of cheap," she said, leaning in close to Andrew's ear. "Did you learn *nothing* from Clinton?" She smiled, spun on her heels, and walked off, head high. Then she turned and gave him a big, juicy wink.

To: Samantha@bite.com
From: Tom@bite.com
Re: Four more!
Meet tonight at APT to plan the four new pages and foolishly celebrate way too early our fantastic success?

To: Liza@bite.com
From: Andrew@bite.com
Re: Secrets
I'll keep yours if you'll keep mine, you hussy.

To: Tom@bite.com
From: Samantha@bite.com
Re: Four more!
Absolutment. Let's see if L&V can make it—just us core edit folks. 9pm?

To: Liza@bite.com, Veronica@bite.com
From: Samantha@bite.com

Re: Tonight
Care to join me and Tom for dinner to plan out these four new pages? 9pm, APT. We may also stupidly toast our success long before we should

To: Samantha@bite.com, Tom@bite.com
From: Liza@bite.com
Re: Tonight
V's here with me, and we'd love to. But I can't stay late—I sort of have a date, and no, I'm not talking about it

Chapter 64

Sam and Veronica spent their lunch sweating through an intense yoga class at OM. To their relief, Gwyneth Paltrow had *not* made her usual appearance, which allowed them to focus on their own misery. Which helped Sam not focus on Veronica's perfect body. She still got hit with horrible visions of Veronica and Chris in bed together. Okay, so one day they'd look back and realize they'd bonded over the whole nightmare, but sometimes it still felt fresh to Sam.

"So what are you doing tonight?"

"Actually," Sam said, as she grabbed her purse out of the locker, "I have a date with Jack."

"Really! Smelling like that?" Veronica teased, toweling herself off with her sweatshirt. Sam couldn't help but be happy to see that Veronica wore white cotton underwear. Still, some men liked that . . . *Stop*. Sam ordered herself. *If it hadn't been for Veronica being with Chris, you might still be hung up on him instead of having a date with Jack tonight.*

"I'm going to go home and shower first, thank you very much," Sam said. "But I think we're both pretty clear on taking it slowly this time."

They headed out into the sunlight on Sixth Avenue and began to walk over to *Bite*'s office. "Here's something I don't get," Veronica said, "How does not having sex 'slow things down'? It seems to me you're either crazy about each other or you're not."

"No, you're totally right," Sam said, "It's just that the sex was so great before, I think that's all I paid attention to. And now I want to pay attention to getting to know Jack."

Veronica pretended to gag.

"Look, I'm not saying it's not the most sentimental schlock you've ever heard out of my mouth," Sam said laughing, "and I hope you won't tell anyone lest you ruin my reputation as a sex goddess. But we shall just have to see with this one. It's worth a shot, I think."

"Oh yeah," Veronica said with a smile. "Let's just see how long you can get him to keep his gun in his pocket."

"Now," Sam said, between giggles, "it's my turn to puke."

Six hours later, showered and dressed in a new Diane Von Furstenberg sundress that was flattering but didn't show too much skin, Sam was sitting with Jack at Le Gamin. They were sharing a bottle of Domaine Ott and a goat cheese salad.

"This is like being in the South of France," Sam said. "It's just perfect."

"There's something worth dreaming about," Jack said with a smile. "Maybe we should think about it."

"I am, I am," Sam said, taking a sip of wine.

"No, I mean there's something *we* should think about. Like the two of us. You've been working like a madwoman, and once *Bite* has taken off, a little vacation might be in order."

Sam's eyes widened. It was amazing how romantic Jack had become. Or maybe he always had been, and she just hadn't been able to see it.

"Too much?" Jack said with a smile. "Did I scare you? Although I have to admit that I'm not too keen on the idea of lounging around Provence with a woman whose idea of romance is a chaste after-dinner kiss."

"That seems like a fair deal," Sam said. "And I love the idea so much I can't tell you. Can I have some time to think about it? You know my instinct is to always say yes to everything too fast, and my instinct is I'm going to say yes to this, as well, but

I think I need to concentrate on *Bite* right now, and go slowly." *Because I'm petrified.*

"I absolutely understand," he said, raising his glass. "To the launch of *Bite,* and the future, whatever that may hold. I have a feeling," he said with a seductive smile, "it's going to be absolutely beautiful."

With the launch only weeks away, the focus in the office was on two very important things: Getting the perfect magazine out the door, and planning the perfect party to celebrate.

When Sam walked into the office the next day—amazing how rested one could be when the night ended with only a kiss at one's doorstep—Trevor, Tom, Veronica, and Liza were arguing in the hallway. "That's the dorkiest thing I have ever heard," Veronica was saying to Trevor. "How could you want to throw a party for the coolest magazine ever at the stodgy Four Seasons?"

"Look, you East Village boho, I know it's a little uptown for you, but it happens to exude an image that the advertisers would really respect, and they're offering us the space."

"This isn't a party for the advertisers," Veronica shot back, as Liza nodded. "This is for us. And who the hell wants to have to have it at the Four Seasons?"

"Hello, children," Sam said as she passed by.

"Sam!" Tom called out. "Get over here. We need your help."

"Not a chance in the world," she said with a smile, opening the door to her office. "I'm Switzerland, baby. All I need is my friends and a martini, and I'll be satisfied."

"Speaking of satisfied," Tom said, breaking away from the huddle and making himself comfortable on Sam's couch. "Are you?"

"What?" Sam looked at him distractedly as she turned on her computer.

"Did . . . you . . . get . . . any . . ." Tom said, speaking as slowly as he would to someone who didn't understand English.

"No . . . I . . . did . . . not," Sam parroted back. "And yes, I feel very satisfied."

"I find this deeply weird," Tom said.

"Frankly," Sam answered, perhaps a bit too firmly, "I'm not sure I care how you find it."

"Well, well, well," Tom said, standing and heading for the door. "Don't kill me for this, but frankly, you were a lot more pleasant when you were getting some."

Sam laughed despite herself and waved him out. She had to admit that she felt a little disoriented in her own skin these days. It was like she was changing so fast that she couldn't keep up with it any more than her friends could. But somehow she knew she was on the right path. She was pouring her energy into a project she really believed in, and she wasn't as unmoored by the uncertainties of silly things like men anymore. *Probably because you have one.*

Mao knocked, and came in bearing an enormous bouquet of lilies from Renny. "Your daily delivery, Madame," she said with fake obsequiousness, bowing before Sam and placing the flowers on the desk.

"What the hell?" Sam said, pulling the card from the flowers. "White lilies represent innocence, so these seemed appropriate," the card read. "But I warn you: passionflowers are coming into season." Sam laughed and immediately called Jack.

"What are you up to?" he said after she had thanked him—both for the flowers and making her laugh.

"Well," she said slowly, with a smile. "I was thinking about checking into airfares to Nice."

The launch was going as planned. Trevor, Tom, and Sam gave interviews to Keith Kelly at the *Post,* who wrote a story that was wildly less pessimistic than it had any right to be. They were in the second half of a double-dip recession, after all, and even though word had leaked about projects several of the big magazine companies were working on, no one else was trying to do it independently. Kelly noted the good advertiser response, MTV's serious interest in doing a reality show on the offices, and the contagious enthusiasm of the Biters. "These Kids Might Just Make It," read the headline. When the newspaper came out, needless to say, the office was ecstatic.

Tom, Trevor, and Veronica were having another round of arguments about the party. Trevor wanted to appeal to upscale advertisers, but advertisers were famously unfun. They were standing in Trevor's office, taking a break from the argument—more because none of them could figure out what to say next.

Mao stuck her head in. "Sorry. Tom, phone for you, a woman, she says it's important."

"Who is she?"

"She won't say. But she scares me." Tom and Trevor looked at each other and started laughing. "I know why you think that's funny, but believe me, this woman's a dragon." Tom told her to patch her through to Trevor's line. Trevor and Veronica both inhaled, ready to start again, when Tom turned white.

"Sanders," said a familiar no-nonsense voice. "Moira McGowan here. Hell yes I'm still annoyed with you. But that will have to wait. Jim Boggs here wants to talk to you and your people. It seems the *Times* is interested in getting back into the magazine business."

"Who is it?" whispered Veronica. "Who are you talking to?"

Tom waved her off. "We're not really looking to sell just yet, Moira."

"Untwist those panties, Sanders. The *Times* wouldn't buy

you outright yet anyway. They want to invest. Get your people here—Wendy! When can Jim Boggs see Sanders? Tomorrow. 10 A.M. Unless you're just going to pull the goddamn rug out from under us, of course."

Tom smiled despite himself. "Moira," he said, "not a day goes by that I don't regret not working for you."

"Ha!" she said. "You son of a bitch. We could have had fun. 10 A.M." As she hung up he could hear her yelling for Wendy again.

Tom gave Trevor and Veronica a suitably meaty pause. "Somebody pinch me."

A few hours later, energized by the news, Tom brokered a peace between Trevor and Veronica. They would book the Starlight Room on the roof of the St. Regis—upscale but with appropriate historical connections, given they'd had their first big meeting there—and hire Stephane Pompougnac to deejay it. "It's uptown, it's downtown, it shows we don't care about those boundaries anymore." Veronica wanted more concessions—photo booths, carnival games, that sort of thing—which Tom actually thought sounded fun, so he agreed. Everyone was happy.

And nervous. Could they really be having this much good fortune?

They could—and more. The next day's *Observer* devoted almost the entire media column to rumblings within Worldwide Media that Ethan's magazine was in trouble. Major rumors about confusion and arguments between Ethan and Chester. Sam and Tom engaged in a good half hour of schadenfreude—after all, it only seemed fair that you be allowed to get joy from another's pain when you were instrumental in inflicting it.

Chapter 65

Andrew came in to talk budgets, pointing out that the *Times* was going to want to know all about their finances. "Tell them it's all on Sam's parents," joked Tom.

"Ha ha," Andrew replied dryly. "Please, no jokes like that at the meeting. We have to seem extraprofessional, not like a publisher with no experience in publishing, a business manager of a bankrupt company, and two editors who have never managed anyone in their lives."

"Ouch!"

"Well, that's how they're going to see it."

Tom hadn't really thought about that, even if he did wear his best suit that day, a tan Dolce & Gabbana that made him look like an Italian Gatsby, or so he hoped. What could they do about it, though? They were who they were. "Maybe we should do some coke before we go in there so we're all juiced up and ready to get down to *biz*-ness."

"Oh God," said Andrew.

"Sorry, another bad joke. No coke. All we can do, Andrew, is sell them on the magazine the way we've sold everyone who works here. We believe in it, and if they're smart they will too."

"Just let Trevor do most of the talking, okay?"

"Thanks, best friend. I'll keep that in mind." Tom looked at Andrew's hair. "Hey, you're going for the messy look?"

Andrew blushed and reached up to his head. "What? No—yeah, I guess I am. Why not? It's summer, right?"

Sam, Tom, Trevor, and Andrew left for the *Times* at 2:45. They decided to walk, then subway, since Tom and Andrew had very strong opinions about sitting in midtown traffic during the middle of the day. Trevor looked back to see if Mao was trailing them; she wasn't above it.

They were nervous. "We have to get excited!" Sam said as they maneuvered around a flock of schoolkids; what the kids were doing in the Meatpacking District was anyone's guess. "We have to make them see that we are going to make this happen!"

Trevor looked at her through his aviator shades. "I don't think so," he said. "We should play it cool. We don't want to come off like a bunch of kids who decided to do this on a whim. Pretend you're Anna Wintour. You look hot—don't look at me like that. You know what I mean. Intimidate them a little bit. It's like the whole thing: make them wish they could be part of us because we're the cool people."

Tom understood what he was saying, but wasn't sure it would work. Sam could be intimidating, he knew that first-hand, but he thought that what made her riveting was her unbridled energy. And if he tried to seem cool, he just ended up looking bored. He'd learned it over the years at gay bars—too many guys would come up to him, when he was trying to seem above it all, and ask why he didn't try smiling. He thought about saying something, but figured it was either going to work or not—it was too late, really, to try to be anything but what they genuinely were.

On the subway, they happened to get into a car with another group of schoolkids, every single one talking at the same time. "What is it with today?" Andrew asked. "They should have separate cars for these field trippers. Like those trucks you see carrying hundreds of chickens."

"It always comes back to chicken, doesn't it?" Tom asked. Andrew harrumphed. Even though his main role was going to be food columnist, he was more familiar with the finances than anyone else, and Trevor had thought it prudent to have him come.

Walking to the *Times* building, they didn't speak. It had become real for all of them. Before now, they had been *Bite,* but in an insular way. Now they were *Bite,* but going to visit a publishing company—another publishing company—on official business. "Just be yourself," Tom whispered to Sam.

"I was thinking the same thing," she replied. "It's too late for us to be anyone else."

He smiled broadly, and gave her a hug. "Back off, bitch!" she said. "No wrinkling the Marc Jacobs." It was indeed hot, a white shift with black daisies embroidered up one side.

He stepped back and laughed. "Maybe Anna Wintour isn't a stretch."

In the elevator, Tom tried to warn Trevor, Sam, and Andrew about Moira, but he wasn't sure they got it. The doors opened, and they gave their names to the receptionist.

Fifteen minutes passed, and they started to get pissed off. Sam: "I think we should leave."

Trevor: "No. It's standard negotiating practice. A little bush league, but not totally surprising."

Sam: "This is wrong."

Trevor: "Calm down. Breathe."

She tried taking deep breaths, but after ten more minutes they sounded pretty huffy. Trevor paced the reception area. "One thing's for sure," he said. "We have way cooler offices."

Sam offered them up an item from Page Sex: *Which actress took a nose dive at the Oscar party in her honor? She left her golden statue on her table to blow her way into the bathroom.* But they were all too preoccupied, and really, it could be anyone.

Finally, the most beautiful woman any of them had ever seen came out to take them in. She was over six feet tall and wearing strappy heels and a black suit that looked poured on. Sam shot Tom a look and he knew what it meant: Anna Wintour was officially dead.

They were led to a conference room, where they did not find Moira waiting for them. Sam started getting huffy again, but Trevor shushed her. "It's what you do," he muttered. "I'd do it too."

"And I'd hate you for it," she said.

Moira and Jim Boggs came in, all smiles. After the introductions, they sat on the opposite side of the table. She was in full Hurricane Moira mode. Jim Boggs was all calm, though—yin to Moira's yang.

"Pardon me for not asking you much about your project," he said. "I've been following it and asking around, and I feel like I get it. Basically, and this stays in this room, you're in a good position. We really want to get involved. The *Times'* readers aren't getting younger, and we could use any method available to get younger ones. We see *Bite* as a great cross-promotional tool. You get subscribers, we send them direct mail about subscribing to the *Times.* Plus, we think you have a great idea. We've got too much cash right now, and we want in."

"Fantastic," said Trevor, a little concerned about all this frank goodwill.

"But I want to get our issues on the table right now. We want no more than a thirty percent investment, and we'd be willing to forgo all editorial involvement—"

"I should hope," muttered Sam.

"—given that you grow at a mutually agreed-upon rate. And we're willing to be generous on that front. In return, we'd be prepared to pour $10 million into the magazine."

The Biters were speechless.

"The issues!" Moira was positively Tourettic. "Those aren't the issues! What about the issues?"

"Thanks, Moira." And he rolled his eyes, much to the *Bite* contingent's amusement. "We have a few concerns. This two-editor arrangement. We'd need to have you two sign contracts agreeing on how exactly the arrangement works, and what happens when you reach points upon which you can't agree. I know that's hard to imagine, but believe me, it will."

Tom and Sam nodded. Boggs was making them feel more like children—his children—but not in an entirely bad way.

"Two. We really want this MTV show to happen. Our involvement isn't contingent on it, but we want to be sure you're pursuing it. More than that, we want to assign a team to work with you on the deal."

Frankly, Trevor was relieved. He believed in it, but hadn't the time or the resources to focus. "That seems workable," he said.

"As for Worldwide Media." Boggs gave them a very stern look. "I first want to be sure you have no intention of trying to sell *Bite* back to them, given your history there." Sam and Tom both started to deny any such thing. "I figured," said Boggs. "And anyway, they're going to be out for blood when they realize how you stuck it to them."

The Biters played dumb.

Boggs shook his head. "Fine. I don't blame you. But believe me, I know Chester and he can be vicious. Be prepared."

Tom, Sam, Trevor, and Andrew had never felt so vulnerable. "Buck up," said Moira. "Even I have faith in you—well, most of you." She shot Tom a look. "Jim, you forgot one thing."

"What?"

She turned back to the Biters. "Get a lawyer. A good one. The best."

"Because of Chester? Or to negotiate this deal?" asked Trevor.

"Both," said Moira. She turned toward Andrew, and gave a crocodile's smile. "But especially if you're going to be fooling around with your interns."

When they got back to the office—after stopping at Pastis for a drink, during which they insisted a still-blushing Andrew tell them everything—Veronica pounced.

"You're not going to believe it!" she said.

Tom: "Madonna's here?"

Sam: "Marc Jacobs is having a sample sale?"

Trevor: "More ads?"

Andrew: "I need an Advil."

"Better!" she said, then aside to Andrew, "My top left drawer." She bounced up and down three times. "Diana called."

Tom clued them in: "She's the photo editor at *Profit.*"

"Ethan's being transferred!"

She made them guess where. They started with fairly reasonable guesses—*Sports News*, *Star Face*, *Homeowner's Digest*—then moved to the ridiculous. *What's Cooking?* "You're getting warmer!" *Golfer?* "Warm!" *Women's Sports News?* "Warm!" *TV Today?* "Still just sort of warm!"

She couldn't take it anymore. "*Sports News . . .*" she paused. *"For Kids!"*

Chapter 66

Liza was about to leave her office when Sam cornered her.

"Liza. I love you, you know that. And I would never ask you about anything I thought you really didn't want to talk about. But I can't stand it anymore!" Liza got up and shut the door. Sam was clearly about to pop. "Are you dating Trevor?"

Liza took a deep breath. She hadn't wanted to talk about it because she hadn't wanted to think about it. She just wanted to let it happen without overanalyzing it, to enjoy the very act of enjoying it. But she understood that Sam's need to know trumped her need to not talk; it was a universal code of female friendship that if a girlfriend was getting some action, it was fair conversational game. She sat down next to Sam on the sofa.

"Yes," she said. "I suppose I am."

"Okay," Sam said. "That's great. That's all I needed to know, and I'm not sure why I needed to know, but I just did, you know?" She stood up as if to leave.

"Oh, Sam, sit back down! If you're going to make me talk about this let's do it right!" She pulled her legs up under her and let out a giggle. "Isn't he dreamy?"

Sam visibly sighed. "He is. He is! How did it happen? How far along are you? What does he look like naked?"

"Jesus, Sam, do you want to get your notebook?"

"Once a reporter, always a reporter."

They talked for a half hour, Liza outlining the relationship as it had happened—"A kitten!" squealed Sam—with both of them stopping every now and then to think about Trevor naked. Liza, surprising herself, felt no trepidation, only a fun sort of relief. She had forgotten how good it felt to talk about a relationship—a good relationship, that is. It made her remember when she was in high school, and she and her friends would kiss boys just so they'd have something to pass notes about.

"Enough!" she said. "What about Jack? Unless you don't want to talk about it . . ."

"It's only fair," Sam said, then dramatically lolled her head back against the cushion. "He's divine. What was I thinking all those years? What was I afraid of? Oh, who cares. I'm right where I want to be, except that if I really think about it where I really want to be is in bed with him."

"Or rammed up against the sink at the Carlyle?" Liza smiled. "But why don't you just go there now? Or are you still not doing it?"

Sam nodded. She didn't think she had ever been so horny in all her life, but as much as it was about making sure Jack knew she was serious about them, and about making him understand she could control herself, she was also terrified that if they jumped back into bed they would lose everything they'd gained. One sex up, two steps back. Or something like that. But at some point—some point soon—she had to give in. Because, really, how could she edit a magazine about taking a big bite out of life when she wouldn't even let herself get laid?

With only a week left before the issue went to bed, Sam, Tom, and Trevor signed a deal with the *Times*—part of which, Tom insisted, include a provision that explicitly forbade Moira from getting involved unless Sam and Tom agreed. He had grown to kind of like Moira, but had no desire to see her in his office, ever. Boggs, on the other hand, they all loved. Being young was great, but sometimes even they had to admit all they wanted to do was let someone older and more experienced make some decisions—or suggestions, anyway.

Sam's parents were thrilled, at least as thrilled as Upper East Side rich people ever get. And anyway, they had never really doubted that Sam's project would amount to something. When Tom insisted she invite them to the party, Sam snorted. "Of course, but I will tell them they can only stay for an hour. The last thing I need is my interns to chat up my parents, and the second-to-last thing I need is my parents seeing me drunk. Or meeting Jack—for which I would have to get drunk."

The St. Regis gave them a sweet deal, which Trevor brokered by offering them a free ad in the first issue and promising they'd get plenty of mouth-watering coverage in the gossip columns (it had been years since anyone downtown had thrown a party there, and they were desperate for press). The party, as had been long planned, would happen on a Thursday night two weeks after the close, the first day they'd be guaranteed to have issues for the guests—no point in throwing a launch party if you can't show off your product.

Veronica and Liza immediately took the afternoon off to shop. They tore through Soho—Prada, Helmut Lang, Dolce & Gabbana, the Barneys Co-op—and found nothing. After Liza insisted, they went uptown, to Madison Avenue, a place Veronica deemed beneath her sensibilities. "What do I want to look like a debutante for?"

And yet. At Calvin Klein, she found a silk dress in a purple so dark it verged on black. "You're going to hate this," Liza said, "but you look unbelievably elegant."

Veronica smiled. "Well, maybe that's not so bad. All my photographers will be there, and you know, I need to look like I'm in charge. But sexy. Does this do that?"

"Um," Liza said. "I believe it *is* cut down to your navel."

Liza, in turn, was set on something different. At Yves Saint Laurent, she tried on a white tuxedo with no shirt underneath. She came out of the dressing room and Veronica gasped. She looked at Liza from head to toe. "Wait," she said, and ran out of the room. A few minutes later, she came back with a pair of black stilettos. She handed them to Liza, no explanation necessary.

Liza put them on, muttering that she hadn't worn heels that high in years, and would probably topple. But she had to admit. They were hot.

"Do I look like Bianca?"

"Who?"

Liza forgot for a moment that Veronica was twenty-five and would have no idea that Bianca Jagger had worn a white tux to her wedding with Mick. "Never mind," she said.

They came back to the office, bags swinging at their sides, to find Sam and Tom fighting. Sam was about to light into Tom when she saw the bags. "Time out!" she said, and snatched the bags away. "What did you get?"

Veronica grabbed the bags back. "No," she said. "It's a surprise."

"But I have to know so I don't do something similar!" Already halfway there because of her fight with Tom, Sam was now in full perturb.

"I will tell you this," Liza said. "You better work, bitch. Because we are going to steam up that room." And as if they'd planned it—which in fact, they had—they walked out.

Sam turned back to Tom, who was laughing. "Don't you dare laugh at me."

"Get your bag, Sam."

"You can't kick me out! Not over this contract thing!" She was approaching apoplexy.

"Get your bag, Sam," Tom said again. "We obviously have some shopping to do."

Sam stopped fuming as if a switch had been flipped. "Oh," she said. "Sorry about that." Tom just smiled. "But if you think you're going to make me forget about this contract thing by taking me shopping . . ."

He took her by the hand. "Come on," he said. "We can talk about it in the cab."

"The contract thing" was, naturally, about the agreement the *Times* wanted Tom and Sam to sign, making clear exactly how the relationship worked, especially in the event of a major disagreement. Andrew had had a lawyer draw up a contract—it only seemed fair to all involved that Andrew find the lawyer, a final payback for him not telling them about Jonas—and had shown it to the *Times* without Sam seeing it.

"Sammy," Tom said calmly. "Seriously. Have you read it yet?"

This was the question that had set her off before. No, she hadn't read it, but didn't want to admit it to Tom, and anyway, that was so not the point. How dare they assume she'd just go along with it? It was her parents' money. But she knew that if she said that he'd go into his when-you-say-it's-the-principle-of-the-matter-you're-being-an-asshole spiel, and she just didn't want to hear it again. Plus, there was no point in her reading the contract because she never understood the language in those things.

"Okay," he said. "Forget I asked that. Just promise me that before you pull the plug on the *Times* deal—and the entire magazine—you'll get a lawyer to read it. I'm convinced you'll be totally fine with it. And it's not like we're ever going to get to the point of needing it anyway."

He paid the driver. Sam was still refusing to speak. *Tom was right, of course. The fucker.*

"Well," she said after they had entered the Gucci flagship on Fifth Avenue. "I suppose it's the right thing to do."

Tom was about to make a crack about Gucci soothing the savage breast, but thought better of it. "And I apologize for not showing it to you," he said instead. "And for not making sure Andrew had shown it to you."

Sam stopped and grabbed his hand. "That's sweet, honey. Thanks." She dropped the earnest expression like a zircon engagement ring. "Now get the hell out of my way." And she took off, working the racks like a woman possessed.

Tom had been expecting all sorts of last-minute nightmares, the kind that make you stay at work until dawn on the day of the close. But they had had enough ramp-up time, and everyone was so excited, that all deadlines were met, sometimes early.

He stayed late the night before, organizing things and looking at the stories. He loved this magazine. It wasn't perfect, but they'd learned a lot about what *Bite* should be—and about each other—and he was certain that they'd created something people would want to read. Even when the stories didn't have much to say—the fashion spreads, for example—it didn't matter. They were fun. The whole issue was fun. As he looked at each layout up on the wall, he remembered pieces of the text and laughed—everything in the magazine had a giddiness about it that was downright infectious.

He looked around. Sam was out with Jack, Andrew was with Jonas, Liza was probably with Trevor, and he beamed. If one year ago anyone had told him he'd be here, at a half-converted fleabag motel on the far West Side, putting the finishing touches on the magazine he'd always wanted to create, working only with people he loved, and apparently making a success of it, he would have laughed in their face.

But here he was. He looked up at the wall again, checking the pacing of the stories, making sure the order was right, rereading the cover lines (tomorrow he and Liza had to go to Kentucky, where the printer was, to oversee the printing). "Child's Play" it read across the front in big letters. Then, underneath: "A new magazine to help you make the most of your life. Hot sex! Barefoot beaches! Amazing fashion! Finger-licking food! And special: All the things you've forgotten you love—Ping-Pong, treehouses, candy, kites, and much, much more."

He was pretty damn pleased with himself. So much so that he did a little jig.

"I appear to be interrupting something."

The joke could wait. "Can you believe it?"

Veronica gave him a hug. "I'm proud of you," she said. "I'm proud of me. I'm proud of us." She looked up at the wall. "And as much as I'd love to redo the Ping-Pong shoot, I'm proud of this."

They stood arm in arm for a second. Tom shook his head. "I keep worrying that if I look away, it'll vanish."

"I know. If you'd told me a year ago—"

Tom broke out with his big laugh. "Would you believe that's why I started dancing?"

"Want to grab a drink?" Veronica always invited Tom out with care, as if she was afraid he'd say no. "My treat."

"Absolutely," he said. "But if you're thinking of putting the moves on me out of pity or something, just because I'm the one person on staff who doesn't have a boyfriend, I have to warn you . . ."

"No worries," she said, slapping him on the ass. "But I'll let you know if I change my mind."

Chapter 67

Tom and Liza were on the plane back from Kentucky, carrying in their hot hands the cover of the first issue of *Bite.* "I don't know why we keep putting it back in the envelope," Liza said. "We're just going to keep pulling it out again."

"It's gorgeous," Tom said. The apple was right in the center, bright red and mighty big. Brighter than any apple had a right to be—Tom was sure it would pop off the newsstand. A foxy man's face was on the left, his teeth sunk into the fruit; coming from the right was a female model, her eyes locked onto the man's, her lips parted. It was very sexy.

She kissed him on the cheek. "Liza," he said, emphasizing the first syllable as if to warn her this was going somewhere serious. "It's none of my business. But I want you to know that if you and Trevor do indeed have something going on—or if you ever do—I'm all for it. You don't have to say anything. And not that what I say matters, but I figure it doesn't hurt."

"It means a lot," Liza said. "To me, absolutely. But to Trevor, too, I'm sure." They sat for a minute stewing in the awkwardness. "He's thrilled to be at *Bite,* you know."

"Is he? I sometimes think that he's here out of a sense of duty." This was something Tom hadn't said to anyone.

"I believe his exact words were 'I'm having the time of my life.' "

Tom smiled. "Don't kid yourself, Liza. He was probably talking about being with you."

She socked him on the arm. "I'll let you get away with

being nice once, Tom Sanders, but if you start treating me different from everyone else I'm going to have to beat the shit out of you."

To: Tom@bite.com
From: Samantha@bite.com
Re: Issue #2
i know you've been worrying about the next issue, and i have too, but i just can't even think about it right now. how about we promise to meet first thing monday? can we trust ourselves?

"Works for me." Tom had snuck into Sam's office and read the email over her shoulder.

"Don't do that!" she screamed. "What if I was writing a filthy love letter to Jack?"

"Then I would unequivocally expect to be copied on it. New rule! All filthy emails must be copied to Tom Sanders. It's not like I'm getting any at home."

Sam felt terrible. While she'd been planning a week in Provence with Jack, she'd completely forgotten about Tom. "What's up with Justin?"

"We've finally made the transition."

"Friends?"

He nodded.

"Honey," she said, "I refuse to believe there isn't someone out there who's loving you right now."

"Well if he is, I think it's only fair he tell me."

She joined him on the sofa. "Look at it this way. You've been obsessing about the magazine, and you've accomplished so much." She saw her mistake immediately.

"So have you," he said. "But you've still managed to fall in love."

"I know, right! Isn't it great?" She stopped herself. "Sorry.

Listen, don't get down about it. Once the magazine hits the street *le tout* gay New York will want you."

Tom wasn't too upset. He felt like it was his prerogative to hold Sam's good fortunes against her, but *Bite* was going so well that it just didn't matter right then. Justin was a friend now; that was nice. But so much had happened in the past year: His life had become both more exciting and also more settled. The experience with Justin made him feel stronger; his relationship with Trevor made him feel more at home. Love would happen—heck, now that he was a big shot he'd probably even go up a level or two in the dating pool. He laughed at himself, and decided to think pessimistically again. "By the way, there will be a backlash, you know. Do you realize that every journalist in New York is going to hate us?"

"Don't kid yourself," Sam replied. "Journalists all over the *world* will hate us."

"They're here!" Veronica came running in the door; she had been camped in the lobby, waiting for the first issues to arrive. It was four o'clock—the press sent the FedEx for afternoon delivery, and Mao had spent a half hour on the phone chewing someone out—and everyone was agitated, like a fifth-grade class waiting for their substitute teacher, Miss Britney Spears.

Sam ripped the box open and held one up, like the trophy it was.

"I can't believe it's finally happened," Tom said.

"We're real," Sam said.

"We're real," Tom repeated.

Tom and Sam had long lost the excitement they used to have when a new issue of *Profit* or *Star Face* would come out, but that was before it was their own magazine. Now they were as excited as the interns, flipping back and forth through the issue, admiring one story, then another, then back to the previous one. They had seen the stories in their minds, and they had seen the stories on the wall. But it was different when it was an actual magazine, something you could envision on a newsstand, right next to *The New Yorker* and *Vanity Fair*—and *Profit* and *Star Face.* This was the big leagues, and it felt right.

"Is it as good as I think it is?" asked Liza.

"It is," Sam said. For a bunch of highly excited people, they were speaking in very serious tones. "It is."

Mao came out with champagne, breaking the spell. "We did it!" she hollered, popping what would be the first of many corks. "Hallelujah!"

Chapter 68

Sam couldn't believe how calm she was. Liza, on the other hand, couldn't believe how calm she wasn't.

"I hate what I'm wearing," Liza was saying to Sam, who had the phone pinned to one ear as she put the post on the other ear's diamond stud—the last thing she had to do before grabbing her bag and heading out to celebrate.

"Right," Sam said absentmindedly, checking the mirror for one last fluff. She looked like an editor, if she said so herself. A sexy, lapis-colored, low-dipping Gucci top, with perfectly tailored black Chloe pants. Understated, elegant, but—she looked down at her feet and gave one a cheerful wiggle—definitely fuckable, judging by her lucky Manolos, the ones with the rhinestones across the toe strap. Maybe tonight?

"Sam. I hear you not listening."

"I'm listening, I'm listening," Sam said with a sigh, turning into the living room to grab her purse and head downstairs. "I'm sure you look fabulous. You never don't look fabulous. What are you wearing?"

"Nice try, Sam! You'll have to wait."

"Fine," Sam said peevishly. "But get your ass out of the house already. Otherwise, I'll be drinking at the King Cole by myself."

Or not, as it turned out. Because when Sam got downstairs, there was a giant white stretch limo waiting outside. Pure high school prom. The door opened, and out stepped Jack, bowing down before her.

"Oh my God," Sam said, holding her hand up to her mouth to mask the giggles. The limo had runway lights stretched along it, fish tanks lining the walls, and a bright-purple-velvet interior. "What have you done?"

Jack beamed. "I thought it was about time the fun started," he said, escorting her into the back. "You've been working too hard, it's been too serious. It's all been too serious. It's time to embrace our inner ridiculousness, don't you think?"

"I do indeed," she said, as she settled into the remarkably comfortable seat. Jack put on the stereo—a little Marvin Gaye—and leaned back, putting his hand over hers. "Sam?"

"Yes, you lunatic?" Sam said, smiling so happily she felt like her cheek muscles were running a marathon.

"I love you." Jack looked deep into her eyes, and much to her amazement, she didn't have a moment of fear, a moment of that feeling she had always gotten, of going blank, numb, until words just echoed in her ears. In fact, she felt nothing but present, and nothing but grateful for the chance to know that she wouldn't rather be anywhere than where she was right now.

"I love you too," she whispered, just before his lips met hers.

By the time Jack and Sam walked into the St. Regis to meet the crew at the King Cole Bar for a precelebratory glass of champagne, Liza was already there looking glamorous, as always. And nervous, Sam had to admit. She definitely looked nervous.

After they had greeted each other and Jack had ordered them drinks, Sam whispered into Liza's ear. "What's up?"

"I'm just a little—well, rattled, I guess," Liza said, nodding at Jack to let Sam know she was comfortable enough to address him as well. "It's like my whole life I was waiting for this, and I just didn't know it. Finally, I found a job I love, I found friends I love, I'm by myself and I'm not frightened. It's all so . . ."

"Perfect?" Sam interjected with a laugh.

"Yes, I guess you could say that," Liza said. "I just keep waiting for the bubble to burst."

"In which case," Jack said, raising his glass to Liza and Sam, "You shall find another job you love, and other friends you love."

Sam playfully elbowed him in the side. "Don't make me start singing that horrible Dionne Warwick song to you, Ms. Liza," Sam said.

Which is exactly what they were doing when Tom and Trevor walked in, laughing in horror at the sounds of "That's What Friends Are For."

"We got here just in time," Trevor said, after giving an especially lingering kiss on the cheek to Liza and sitting down beside her. "To stop you before the next verse, that is."

"For our next project," Liza joked, "we're going to form a band."

"To our lives as rock stars!" Sam said with a laugh, raising her glass to her friends. "Wait—where's Veronica? We can't begin the celebration without her."

"Veronica's the original rock star," Tom said. "She'll keep the audience waiting until the last minute."

"Fair enough," Liza said, "but let's enjoy the opening act." She placed her hands on the table, offering them to Trevor and Sam. Everyone did the same, until it appeared they were holding a séance.

"What the hell is going on here?" Mao had arrived, dressed in leather hot pants, a halter top, and black fishnets with go-go boots.

"Dear Lord," Trevor sighed. "Just a little something you wore to the Duane Reade Christmas party?"

"This is my dancing-on-the-bar outfit," Mao growled. "Prepare yourselves."

"Is this the sex addicts anonymous meeting?" a voice boomed out from the entrance. The whole bar turned—R.J. had arrived. He went the opposite direction from Mao, and had duded himself up in a double-breasted, metallic blue suit. "The devil wore Prada," he said. "But God wears nothing but Gucci."

"Get over here," Tom said with a laugh, standing to hug R.J. Then Veronica appeared, radiant in purple. She did a piroutte, and they applauded. Dael was right behind her, in a sharp navy suit.

"Have you ever seen such a glamorous table?" Sam asked.

"Well . . ." Tom said, winking at Mao. "Except for the lap dancer sitting over there."

"Cheers!" Sam suddenly yelled, "To us! To our party!"

"Speaking of the party, this is probably one we shouldn't be late to," Liza said. "Should we go check out the room?"

Trevor got the check and the group boarded the elevator to the penthouse. When the door opened, they all gasped. It was perfect. Hundreds of votive candles lined the room. The caterers were busy opening the bottles of champagne and arranging the tins of caviar.

"Come on R.J., let's check out the sturdiness of the bar," Mao said, pulling him away.

"And we'll check out the sturdiness of the champagne," Trevor said, leading Veronica, Jack, and Liza toward the side table.

Tom and Sam just stood in the middle of the room, slowly absorbing what they had done. Ahead of them, the balcony door was open, the tiled floor covered in thousands of white-rose petals. Without a word, the two joined hands and stepped outside.

Below them, New York looked like it had put on its finest and brightest lights just for the occasion.

"Tom," Sam whispered, "doesn't it look like the whole city is there, just for the having?"

"We're having it, honey, we're having it."

Sam felt a grin spread across her face. And so they were. Maybe it was just the beginning, she thought, but it was a damn good way to start.